Love
mom + Dad

V.G.

The Far-off Rhapsody

A novel by

Anne-Marie Sheridan

SIMON AND SCHUSTER
NEW YORK

Library of Congress Cataloging in Publication Data

Sheridan, Anne-Marie.
  The far-off rhapsody.

  I. Title.
PZ.S5516Far3 [PR6069.H456]   823'.9'14   76-54898
ISBN 0-671-22601-0

PART ONE

The Distant Airs

1

It was on Thursday, 25th February 1847, that the door-keeper of Penruth Workhouse in the Duchy of Cornwall opened up in answer to the bell and found me there on the step, a newborn baby wrapped in a clean blanket. For this reason, I was given the surname of Thursday. My first name—Tessa—was thought of by the then parish parson, and it was considered by his fellow members of the Workhouse Board to be rather on the fancy side for a foundling; but the parson stuck to his guns, and Tessa I have remained.

I survived childhood with no more than the usual child's complaints, though many of my fellows did not. The provisions of the Poor Law were made with the view in mind that poverty was a crime and the result of vice and indolence. Relief was given only in properly regulated workhouses, where the living conditions had to be inferior to those of the most wretched laborers outside—that was the law. It is scarcely surprising that the young and the weak went under, through poor diet, lack of warmth, and overwork.

At six, I was examined by the Workhouse Board, who decided that I was strong enough to be put to some form of labor; so I was made to work twelve hours a day, six days a week, in a factory on the edge of Wendron Moors, which is above Penruth.

Six mornings a week, I was roused from the common mattress of straw that I shared with five other boys and girls. There was no getting dressed—we slept in what we stood up in—and four o'clock of a winter's morning is no time to go blundering in the dark for the yard tap; none of us were so fastidious as to be *that* much in need of a wash!

Breakfast, winter and summer, was always the same: a

preparation of bread and hot water flavored with the drippings of a teapot, which went by the name of "sop" and was greatly esteemed by us. There was scarcely time to bolt it down before the carts arrived to take us, barefoot and still heavy-eyed, through the sleeping town and up into the cold rawness of the moor.

The factory was owned by a Mr. James Martel, a native of the Midlands, who had seen an opening for the manufacture, in West Cornwall, of iron chains of every variety for the fishing fleets of the peninsula. The work, which was done in an old quarry building, was exhausting, unhealthy, and dangerous, especially for the men who worked at the big furnaces, and whom lung disease carried off at an early age. These men were forever covered with burns and sores, for it is easier to catch a flea than remove a flying fragment of red-hot iron from the skin or clothing. The risk of succumbing to a sudden chill was the most dreaded of all: after twelve hours at a baking-hot furnace, men have gone out into the wintry moor, got wet, and been dead the next morning.

For the women and children it was utter wretchedness. The passing years will never shut out my memories of those poor creatures. I can still see the haggard faces of the women, some with wizened infants slung on their backs as they plied their hammers, some with little ones clinging to their skirts and crying from hunger and weariness, some with their babes dangling from swing chairs nearby, so that they could be rocked between hammer blows.

The work of chain-making consisted of heating iron rods to redness, bending each piece, cutting and twisting it into links, then closing the links with repeated blows of a hammer. The women worked on the smaller chains, and the metal for these was heated in forges supplied with bellows.

I was a bellows-worker, which meant that I stood with one foot on a pivoted plank and bore it up and down with all my weight. This moved a rope fastened to the other end of the plank, which opened and closed the bellows, supplying gusts of air to the forge. I did this for twelve hours a day, with only a short midday break for a basin of skilly, six days a week. For this I received threepence a day, which was paid directly to the Penruth Workhouse and set against my upkeep.

That, then, was my early life. It was far removed from the picture of childhood as imagined by folks who eat four meals a day and wear shoes on their feet; but somehow I found time and energy for the lighter things of existence. I sang at my work often, as did many of the others. I enjoyed the company of my fellows. The smaller children were a delight to me: I loved to care for them; I was broken-hearted for those who sickened and died. And I had a best friend in a girl named Mary Allen.

Mary was two or three years older than I, not a foundling but a workhouse orphan, and was apprenticed at the age of fourteen to the trade of chain-making at a wage of two shillings and sixpence a week—in return for which she was bound by a solemn undertaking, during her apprenticeship of seven years, not to frequent taverns or playhouses, or to squander her wages on "playing at cards, or dice tables, or any other unlawful games."

Poor Mary, whose arms were like matchsticks, forged dog chains from dawn till dusk and was obliged by the terms of her apprenticeship to satisfy her master's demand of six completed chains a day—a task that she performed with cheerful willingness. Of what was left of her miserable wage, after she had paid for her lodgings at the workhouse, I do not suppose much went in low taverns or was squandered on games of chance!

At fourteen, I too would be faced with the prospect of entering into the apprenticeship—a prospect that I viewed with some dismay. And for a very particular reason.

It all came about at the Christmas of my thirteenth year, the Christmas that the mummers came to Penruth Workhouse.

"You know 'tis Christmas coming?" said Mary.

"Of course," I replied. We were well schooled in the religious calendar, for Sundays were given over entirely to chapel services, Bible readings, and instruction from the parson and his volunteer ladies from the town. Yes, I had learned all about Christmas from a very early age: it was the one day of the year on which we were given a holiday from work—providing it did not fall on a Sunday; then the day's holiday had to serve for both Christmas and the Sabbath. And this year of 'sixty, as I had ascertained from the big calendar from the local corn chandlers that hung just inside the workhouse master's office door, was blessed with a 25th of December that fell on a Tuesday.

"Well, there's to be a treat for us on Christmas Eve. Do you know that?"

"A—*treat?*" It was not a word I had heard bandied about very much in my thirteen years, nor Mary either, though we both vaguely knew that a treat was something you got for nothing.

"The mummers are coming!" cried Mary.

"What's mummers?" I demanded.

"They act out all the old tales," she explained. "About Robin Hood and Marian, and the Fool. Then there's Blue Breeches and Pepper Breeches, the Doctor, Mrs. Allspice, and Candy. I've seen them before. I saw them at Bodmin Fair when my Mam and Dad was alive and did take me. It was many years ago, but I never did forget the mummers, Tessa."

"And we'll see them—at the 'house?" I asked wonderingly.

She nodded. "On Christmas Eve! After supper. All dressed up, with colored lanterns, music and everything. 'Tis something you'll never forget, Tessa!"

It was at that moment that Mr. Martel smote the downstairs door with his knotty walking stick, signaling the end of our dinner-time break; so I heard no more of the coming treat on that occasion, but returned to my bellows-arm for the remaining half of the seemingly endless day.

And all the while, as I leapt on and off the plank, bearing down with all my puny weight to make the bellows open and close, the thought—new, precious and infinitely zestful and exciting—ran through my mind: *The mummers are coming . . . I'm going to see the mummers!*

The Penruth Workhouse—happily long since gone, its very site all but forgotten save in musty deeds and ancient maps—stood at the top of the town, the most exposed part that takes the worst of the southwesterly gales. In later years, when the urge for scholarship moved me, I took the trouble to discover that it had been built after the model of the famous, not to say infamous, Newgate prison in London. Its appearance comes back to me as some monstrous dolls' house: square-cut, uncompromisingly grim, with blanked-off, eyeless windows and a great pair of iron-studded gates. The gates led directly to a courtyard, and from there through double doors into a vast hall running all one length of the building. This chamber was known to all, both staff and inmates, as "The Walk," and was so called because it provided a place of general promenade for an hour on Sundays, and the only opportunity for husbands, wives, and children to meet all together and exchange a few words. It also served as a communal eating place for all: children at one end, next to them the women, then the workhouse master and his assistants separating the adult male inmates from the rest. Apart from the short Sunday promenade, the men were not allowed to mix with their families: this was to encourage them to find regular work outside, and so relieve the parish of the burden of them. Only there was not enough work to go round in West Cornwall.

It was to be in The Walk that the mummers would give their performance on Christmas Eve. We were officially informed of the coming treat by the workhouse master, Mr. Pendleton, over our supper of skilly that night. Christmas Eve, he said, being on Monday week, all out-workers would be let off early, so as to be back in the 'house for a special supper before the mummers' performance. I can remember downing the last dregs of my skilly, wiping out the basin with my fingertips, and thinking I should never find the patience to live through one whole week.

The next day the winds died over Penruth and the Wendron Moors, and the great silent snowflakes came down, blanketing our remote world of West Cornwall, closing the roads, making it impossible even to descend the hill from the workhouse gates. The lane that led up to the moor and

Mr. Martel's factory completely vanished; I still have a clear recollection of scores of parish paupers—men and women both, dark figures against the startling whiteness—laboring to clear it with shovels. It was never opened again before the New Year.

The impossibility of our getting to the factory must have thrown the authorities into confusion. There was plenty of snow-clearing work available, but only for the men and the stronger of the women. The lack of warm clothing and boots—all of us children and many of the women went barefoot the whole year round—would surely have put the majority in hazard of death and injury from frostbite and exposure, for which even the harsh Poor Laws had made no provision. It must have been for this reason that we were allowed to do nothing but simply hang about the 'house, eat our meager fare—and dream of the coming treat on Christmas Eve.

It was Mary Allen—with a shrewdness beyond her years and a short lifetime full of disappointments—who first voiced the terrible doubt amongst us: *"What if the mummers can't get through to Penruth?"*

When that had been said, the formerly blessed snow became our enemy, and every morning we children sought for signs of its going. Even the dawn drive up to the moor, even twelve hours a day in the chainworks, the flying sparks, the choking heat and fumes, the labor at bellows and anvil—better to bear all those than to be deprived of our Christmas Eve treat.

The dawn of Christmas Eve revealed the snow to be as firm and glistening white as ever, and the leaden sky gave no promise of any change. Nor was there any, through all that day.

Supper that evening—the special festive supper—was provided by the people of the town in their seasonal charity. There was boiled meat, potatoes, carrots, swedes, and big dumplings all swimming in gravy. Being unused to meat, most of us left it on one side and addressed ourselves to the dumplings, which were more to our taste. I had no appetite for this, the only substantial meal I had faced in a twelvemonth; my thoughts were all on the mummers, and whether by some miracle they would find their way through the choked roads to perform for us. It was pitch dark outside, and new flurries of snow were plastering the small, high windows of The Walk. In the great open fireplace, a single log burned sullenly with a strange green flame that tells of frost; and you could see the rising plumes of all our breaths, we hundred and fifty-odd parish paupers and our benefactors.

"Let the mummers come—let them get through to Penruth!" I prayed.

Suddenly there came the sound of the bell at the outer gates, and the noises of eating and chattering died on the instant into a breathless silence. We heard the doorkeeper's hobnailed boots clatter over the cobbled yard, followed by the drawing of the bolts, the taking off of the chains, the groan of the key in the great lock, the rusty creak of the gates.

Then—voices and many footfalls crossing the yard. I held my breath and looked down the table to Mary. Her eyes were wide with hope, and she was soundlessly mouthing something to herself.

They came into the hall, bringing with them the icy gust of the outside and a carpet of snow that they stamped from their boots. We greeted them with stony silence.

I could have wept. I think I *may* have wept a little. Were *these* the mummers for whom we had been waiting with such hopes and fears? Just a group of ordinary-looking men and women, some old, some young; all wrapped in scarves and shawls, the men in tall hats, the women in plain bonnets, and all on the shabby side. It takes a pauper to spot the signs of seediness.

The leader of the party—he was a tallish man with a mane of gleaming black hair below his hat brim; but his back was to me, so I only caught tantalizing glimpses of his profile—was greeted with handshakes from the workhouse master and the chairman of the Parish Council. There was a ripple of talk between them, and a burst of deep-throated laughter from the spokesman of the mummers. The party was then conducted to the far end of the hall, to the great staircase. They were followed by some of the male paupers carrying clothes hampers that the mummers had brought with them.

Near the foot of the stairs, where the floor was stepped up in a wide platform like a stage, the mummers' leader turned and looked back down the length of The Walk, staring out across what must to him have appeared as a mass of regarding eyes. I was quite near to him—near enough to see the threadbare cuffs of his coat and the cracks in his well-polished boots—and I received an immediate impression of a strange power.

He was quite young—in his early twenties was my inexpert reckoning—and startlingly good-looking in a swarthy way, though, surprisingly, the eyes that scanned us were of a deep and luminous blueness. For all of a minute, while his companions passed behind him and on up the staircase, he swept us with his glance, looking to and fro, almost as if he was searching for a familiar face.

There was power in that glance, and an arrogance in the pose of his figure; but it was a power and arrogance that was lightly carried. When he had seen all he needed to see, a brilliantly good-humored smile illuminated his handsome face, and he doffed his tall hat to us with a courtly flourish.

"I wish you a good evening, ladies and gentlemen," he said in a deep quiet voice that carried every syllable. Then he smiled toward the children's tables. "Not forgetting the younger ladies and gentlemen. My name is Oliver Craven, and it will shortly be my inestimable pleasure to present to you a little entertainment of mime and music that my troupe and I have devised for your delight. I ask you, please, to forgive our late arrival, which was due to the present inclement weather, and to bear with us for a few minutes longer till we have changed into our costumes. I thank you, ladies and gentlemen."

With that, he bowed, replaced his hat, tapped it on with the knob of his cane, and marched up the stairs with a light tread; leaving his audience of parish paupers to wonder at the novelty of being addressed as "ladies and gentlemen" and being apologized to by such a splendid-looking person, for all that his clothes were shabby and his shoes down-at-heel.

Scattered pockets of muttered comment died away into a stark silence of expectancy. All eyes were directed toward the staircase and the shadowed hallway above, where the otherworldly creature—he who had introduced himself as Oliver Craven—had vanished. I hugged myself against the cold and watched and waited also . . .

I tell about what followed—as about everything that took place in those early days—with the imperfect understanding of a thirteen-year-old parish foundling who could barely spell out her own name, and this overlaid with a slight wisdom of hindsight and the added knowledge of the years between. I have garnered a mixed store of memories since then: memories as fragrant as summer days, and living nightmares that bring unease in the empty hours before dawn; but while I live, nothing will outshine the remembrance of the mummers' performance on that enchanted Christmas Eve, when the great hall of Penruth Workhouse became a fairyland.

First came mummers dressed as animals, bearing colored lanterns: feathered birds and gauzy butterflies, gray moths and furry bears, lining the sides of the staircase with a soft glow of rainbow light.

Then, down the stairs, in and out of the lamplight and the shadows, flitted a lady dressed all in white, with a coronet of glittering stars. She was beautiful beyond wonder as, to the distant music of a pipe and drum, she began slowly to dance. Turning, turning all the while, she spoke to us with fluid gestures of her hands and arms; of her head, neck, and shoulders. Her message was clear and simple to understand, even for the youngest of the children, gazing up at her, wide-eyed.

Soundlessly, she told us that she was a princess in love with a shepherd, and that her royal father had forbidden her to set eyes on him again. Yet, though of humble birth, she told us, her lover was good, brave, and kind, and handsome as no other man in the world . . .

I gave a start at the touch of a hand. Looking down, I saw Mary's thin fingers twining in mine. She had moved to sit beside me. Her eyes never left the vision in white. I squeezed her hand.

Presently, the unearthly music of a flute announced the arrival of her lover. He came down the stairs, tall and fine, with a wreath of vines and roses circling his mane of jet-black hair, in a tunic splattered all over with embroidered flower-heads, and golden sandals on his feet. The power and the arrogance were still there, and carried as lightly and good-humoredly as before. It was Oliver Craven, of course.

The lovers greeted each other. He mimed amused indifference when the princess told him of her father's cruel decree; laughed her gently to scorn when she warned him that he was in danger of his life from the king's soldiers, and must flee. Then a distant trumpet call summoned the princess back to her father's castle. There was a poignant parting. And the shepherd was alone.

But not for long! . . .

A hundred and fifty-odd assembled paupers should have been enough to warn him. Our frenzied cries told him of his danger as the king's cruel soldiers crept stealthily down the staircase toward him; but he seemed both unconscious of the threat and deaf to our warnings. I covered my eyes to shut out the horror—as they fell upon him with cudgels. When I opened them, he lay stricken and senseless at the foot of the stair, and all the little children in the front rows were sobbing, while the adult paupers shook their fists and shouted curses at the sneering soldiers as they swaggered back the way they had come.

We need not have upset ourselves. . . .

It was the animals—the birds and butterflies, the moths and the kindly bears of the forest—who restored the shepherd to life, tending his hurts, fanning his fevered brow with their wing-beats, bearing news to the princess for her to come.

The play ended, as all plays should, with the reuniting of the lovers, reconciliation with the father, embraces. The end found us all unashamedly in tears. There followed other diversions: our tears turned to laughter at the antics of Fool and the absurdities of Blue Breeches and his cronies; we wondered at the marvels of the tumbling, the mysteries of the juggling and sleights-of-hand, the elegancies of music, dance, and colored lights. In this manner, I was shown a vision of a world beyond the drab walls of the workhouse, and a way of living that was as different from the mindless toil on the bellows-arm as the flight of a butterfly differs from the slow, hard trail of the slug.

In that moment was born my ambition—to be an artiste of the mime, like Oliver Craven's beautiful princess.

The treat was over and the children were being sent to their hard mattresses. I managed to creep away unseen, risking detection and certain punishment if I was discovered.

At the top of the big staircase were various large chambers given over to workrooms for the women who labored at piecework for various dressmakers in the town. It would be one or more of those rooms, I told myself, that the mummers would surely be using to change in and out of their costumes. No use to walk straight up the main staircase in full view; I should soon be spotted and brought down with a flea in my ear. There was a smaller, spiral stair leading to the upper floor and conveniently close at hand. I took it, and was soon standing only a few yards from the open door of the nearest workroom, from which issued a broad fan of lamplight.

Tiptoeing barefoot, I moved to the door and looked inside. One glance was enough to make me catch my breath. In the center of the room was my princess in all her glory of shining white and glitter. A second glance showed me that she was headless—not my princess in real life, but her fairy-tale gown set upon a dressmaker's dummy that the piecework women used!

I heard a voice from inside the room: a woman's voice, and speaking in some foreign language. She sounded angry. Peering round the side of the door, I met her suddenly surprised eyes. She was standing just beyond the lamplight, partly in shadow. Her companion was behind her, doing something to the back of the speaker's gown.

"What is it you want, child—hein?" came the sharp challenge. She spoke English with a marked accent. "Come here. Come and help me with this fastening."

I obeyed. As I crossed the room, my legs began to tremble

with nervousness. As I drew near to the speaker, she moved slightly forward, into the lamplight. The shock of recognition robbed me of my breath.

She was the princess—*my* princess—but greatly changed from the vision that had descended the staircase in the flatteringly colored lights. Here was a woman—once beautiful, indeed—but past her prime. An overblown rose, with some petals already fallen. Wrinkles of irritation surrounded the heavily kohled eyes; the fleshy, voluptuous mouth was petulant.

"Oh, do hurry, child," she wailed. Then, turning to her companion, who was still fiddling with the fastenings at the back of her gown: "Clumsy! Stupid! Leave that for the child and pour me some cognac!"

She turned her back to me, presenting the line of unfastened hooks and eyes. My fingers, though trembling, made quite swift work of them. There was enough light to see that her gown—which was of burgundy figured velvet—was threadbare at the elbows and seams, and that her lace collar was none too clean. She smelled strongly of scent, and also of spirits.

"Have you not finished, child?"

"Nearly, ma'am," I faltered.

"Where is that fool with the cognac?"

My task completed, I had the opportunity to look about me. Close by the wall there was a long table set as a workbench for the sewing-women, and it was there that the "princess's" companion now stood: a hunched and wizened figure dressed in shapeless black, with a bonnet pulled down all round the sides. She was pouring from a black bottle into a glass. A bright spark of light burned in the center of the shadowed profile, and I caught the familiar whiff of strong tobacco such as the chain-workers smoked. She did not remove the clay pipe from her lips, nor speak a word, when she shuffled back and handed the brimming glass to the princess. The latter drained it down in one mouthful.

"My dear Jeanette, your partiality for the brandy bottle is going to be the ruin of your complexion—if not your distinguished professional career!"

The voice—deep, quiet, and clear in every syllable—came from the doorway. My heart leapt before I looked.

Oliver Craven was back in his shabby street clothes again, but he carried them like a prince. Tall hat cocked jauntily on one side, the knob of his cane tapping his cheek, he regarded the woman he had addressed as Jeanette with a quizzical smile.

"Damn you, Oliver!" she retorted angrily. "How dare you spy on me?" Then she gave a sob and continued in a whine, "You shouldn't talk to me so. I can't help it. I am so cold and miserable in this Cornwall. Everything I have to do for myself. That one—her!"—and she pointed to the old crone, who had retired back into the shadows, puffing at her clay pipe—"she is so lazy, so stupid. Why do we not send her back to France? Call her a dresser—ha!" And she began to cry tipsily.

"Jeanette, Jeanette," said Oliver Craven, moving forward and reaching out a comforting hand. "Don't take on so, dear. It was very remiss of me to be so rude to you, particularly since you gave such a splendid performance tonight. Why, I came in to congratulate you—how's that?"

Jeanette sniffed and clutched at his arm, her swollen eyes searching his, appealingly. "I was beautiful, wasn't I, Oliver? Tell me that. There is no one like Jeanette, hein?"

"No one like Jeanette," he repeated comfortingly. "The performance of your life, my dear—albeit that it was a charity performance, for which we gain not a penny. Still, we shall be rewarded in heaven for our charity."

"Money!" she cried. "Money—how miserable it is, to have to count every sou! Oh, Oliver, tell me we shall one day be rich and famous!"

"One day, my dear," he responded, "we shall be the toast of London, Paris, and New York."

She flung her arms about his shoulders in a wild gesture of delight. "And then, Oliver—then we shall be married, just as we have planned, hein? Tell me that—just once more."

From where I stood, in the shadow of the fairy-tale gown on the dressmaker's dummy, I saw the effect that her request had made upon him. Instantly, his face took on a blank and empty expression, as when a small child is told he must be punished, and is aware that no amount of protestation will spare him. This, Jeanette could not see, because he was close to her, in her embrace, and looking over her shoulder.

"Tell me again, Oliver," she pleaded. "Just once more . . ."

"When we are rich and famous," he began, "just as we have planned, we shall—"

And then he saw me, peering at him round the side of the dressmaker's dummy!

"Who in the deuce are you, young woman?" he demanded, gently freeing himself from his companion's embrace. "And how long have you been standing there, might one ask?"

"Please, sir . . . I . . ." Dry-mouthed, I could not have framed an answer, even if my brain had provided it.

"Oh, that child?" said Jeanette carelessly. "She is, I suppose, one of the young people here. She is not important. You can go now, child."

Those deep blue eyes never left my face, as Oliver Craven gestured with his lean hand for his companion to be silent and me to remain.

"What is your name, young lady?" he murmured quietly.

"Tessa Thursday, sir," I managed to reply.

"Tessa Thursday—aaaah. And how old are you, Tessa?"

"I—I'm something like thirteen, sir."

"Something like thirteen?"

"I—I came here . . . was found on the step, by the front gates, on the twenty-fifth of February, eighteen forty-seven," I whispered.

"Found on the step—I see." He reached out his hand and cupped my chin, lifting my head higher, so that it was turned toward the lamplight. "What a remarkable countenance," he said. Don't you think she has a remarkable countenance, Jeanette?"

"She is—quite pretty," replied the other huffily.

"I see more than mere prettiness here," replied Oliver Craven. "Let a very few years pass, and I promise you that young Miss Thursday here will be a very considerable beauty. Just look at that bone structure.

20

Jeanette sniffed. "She is *all* bone, that one. Too skinny by far!"

"She will not always be skinny," replied Oliver Craven dryly. "Given a little time and a little nourishment, and great changes will be wrought upon our young friend, I assure you, my dear."

But Jeanette was not interested in me, and showed it. She slumped down upon a chair, breathing heavily and calling to the old crone for her glass to be refilled: the demand was clear, though made in the foreign language, which I had by then decided must be French. Oliver Craven took his fingers from my chin, patted my shoulder encouragingly, and turned to leave the room, motioning me to follow him.

"Well, my dear Jeanette," he said from the door, "time for us to pack up and go, if we're ever to reach Truro tonight before the road is closed again. I will see you downstairs in a while."

She did not reply. The last I saw of her, she was still slumped in the chair, gazing morosely into her glass—which was empty again. The old woman had lifted the princess's gown from the dummy and was laying it in a hamper.

Out in the corridor, two of the other mummers were carrying a loaded hamper toward the staircase. Oliver Craven paused to let them go past. When they were gone, he looked at me with a quizzical smile.

"So we say goodbye, Tessa Thursday," he said. "Till next time."

"You—you'll be coming here again, sir?" I breathed.

"You enjoyed the plays?"

"Oh, yes!" How could I begin to explain the wonder that had been brought into my life that night? Then I thought—how better than by telling the truth? "When I'm older," I blurted out, "*I'm* going to be a mummer!"

"Are you now?" His face was quite serious, with not a hint of mockery or derision. "Well, that's a very worthy ambition, Tessa. And how long have you had this ambition?"

"All the evening, sir," I told him.

21

He could have laughed then; instead, he continued to look at me with sober interest.

"Since you saw the performance."

"Right from the first moment, sir," I replied. "From the time that the princess came down the staircase."

He did not answer at once. I looked steadily at him, trying to make a picture in my mind so that I should not forget his face. The dark hair coming to a pronounced widow's peak that showed when his hat was pushed back on his head, as it was then. Dark eyebrows, deep blue eyes. He had a habit, when speaking, of sometimes flicking his right eyebrow with the second finger of his right hand. It was, I told myself, a strong and noble face; I knew that I should never forget it for as long as I lived.

Presently he stooped and placed his hands on my shoulders, regarding me closely, eye to eye. And he said, "Well, if you have an ambition to act, Tessa, then we must see what can be done."

"Sir! You mean . . ."

"I promise nothing," he said. And he took hold of my hands, looking at the callouses on my fingers and palms, at the ground-in tar from the bellows rope that no cold water would erase. "What do they make you do in this place, Tessa?" he asked quietly.

"I'm at Mr. Martel's chainworks, up on the edge of the moor, sir. I'm a bellows-worker."

"A bellows-worker." He nodded gravely. "And can you read and write, Tessa?"

"I know my letters and I can write my own name," I told him. "I learned that at the Sunday school, just by asking questions of the lady teacher."

He tapped my shoulder with his forefinger. "You'll have to do better than that, Tessa," he told me. "To be an actor, a mummer, call it what you will, you will have to be able to read and understand the parts you play, to have a knowledge of the world outside your own time and place. These things are learned from the world of books. Do you understand?"

I nodded miserably. Suddenly my fine ambition seemed to drain away, like water between my fingers.

"We aren't taught proper reading and writing at the Sunday school," I said. "Only to recite the books of the Bible, and about Adam begat Seth, and Seth begat Enosh, and Enosh begat Kenan, and Kenan begat Mahalalel, and . . ."

"Enough, enough!" He raised his hands in mock protest. "Your erudition impresses me mightily! But you must widen your knowledge, Tessa, to include reading and writing. You must request to be taught, for I assure you it is your right under the law. And if your requests are not met, you must *demand!*"

"Du-demand, sir?" The idea of making any kind of demand on the authorities who governed Penruth Workhouse was something my mind simply could not encompass.

Oliver Craven exhaled deeply through his nose, flicked his right eyebrow, then paced a few steps away and back. And all the time, he stared at the floor in front of his feet, deep in thought. He paused in front of me again, and took a deep breath.

"Tessa," he began. "I would help you if I could, believe me. But I am a poor man—" he held out his hands to show his frayed coat cuffs, the patched and oversewn edges of his shirtsleeves—"as you can see! Most actors are poor. You have chosen a most precarious profession, of which profession I and my company of strolling players are perhaps among the poorest of the lot. It's scarcely conceivable that you should want to be one of us, but if you do, you have my blessing—no, don't bother to thank me; you may yet live to curse me—you have my blessing, but I am in no position to give you any assistance.

"You must shift for yourself, Tessa. From this time forth, until you take up your chosen profession, you must work to improve yourself, your knowledge, your understanding. You must seize every opportunity for self-improvement. If those opportunities are not forthcoming you must *make* them, Tessa. You must snatch them from the empty air!"

"Oh, I will, sir—I will!" I cried, inspired.

He smiled down at me. "I believe you will, Tessa Thursday," he murmured. "I truly believe you have it in you to prepare yourself, in the years immediately ahead, for the calling of your ambition. And now, we truly say farewell. We shall meet again. I would be deceiving you if I made any promise as to when this will be, or in what circumstances. But return I will." So saying, he stooped and kissed me tenderly on the brow. It was a kiss such as a more fortunate girl might have received from an older brother. Or her father.

Raising his tall hat, he backed away a pace, turned, and walked swiftly toward the great staircase, down which he disappeared without a backward glance.

I waited till the echo of his footfalls faded away in the vastness of The Walk below. His sonorous voice was raised in a brisk command to someone. Then—silence.

As I crept toward the spiral staircase, I heard the woman Jeanette tipsily berating her dresser at the other side of the workroom door.

Being thirteen, I no longer slept on a communal mattress, but shared a small, cell-like room with Mary Allen and two other girls of about my age. We each had mattresses of our own, together with certain other privileges: such as a hand wash-basin and water jug, a cake of carbolic soap, and a single candle that had to be doused at nine-thirty "lights out."

The others were asleep when I entered—for even the excitement of Christmas Eve and the mummers could not keep them awake, undernourished and drained of energy as they were—and the candle had been snuffed. By moonlight from the frosted window, I washed my hands in the icy water from the jug, in the hope that I might make a start on getting them as white and soft-looking as I had observed Jeanette's to be. The hands of an actress. An *actress*—I thrilled to the word, and resolved to use no other; much better-sounding than "mummer."

Alas for my efforts! The chill water and the poor lather had little effect on the state of my hands, save to turn them red and swollen with the cold. But a start had been made.

Under the coarse blankets, I lay awaiting sleep and passing the events of that memorable evening before my mind's eye. First, the performance, beginning with the entrance of the princess—no!—first the part where Oliver Craven turned and introduced himself to us at the foot of the staircase . . .

After the performance, the strange scene in Jeanette's dressing room: her tipsy behavior, the old crone with the clay pipe, the arrival of Oliver Craven . . .

So he and Jeanette were promised to each other in marriage!

It was scarcely believable that one so young as he could possibly become affianced to such an old woman. Why, she seemed almost old enough to be his mother. What's more, she drank and had a very tetchy and irritable disposition.

Trapped! That must be it—he must have been trapped. I had heard of such things, from listening to the gossip of the women in the 'house: how so-and-so was trapped into being wed to so-and-so, and how she—it was nearly always the woman—had lived to regret it.

Yes, and that accounted for the expression on his face when she had demanded that he repeat his promise to marry her when they were rich and famous: it was the face of a man who had allowed himself to be snared, but who is too honorable to go back on his word. I found the explanation strangely comforting, and it was the last thing I remembered before sleep overtook me.

I was bound hand and foot, unable to move or help myself. It was dark, and I was freezing cold and terrified. I screamed into the blackness till my whole body ached with the effort; but no one came in answer to my pleas. I was forgotten, abandoned. The helplessness, the darkness, the cold, and the hunger—they were without end. But still I screamed.

Next there was a tiny light coming out of the blackness, coming toward me. Fascinated, I ceased my cries, looked toward the light, imagined warmth, food, comfort.

The light blotted out more of the dark and showed the looming outline of a figure standing over me where I lay. The figure was shrouded with blackness, but strangely familiar. I gazed up at it, something like hope beginning to take the place of the unreasoning panic. For a short while, I felt almost happy, anticipating pleasure and contentment.

Then the voice assaulted my senses.

It struck me with the force of a blow: loud, angry, filling the empty silence.

It was worse—infinitely worse and more terrifying—than the eternity of cold and darkness that I had known. I wished for the darkness to come again, to shut out the awful sounds that filled my whole world.

I began to scream.

The shouts continued. Increased. Rose above my screams.

Next, something was descending upon me. If my arms had been free, I might have raised them, to ward off this thing. But my arms were bound.

A softness on my face. Gentle at first, almost caressing. Relieved, I murmured with delight at the warmth, the fondling touch.

Next, my mouth and nostrils were enveloped in the softness, and I was gasping for air. And, above the sudden roaring in my ears, I could still hear the voice shouting in fury.

I woke up, choking on my own screams.

The other girls who shared the little room—Mary, Ethel, and Betsy—were already sitting bolt upright on their mattresses, hugging their blankets to them, eyes wide in the thin moonlight.

"What's amiss, Tessa?"

"Mercy! I thought you were being murdered in your sleep!"

" 'Tis that dream of hers—she's had that bad dream again. Isn't that it, Tessa?"

"Yes," I replied, when wakeful reality had come flooding back to me with all its blessed release. "Yes, I had that dream again."

" 'Twas the meat," said Ethel sagely. "Them as isn't used to meat shouldn't take it. Very heavy on the innards, is meat."

"The dumplings, more like," said Betsy, in her superior way. Betsy, the orphan of a clergyman, never let us forget that she had known a better life than that of Penruth

Workhouse. "We ate meat every day at the Rectory, and I never suffered from nightmares till I had to exist on workhouse slops."

Mary was already crossing the room, carrying her blanket. She snuggled in beside me and laid her covering on top of mine, her arm enfolding my shoulders.

"There, there, Tessa," she whispered. "Stop your trembling. Nothing to hurt you now. Was it very bad?"

"Yes." I nodded against her thin shoulder.

"Want to tell?"

I shook my head. How to begin to tell about a recurring nightmare that had haunted my sleep ever since I could remember? An evil hallucination—forever changing in matters of detail, always the same in essence—that had become so much a part of me that I had come almost to accept it, as the sufferer from some dreadful physical deformity will grow to live with what he cannot alter.

No—decidedly, I did not want to share it with Mary, or with anyone else. What would she, or anyone, think of a girl who constantly dreamed that she was a baby in a cot and that someone was smothering her with a pillow?

They would think that she was mad, perhaps.

New Year brought the release of a thaw. An early spring revealed Cornwall in its glory of high blue skies and the abundance of wild flowers in hedgerow and moorland. On those mornings, we sang on our way to work, luxuriating in the warmth of the new sun. That spring, also, I grew to ripeness in myself. It seemed to me that my uninteresting mid-brown hair took on a new and becoming luster and my body an unaccustomed and welcomed roundness. And my hands—thanks to twice-daily attentions from an old scrubbing brush that I had begged from one of the 'house cleaners—were slowly winning the fight against the bellows rope.

My resolve—to become an actress—had not faded with the passing months; indeed, it became a constant obsession, shutting me off from my companions. I often saw Mary glancing wistfully at me: she would be wondering why I so seldom responded to her gaiety; how could she know that I had discovered a private world of daydreams about a bright and entrancing future? Poor Mary.

There remained the problem of my coming apprenticeship. Sometime during the year the parish would wish to bind me to Mr. Martel for seven years' indenture to the trade of chain-making. At the end of it, I should become like any one of the miserable wretches who slaved out their days at the forge and anvil.

It had to be avoided at all costs—but how?

There was the other thing: the matter of learning to read and write. I never forgot Oliver Craven's words: *"You must request to be taught . . . it is your right under the law. And if your requests are not met, you must demand!"*

Fine words. Brave, inspiring words—but to whom did I make my request, and of whom my demand? Apart from the workhouse master, Mr. Pendleton, whom I occasionally saw from afar, I had not the remotest contact with the faceless ones who regulated my life; not since the age of six had I been before the Workhouse Board. As for the staff of the 'house—poorly paid employees of the parish, who were scarcely less wretched than the paupers they kept in order—any such request or demand addressed to that quarter would only have earned me a box in the ear.

But out of the blue, shortly before Easter, the dame who had charge of the girls' rooms brusquely ordered me to have my dress washed out and my hair cleaned and combed for inspection by her on the following Monday morning—for on that morning I was to appear before the Board.

On that fateful Monday, I stood for an hour in the drafty passage outside the master's office. As the last chimes of nine o'clock rang out from the clock above the gateway, the door opened and a finger was crooked at me to enter.

I went in; stood, barefoot in my clean dress, dry in the mouth, before a row of faces set behind a long table.

"Tessa Thursday. Foundling. Deposited in charge twenty-fifth February, 'forty-seven. Parents unknown. Employed since 'fifty-three at Martel's. Hard-working and of sober habits. No known diseases. Recommended for apprenticeship." The introduction was delivered by Mr. Pendleton,

who sat at the far right-hand end of—as I by then had had
time to count—a row of six, two of them women.

"Any observations?" This came from the man seated
roughly in the middle, in a bigger and more important-
looking chair. He was bald, all in black, with a clergyman's
twice-about collar, and heavy whiskers.

"Foundling, eh?" commented the man on his left. He was
very fat, with an eyeglass, through which he looked at me
with distaste. "Too many of *that* sort by far! What steps,
if any, are presently being taken to prevent these unwanted
creatures from becoming burdens of the ratepayer?"

"Extensive inquiries are made by the police, Squire
Haworth," said Mr. Pendleton, "in respect of all foundlings.
But, in the nature of things, the worthless mothers of these
unfortunates spare no effort at concealment."

"Humph!"

"Any further observations, ladies and gentlemen? No?"
The clergyman turned to the person on his right, who was
scribbling on a piece of paper. "You will appreciate, Mr.
Sewell, that this is a very straightforward case. The young
person will be placed in apprenticeship and will continue
to lodge in the 'house till the indenture is completed."

This Mr. Sewell did not bother to look up, but simply
retorted, "Quite, quite."

I clutched my hands together very tightly.

"Then, if we are all satisfied, ladies and gentlemen . . ."

There was a mumble of agreement. One of the ladies—a
stout person with a bird of paradise on her bonnet—took
a tiny mirror from her reticule and covertly examined her
side curls.

I took a deep, shuddering intake of breath.

"Very well. Then, Mr. Pendleton, you will proceed to
have the indenture drawn up."

"Yes, Mr. Chairman."

Mr. Chairman glanced at me for only the second time
since I had entered the room.

"And now, young woman. Now—er—Tessa Thursday,
you will no doubt wish to thank the Board for their
favorable decision in your case. An apprenticeship to a
skilled trade is not lightly entered into, and . . ."

I let all my breath go in one great gust of sound:

"I DON'T WANT TO BE AN APPRENTICE! I RE-QUEST TO BE TAUGHT TO READ AND WRITE!"

"Good gad!" exclaimed Squire Haworth, with the eyeglass.

The lady with the bird of paradise dropped her mirror onto the table top.

"Insolent creature!" cried the other, younger lady.

"Girl, have you gone out of your mind?" demanded Mr. Pendleton.

"The young woman must be sick," said the chairman. "It is the only charitable construction one can put upon her wild behavior." He turned to the man on his right, who had looked up from his writings at my outburst. "Mr. Sewell, you are our guest here today. On behalf of the Board, I can only tender my most sincere apologies."

In response to that, Mr. Sewell made a noncommittal gesture with his hand—and continued fixing me with an inscrutable, pale-eyed stare.

"Damned foundlings!" exclaimed Squire Haworth. "This is what comes of raising unwanted brats at the expense of the ratepayer. Confounded creatures rear up and bite the hand that feeds 'em. Haven't I always said that the law should be changed? But no one listens to me, nor will, till it's too late!"

"I totally agree!" cried the younger lady shrilly.

"Ladies and gentlemen, please," said the chairman soothingly, with an anxious glance at Mr. Sewell, who still stared at me. "Out of consideration for our guest, let us not perform our—ha—ablutions in public. It is my suggestion that the case of the young person before us be postponed till another and more suitable date."

There was a general shuffling of papers and a distinct air of relief at the chairman's suggestion. I clutched my hands very tightly behind my back.

"Tessa Thursday," said Mr. Pendleton severely. "You will leave the room. The Board has finished with you."

I took another deep breath.

"Did you hear me, girl?" snapped the workhouse master.

"I *DEMAND* TO BE TAUGHT TO READ AND WRITE!"

"Wha-a-a-t?" From the chairman.

"Outrageous!"

"Get rid of her! Send for the doorman!"

"IT IS MY RIGHT, IN LAW!"

There was a thunderstruck silence, broken only by Squire Haworth's heavy breathing. Someone rustled a paper, and it sounded like an intrusion.

And then a quiet voice said, "She's quite right, you know."

Everyone looked at his or her neighbor, till all eyes came to rest on the gentleman on the clergyman's right.

"*What* did you say, Mr. Sewell?" cried the latter.

"I said, Mr. Chairman," replied Mr. Sewell, "that the girl is quite correct in her assertion. Commencing from the Act of 'thirty-four, Poor Law officials have a responsibility for the elementary education of all children under their care. If this young person is illiterate, the blame lies at your door."

"Goodness gracious!" exclaimed Mr. Chairman.

"Poppycock!" cried Squire Haworth, loudly, to everyone in general. "Confounded impudence of the fellow, coming here from London to try and teach us our business!"

"Squire, I beg you to moderate your language," said the clergyman hastily. "Mr. Sewell is our guest, and . . ."

"With respect, Mr. Chairman," interjected Mr. Sewell calmly, "I am here as a representative of the Home Secretary. I am grateful to be treated as your guest, but your courtesy makes no difference to my *official* position here."

"I'm damned sure," growled Squire Haworth, "that the Home Secretary didn't order you to come here to try and make us look a pack of fools!"

Mr. Sewell gazed mildly at the red-faced squire, and replied, "Sir George Cornewall Lewis *requested* me to visit the Poor Law authorities of the West Country, to investigate certain irregularities. I have already ascertained that you have not complied with the Act of 'fifty-three by having your people vaccinated against smallpox. I now

31

learn that you have evaded your responsibilities in the matter of this young person's elementary education. If, incidentally, I have made you look a fool, sir, I am sorry. The fault lies elsewhere than in me!"

The squire subsided in blustering silence, and Mr. Chairman coughed nervously, eyeing his disturbing guest with great trepidation.

"Hem, if I may make an observation, Mr. Sewell," he said. "We—that is, the Board—have tried in the past to introduce the children of this institution to the benefits of education, but have found that they infinitely prefer manual work to school work. They play truant from school, never from their labors. They do not enjoy exercising their intellects, and they do not relish being caned for refusing to do it. Children of this class, sir—the lowest possible laboring class—are happier with simple, mechanical tasks, for which a formal education is not only a superfluity but a burden."

Mr. Sewell nodded reasonably. "There is some truth in that, Mr. Chairman," he said. "But the argument does not relieve you of your responsibilities under the Act. And as for the young person standing here before us—as for the outspoken Miss Tessa Thursday—I doubt very much if any part of your argument applies at all. Oh, no, Mr. Chairman, I think Miss Thursday will get her education. . . ."

He smiled conspiratorially at me.

I got my education, and I seized it with both hands, gulping it like a traveler dying with thirst who comes upon water in the desert wilderness.

My apprenticeship was set aside—"deferred" was the expression used—but I knew, if the Workhouse Board did not know, that I would never again set foot in Mr. Martel's chainworks. From then on, the school would be my whole life—until Oliver Craven returned, as he had promised to return.

They sent me to the local Board school in the town, together with six other children from the 'house. We were immediately subjected to the most cruel persecution not only from the regular pupils at the school but from their parents, particularly the mothers, who violently objected to their offspring being contaminated by contact with what they called "workhus brats," "chance brats," and similar epithets. The persecution, added to the rigors of learning, discouraged most of my companions, none of whom had ever wanted to go to the school in the first place. As the chairman of the Board had told Mr. Sewell, they played truant, misbehaved in class, struggled like tigers when threatened with the cane. Finally all save one other girl were withdrawn from school and sent back to work. The other girl—Betsy, the clergyman's orphan—was carried off in a galloping consumption in the early summer. Then there was only me. And not all the persecution in the world was going to dislodge Tessa Thursday.

It was the teacher, Miss Cribbenshaw—a muscular and capable lady in her mid-forties—who rescued me from the persecution. She quickly espied in me someone who was on her side, on the side of learning. From that moment, she became my ally and friend. The boys who waited in the alleyways behind the school to pull my hair when I came out—they were soundly boxed on the ears by the heavy hand of our teacher. Mothers who nattered about my parentage and upbringing were loudly and publicly reminded of their own shortcomings—such as that of allowing their precious darlings to come to school with nits in their hair, or with a vocabulary of foul language that could only have been picked up in their well-ordered homes. The persecution quickly abated and died.

Armed with the knowledge of my letters, which I had gained at Sunday school, I learned to string words together and was reading simple sentences within the month. By the end of that summer, I was spelling my way through *"Westward Ho!"* by Charles Kingsley. In that summer, also, I was able to read, in Miss Cribbenshaw's copy of *The Times* newspaper that she had sent from London, of the terrible Civil War that was being waged between the Northern and Southern states of America, how Fort Sumter had fallen to the Confederates, and of the Southerners' victory at the Battle of Bull Run.

Remembrances of that year of 1861 are all overshadowed

33

by the tragedy at its close: a tragedy which I was able to follow day-by-day in the newspaper reports. From the second week in December came reports that Prince Albert was taken ill of the fever at Windsor. At first, there was no hint of the seriousness of the Prince's condition; but when the young Prince of Wales was telegraphed for from his studies at Cambridge, I had a premonition of disaster. Next day came news that the invalid had rallied slightly during the night—a ray of hope that was brutally quenched in the next issue of *The Times*, where we were told that Albert the Good had departed this life and that our dear Queen was a widow and her nine children fatherless. The whole countryside was plunged into mourning and the school was closed for two days. My recollection of those two days is that I spent them reading the first chapters of *Barchester Towers* by Anthony Trollope, a book that memorably brought me to the close of my fourteenth year.

At fifteen, I was the oldest pupil in the school by six months and the one making the swiftest progress, save in the subject of arithmetic. I never possessed a head for figures, nor ever shall; but in reading and writing I forged ahead by leaps and bounds, devouring every book, periodical, handbill, tract; tradesmen's broadsheets, public notices, banns of marriage—every printed page that I set eyes on. And, as Oliver Craven had promised me, my knowledge and understanding of the world, far and near, of my own time and of other times, increased also.

In the spring of 1862 Miss Cribbenshaw recommended to the School Board that I should be appointed pupil-teacher under her at a wage of £15 per annum, an event that brought me much joy. So it was that the "workhus brat" —now completely accepted—was able to pass on her skills to the children of the town. I still lodged at the 'house, that being the only place I could afford on my meager earnings. I shared a room with Mary Allen, then halfway through her harsh apprenticeship and already crippled with bronchial trouble due to her conditions of work. No longer classed as a child at the 'house, I ate with the pauper womenfolk and learned much about their problems, which mostly stemmed from ignorance, drink, and an inability on the part of their husbands to secure regular work. On the Sunday promenades, too, I was able to converse with the menfolk, many of whom were more worthy than the wretchedness of their situation implied. There were several discharged soldiers—men who had served the Queen in many a distant clime—who were unable to live on their meager pensions and were reduced to accepting the grudging charity of the parish; these I found to possess qualities of gentleness, kindness, and courtesy as you would expect to find only in gentlemen of the very highest order. There was one old soldier whose condition disturbed me greatly, who would sit most of the time with his face turned toward the wall, with slow and bitter tears running down his leathery cheeks. When I asked, his comrades told me that "Corporal Bert," as they called him, had been among those of the 19th Regiment who had volunteered to go to India at the time of the terrible Mutiny. On landing at Calcutta, his regiment had marched straight to Cawnpore, arriving only some forty-eight hours after the massacre of the women and children there. What Corporal Bert had seen in Cawnpore was so horrible that it could be neither explained nor described; such evidence of cruelty and dishonor that it had struck him to a silence that he had not broken for nearly five years; had left him in perpetual anguish, in which he was likely to remain for the rest of his life.

It was with great relief that I finally turned my back on the Penruth Workhouse in the September of that year. It came about this way: Miss Cribbenshaw had been living with her widowed mother in a small house in the town, and on her mother's death she offered me the spare bed at only one and sixpence a week. I was more than happy to accept, and informed the workhouse master accordingly. Mr. Pendleton, who, to his credit, had never showed me any resentment or ill will following my behavior before the Board, received me in his office on the day of my departure and—of all things—treated me to a glass of homemade parsnip wine and a biscuit. We chatted amicably for a short time, and he referred to me as one who was a credit to the 'house and a shining example to those foundlings and others of the establishment who might wish to improve themselves by snatching at the manifest opportunities that were made available to them through the kindness and generosity of their benefactors. When I thought by how narrow a margin I had escaped poor Mary's fate, and how I had to stand up and fight for my right to be educated, I could scarcely suppress a wry smile.

It was then that Mr. Pendleton opened a drawer, took out a small cash box, unlocked it, and produced—a pendant on a chain.

"This is yours, Tessa," he told me. "You were wearing it round your neck when you were taken up from the doorstep. It was—save for the blanket you were wrapped up in—the only thing you brought with you. The blanket, I'm afraid, has long since worn out; but the pendant, as you see, is intact. I should like your signature for its receipt, my dear, if you please."

The pendant itself was some kind of silver coin bearing the impression of a lady's head—a rather severe-looking lady with an antique hair-dressing. There were words written round the edge of the piece, which seemed about the size of an English crown piece—though the crown was not a coin with which I had much acquaintance.

The words read: ". . . *REG. M. THERESIA D.G.* . . ."

That was all—for the coin had been cut roughly in half, and in a peculiar sort of way.

Mr. Pendleton said, "It is half of a Maria Theresa thaler, or dollar. An Austrian coin, which, though neither rare nor of any considerable value, is a coin with an interesting history. This much we know because the then rector of this parish and chairman of the Board was a collecter of coins and identified it immediately. The lady represented on the face is the Empress Maria Theresa, and it was for this reason that Mr. Lancing, the then rector, decided—much against the inclinations of the rest of the Board—that you should be christened with the somewhat fanciful name of Tessa, which is a corruption of Theresa."

"But—it's been strangely cut," I said.

"As to the unusual shape of the cut," said Mr. Pendleton, "it was done in what is known in the carpentry trade as a 'dovetail joint,' where two pieces are connected by what are referred to as the—hum—the 'male' and 'female' ends of the joint. What you have there is, in the parlance of carpentry, the female part of the dovetail joint.''

"Then somewhere there must be the other half!" I cried.

"Ah, that is entirely possible," said Mr. Pendleton, looking away in an embarrassed manner.

"The—male part."

"Quite so."

"Then that must mean—may mean—that my mother, whoever she was, and my father—whoever *he* was—had the coin cut as a keepsake, to share between them."

"I should think it not unlikely," admitted Mr. Pendleton.

"Then," said I, "I have only to find the other half of this Maria Theresa thaler, as you call it, and I may discover who my father was, and perhaps my mother also."

The workhouse master summoned up his courage to look me in the eye and address me in a voice of real sincerity.

"You might think that such knowledge would bring you happiness, Tessa," he said. "But, from my own personal experience of these painful matters, I would say that you would do better not to probe into your origins. Consider the painful truth of it, my dear: you were left here as a babe, alone, unwanted. It is scarcely possible that the passing of the years would make you any more welcome if you intruded—unasked and unannounced—into the lives of those who cast you aside when you were most in need. Take my advice, Tessa: make your own way in the world, and let the unknown look after itself."

Staring down at the mutilated coin in my hand, I could only agree with Mr. Pendleton. So, without any deep regrets, I resolved to forget the other half of the dovetail and wear the pendant always, but only as a keepsake for myself: the only possession I had brought with me, and my sole inheritance.

Sharing house with Miss Cribbenshaw was not without its drawbacks, for she was a hard taskmaster both in and out of school, and I was obliged to help her in keeping the little four-roomed terraced house as neat and tidy as a well-kept sewing box. The cat, Orlando, had to have his paws wiped clean and dry before he was permitted to walk over our holystoned front step and relax upon his favorite chair with its spotless loose covers and antimacassars. A fervent freethinker, anti-cleric, and feminist long before her time, Miss Cribbenshaw was a soul of good charity, and fed four old men and women of the parish a Sunday dinner every week at her own expense. This meant my rising early to help prepare a shepherd's pie or Cornish pasties, with potato cakes, vegetables in season, followed by apple pudding and custard. The old folks also were subjected to a similar discipline as the cat Orlando, and were obliged to leave their boots just inside the front door.

But if Miss Cribbenshaw was a bit of a martinet—and she was—and if she was the sort of person who found it difficult to make a warm personal contact with a fellow human—and she was—there existed a richness of good qualities within her forbidding exterior. Being aware of my avid thirst for knowledge and self-improvement, she was extravagant with her help to the point of recklessness, dipping into her own slender purse for books for me to read, working all hours to instruct me in anything I wanted to learn. And she was a mine of knowledge far beyond the needs of a country town Board school teacher, being conversant with all branches of mathematics; with history, geography, the natural sciences; as well as the Spanish, French, and Latin languages.

In the winter of '62 and '63, when we were snowed up in West Cornwall and the school was closed for a whole month due to inadequate heating facilities, Miss Cribbenshaw taught me enough French to permit me to find my way through most of Dumas's *Three Musketeers* in the original. Further to assist my French studies, she took out a subscription to the Parisian journal *Le Figaro*, which arrived in weekly packets from the capital city of France, bringing with it—in everything about it: wrappings, pink string and sealing wax, foreign postage stamps—a heady whiff of Gallic enchantment to my remote and narrow world in West Cornwall.

In the pages of *Le Figaro*, I perfected my French by keeping abreast of the great developments in the outside world—as, for instance, the progress of the dreadful Civil War in America; the triumphant career of Napoleon III, Emperor of the French and himself a descendant of the first great Napoleon, who had held all Europe in dread and against whom many of the ex-soldiers at the Penruth Workhouse had fought at Waterloo.

In *Le Figaro*, also, my eye lit upon an item of news on the theater page that brought me mingled joy and despair. Translated into English, these words read:

NOTED ENGLISH MIME COMPANY
FIND NOBLE PATRON

The mime company of Mr. Oliver Craven, who have been playing a season of English traditional mime plays and classical French mimes of the 17th Century at the Comédie Française, are to receive the patronage, it is stated, of Monsieur le Comte Robert de Brassy.

M. le Comte, as will be known, resigned his commission from the Army following a serious wounding at the siege of Sebastopol during the Crimean War, and is now devoting himself to the support and patronage of the arts, particularly the theater. To our correspondent visiting the sumptuous Hôtel de Brassy in the rue du Faubourg St.-Honoré, M. le Comte had this to say of the English mime artiste: "Mr. Craven's art is in a direct descent from the Greek and Roman origins, in that it transcends nationality, and speaks to all men. It is my intention to obtain a Parisian theater for the sole use of Mr. Craven and his company so that the world may benefit from the richness of their art. . . ."

So Oliver Craven had found his fame and fortune at last. And now, I supposed despairingly, he would have to marry that dreadful Frenchwoman, that Jeanette, who had trapped him into it. With such success—and so far away—it was almost impossible that he would now carry out his promise to return to Penruth. What hope of it, when his new wife would almost certainly prevent him. I remembered well enough—it seemed so long ago, but it was only three short years—the incident in the changing room, when Oliver Craven had spoken of my looks, and how Jeanette had seemed bored and resentful. No—decidedly, it was no longer worth looking to that quarter for help in my career. Having decided that, I broke down and cried.

I think it was one of the bitterest disappointments of my life so far; but fate had yet another blow to deliver at me. And soon.

The engagement of the Prince of Wales to Princess Alexandra of Denmark had caught the imagination of the British people, and was a daily topic in *The Times*. The marriage was set for 10th March, but the Queen, who was still in deepest mourning for the Prince Consort, had stipulated that the ceremony must take place in the privacy of St. George's Chapel, Windsor, instead of publicly and splendidly at Westminster Abbey. But if Her Majesty was determined on maintaining an atmosphere of gloom and mourning throughout the nuptials, not so her faithful subjects. The dashing young Prince was quite a favorite with the public, and his beautiful bride-to-be everything that a Cinderella princess should be—even down to her comparatively penniless royal parentage (why, the poor girl even had to do her own dressmaking!); so it was a popular move when the Penruth town council voted the unheard-of sum of two hundred and fifty pounds for the proper celebration of the Royal Wedding, to include street decorations, the fife band of the Cornwall Yeomanry, fireworks, and a slap-up high tea for all the children and old folk of the town.

Naturally, with her energy and enthusiasm, Miss Cribbenshaw was caught up in the organizing of the festivities, which meant I was too. Our responsibility lay with the supervision of the tea party, which was to take place—weather permitting—in Fore Street, the main street of the town, where trestle tables were to be laid right down the center for an estimated one hundred and thirty sitters. Miss Cribbenshaw appointed herself general director of the feast and keeper of order. My personal chore was largely connected with the four huge tea urns that were to be set up conveniently near to the public water fountain.

Tuesday, 10th March, dawned with a slight drizzle and

a wind from the southwest that presaged a day of rain. Miss Cribbenshaw, who had been up since five o'clock cutting extra sandwiches in the quite mistaken belief that we should run short, put on her bonnet and shawl as soon as it began to get light and set off to supervise the men who would be setting up the tables and hanging the decorations in Fore Street. She left with an injunction to me not to tarry, but to be there for the arrival of my tea urns at nine o'clock. Tea would be served at three p.m. promptly. And there was much to be done in the meantime, she said.

Obediently, I left the house at a quarter to nine and made my way to Fore Street, where I found a group of men from the workhouse who had been pressed into service as laborers. They lolled around the street corners, smoking and idling, while the trestle tables were still stacked by the water fountain, and of the decorations there was not a sign. Nor any sign of Miss Cribbenshaw.

Had they not seen Miss Cribbenshaw? They took clay pipes out of their mouths, scratched their heads, shook their heads, and went back to their gossiping. She had not turned up. But why?

I had an immediate premonition of tragedy. Heart pounding, I retraced my steps—back the way she must have come. At the junction of Fore Street and Station Street, where the road ran under the railway bridge, I chanced to notice something that had escaped my eyes on my way past earlier: a small knot of women standing at the open doorway of a house on the corner. They were talking together excitedly and pointing in the direction of the bridge's arch. With a sick, dull feeling of despair, I went over to them.

Some of them recognized me at once—as the young teacher-lass from the school. There was deep concern in their glances. And something else.

I asked them if they had seen Miss Cribbenshaw—half expecting their answer, yet not suffering the less shock and horror for that. They had not much to tell . . .

Hurrying to her self-appointed task, in the dawn darkness, my friend and mentor had slipped on the wet cobbles while crossing the road by the bridge. A two-horse dray, coming through the archway at speed, had run over the prostrate woman. She had been taken to Penruth Infirmary.

They took me in a donkey cart to the grim-walled infirmary. Miss Cribbenshaw had died on her arrival there; but an attendant turned back the cover so that I could see her face: serene as if in sleep; all her wisdom and wide knowledge, all her boundless kindness, vanished with the new dawn.

Oddly enough, the wind changed and the sun came out, drying off the streets. Because Miss Cribbenshaw would have wanted it that way, I took charge of the men and ordered them to put up the decorations and set the tables in place. And, somehow, it was done. Three o'clock found the children and old people seated in the sunlight and shade, under the red-white-and-blue flags, the gay rosettes, pictures of the Happy Couple framed in paper lilies, a portrait of our Queen wreathed in the Union Jack.

I said nothing to the children about Miss Cribbenshaw, for she was well-loved by them, and it would have ruined their day. The old people knew, for news of death passes swiftly among the elderly. They, too, kept it from the little ones.

When they had all been served—when everyone had their heaped plate of sandwiches, pasties, biscuits, plum cake, and a steaming mug of tea—I let myself give way to tears.

No one saw me, over by the tea urns, while the Cornish Yeomanry marched and counter-marched to fifes and drums, under the colored bunting and the wide blue sky.

Miss Cribbenshaw had gone, and now there was a hole in my life that surely no one else would be able to fill. The new teacher would like as not be a man. And where would I live? Did this mean that I should have to go back to the 'house? Perhaps even return to work for Mr. Martel, if the new teacher did not approve of me? Self-pity battling with grief, I stared unseeingly down the crowded street.

A voice at my elbow said, "Could I trouble you for a cup of tea, please, ma'am?"

I gave a start and turned toward the sound. Through

my tear-blinded eyes I could make out only the wide shape
of his shoulders and the tall hat he wore. I blinked away
some of the tears—as he took off the hat and revealed the
dark mane of hair coming to a widow's peak in the middle
of the wide forehead. Deep blue eyes swam into my view,
regarding me searchingly.

"You!" I cried.

"I've kept my promise, Tessa Thursday," said Oliver
Craven. "And I've come to take you away—if that is still
your wish."

2

"From now on, my dear Tessa, you will call me Oliver."

I nodded eagerly. I would have agreed to anything on that day of days, when the enclosing walls of my life had fallen down and the wide world had opened up for me; and my only regret was that Miss Cribbenshaw, to whom I owed so much, had not been there to see me off at the railway station. I looked back, out of the carriage window, to the low hills of mid-Cornwall fading away in the west. Would I ever go back? I wondered.

"Oliver," I murmured, trying it on my tongue. "Oliver."

"Excellent," he said.

He had not changed much in the three years; all that had changed was my judgment of age, which had become more practiced and mature. Oliver Craven was older than I had thought him at our first meeting. The slight touch of gray at the temples and about the ears accented this. I guessed, now, that he must be in his late thirties. Truly old enough to be my father.

"So we're going to France," I said, shaking my head. "I just can't believe it. I really can't. To think of it—me . . ."

"We stay overnight in London," he said, "at Morley's Hotel in Trafalgar Square, where the rest of the company and I have been staying during our short season at the Theatre Royal. Then tomorrow we depart by rail for Southampton, where we take the cross-Channel packet for the French port of Le Havre, we proceed by rail to Tours, where, on Monday evening next, the company opens at the Opera House in that city, in a gala performance to be given before—would you believe it, Tessa?—the Emperor and Empress of France. Now, what do you think of that?"

"It—it's like a dream," I told him.

"And you shall be there, Tessa," he told me. "You shall

see the gala performance and no doubt witness the scene when my patron, Count de Brassy, presents the company and myself to their Imperial Majesties. That will be something to see, eh, Tessa? A far cry from our performance at the Penruth Workhouse on that Christmas Eve, eh?"

I glanced sharply out the window, to hide my sudden hurt.

"It was—a very nice performance, that Christmas Eve," I whispered.

"Tessa, Tessa . . ." He moved quickly over from his seat opposite and sat down beside me, taking hold of my hand. "That wasn't what I meant, my dear. Of course, that was a memorable occasion, if only for the fact that I found you, Tessa. But—don't you see?—this gala performance before their Imperial Majesties is going to set the seal on the company's success. From next Monday, I assure you, all France will be at our feet. And soon all Europe and America. That's the way it will be, Tessa. Don't you see?"

I nodded. And then, I dared to put to him the question which had been faltering on the tip of my tongue almost since the moment he came back into my life.

"I suppose, now you're a great success, that you and that French lady, Miss Jeanette, will be married?"

"Jeanette?" He stared at me in surprise. "Oh, of course you didn't know. How could you? Poor Jeanette passed away. It was a terrible tragedy. It happened this way: soon after we left Cornwall that winter, the company had an opportunity to do a European tour. It sounds rather grand, but, in fact, it was the poorest thing imaginable: giving performances in back-street taverns and music halls in Marseilles, Genoa, Naples. We were in Naples when an epidemic broke out. Poor Jeanette fell ill and died there. It was terrible. I was with her at the end. I would have married her—indeed, I sent for a priest to perform the ceremony—but she slipped through our fingers before his arrival."

"I'm sorry, Oliver." I laid my hand on his, and was stricken with sympathy to see a tear course down his cheek.

He said quietly, "You never saw her in her great days, Tessa, before disillusionment and drink brought her low.

Oh, she was able to put on a good performance right to the end—as you saw her doing at Penruth—but, ah, you should have seen her ten, fifteen years ago. What style! What artistry! She should have been another Mrs. Siddons, another Peg Woffington; but that poor creature—so full of vivacity, beauty, talent—was dogged by evil luck her life through. Right to the end. She never tasted the success she so richly deserved."

"You must miss her very much," I murmured.

He took a deep breath. "I never—loved her," he said. "I esteemed her—yes. I admired her beyond all others for her artistry. In the end, I pitied her. But I never loved her, Tessa, though I'm aware that her feelings for me were of a more—profound nature."

Any further discussion was cut short by a piercing note from the locomotive's whistle, and the train slackened speed and came into a wayside station. There was much hissing of steam, opening and closing of doors, and shouting of orders. Into our first-class carriage—which we had had to ourselves since we left Penruth—came a red-faced gentleman in a tall hat of enormous size, carrying a hamper and a carpetbag, which he placed high on the luggage rack. He then took out a snuffbox and a newspaper, snuffed from the one and quickly proceeded to nod off to sleep over the other. I took the opportunity of the break in our conversation to consider Oliver, who was looking out the window as we pulled out of the station.

As I have mentioned, he looked older. But none the less handsome and commanding. And his clothing was faultless. Coat of the finest-looking material, light and soft. Shirt of pin-tucked linen. Cravat and waistcoat both silk. On the little finger of his left hand he wore a thick ring engraved with a monogram, and there was another ring that winked like a diamond—or so I supposed diamonds to wink—on his other hand. Signs of prosperity were written large on Oliver Craven; but he wore them, as he had worn penury and obscurity, lightly and without effort. I thought back to his arrival in Penruth: how he had swept me off my feet with his dramatic energy, commanding my life by arranging for my immediate departure for London and beyond. I needed, he said, a complete new wardrobe; but there being nothing but the poorest stuff to be had ready-made in the town's only general store, we must settle for a couple of changes of costume and leave the rest till we reached more civilized parts. His intent had been to leave by train that same afternoon; but I had jibbed at leaving without paying my last respects to Miss Cribbenshaw —a protest that he had taken in his stride by arranging, at such short notice, for a funeral on the following morning, of the sort that must seldom come the way of such as poorly paid Board teachers, with the finest hearse that Penruth could provide, plumes, flowers, and choir and organ. We had left immediately after the ceremony. I had placed the cat Orlando with good neighbors. And now we were steaming eastward.

At the signal of our new companion's second reverberating snore, Oliver leaned forward and said, "I must tell you about my patron, Count de Brassy."

"I know," I replied, "that he has a sumptuous *hôtel particulier* in the rue du Faubourg St.-Honoré, because I read about it in *Le Figaro*."

An expression of amused incredulity crossed his face, and he grinned at me.

"Bless my soul!" he exclaimed. "This really is too good. Would you be so kind, my dear Tessa, as to repeat that, please?"

I had thought that he was teasing me. "Repeat what?" I demanded suspiciously.

"The French bits," he explained. "Hotel whatever and rue de thingummy."

I obliged him, puzzled. He shook his head in wonderment.

"You're a marvel," he said. "My French is atrocious and my accent a joke. And here's you, sounding for all the world like a Parisienne born and bred. By jove, you haven't been wasting these last three years, Tessa. You said you'd do it, and by thunder you have!" And with that, he rose to his feet, and, crossing over, he took me by the shoulders and gave me a resounding kiss on the forehead. "Well done, my girl!"

"Miss Cribbenshaw taught me all I know," I said, modesty

and pride of achievement struggling for supremacy in my mind. "And she was particularly strict about French accent and pronunciation."

"She had a confoundedly good pupil," was Oliver's rejoinder. "But I was telling you about De Brassy. He's a splendid fellow. An aristocrat to his fingertips—one of the ancient nobility, but no trace of the snob for all that. A man of action. Soldier and sportsman. Used to ride to hounds like the devil himself, so I'm told—in the days before a Russian musket ball lamed him in the leg before Sebastopol. Now he limps around with a stick, and is only able to indulge his passion for the arts. He's a fine musician: plays pianoforte and flute in masterly fashion. And he is of the opinion, my dear Tessa, that Oliver Craven is one of the finest of living actors and certainly the greatest mime artiste—and I'm of the opinion that he's right!"

His statement, free of any false modesty or sly conceit, made me smile nevertheless. "You're the only mime artiste I've ever seen," I told him, "but I never expect to see better."

He flicked his eyebrow with his finger, the way I had always remembered. "Then we are all in agreement," he said.

We both laughed, and our traveling companion stirred in his sleep and snorted. Oliver put a warning finger to his lips.

In the silence while our companion resumed his slumbers, there came to my mind the serious question that, sooner or later, I must put to Oliver. As well now as later. I glanced at the sleeper, steeled myself, and began:

"Oliver . . ."

"Yes, my dear?"

"What's going to happen to me next?"

"You mean—in your immediate future, this year, next year?"

"Yes."

Oliver smiled, took from his breast pocket a leather case, and from that a slim cigar, which he lit with a lucifer match: watching me all the while with his blue eyes half closed. He drew a mouthful of smoke and exhaled it in a thin plume.

"The valley of the River Loire," he said, "as I am sure that you, with all your learning, will know, was once one of the great centers of power in France. It was on the banks of the Loire that mighty kings, and nobles scarcely less mighty, built vast castles as monuments to their pride and wealth. One such castle—and one of the most notable —is the Château Brassy, ancestral home of my patron's family since the fifteenth century. It is a place of almost unbelievable beauty and splendor. And, my dear Tessa, it is to be your home till you come of age."

"My home—a castle?" I stared at Oliver in flat disbelief. "But how—why?"

"My patron has ordained it," he replied. "With scarcely any prompting from me, Count Robert has said that you will go to live in the château and be treated as a permanent guest. I should tell you that the custom of patronage is commonplace among the continental nobility. The present count's father, for instance, maintained a five-piece string orchestra—and their families and dependants—for over twenty years. At a neighboring château, a distinguished but impoverished painter and his wife have enjoyed half a lifetime of unstinted patronage. The likes of Count Robert do not regard artistic patronage as charity but as one of the obligations of the life aristocratic. Do you understand, Tessa?"

"But why should he do all this for *me*, Oliver?" I persisted. "He hasn't even seen me. Why, he might hate me on sight."

"It's scarcely likely," smiled Oliver indulgently. "I should think he will succumb to your charms as soon as you walk in through the château door."

"But why me? Oliver, what did you tell the count that made him so willing to accept me almost as a member of his family—me, a foundling, brought up in a parish workhouse in far-off Cornwall—without even setting eyes on me?"

"The point is well-taken, my dear. You have a shrewd head on those young shoulders. I can see that I shall have to unburden myself of the truth of the matter—which is a pity."

"Why a pity?" I asked, puzzled.

"Because," he said with a smile, "I had hoped to spare you from a grave sin."

"A grave sin? I don't understand you, Oliver. What sin?"

"The sin of—conceit!"

I shook my head at him. "Please, Oliver, don't tease me."

Slowly, deliberately, he blew a perfect smoke ring and watched it rise to the carriage roof and be dispersed. Then, eyeing me evenly, he said, "Why do you imagine I came for you, Tessa? Why do you think I made the promise three years ago, to come back to Penruth?"

"I've thought about that many times," I replied. "And it must have been because you were impressed by the sincerity of my ambition to become an actress. For even though the ambition only came to me that night, suddenly, it came with tremendous force. I felt it in myself. I tell myself that you felt it also."

He nodded. "That's true, Tessa. I did feel that force which had sprung to life within you. As an artiste, a man of acute sensibility, I could scarcely have missed it. But there were other impressions I received: impressions of which you cannot have been aware. Even poor Jeanette missed the most important of them—but that was because her artistic sensibilities were already far eroded by drink and despair."

"What were these—impressions?" I asked him falteringly.

"The most forcible and obvious—and I think, to her annoyance and possible jealousy, that even Jeanette must have discerned it—is that you were a young girl with the promise of a most outstanding beauty. Half-starved as you were, pale and unkempt, your hands grimed and callused seemingly beyond redemption, this promise shone within you like a lantern hidden from sight under a cloak.

"I said that you would become a beautiful woman, Tessa. That promise is now all but accomplished!"

I stared down at my hands and found they were trembling. No one had ever spoken to me so directly about myself. As I was not a self-regarding person, the idea of my having any pretensions to beauty was something that had never crossed my mind. My hands—they were a different matter;

had I not labored for three years to undo the damage wrought by the bellows ropes? And with some success: as I looked down at them, to cover my confusion, I was gratified to note that they were now quite clean. Not white; all the scrubbing in the world would never tone down their russet, countrywoman's color. Not smooth and soft; coarse carbolic soap is no great aid to the care of the skin. But they were undeniably clean and free of calluses.

What was Oliver saying now? . . .

"Beauty—great beauty, of the kind that you, my dear Tessa, will be commanding in the full flowering of your womanhood—is almost sufficient to sustain the career of a leading actress. Indeed, many have done it, and are still doing it, with considerably inferior physical equipment. The promise of beauty that you displayed as a young girl of thirteen would almost have been sufficient to have attracted my interest. But there was something else . . ."

"Something else?" I looked up at him sharply, my embarrassment overcome by a sudden, new curiosity. "What else, Oliver?"

"Artistry—the artistry of the great actor—is difficult to define, but is quite unmistakable. Physical equipment plays a large part. The great actress of the last century, Sarah Siddons, was of superb appearance, with large and eloquent eyes, magnificent voice, faultless diction. Added to these, she had the magical quality of power over her audiences. Do you follow me, Tessa—can you imagine what I mean by this strange power?"

I nodded. Did I not follow him very well indeed? Had I not been conscious of this strange power in Oliver himself, from the very moment that he turned to regard us paupers—his audience—that unforgettable Christmas Eve? But what had this to do with me?

"This quality, this power," he said, "is either there or it is not there. It cannot be counterfeited. An actor may enjoy a middlingly successful career on the boards without possessing it; but he will never—he cannot ever—be a great artiste. Are you still following me, Tessa?"

"Yes, Oliver," I whispered. The presentiment of a strange

wonder flooded over me, and I felt my skin prickle with the beginnings of an almost physical shock.

He watched me evenly, and said, "Three years ago, I thought I saw the beginnings of that quality in you, Tessa. And I was not wrong. It is still there—shining even more brightly."

"In—*me?*" I breathed.

"Unmistakably," he said. "It needs to be developed, of course. Carefully nourished, lest it wither and remain just empty promise. It is for this reason that you are going to spend the next few years—till you are twenty or so—at Château Brassy. For, as I told my patron, and he was entirely in agreement, there is no place in Europe where you could better finish your education than in the elegant and cultured atmosphere of a Loire château, with its magnificent library, its works of art, its air of gracious living and effortless ease. Perfect conditions, my dear Tessa, to prepare for a career of the first magnitude."

A career of the first magnitude! Was this *really* being said to *me?* Dizzy with the splendor of it, I rested my head back against the antimacassar of my seat and stared at my companion, fearful that he might cruelly be teasing me. But there was only intense sincerity in his glance. I closed my eyes and felt the prickle of tears.

"Borrow my clean handkerchief, my dear," murmured Oliver, reaching to tuck it between my fingers.

Further conversation between us was prevented by the awakening of our traveling companion, who rose and, stretching himself, ventured the opinion that we should be at Paddington within the hour. He then reached down his hamper and took from it a large black bottle and a glass, a dish containing some sort of meat pie, a roast fowl wrapped in a napkin, and half a loaf. These he proceeded to attack till they were entirely consumed.

All the rest of the way to London, I sat in a dream of delight and wonder, with the magical thought running through and through my mind: that Oliver Craven had discerned in me the beginnings of that magical quality which he himself possessed to such a very high degree.

I was going to be a great artiste, with a career of the first magnitude! . . .

Holding this thought tightly with me, I sat with my eyes closed, till the events of the previous two days bore down on me and carried me off into a deep and dreamless sleep, from which I was awakened by Oliver's touch and the sound of a raucous voice outside the carriage.

"Paddington—this is Paddington! All change, ladies and gentlemen."

"We're here, Tessa," said Oliver.

The red-faced gentleman took down his carpetbag and smiled across at us.

"Your daughter has soon discovered the best way to reduce the tedium of railway travel, sir," he said to Oliver.

Out of the soaring glass-and-iron cathedral of Paddington Station, with a trio of porters carrying our luggage.

"We'll take a hansom cab to Trafalgar Square," said Oliver.

As if in a dream, I took my place in the cab and had a thick rug laid across my knees against the cold. It was raining in London. A sea of tall hats and bobbing umbrellas swept in and out of the great entrance arch. In the roadway beyond, the gas lamps had been lit against the evening overcast. I had never seen so many people together in my life before.

Out of the station, the wind drove featherings of the rain under the canopy of the cab, stinging my cheeks. The horse was gleaming with wet, and steaming. Clip-clop on the cobbles. Iron tires trundling loudly. Past long rows of town houses with basements all lit up, holystoned steps, and polished door handles.

"Hyde Park," said Oliver, pointing to a wide green sward. "See how the trees are still bare here. Not like the West Country. Over yonder, beyond the Serpentine lake, is where the Crystal Palace was built for the Great Exhibition of 'fifty-one, but the building was taken down and set up again in Sydenham. Are you quite comfortable, Tessa?"

I made no reply, but he did not seem to notice, and

continued to point out places and scenes of interest as we went through Mayfair, along Piccadilly. By then, the late afternoon had tired of battling with the overcast and had resigned itself to the coming night. The gaslights were all on in Piccadilly: long chains of diamonds stretching out of sight in a dramatic curve. The shops were ablaze, reflected from the glistening pavements, where the umbrellaed crowds swarmed.

I glanced out of the corner of my eye at Oliver, who was looking directly ahead, his tall hat tipped low over his brow against the flurries of rain that swept in on us from gust to gust. He seemed unaware—or unconcerned—that anything was troubling me.

We joined the throng of cabs and carriages skirting a place of lights and dazzling movement at the end of Piccadilly, with Oliver pointing here and there, to draw my attention to a notable building, a colorful shop, the flower-women lining the pavements with their huge baskets of brightness. I scarcely paid any attention.

The rain slackened when we drew near to our destination: a great open space dominated by a towering column.

"There stands Lord Nelson," said Oliver. "And that antique barracks of a place yonder is the town house of the Duke of Northumberland. Its gardens reach right down to the river, and it's to be wondered how much longer His Grace will be permitted to lord it over quite so much of central London. Ah, here's Morley's Hotel just across the way. Did you enjoy the drive, Tessa? Didn't get too wet, I hope?"

It had to be said now, while the memory of that casual remark by the gentleman in the train still lay freshly between us: let even another hour go past and it would be almost impossible to reintroduce the subject. Now was the time: while the cab was slowing to a halt before the hotel's entrance porch, and liveried footmen were moving out from the lamplit warmth to see to us and our baggage.

"Oliver . . ." I laid my hand on his arm. I had to have his whole attention, with him looking into my eyes.

"Yes, my dear? Heavens, is something amiss, Tessa?"

"Oliver, am I your daughter? *Am* I?"

I would have sworn that there was not the slightest flicker of hesitation of the kind that betrays someone about to tell a lie; just a moment's pause of genuine surprise, and then:

"Why, no, Tessa, you are not. And more's the pity, I say!"

My room was on the third floor, with a window that overlooked Trafalgar Square and Nelson's Column, the moving tide of people, wheeled traffic of every conceivable kind, lamplight, and a new downpour of rain. I closed the tasseled velvet curtains and shook my head in wonder.

It was seven o'clock and Oliver had said we would dine at eight. This would make the second occasion that I had dined in the evening in all my life: last night had been the first, with Oliver at the Post Inn, Penruth.

What to wear? My choice was not wide, for I had only the three changes of costume that Oliver had bought for me before we left Cornwall: two day dresses of grosgrain, one in bottle green and the other in brown (I was wearing the latter), and a more formal garment of deep blue terry velvet. I plumped for the velvet, mostly for the reason that it was to be worn over a crinoline instead of over petticoats—and it was the first crinoline dress of my life.

In it, and with my hair drawn back in a tight chignon, I took stock of myself in the long mirror. The dress suited me very well, for all that it was the best that the Penruth emporium—no purveyor of the latest Paris fashions—could provide. Its unaccustomed round neckline revealed the chain I had worn ever since leaving the workhouse. For the first time, I felt inclined to lift out my half-thaler pendant and let it be seen; till then I had instinctively kept it secret from the eyes of the world.

I gazed at my reflection dispassionately. Oh, Tessa Thursday, I told myself, you look older than your tender years. Why, you could pass for twenty in that crinoline. And your complexion isn't at all bad, and your hair has a good shine. Clear eyes of deep brown. Good teeth. Nose inclined to be a little perky: what the French would call *retroussé*. Not bad, my girl.

But a raving beauty, now or in the future?

Sorry—no!

"I just don't see it," I said aloud.

Nor did I. In that, if in nothing else, Oliver had been wildly overoptimistic in his judgment. "Pleasant," "wholesome," "interesting"—these were the sort of qualities I could with candor, and in the privacy of my room, apply to my appearance. "Outstanding beauty of the future"? Not so.

As for the remark by the gentleman in the train: from every angle that I viewed myself, I bore not the slightest resemblance to Oliver, either in form or in coloring. The remark had been loosely made. But, strange how it had affected me.

Was I sorry, after all, that Oliver's interest in me stemmed from nothing more than a professional interest? Would I have preferred it if he had turned out to be my natural father?

On the whole, I decided I was glad he was not. Whoever my father, I owed him nothing—and certainly not my esteem. I greatly esteemed Oliver, and wished to keep it so.

The clock on the chimney piece tinkled the hour. With a sigh, I gathered up my unaccustomed wide skirts and edged out the door to the broad stairway that led down, past gilded gas brackets and on a carpet of yielding softness, to where Oliver was waiting for me in the hallway.

"Beautiful," he said, holding out his hands for mine. "You look truly beautiful, Tessa."

"Thank you, Oliver." A compliment was no less acceptable for being an exaggeration, I discovered.

The crowded dining room was as full of sound as an overturned beehive, with waiters bustling about the needs of half a hundred people seated at tables about the vast, chandelier-hung chamber, under a painted ceiling adorned with fat cupids and tumbled clouds. A personage with loops of gold cord about his shoulders, a powdered wig, and whiskers of excessive size signaled Oliver from a table for three in the center of the room.

Oliver handed me into my seat and took the place opposite. There remained a vacant seat on my left.

"Mirabel will be joining us," he said. "She is not the acme of punctuality, bless her."

Mirabel, as he had already told me, was the leading actress of the company: the "princess"—she who had replaced poor Jeanette.

"What about the rest of the company?" I asked him.

"They are all over there, at the table by the window at the end," said Oliver. He waved to a group of people—three men and three women—all of them young and amiable-looking. They smiled and waved in return.

"I will introduce you to them after dinner," said Oliver. "They are all new to the company. I must have made at least two complete changes of artistes since the time you saw us in Penruth. Which brings me to another point, Tessa. I have said nothing, out of consideration for your feelings, about your origins. Nothing about your being a foundling, nothing about the—place—where we first met. As far as Mirabel and the others are concerned, you are an orphan, you lived in Penruth, and we are distantly related." He smiled brilliantly and flicked his eyebrow with his finger, adding, "I hope you are not annoyed at my presumption in attaching myself to you as a distant uncle, dear niece?"

"I'm very flattered," I replied. "But, I promise you, Oliver, I don't mind being a nobody, I am what I am, and nothing I can do or say will change that."

"Your honesty does you credit, Tessa," he replied seriously. "I am not suggesting that you tell lies; merely that you abstain from certain truths. The facts of your background are known only to Count de Brassy and myself. Oh, and the Count's young nephew, who also lives at the château. For the time being, at any rate, I should prefer to keep it like that." He smiled again—that winning, irresistible smile. "If you're not angry and offended by the suggestion."

"Of course not," I assured him. To tell the truth, the prospect of turning my back on Penruth Workhouse and all its memories had suddenly given me a heady sense of new freedom, and the idea of being Tessa Thursday, formerly of Penruth and niece to the distinguished actor Oliver Craven was like ceasing to be nobody and becoming a somebody.

I was reflecting on this when there was a sudden stir in the dining room: a shifting of movement and a changing note in the sounds. Then an awed silence.

"Here comes dear Mirabel," said Oliver with an amused inflection in his voice. "And all dolled up like the Carnival of Venice!"

I turned, gasped, and stared . . .

She was tall and splendidly made. A vision in pink flame. Hair of flaming auburn, dressed in an elaborate chignon and falling in ringlets behind a tiara of pink roses and brilliants. The pink silk ball dress—at that time, I did not have the language to describe it; subsequent acquaintance with the "creations" of Mr. Charles Frederick Worth, the English dressmaker who had inspired all Paris, help me to recall that it was embellished with escallops and pleated flounces, roullets and ruches; lavishly decorated with handmade lace and enough artificial flowers to shame a conservatory; with a crinoline wider than any ordinary door known to man. The vision was preceded by two waiters clearing a path, and two more setting in order the things that had been disturbed or overturned in its passing.

"Oliver, lovey! Oh, it's nice to see you back. Give us a kiss, dearie." Her voice, loud and raucous, echoed from the far recesses of the silent dining room.

"Hello, Mirabel dear," murmured Oliver, standing to deliver a cool kiss on a painted cheek. "You're looking very splendid, as usual. This is Tessa Thursday, of whom I spoke. Tessa dear, I'd like to introduce you to my leading lady, Mirabel Ducane."

"Pleased to meet you, Miss Ducane," I said, holding out my hand.

"Oh, Oliver. She's lovely—lovely," cried Mirabel Ducane, ignoring my hand and taking me by the shoulders. "Oh, and I can see the family resemblance all right. Oh, yes, lovey—you're a chip of the same old block and no mistake." So saying, she enveloped me in her arms and, burying my face in her bosom, proceeded to cover my forehead with cachou-scented kisses. When I managed to win free, I met Oliver's gaze over her shoulder and he rolled his eyes and hunched his shoulders in a gesture of helplessness.

"Sit down, my dears," he said mildly, "then everyone can go back to enjoying their dinners."

"Champagne is what I'm having before I eat a morsel," declared Mirabel Ducane, "for I've a thirst on me as would not shame a Billingsgate fish porter." She turned to me and laid a hand on my arm. Her eyes were large, green, and glittering. "You may keep your claret wine and your Burgundy wine," she told me, "likewise your stouts, your ales, and your beers. When it comes to laying a thirst, there's nothing can beat a drop of fizz!"

"Er—yes," I murmured in some confusion.

"You shall have your champagne, Mirabel," said Oliver, giving a signal to a passing waiter and making his wants known. "But what have you been doing today, my dear, that has reduced you to such a state of thirst?"

"Why, shopping, Oliver," responded the other, patting the corkscrew curl that hung down before her left ear. "Traipsing all over town for a pair of green-silk button boots to match my new outfit. And not a cab to be had. Would have stopped in for a can of ale, but the public houses was all full of drunken Welsh and Irish. Then what do you think? I gets back to find that fool of a woman— that so-called dresser—has burnt a great hole in the skirt of my new ball gown, the one as Worth made me for sixteen hundred francs, not the magenta silk but the lilac satin. She'll have to go, Oliver, she really will. Ah, here comes the fizz. Capital!"

The sparkling, pale wine was poured into three tall glasses, one of which was set before me. I eyed it doubtfully.

"Lovely!" cried Miss Ducane, raising her glass. "Chin-chin as the Chinee say, and the best of health to my father's only daughter." She downed half the glass.

"She can't go," said Oliver brusquely. "I can't get rid of old Gigot after all these years. Why, she's the only original member of the first company I took on the road." He tapped my hand. "You will remember Gigot when we performed at the—er—Theatre Royal, Penruth, my dear Tessa. She was dresser to poor Jeanette as she now is to Mirabel."

59

"Yes, I remember her," I replied. And I had a recollection of a humped creature in a floppy-brimmed bonnet.

"But, of course, *she* wouldn't remember you, Tessa—not after all these years," said Oliver, and he gave me a knowing look.

"If it was left to me, she'd be sent packing this very night," declared Mirabel without heat. "Now, one more glass of fizz and I shall be ready to eat. Where's the menu?"

A waiter brought three cards upon which were written the list of fare. Mirabel took another glass of champagne and, pointing to the half-empty bottle, winked to the man to bring another.

"Are you in good appetite, Tessa?" asked Oliver.

"I think so," I replied, scanning the menu, which seemed to aim at confusion above all things.

"Why does it always have to be in French?" cried Mirabel. "I'm bad enough at the Froggy lingo, but what's this poor child to do?" And she beamed at me indulgently over the rim of her wineglass.

"In fact, Tessa has a splendid command of the French language," said Oliver. "Considerably better than mine. The tremendous advantages of an excellent education," he added, smiling mischievously into the menu and avoiding my eye.

"Oh, aye?" said Mirabel, sounding none too pleased. "All right for some; but speaking for myself, I never had any fine schooling—nor any schooling at all, for that matter."

"I—I'd be very happy to help," I faltered, feeling that it was quite the wrong thing to say.

Mirabel sniffed, consulted the menu, and addressed her next remark very pointedly to our companion. "Aw, I think I'll try the third one down. The thing called 'fillets dee something'—what's that, Oliver?"

"*Filets de plie et crevettes,*" mused the latter. "That will be fillets of some kind of fish, perhaps. Any ideas, Tessa?"

"I think *plie* is plaice," I said.

"Quite right," replied Oliver. "Plaice it is. I remember now."

Mirabel gave a sniff. "I quite like plaice," she said. "But what's the other thing that goes with it, Oliver?"

"*Crevettes*—mm! Know what that is, Tessa?"

"I—I think it's shrimps," I said in a very small voice.

"Tessa says it's shrimps, Mirabel," said Oliver, with a note of mischief.

"Don't like shrimps!" snapped Mirabel, throwing me a savage glance.

"Then let's think of something else," said Oliver smoothly, returning his amused gaze to the menu. "Let us consider the possibilities of—shall we say—*caneton*? Jog my memory, dear Tessa, and tell me what *is* that?"

"Duckling," I breathed. I think, at that moment, I could cheerfully have thrown a plate at Oliver Craven.

"How do you fancy duckling, Mirabel dear?"

This won another angry sniff from his leading lady.

And so it went on. It was quite clear that Oliver was teasing Mirabel, and that she was not the amiable creature that she appeared at first sight but had more than her share of human failings, one of which was her resentment of someone with a superior knowledge of the French language. It seemed a very small thing to get upset about.

Finally we settled our choices—plain roast fowl for all —and, after having drunk another couple of glasses of champagne, Mirabel appeared to calm down.

After a while, she said, "That's an unusual thing you're wearing round your neck, lass. What is it?" She pointed at my pendant.

"Yes, Tessa, what is it?" repeated Oliver. "I don't think I've seen you wearing it before."

"It—it used to belong to my mother," I said hesitantly. Then I went on to explain as best I could: "It's half a coin—a Maria Theresa thaler." Then I took a deep breath. "And my father had the other half."

"Well, what a lovely idea," cried Mirabel. "Don't you think that's a lovely idea, Oliver?"

"May I have a look at it, Tessa?" asked Oliver quietly. I unfastened the hook that joined the chain, and handed chain and pendant across to him. He took the half-thaler between finger and thumb and examined it closely on both sides. Presently, he said, "Oh, yes, of course, I remember very well that your mother and father had the coin cut in half when you were born. It quite slipped my mind. Have you any idea what your father did with the other half, Tessa?" He looked at me intently: it was a serious question.

"No, Oliver," I replied in all honesty. "I think he—took it with him."

" 'Took it with him'?" demanded Mirabel. "Where did he go, then? Off to sea? Was he a sailor, then? I know what sailors are!" She gave me a tipsy laugh.

I looked to Oliver for assistance.

"Will you please spare us your vulgarity, Mirabel!" he snapped.

"Oy, don't you talk to me like that, my fine . . ." she began.

"Shut up!" A bright spot of red had appeared on each of Oliver's cheekbones and a vein stood out, lividly, on his brow.

"Ooooh!" Mirabel's painted face crumpled and she took out from her corsage a scrap of lace handkerchief.

Instantly, Oliver was all contrition. "Dear, I'm sorry," he said, reaching out to touch her shoulder. "I shouldn't have said . . ."

She shook him off. "No need to crawl to me, Oliver Craven!" she cried. "I know I'm nobody, with my ignorant mind and vulgar way of talking. Not fit to sit at table with your fine lady niece, I don't suppose."

"Mirabel—please!" appealed Oliver. "Everyone's looking at you, my dear."

"Let 'em all look!" she shouted. "I ain't ashamed of what I am . . ." She turned, swollen-eyed, to the people at the nearby tables, who were staring at the three of us with renewed interest. "Do you hear that, all of you? I ain't ashamed, so there!"

"I think," said Oliver, "that you feel rather tired after your busy day, Mirabel dear. I suggest a nice early bed . . ."

" 'Mirabel dear—Mirabel dear,' " she mocked. "Don't call me that. You know it ain't Mirabel Ducane! Minnie Duggan's my real moniker. Minnie Duggan from Hackney Wick—that's me, ladies and gents. I don't ask for to be told how to behave, nor how to talk the Froggy lingo either.

So there!" She rose regally to her feet, turning her head to eye me with a glance of cold disdain. "Put *that* in your pipe and smoke it, Miss Clever—you with the fine schooling and your airs and graces!"

With that, she picked up her reticule—sweeping a wine-glass and some cutlery onto the floor as she did so—and walked with monumental dignity toward the door, with every eye in the place upon her and in total silence. She paused at the door, turned, treated us to a last, withering glance. Then, with a haughty toss of her head, she disappeared from view. The dining room was left gasping.

In the hubbub of excited comment that filled the awesome silence following her departure, Oliver beamed across the table at me. He seemed completely to have recovered his composure, together with his good humor.

"What an exit!" he cried. "Now you see, Tessa, why Mirabel is hailed as one of the finest mime artistes in the country. That exit—it was the essence of mime: what economy of means, what richness of feeling. Why, even the back of her head expressed disdain, and the very bend of her elbows a supreme contempt for all present. A great mime artiste, Tessa. What a tragedy she ever opens her mouth!"

"You teased her," I told him severely. "What's more, you were very rude to her. And it wasn't necessary."

He looked contrite. "You are quite right, Tessa," he admitted, "and I stand corrected. Happily, our Mirabel, though of somewhat mercurial temperament, does not bear a grudge for long. Mark my words: tomorrow morning she will be begging forgiveness for having been rude to you. Me she will have forgiven by the time she lays her head on her pillow."

"I think she's very nice," I said. "Though rather—difficult."

"She's a grown-up waif," he replied. "Reared—if you can call it that—in the worst slums of the East End. Minnie Duggan learned her art as an aid to begging for pennies—and thieving them too, I shouldn't wonder. As you have gathered, she did not even have your slender opportunities for honest work, with a settled existence and a chance to learn. She had nothing but her instinct for survival. And it was her art that saved her from the gutter."

"I'd like to think," I said wistfully, "that I could be as good as that one day."

"Don't think of it," he said. "There is no intelligence behind her acting; it is pure instinct. Mirabel acts the way a bird flies. You will be quite different; what will develop you into a great artiste will be your sensitivity, your high intelligence."

"I—I hope you're right, Oliver." And I bowed my head in confusion at his praise. I thrilled to the sound of it—but it all sounded so unlike me.

He had picked up the half-thaler again when next I raised my eyes, and was twirling it round thoughtfully on the end of its chain.

"This fascinates me," he said. "You say it belonged to your mother?"

"It was round my neck when I arrived on the workhouse doorstep," I told him. "Mr. Pendleton, the master, gave it to me on the day I left."

"It can't be worth a great deal, but I wonder that it ever found its way back to you," he said dryly.

"No one would have stolen it," I told him. "They were hard, the workhouse staff, but very honest."

"And you merely assume that your father possessed the other half?"

"Doesn't it seem likely?" I asked.

He nodded gravely. "Yes, it does, Tessa."

"And would you say that, if . . ." I hesitated, confused.

His searching blue eyes were fixed on me. There was all the sympathy and understanding in the world within their glance.

"If what, Tessa?"

"If I found the owner of the other half, I should know the identity of my father, do you think?"

"Do you want to know his identity, Tessa?"

"No, Oliver," I said with honesty. "And I decided that a long time ago. Only, I'd like to know what the chances are if I stumbled across it. After all—there may be other

Maria Theresa thalers that have been divided in the same way. Perhaps it's an old custom."

"Not divided quite like this one," he said, shaking his head and holding up the mutilated coin. "You see how the dovetail joint has been cut in a particular sort of way? Not straight across the center, nor from top to bottom, but in a roughly diagonal line. And the sides of the joint are slightly irregular.

"Oh, yes, Tessa—only one other half-thaler in the world would ever fit snugly into this one.

"Find it and—though you may not wish to—you will probably have discovered the secret of your birth!"

They had built up the coal fire in my comfortable bedroom on the third floor: its companionable glow greeted me when I entered; that and the musical chimes of the clock on the chimney piece as it struck the hour of ten. It was immediately echoed by a deeper, rounder chime from somewhere out in the night. Crossing to the window, I drew back the edge of the heavy curtain and looked down. There was not so much traffic about: no more than half a dozen carriages and cabs moving down there in the lamplight, and scarcely anyone out walking. The sound of the chimes must have been lost to me earlier in the rattle of many wheels on cobblestones.

Nine—ten—eleven. Silence.

I gave an involuntary shudder and stole a frightened glance behind me. Had something moved in the shadows by the head of the bed? No, that was surely caused by the flickering of the candle flame on the bedside table. Across the room I saw my full-length reflection in the pier glass: it made me look very young and vulnerable, despite the grown-up crinoline and rounded neckline. I tried to summon up a brave smile; it came back as a strained grimace.

"You really must pull yourself together, girl," I told myself aloud.

Easier said than done. I had never slept in such grandeur and solitude before. At the workhouse, it had been a crowded mattress, later followed by a cubbyhole for four.

Even when lodging with Miss Cribbenshaw, though I had a tiny room of my own, the paper-thin walls had in no way muffled the heavy snoring from my teacher and friend. This place of cosseting warmth and snowy-white sheets was larger and emptier than any resting place I had known in my life. And, save for the faint ticking of the little clock on the chimney piece and the thudding of my heart, a breathless stillness lay like a blank wall against the world.

In silence, I undressed to my shift, washed in the basin, and climbed into the huge bed. The candle was burning low, so I snuffed it. The warm firelight cast greater shadows in the gloom. I clutched at the pendant round my neck as if at a talisman against the night's evils. And my last waking thoughts were of Oliver's watchful, compassionate eyes.

The dream came upon me unawares . . .

At first I was lying in long grass, with the smell of summer and the sound of bird songs all about me. It was only when I tried to raise my arms and stretch myself that I found myself constricted by a winding-sheet. Then it was suddenly dark, and the familiar coldness and terror closed down upon me.

For once I tried to hold back the screams, knowing that no one would come to my aid, and that the slightest sound would attract the figure that always came out of the darkness to destroy me; but the agony was too great, and I began to cry out.

The familiar figure was soon with me, looming down upon me. The suddenness of its appearance shocked me into sudden wakefulness, so that I was able to half sit up and raise a hand to protect myself. I was screaming anew, when a pillow was thrust against my face, forcing me back again. Choking, I clutched at anything that offered itself—and felt warm flesh shrink from the touch of my raking fingernails.

Next instant, the deadly pressure was relaxed. I choked on a mouthful of air as I brushed the pillow aside.

I saw a dark figure with a swirling skirt framed briefly in the lighter shape of the doorway, then it flickered from sight.

The chimes of the clock on the mantelpiece came out of the darkness, and they were echoed by the distant great bell of the night.

I knew then that my dream had become a reality.

Presently, there were excited voices in the corridor outside, and the sound of doors being opened. Figures appeared, bearing candlesticks. A man's face was thrust into my doorway, grotesquely lit by candle flame.

"Are you all right, missie? That awful cry—!"

"Someone came into my room," I blurted out.

Others appeared in answer to the man's summons, filling my room with reassuring light and shocked faces. I recognized some of the members of the company to whom Oliver had briefly introduced me after dinner.

Then Oliver came.

"Tessa, what's amiss?" he cried.

"I heard a scream," said the first man. "Enough to wake the dead . . ."

"I had a nightmare!" My voice sounded shrill.

"Said someone came into her room. The door was open."

There was now a row of faces all round my bed. Men with their hair awry, women in plaits or curling rags; most in their nightshifts, some still fully dressed. In most of their faces, I saw resentment and suspicion; and a couple of the women at the back were sniggering and remarking to each other out of the corners of their mouths.

"I—I must have imagined it," I said weakly.

"But, Tessa, this gentleman says the door was open," said Oliver, perching himself on the edge of the bed and taking my hands in his.

"It could have blown open easily enough," said a woman flatly. "The draft in that corridor would freeze the dead. I'm off back to bed."

There was a general movement toward the door, with many vexed backward glances at me; but the exodus was checked in a most dramatic fashion.

"What is it then? Merciful heaven, what's happened to that poor child?" A familiar voice: loud, raucous, and penetrating.

Elbowing all aside, Mirabel Ducane swept in with a

swirl of billowing pink and vermilion, silks and plumes; and all fell back in awe at her passing. She wore, over her red nightdress, a rose-colored peignoir trimmed at neck, cuffs, and hem with ostrich feathers. Her auburn hair was piled high in a most elaborate confection, with pink bows, and the heady scent of patchouli preceded her person. One plump hand was laid gently on my forehead.

"Why, the poor little creature is afire with the fever," she cried. "All of a raging perspiration." She turned to the audience, who had paused in their departure to feast their eyes upon the new arrival. "Be off with you! Don't you have any shame, to stand there a-leering at a sick child?"

"She had some kind of nightmare," explained Oliver, when the door had closed on the last of the others.

"What sort of nightmare, lovey?" asked Mirabel. It was as if the virago of dinnertime had never been. She hugged me to her, patting my cheeks and smoothing my brow.

"I thought someone—came into my room," I said. "But it was all a bad dream."

" 'Twas the sage and onion stuffing as went with the fowl," she declared. "I had a notion myself as it smelt a bit off. Upset you, it has, but all will be well by morning, never fear. Lie back, lovey, and Mirabel shall tuck you up."

This I did, and she folded back the sheets and tucked them in, smoothing my pillow and dropping a kiss on my brow with all the tenderness of a fond mother.

"Back to sleep with you, Tessa," said Oliver. "Shall I leave you my candle?"

"Yes, please," I said fervently.

"Good night, then." He gave my shoulder a companionable squeeze.

"Good night, Oliver," I replied. "Good night, Mirabel."

"Good night, ducky. Just one thing I would add, like . . ."

"What, Mirabel?"

"Allus remember this in your dealings with me, lass: Mirabel's bark's worse than her bite by far—'specially when she's been at the fizz!" She winked at me, and was gone in a swirl of silks and plumes. Oliver followed.

In the silence that took over, I lay watching the flickering candle flame, whose length, I reckoned, would provide me with light till dawn. Blessedly—for I knew that I would never dare to close my eyes in that room again, in case . . .

A terrifying thought had me swiftly out of bed and rushing to the door. There was a key in the lock. I turned it and brought the key back to my bedside table. It was then that I noticed my fingernails.

I stared down at them, trembling uncontrollably as the meaning was borne in on me . . .

The second and third fingernails of my right hand were moist with bright carmine, and so were those of my left hand.

It all but had me screaming anew, this proof that—despite what I had told the others, because I had so desperately wanted to believe it myself—the recurring nightmare that had haunted all my childhood had, that night, become a living and wakeful reality.

Someone had indeed come into my room, and with intent to destroy me; and in my frantic struggle for life, I had clawed at that someone and drawn blood!

We left London for Southampton the following afternoon Mirabel had insisted on my spending the morning in bed, and I had had a few hours' sleep, comforted by the fact of her presence in the room: she sat over by the window playing Patience. Heavy-eyed, still, I stared blindly out the railway carriage window, only half-seeing the prim new suburbs and the lush green downlands beyond, the ancient market towns, the squat tower of Winchester Cathedral that Oliver pointed out to me.

What should I do? I must have repeated the question, over and over to myself, a thousand times.

Tell Oliver? I thought not: my mind was already beginning to doubt the evidence of my own eyes, for I had been quick to wash the faint traces of blood from my fingernails—and had they not been of my imagining after all? Better, perhaps, not to draw attention to myself as a some wild and hysterical creature, or Oliver and his patron the Count might think twice about taking on the responsibility for the foundling Tessa. Yes, better by far to forget it.

If only I could . . .

"Southampton Water!" cried Oliver. And there lay a glistening stretch of blueness and the masts and funnels of many vessels lying there, where white gulls dipped in the low-cast sunlight, wheeling and turning on the light airs. "By look of it, we shall have a smooth crossing to Le Havre."

"Lor' love us, I hope so!" cried Mirabel. She was wearing a traveling costume of green velvet trimmed with orange ruffles, with a crinoline so wide that she had got in through the carriage door only with the greatest difficulty. "When I remember how ill I was the last time we came back from Calais. What sort of sailor are you, lovey?" she demanded of me.

"I don't think Tessa has ever been to sea," interposed Oliver. He could have added, indeed, that I had never before even *seen* the sea.

"I only hope it's a big boat," said Mirabel. "One as will ride the waves without lurching about like a drunken drayman."

The Channel packet steamer *Princess Royal* was big enough to have taken up the whole of the main street of Penruth from the workhouse to the Baptist chapel, with paddle wheels twice the height of the waterwheel that provided the power to Mr. Martel's chainworks. It had been named—so the brass plate in the main saloon informed us—after the present Princess Royal, the Queen's firstborn, who was now married to the Crown Prince of Prussia; was of 2,000 tons gross; and was built on the River Clyde. I fervently joined Mirabel in hoping that this impressive vessel would live up to its appearance during what was to be an eight-hour crossing to the French port of Le Havre.

They ushered me to a trim cabin on the main deck: all flowered chintz and mahogany. The view from the single, round porthole gave out onto the deck, so I drew the curtains to prevent passersby from looking in. To my slight dismay, they did not quite meet in the middle.

We had tea in the saloon, Oliver and I and a couple of the company. Mirabel sent word that she had retired early with a sleeping draft of laudanum and did not wish to be called before we arrived in France. Despite my secret fears and my own misgivings about the coming voyage, I joined the others in a laugh over poor Mirabel.

The *Princess Royal* sailed with the tide at sunset, so I saw little of Southampton Water, or of the wide Solent beyond; only the necklaces of colored lights strung along the quays and streets, the lanterns of passing ships, and the probing finger of brightness that marked a distant lighthouse on a headland. I stood on the ship's rail with the others—close by the great paddle wheel, our faces lit up by the strange luminosity of the churned-up water—till we were out in the open sea and the night wind made me shiver. Then I said good night and retired to my cabin, locking the door.

I had scarcely taken off my bonnet when I received the unmistakable impression that I was being watched!

On that instant, I felt my skin prickle all over with gooseflesh and my breath quicken. Fearful of what I might see there, but unable to prevent myself, I slowly turned my head to look at the porthole with its drawn curtains that did not quite meet in the middle.

Nothing there to be seen—but there could easily be a questing eye in that narrow strip of blackness. I felt my limbs begin to tremble at the thought, but willed myself to cross to the wall—the same wall as the porthole—and stand with my back pressed to it. There at least I could not be seen by any watcher from outside. I waited for a long time, conscious of the drumming of a vein in my temples, turning the situation over in my mind. One thing was sure: it would be out of the question to lie down, dressed or undressed, for the bunk lay directly in the line of vision of anyone who looked in on me. And the very idea of extinguishing the oil lamp that hung in the bracket above the bunk—to reduce the cabin to a terrifying blackness—was unthinkable.

It was at that moment in my speculations that a most heartening sound reached my ears: the stamping of booted feet on the deck outside, accompanied by someone whistling the tune of "Tom Bowling" at a brisk tempo. Impulsively,

I unlocked the cabin door and stepped out. A tall figure in a capacious brass-buttoned coat strode past me, his rosy face and pepper-and-salt whiskers reassuringly solid and friendly in the light from my open door.

"Evening, missy." He touched the peak of his cap with a forefinger. "Fine night for the crossing, ain't it?"

"Good evening," I replied. Then he was gone, and I saw him pass in and out of the glow of the lamps strung at intervals down the long deck, and his merry whistling came back on the night breeze. Before he went out of sight, I heard the clang-clang of a bell from somewhere above. Looking up, I saw a group of figures—their heads and shoulders—on the high steering platform, and heard a crisp order being delivered and acknowledged.

I breathed a sigh of relief. Out there, in the clean air of the night, there was nothing to fear. What possible harm could come to me on the deck of a busy ship? In the cabin I was caught like a mouse in a cage-trap; outside, I was free to run where I willed—and the staunch crew of the *Princess Royal* was near at hand.

Leaving the cabin door ajar, I gathered my shawl more closely about my shoulders and set off down the deck in the direction of the paddle wheel, where I had earlier stood with the others. It lay halfway down the vessel and was brightly illuminated by a cluster of lamps that also marked the entrance to the saloon where we had had supper. It was then I decided—with a considerable lifting of my courage—that what I wanted to do most of all was to spend the rest of the voyage in the spacious and brightly lit saloon, where there would certainly be other passengers, perhaps even Oliver and other members of the company.

The decision having been made, I quickened my pace.

And heard footfalls behind me—as they quickened also!

I turned to see who it was, lost my direction, and collided with a curved beam of metal that supported one of the big lifeboats that were hung above the deck. Suddenly I felt trapped, confused.

"Who's that—who's there?" I cried into the shadows.

There was no one: a distant lamp revealed a clear space

of wooden deck stretching as far as I could see. From where, then, had the sound of the footfalls come? I began to tremble, like an old person with the ague.

"Where are you? Show yourself!" Was that frightened voice my own?

No answer.

Loath to turn my back on the possible pursuer, I edged away, facing the direction from which I had come. Not far behind me—a mere fifty paces—was the paddle wheel and all the light in the world. I had but to make one short run and safety would be mine. One last look around, and I would risk all on one wild dash for the light. I probed the shadows, peering among the clutter of gear that littered the deck: the supports of the lifeboats, pillars and posts, a baffling array of holes and corners, each with its private piece of concealing darkness. Nothing to be seen. Nothing that moved or gave sign of being able to move.

I looked up, to the rails of the deck above—and saw a dark figure staring down: the figure of a woman dressed all in black.

She was by the rail almost immediately above where I stood, and it was clear that it was her footfalls that I had heard: she had been following my progress from on high.

How to describe her? That is simplicity itself: my encounter with the "Woman in Black" could not have lasted for more than the space of half a dozen frightened heartbeats, but I shall carry the image in my mind's eye for as long as I live . . .

Tall—because of my low viewpoint, she loomed on high like an avenging angel. A shroudlike garment of black covered her from throat to foot, and the shawl that draped her head and masked her features was of the same somber tone. All this I saw in the time it takes to draw breath for a scream; but my scream died in a whimper—*as the unearthly figure reached out a hand and pointed down toward me!*

I turned and ran blindly. I think that, in my terror, I would have leapt into the dark sea if no other way of escape had offered itself. All that mattered was to get out of sight and out of reach of the thing up there. I raced through the shadows, my eyes fixed on the lights ahead— suddenly seeming so distant. Then something came out of the darkness at me. A blinding light behind my eyes. A nauseating wave of pain. Oblivion.

3

When I came out of nothingness, there was a dreamlike state in which people and things were very far-off, though pain was with me all the time. In this state, I was sometimes aware of movement: as of being carried, or lying in a traveling vehicle like a train or coach. People's voices came to me from a distance; even so, they were sometimes so loud that the pain in my head reverberated in time to the sounds. One morning, I opened my eyes to daylight—and knew reality again.

I was lying in a snowy-white bed, with an embroidered counterpane, under which I could see the shape of my own legs and feet. Beyond the end of the bed, there was a large window covered with a shutter, through which came narrow rays of sunshine tinged with greenness—as of light through leafy trees. To my ears came the distant sounds of a busy street beyond the closely shuttered window.

"You're awake, Tessa. Good." Oliver's voice. He leaned forward over me. "Feeling better, my dear?"

"What happened to me?" I breathed.

"I'm afraid you knocked yourself out by walking into one of the ship's lifeboats. And you must have been going at quite a rate, to raise the bruise you have on your brow, Tessa. Isn't that so, doctor?"

Another figure swam into my view: an elderly man with white whiskers and pince-nez, who spoke English with a slight trace of the French accent. He lightly touched my right temple, causing me to wince with sudden pain.

"Indeed so, monsieur," said the doctor briskly. "However, I am not much concerned about the bruise; the warm bread-and-water poultice in moist flannels has suppled the skin, and the application of the leeches has drained out the morbid blood. The slight concussion of the brain might

75

have led to violent inflammation of the cerebral tissues themselves, but the symptoms of crisis are now withdrawn, and our patient is on the mend. I will prescribe a fever mixture, and she is to be kept on a low diet. No exercise or excitement for a day or two. I wish you a good afternoon, monsieur. And you, mam'selle." He bowed and moved out of my vision. A moment later a door closed behind him.

"Oliver," I whispered. "Do I still have—leeches attached to my head? I—I can't bear the horrible things."

"No, my dear," he replied. "That was all done while you were slipping in and out of unconsciousness, last night."

"What day is it now?" I asked him.

"It's Saturday afternoon, Tessa. You've been stricken down for about forty hours."

"And we're—in France?"

"At a hotel in Tours, my dear. I've sent a message to Count Robert at the château, and he's replied expressing a wish to call and see you on Sunday afternoon, with his young nephew. If all goes well, you will take up residence in your new home immediately after the gala performance on Monday."

I felt a sudden prickle of unease. I looked at Oliver, but his bland eyes told me nothing.

"You say 'if all goes well.' Does that mean I shall be—on display on Sunday afternoon, and that if I don't come up to expectations . . ."

"Put the idea right out of your mind, Tessa!" he cried. "I've told you that the Count has accepted you without reservation, on my recommendation. What more natural than that he and his nephew should want to see you, to pay their respects, to inquire after your recovery from the accident? When I said 'if all goes well,' I was taking into account the possibility that you might not be sufficiently recovered to attend the gala performance, or to be moved to the château. Don't you see, silly girl?" And he gave my hand an affectionate squeeze.

"I want very much to see your gala performance," I told him. "It will be your moment of triumph, Oliver. I know how much it must mean to you—to be presented to the Emperor and all."

"The Emperor," he said excitedly, "arrived in Tours yesterday, by train, on his way to the royal château of Amboise. There was a procession of carriages through the streets. Oh, Tessa, you should have seen it: such splendor and pageantry; the escort of cavalry in their plumes and shining breastplates; their Imperial Majesties, and their guests, the Austrian Archduke Maximilian and his wife— she is reputed to be the most beautiful woman in Europe, and I would not argue with that. And tomorrow, Tessa—I shall have some splendid personages seated before me, in the darkened opera house . . ." At these words, Oliver rose to his feet, his eyes shining with a mystic light, his whole person taking on the strange power of attraction that I had first seen in him on the unforgettable night of his appearance at the Penruth Workhouse. "I shall be bending their minds, their emotions, Tessa, to my very will, leading them through sublime ecstasy, to terrors unknown, to blissful climes beyond the imagining . . ." Now he was on his feet, his hands and eyes expressing the meaning of his wild words, so that they carried a total conviction, and I knew the true meaning of an actor's power over his audience.

He stood poised for a few moments in utter silence, his expressive hands extended. I had an impulse to applaud, but it would have been like applauding in church. Next instant, the spell was broken: he gave a light laugh, hunched his shoulders in a carefree gesture of resignation, flicked at his eyebrow.

"Well," he said. "That's the way I *hope* it will turn out, Tessa dear. One small consolation a poor actor has to offer himself: if he gives a bad performance before personages of such exalted rank and such impeccable breeding, he can at least expect *not* to be pelted with the overripe and inexpensively priced fruit and vegetables of the lower orders."

"Oh, Oliver!" I cried. "That could never happen to you —never!"

He smiled wryly. "You think not, Tessa dear? I assure you that it already has—several times." His face took on a strange expression that I had not seen written there before

—determination mixed with something else: bitterness? "But one thing I promise you, Tessa, as I promise it myself . . .

"It will never happen to Oliver Craven again—*never!*"

My pretty, airy room in the Hôtel Voltaire, overlooking the tree-lined principal boulevard of the city of Tours, became the scene of many comings and goings in the next twenty-four hours. First came Mirabel and the ladies of the company, who had been shopping in the boulevards. They brought me flowers and chocolates, glazed chestnuts, sugared almonds in the prettiest shades of pink and violet, and a woolly toy dog. They also brought me a peignoir: a dazzlingly useless thing of silk and bows in stripes of lemon and cream—for me to wear when I "received the Count de Brassy," as they put it.

They dressed me in the peignoir that Sunday afternoon, and Oliver carried me to a glass-walled conservatory, at the rear of the hotel, that was banked high with whispering ferns and lush tropical plants. An artificial stream ran through the middle of the conservatory, fed by mechanical means and filled with carp, goldfish, and other exotic water-creatures. I was set in a richly fashioned, high-backed wicker armchair: my hair simply dressed in a single plait and shining through the attention of Mirabel's brush; my feet encased in a par of Oriental slippers—a gift from Oliver.

Oliver looked at his watch. "Three o'clock, less only a couple of minutes," he said. "If you would be so kind as to leave us, ladies, please."

Mirabel dropped a kiss on my brow. The others blew kisses and swept out of the conservatory. Oliver took a hard-backed chair and set it facing me, a few paces distant. Another glance at his watch, and he stood there, waiting, one hand resting on the back of the chair.

After a short space of time, a nearby clock in the hotel chimed the hour of three. Immediately after came the sound of footsteps in the hallway beyond the conservatory doors.

Oliver smiled at me and nodded. "The Count is the most

78

punctual person I have ever come across in my life," he said. "It is a virtue that actors—and their audiences—greatly appreciate. Cheer up, Tessa dear. The Count won't bite you, though you may find his manner a trifle daunting at first."

The glass doors were opened by two young men—both about my own age—who held them back, with a considerable show of deference, to allow their companion to enter. This he did slowly, leaning heavily on a walking stick. A large, wolfish-looking hound paddled silently at his heels.

"Good day to you, Craven. How are you, and how went the season at Drury Lane?" The question was delivered in perfect, unaccented English.

"Good day, Count," responded Oliver. "And, in reply to both your questions—very well, I thank you."

"Humph!" grunted the other.

His eyes—dark, brooding, and of disconcerting intensity—met mine. They stared out unwaveringly from a powerful, craggy countenance, and were all the more arresting because their clear whites contrasted so markedly with his bronzed and weatherbeaten skin. It was the face of a man of action: a seafarer, a soldier, an explorer of far-off places. I remembered that the Count had been wounded in the Crimean War. He doffed his tall hat; I experienced a shock to see that his thick thatch of hair was so heavily streaked with gray as to be almost white, though he could scarcely have been more than a year or two older than Oliver.

"The young lady from Cornwall, I perceive. Be so good as to introduce us, Craven."

"Miss Tessa Thursday, may I present Count Robert de Brassy; Count, this is Tessa Thursday, formerly of Penruth, in the Duchy of Cornwall."

Seated as I was, I had no idea if I should offer my hand to the Count, which would mean that he—senior by rank, by age, and also crippled—would have to limp forward several paces to take it. He resolved my dilemma by bowing his head stiffly, muttering a gruff greeting, and seating himself in the chair that Oliver had provided. The great hound, after turning round and round several times, sank to the floor at his feet and regarded his master, tongue lolling.

"Miss Thursday," said the Count, indicating the young man who had taken up a place at his right hand, "this is my nephew, Philippe de Brassy, who is at present at school in England, together with his friend and companion here." This introduction done, the Count leaned back in his chair and let his hand fall upon the hound's head. I watched his fingers—surprisingly long and slender—toying affectionately with the beast's ears.

Philippe de Brassy darted forward eagerly. He was, like his uncle, middling tall and dark-eyed, with jet hair to match, and the Count's rugged cast of features. He took my proffered hand and, to my embarrassment, lifted it to his lips and planted a kiss—not upon my hand, as I was surprised to note, but upon his own thumb, treating me to a dazzling smile as he did so, a smile that was enhanced by his flashing, gypsy-like eyes and the perfect whiteness of his teeth.

"*Enchanté de faire votre connaissance, mam'selle,*" he murmured in formal French, continuing in English, "And may I have the honor to present my friend Otto von Stock, from Prussia."

"*Enchanté, mam'selle.*" The Prussian boy was the complete contrast to his friend: with sky-blue eyes, pink-and-white complexion that would not have shamed a milkmaid, flaxen hair cut close to his neatly shaped head. Like his friend, he took my hand, but carefully brushed his lips against his own thumb instead of, as I supposed, offending my fastidiousness by defiling my delicate skin! Not for the first time, I marveled at how far Tessa Thursday had traveled from the workhouse in Penruth—not to mention the bellows-arm!

"If the young gentlemen," said the Count in a loud voice, "would be so kind as to return to their places, in order that I may more closely examine this young lady, this— *paragon*—from Cornwall."

There was an edge of mockery in the Count's tone that made my skin prickle with sudden unease. I cast a swift glance at Oliver, who was examining his fingernails. No help from that direction . . .

"Look at me, miss," commanded the Count. "Lift your head."

I obeyed. He had replaced his tall hat, hiding most of the grayness. His eyebrows were heavy and as black as his eyes.

"Yes, sir?" I murmured.

"Pray, are you recovered from your accident?"

"Yes, thank you, sir."

"Address me as Count Robert, miss."

"Yes—Count Robert," I responded meekly.

The dark gaze flickered toward Oliver.

"Who attended her?" he demanded.

"Er—Dr. Bourienne of Tours, Count," replied Oliver. "He—he was very highly recommended by the hotel, and . . ."

"Bourienne is a bungling fool," said the Count without heat. "You will dismiss him, Craven. Instruct him to send his bill to my bailiff. My personal physician will assume the care of the patient. She had better rest till Tuesday or Wednesday in the hotel and then be brought to the château."

"BUT I WANT TO GO TO OLIVER'S GALA PERFORMANCE!"

The shouted words were out before I could check myself, or at least persuade myself that they should have been delivered in less raucous tones. My hands flew to my lips, and I pressed them there, staring across at the Count, trying to assess what effect my outburst had had on him. I was uncomfortably aware of Oliver's outraged face on my right; behind the Count's chair, his nephew and the Prussian boy were gazing at me in wide-eyed fascination, as at a horse that had taken upon itself to contradict its rider.

The Count's right eyebrow had risen so high that it was right out of sight under the curly brim of his tall hat.

"Count, I really must apologize for Tessa," blurted Oliver. "It's been a very trying time: the tragic death of her friend, the accident on shipboard . . . I beg you . . ."

The Count silenced him with a brusque gesture. His brooding dark eyes never left mine.

Presently, he said, "What now, Napoleon Bonaparte, are you going to overthrow us and set yourself up as Emperor of the French? By heaven, miss, you have old Bonaparte's style—which is more than can be said for our present most gracious ruler, his nephew. So, now, you *demand* to be taken to the gala performance, is that it?"

"Tessa would greatly like to attend," interjected Oliver smoothly. "And in view of her special interest, Count, the matter of her future career . . ."

"Ah, the great career!" The Count raised his walking stick and pointed it straight at me. Seeing this, the hound at his feet growled menacingly and bared its long fangs in my direction. "I am told, Miss Thursday, that we have only to bear ourselves in patience for a few years, and you will develop into one of the greatest actresses of your generation, beside whom that young person who made such a sensational *début* at the Comédie Française—what was her name, Craven?"

"Ah, Sarah Bernhardt, Count," supplied the latter.

"Beside whom Sarah Bernhardt will be merely a passing caprice of the theater critics. An actress fit to be mentioned in the same breath as your late, distinguished countrywomen Mesdames Siddons and Woffington. I beg you not to stare at me as if I had taken leave of my senses, miss—I am merely repeating what I have been told. Answer me—is it true?"

"Count, I assure you . . ." interposed Oliver.

My tormentor silenced him with a gesture. "No, Craven," he snapped. "Let her speak for herself. Declare yourself, miss: are you the paragon whom I have described?"

The bruise in my temple was throbbing painfully to the rapid beating of my heart. My racing mind assembled something to say. Dry-mouthed, I tried to utter the words. "Count Robert, I . . ."

"Yes? Please continue." He leaned back in the chair, one hand on the silver knob of his stick, the other stroking the great head of the seated hound. His dark eyes were inscrutable, but I would have sworn that he was enjoying the situation, delighting in my embarrassment.

"I want to be an actress more than anything in the world. I've worked very hard so far, and I shall carry on working hard till I succeed, and that's all I can say!" I blurted it all out in one breath.

"Excellent sentiments," said the Count flatly. "But aspiration is not all; there must also be the ability, in other words the equipment. Are you equipped for the task? Show me. If you are an actress, miss—then act!"

"Count, Tessa is not prepared for a trial hearing," said Oliver hastily. "And she is still too unsteady to stand."

The Count spread out a hand and shrugged his shoulders. "We are informed that she has worked hard," he said. "Are we not then entitled to listen to some of the results. Can she not deliver a few lines in a seated posture?"

Oliver looked down at me inquiringly. I nodded to him.

"I—I will speak some lines from *Antony and Cleopatra*, by William Shakespeare," I said falteringly.

"Excellent," said the Count. "Please proceed when you are ready."

Now, I knew Cleopatra's dying speech as well as I can recite the first thing I ever learned at the workhouse Sunday school, which is the list of books of the Bible. Miss Cribbenshaw had coached me in the reading, helping me to appreciate the gulf that lay between my own humble, youthful state and that of a doomed woman of mature age —and she a mighty queen of antiquity. I prided myself that I had come some considerable way toward bridging that yawning gulf. I closed my eyes to compose my thoughts for a few moments. Then I began:

> *Give me my robe, put on my crown;*
> *I have*
> *Immortal longings in me. Now no more*
> *The juice of Egypt's grape shall moist this lip. . . .*

With that line—as I had been advised by Miss Cribbenshaw, who had seen the play acted professionally in London

—I reached out my hand to take hold of an imaginary wine cup that was being served to me by an imaginary attendant. And met the eyes of Count Robert. Immediately, the absurdity of my gesture struck home at me. I felt gauche, awkward. All fingers and thumbs. The words died on my lips.

The Count coughed discreetly, and prompted me:

> *Yare, yare, good Iras; quick. Methinks I hear*
> *Antony call; I see him rouse himself . . .*

I licked my dry lips and tried to continue:

> *To praise my noble act; I hear . . . I hear . . .*

The Count's relentless voice took up the speech again:

> *I see him rouse himself*
> *To praise my noble act; I hear him mock*
> *The luck of Caesar, which gods give men*
> *To excuse their after wrath.*

In the silence that followed, I looked down at my hands and saw a slow teardrop splash onto them and trail away down my wrist.

"It is a very difficult role to interpret," ventured Oliver. "And perhaps somewhat beyond Tessa's range at present."

"You may be right," said the Count distantly. "Well, gentlemen, we will take our leave. I thank you for receiving us, Miss Thursday, and for your—entertainment. I greatly look forward to your performance on Monday evening, Craven."

"Thank you, Count," said Oliver. I could have thrown something at him, for his meekness to that insufferable and overbearing man.

"You will see to it that Miss Thursday is delivered to my box before the performance," said the Count.

I glanced up with a start. He was not looking at me.

"Er—you wish her to be present, Count?" asked Oliver, puzzled.

"Naturally," replied the other blandly. "She will most

conveniently learn her chosen profession by observing the work of the best artistes—and who better than you and Miss Ducane? Come, gentlemen. Walk to heel, Roland."

He limped out of the conservatory without so much as a backward glance or word in my direction, his wolf-hound loping after. The two young men bowed and smiled at me, and expressed their hopes of meeting me again at the gala performance. The Prussian, particularly, by the warmth of his glance, seemed to be trying to convey some private message to me. I was almost too embarrassed and sick at heart to notice.

And when they had all gone, I rounded on Oliver.

"I want to go back to Penruth!" I cried. "I won't go and live in that man's home—not if he offered me fame and fortune enough to last a lifetime!"

"My dear Tessa . . ." he began.

I had more to say. Much more: "You deceived me!" I accused him. "You denied that I should be on trial this afternoon; but that's exactly what happened. That horrid man—that hateful creature with his title and all his power and riches—treated me like an animal at market, or a scullery wench at a hiring fair. I wasn't a human being to him at all; I was just—chattel. He looked me over, and decided he didn't like me. Well, I can tell you it's mutual!"

Oliver was watching me with a quizzical smile on his lips, humorous blue eyes dancing. When I paused for breath, he raised his hands and clapped me loudly!

"Bravo!" he cried. "Bravo, Tessa! By thunder, what a delivery! In matters of technique, what phrasing, what breath control. As regards emotional qualities, it would cast a pall of awestruck silence over the most discriminating audiences in Europe and America. With all my heart, I wish that the Count had remained to hear it."

I eyed him with the deepest suspicion. "Oliver Craven, you are having me on," I cried.

"I am not, I swear it," he responded. "With my hand upon my heart, I promise that you have just displayed to the full the artistry that I saw hidden in you from the first."

"You're not saying that—just to make me stay?"

"No, I am not, Tessa. But you *will* stay?"

I thought of Penruth without Miss Cribbenshaw; tried to imagine what it would be like working under another teacher; perhaps having to go as a day laborer at Martel's chainworks. I saw again the flying sparks of burning iron; smelled the mixture of unwashed humanity, furnace smoke, stale water, rotting food. And I shuddered.

"I don't have much choice," I admitted. And then, on an impulse: "Yes, I'll gladly accept the Count's high-handed hospitality, and give thanks for it. But what happened this afternoon will only steel my resolve: to be everything you promised I would be—an artiste with a career of the first magnitude. And not only to repay your faith and trust, but to prove to that insufferable man with the limp that he was wrong about me!"

Oliver was smiling broadly and clapping me anew.

"Well done!" he cried. "Let another year pass, and Sarah Bernhardt will have to look to her laurels!"

That night, before composing myself for sleep, I attempted the few steps to the window of my room—accomplishing them pretty well—and gazed out into the lamplit boulevard in the rain; watched the carriages speeding past, between the trees. My mind was curiously calm. By now I had asked myself all the questions and provided myself with the answers, and had laid all my fears to rest.

The matter of the strange and frightening incident in the London hotel I dismissed in one of two possible options: either I had dreamed the whole thing—which was most likely—or there had indeed been an intruder and he had been a hotel thief. It was Oliver who had mentioned the possibility of the latter—a class of criminal of whom, of course, I had never heard—during tea aboard the Channel packet. On the whole, I preferred the former option; but the latter offered an explanation for the blood on my fingernails—if blood indeed it had been.

As to the "Woman in Black" (I had by then given her this title in my mind): it was quite obvious that, in my nervous and pent-up state, I had wished a totally false role upon a perfectly innocent and well-meaning onlooker. Certainly, the woman had pointed to me, and on reflection,

I was pretty certain that she had said something (though what, I could not remember—even supposing that I had heard the words). What more likely than that she had uttered a warning cry against my doing just what I did—collide with a hanging lifeboat?

These matters neatly disposed of, my mind was free to roam over the events of the afternoon. And there was certainly plenty upon which to speculate. . . .

Count Robert de Brassy, no matter what Oliver might say, was an ogre—that much was sure. It was also certain that I had not measured up, in his estimation, to the glowing report that Oliver had given of me. A tremor of embarrassment accompanied my remembrance of that dreadful rendition of *Cleopatra*. What a booby he had made of me! I clenched my hands and gritted my teeth. How could I have let myself be betrayed into stumbling and falling so badly? Would I have done better to have chosen a piece more nearly fitting my age and character: such as, say, the maid Maria in *Twelfth Night*, or some other Shakespearean ingenue? I thought not—for Miss Cribbenshaw had many times told me that my interpretation of the Cleopatra role, considering my age and inexperience, was the most impressive thing in my small repertoire.

And I had let that man—that sneering aristocrat—cheat me out of my brief moment of glory. I was almost as furious with him as I was with myself.

But one consolation remained: as I had sworn to Oliver, the humiliation would act as a goad upon my ambitions. The fruits of future fame would be all the sweeter for knowing that I was enjoying them before the astonished eyes of Monsieur le Comte de Brassy. With which malicious reflection, I betook myself to bed.

Sleep was long in coming. There were thoughts of the gala performance the following night, when I might see the Emperor and Empress of France at quite close quarters. Another pleasurable consideration came to mind—and was instantly quenched in an excess of guilty shame, so that quite five minutes passed before I could bring myself to take it out and examine it again. . . .

The young gentlemen who had accompanied the Count;

they also would be at the performance, and presumably sharing the Count's box. Philippe de Brassy was—very nice. A bit like his uncle to look at (come to think of it, a great deal too much like his uncle!), but well-mannered with it.

And . . .

It was upon the other, the young Prussian with the melting smile and the eyes of china blue, that my thoughts were fixed—nervously, hesitantly, and in a sort of way in which I had never before dreamed of regarding a male person—when sleep took me away, unasked.

I did not dream that night, or at least I have no remembrance of doing so. Certainly, I did not have the nightmare that had haunted me since the very beginning.

Curiously, after the experience in London, whether real or imagined, I never was cursed by that nightmare again. Ever.

Because of my accident, there had been no opportunity to have a dress specially made for the gala performance—which had been Mirabel's wish. However, she hung up my blue terry velvet from Penruth on the Monday morning and subjected it to her critical eye. What it needed, she decided, to make it a garment suitable for an Imperial occasion, was more embellishment. Flounces were called for, she declared, not to mention roullets and ruches. Mindful of her own taste in dress and of the extravagant effect that her appearance always created, I was full of doubts. But there was little I could do against her forceful kindness. After luncheon, she planned to go out and buy suitable materials and herself sew on the embellishments.

Happily, disaster was averted by Oliver, who bore Mirabel off in the afternoon to a special dress rehearsal at the opera house. I am more than half convinced that, with his tact and diplomacy, he specially arranged that rehearsal for my sake!

Seven o'clock, then, found me in my plain blue terry velvet crinoline—unadorned. The company's *soubrette*—a sweet French girl of twenty named Joëlle Romy—arranged my hair in a chignon, with small blue bows to match my dress. As on the night of my dinner at the London hotel, I wore my only piece of jewelry, the Maria Theresa pendant. And, at seven-thirty, the carriages called to take the company and me to the opera house.

I traveled with Oliver and Mirabel in the leading carriage, through the starry evening, to an imposing, brilliantly lit building at the end of a long boulevard. As we drew up before the arcaded front, my heart gave a leap. From out of the porch darted two tall male figures in evening dress, one dark as a gypsy, the other blond as a Viking.

"Bonsoir, mam'selle," cried Philippe de Brassy. And Otto von Stock bowed stiffly, clicking his heels.

"We leave you in good hands, Tessa," said Oliver. "Mirabel and the rest of us must now go and change into our costumes for the opening scene. The curtain goes up soon after their Imperial Majesties arrive at eight. We will see you at the presentation during the interval, my dear." He handed me down from the carriage, squeezed my hand, and was gone.

"How are you?" asked Philippe de Brassy gaily.

"We were told that we should probably have to carry you up to the Count's box," murmured Otto von Stock, with a note of regret.

"I'm much better, thank you," I told them. "And quite well able to walk, as you see." And I offered them both my hand to kiss; Philippe first and then Otto. When the latter released me, I felt a butterfly of paper nestling between my fingers, and had the presence of mind not to stare at it nor to show it, but to slip it into my glove as they guided me to the great open doors and into the brilliantly lit, crowded lobby of the opera house.

I avoided Otto's glance and stared calmly before me, as Philippe led the way up a red-carpeted staircase to a curved corridor that ran round the rear of the first-tier boxes. I still looked to my front as my blond admirer drew back a curtain and admitted me into the box—where instantly I drew a breath of awe and wonder at the splendor of the scene before, below, and above me: the sweep of gilt and crystal, of scarlet plush and dazzling gaslight; the hum of many hundred voices; a million jewels, brilliant gowns, uniforms, and pageantry.

"It's beautiful—beautiful!" I could not prevent myself from exclaiming aloud with awe.

"And opposite us, you see, is the Imperial box," said Philippe, pointing across the dazzling void to an unoccupied box that was hung with swags of blue velvet adorned with golden honeybees; a golden plaque with the monogram *N III* surmounted by a crown; and pillars at each side of the box, surmounted by golden eagles.

"Napoleon the Third," I breathed.

"All the trappings of the first Napoleon have been brought out of the opera house cellar," said Philippe, with a touch of malice in his voice, "where they have been lying since your countrymen brought that gentleman's noisy career to an end at Waterloo nearly fifty years ago. The bees represent the initial B for Bonaparte. The eagles are a reminder of the glories of ancient Rome. The first Napoleon had ambitions to turn Paris into a modern Rome, dominating all Europe by the sword."

I nodded. Determined to show that, thanks to *Le Figaro*, I was well-read in the affairs of present-day France, I said, "But your present emperor says that the true Napoleonic idea has nothing to do with war. He believes in advancing France by peaceful means. Through the building of railways, through industry, through social improvements."

Philippe looked at me in surprise, his dark eyebrows raised. "Does he now?" he replied. "Well, I'm not well informed on the Emperor's doings, so I won't argue with you. But I think you will find Uncle Robert hard to convince that our fine emperor is anything but an adventurer!"

I shook my head in puzzlement. "In that case," I demanded, "why is Count Robert honoring the Emperor by attending this gala performance tonight?"

"Solely on account of Oliver Craven," was the reply. "In the cause of advancement of the arts, my uncle would sup with the devil. But I will tell you one thing—he will not arrive in this box till . . ." and Philippe took a gold watch from the pocket of his white waistcoat and consulted it . . . "till three minutes after eight o'clock precisely."

"But," I said, remembering, "the Imperial party arrive at eight."

"Exactly," smiled Philippe. "And the Bonapartist anthem, which will strike up when they enter, takes three minutes to play. My Uncle Robert would rather go to the guillotine —like so many of our forebears during the Great Revolution—than stand in honor of *that* unfortunate melody."

Otto, who had been hovering at my elbow during the preceding conversation, broke in with a light laugh. "Ha, the ways of French politics are puzzling to us foreigners, mam'selle."

"There is no puzzlement," said Philippe with a touch of sharpness, his dark cheeks reddening. "We De Brassys make no secret of our sentiments. We are Royalists and owe our allegiance to the rightful king of France, not to that self-styled emperor."

"But my dear Philippe," smiled Otto, "even you Royalists don't seem to be able to make up your minds who *is* the rightful king of France."

"I have explained to you many times," snapped the other, "that we De Brassys are Legitimists . . ."

"Your neighbors, the Duchanels, who are also Royalists, describe themselves as Orléanists . . ."

"I would have thought," cried Philippe, "that even you —*a foreigner*—would be able to distinguish between . . ."

"I think I feel a little faint," I broke in hastily. "And I should like a drink of water."

"Of course, of course," cried Philippe. "How neglectful of us. What are we thinking of? Otto, my dear fellow . . ."

"I will fetch mam'selle a glass of water," said the Prussian, with an anxious and adoring glance into my eyes.

Phillippe fussed about me, arranging my silk shawl more comfortably about my shoulders, and inquiring if I felt a draft. It was this—his typically French obsession with drafts—that sent him out of the box to see if there was a door open in the corridor beyond, and gave me the oppor-

91

tunity to unscrew the butterfly scrap of paper that Otto von Stock had pressed into the palm of my hand when he had taken it to kiss.

I looked down—and felt some disappointment. I supposed that the words were in his own language:

"Du bist wie eine Blume"

How should I ever learn what they meant?

At eight o'clock promptly (with my two cavaliers on friendly terms again, and no longer arguing the tangled politics of France), the vast auditorium echoed to a nearby fanfare of trumpets and shouted words of command. Immediately, the entire audience rose to its feet, myself and my companions included. A silence followed the silvery trumpet notes: a silence of expectancy, with every head in the vast space turned, and every eye fixed upon the empty box.

Then a murmur of voices ran through the huge audience, repeating over and over again a single phrase that became more clear as people took up the rhythm:

"Vive l'Empereur . . . Vive l'Empereur!" The murmur rose to a concerted shout.

I glanced at Philippe de Brassy. His rugged profile was set in an expression of sullen silence, his firm lips pressed tightly together. There were deep frown lines between his brows, and a vein pulsed visibly on his temple.

"And here, mam'selle, is the Emperor," murmured Otto von Stock close to my ear.

The Emperor of the French was the first to appear in the box opposite. He raised one hand in salutation to his rapturous subjects. And I suffered an immediate pang of disappointment.

Napoleon III was not a handsome man. Even from a distance, I was able to observe that his head seemed too large for his smallish body and that his features—particularly the prominent nose and drooping eyelids—were too pronounced. His hair was fair, his complexion rather sallow, and he wore a goatee beard that was set off by moustaches waxed to such long and spiky points as to be almost ridiculous to my eyes (a fashion, this, that I later learned was called the "imperial"). He wore a dark blue uniform tunic with heavy epaulettes and a scarlet sash across the right shoulder, and a line of decorations winked and glittered on his breast when he bowed stiffly in response to another round of plaudits from the audience.

"Here comes the Empress," murmured Otto.

She was preceded by two flunkies in blue and in scarlet, who stood aside and bowed at her entrance. The Empress Eugénie was half-Spanish, half-American—this I already knew. What I was not prepared for—for she was, as I had calculated, a woman in her late thirties—was the youthfulness of her dazzling auburn-haired, blue-eyed beauty. She was dressed in a gown of ivory silk, very *décolleté*, and wore four strands of perfectly matched pearls and a tiara of diamonds that glistened with a thousand eyes as she looked about her and nodded and smiled to the assembly. She was accompanied by a gentle-looking boy of about seven or eight, who wore a miniature of the Emperor's uniform. This, I decided, would be their only child, the Prince Imperial.

When the remainder of the dazzling party had entered the box, the orchestra struck up a lively anthem. I took another look at Philippe, and was amused to see that he had closed his eyes and wore a martyred expression.

The anthem over, the Imperial party were seated, and we followed suit. Immediately after, the great gaslit chandeliers were dimmed, and the flutes and violins sketched the theme of an overture. There was a rustle of curtains from the rear of the box, and my skin pricked with a strange chill as, from out of the corner of my eyes, I saw Count Robert de Brassy enter and take the vacant seat behind and to my left.

It was as Philippe had said: three minutes after eight precisely!

The curtain rose in a glow of rose-colored light, upon a scene of such heart-warming loveliness as to bring an involuntary gasp of delight from the entire audience. We were presented with a forest glade at sunset, with real trees, real tussocks of grass, and a real stream running through the center. Over all hung the great glowing sphere of the descending sun, which bathed the scene in its warm light till it dipped below the distant horizon, when, by some miracle of stagecraft, myriads of bright stars appeared in the deepening blue of the evening sky.

Softly the orchestra took up the theme of impending night with a slow and mysterious tune led by a solo violin. As the piece rose to a crescendo, I experienced a sudden sense of familiarity with it: somewhere in the past I had heard those strains before.

In the past—on an enchanted Christmas Eve . . .

Through my tears, I saw them again: the mummers dressed as birds and butterflies, moths of the night and bears of the forest, flitting in and out of the trees—as they had once descended the staircase at Penruth Workhouse.

And then—the princess. Slowly pirouetting out of the shadows, speaking to us with the soundless gestures of the mime. Now it was Mirabel, as it had been the tragic Jeanette all those years before.

And I guessed that Oliver had arranged it for my sake: that the opening mime should be the one that I had first seen as a barefoot foundling, and through which I had been led into a world of enchantment that was with me still.

The tale of the princess and the shepherd was greeted with rapturous applause, and Mirabel and Oliver were obliged to reappear again and again before the curtain. The Emperor himself rose to his feet and clapped most enthusiastically, and posies were thrown upon the stage from the people in the stalls.

The remainder of the first half of the program was devoted to mimes which had been devised from classical legends of ancient Greece. It was Otto who drew my attention to a note on the printed program which informed us that "the above legends have been translated from the original Greek sources by M. le Comte Robert de Brassy of the Académie Française," which caused me some surprise, since I had not regarded the Count as a scholarly person— for all that he had been able to prompt me with the lines from *Antony and Cleopatra*.

The curtain fell upon Mirabel and Oliver in a mime of

the tragic love of Narcissus and Echo. The lights went up, and the audience rose to its feet, chattering excitedly and looking toward the Imperial box.

"The presentations are taking place in the foyer," came a deep voice at my elbow, and I turned with a start. The Count was addressing me. "The general public will not be admitted there, but certain persons—yourself included, miss —will be permitted to watch from above. The young gentlemen will escort you there." With that, he bowed and left the box.

"Come, Mam'selle Tessa," smiled Philippe, offering me his arm. And Otto did likewise.

"Thank you, messieurs," I responded gaily, taking both their arms. In this manner I was escorted by my two cavaliers to the Imperial reception, which we were to witness from a balcony in the main foyer, or entrance lobby, of the opera house.

Philippe explained the brilliant scene below us, where two lines of soldiers were drawn up, the lights of the great chandeliers dancing in pinpoints on their helmets and breastplates, their drawn sabers. "The Imperial Bodyguard," he murmured close to my ear. "They comprise eleven officers and one hundred and thirty-seven men, all of them over six feet tall. They guard the Emperor constantly; till recently, one of their officers slept outside his room every night. Here come Mr. Craven and the company."

Oliver, Mirabel, and the others, still wearing costumes, were guided by flunkies to the open space immediately below us. Oliver's eyes flickered upward in search of me, found me, and he waved.

"Did you enjoy it?" From where he was standing, I could hear him quite clearly. "Did you enjoy your surprise?"

"It was beautiful," I called down to him. "And I had hoped you'd arranged it for my benefit."

Any further conversation was checked by a single shrill note of a trumpet—and the Imperial party descended a wide staircase into the foyer, between two lines of saluting bodyguards.

"Behind the Emperor and Empress come the Archduke Maximilian of Austria and his lady," whispered my guide.

"He is the tall fellow in naval uniform, with the fair hair and beard."

"His wife's very beautiful," I said.

"There's some talk that he's to be offered the throne of Mexico," said Philippe, "and that our fine emperor will push him into it if he can. Napoleon has ambitions for France to spread her wings in the New World. Look, Uncle Robert's moving forward to receive the Emperor on behalf of the nobility of the Loire. Watch him: watch how he will flavor the deference due to the Emperor of France with the touch of contempt that he feels for an upstart—a bit like a dash of vinegar in a bowl of cream."

The Count, tall, lean, with a single bright star pinned to the breast of his evening coat, halted some way from the foot of the stairs and stood leaning heavily on his cane. Seeing him, the Emperor paused, as if expecting the other man to step forward the few paces that would close the short distance which separated them. Count Robert made no such move, but remained leaning on his cane, regarding his sovereign with his white-maned head slightly on one side, almost—mockingly.

Napoleon III seemed nonplussed for a moment. I saw his beautiful wife's rather prim lips purse with annoyance and she whispered something to him. This drew a smile and a resigned shrug from her spouse, and he walked forward with dignity to greet the Count, his hand extended. The Empress made an attempt to pluck at his sleeve and check him—too late.

"Did you see that?" whispered Philippe. "To give the devil his due, the Emperor's big enough to overlook Uncle Robert's slight; not she, being a typical nobody."

"I think the Emperor looks rather nice," I said.

"He's well-meaning," said Philippe. "Make a good mayor of a provincial town like Tours—but I would not rate his abilities any higher."

The Count appeared to take his sovereign's proffered hand agreeably enough, bowed his head stiffly, and replied gravely in answer to a question from the Emperor, who then presented the Count to the Empress and the rest of his party. The Austrian archduke and his lady were all affability; not so the Empress Eugénie, who not only did not offer her hand to Count Robert, but stared straight past him with her nose in the air.

"I don't think I like Eugénie very much," I confided to Philippe.

"Pah—she is a nobody!" he replied.

This nettled me somewhat. "What's that got to do with it?" I demanded. "*I* am a nobody—as you very well know, monsieur."

"But *you* do not preen yourself as Empress of the French," he retorted with a smile.

By now, Count Robert and the Emperor had reached the end of the line of waiting actors. The most junior members of the company were first to be presented, the menfolk bowing and the women making deep curtsies, as the Emperor paused by each, shook hands, exchanged a few words, and passed on. As he drew closer to Oliver, who was waiting immediately below me, I was able to overhear that he was addressing them in quite passable English and that his remarks to the females were of a somewhat playful nature, even a trifle flirtatious. He obviously fancied himself a ladies' man.

At closer quarters, indeed, despite his lack of height and a tendency to portliness, and although he was by no means handsome, Napoleon III struck me very forcibly as a man of considerable charm. His manner was warm, affectionate. His eyes, which appeared expressionless due to a drooping of the lids, brightened wonderfully in conversation: a typically pert retort from Mirabel Ducane had them flashing with mirth, blue-gray and brilliant; one could see that there was a fire burning within that bland and amiable exterior. I remembered from my reading that this was a man who, beginning as an exile, had fought and intrigued his way first to the Presidency of the French Republic and then to the leadership of the Second French Empire.

He came to Oliver and held out his hand.

"We thank you, Monsieur Craven," he said, "for a most enjoyable experience. Pure artistry."

"Thank you, Imperial Majesty," responded Oliver.

97

"When you are established in your new theater in Paris, you must put on a performance before us at the Tuileries."

"It will be an honor, Imperial Majesty."

"Meanwhile, we look forward to the second part of tonight's truly delightful entertainment."

"His Imperial Majesty is most kind," responded Oliver smoothly, bowing again.

The Emperor passed on, with Count Robert at his elbow and the rest of the party following. I had a hope that the Emperor might look up, in which case I had steeled myself to wave and cry out *"Vive l'Empereur"*—but he did not. Nor did any of the Imperial party, save the beautiful Austrian archduchess, who caught my eye and smiled in a most friendly manner.

The presentation was over.

"Shall I fetch you a water ice?" asked Philippe.

"A glass of champagne?" asked Otto.

I saw an opportunity of being alone with my Prussian admirer—and fled from the idea in breathless panic.

"I think I should like champagne," I said hastily. I, who had only tasted the stuff once before in my life, and that only briefly, during that first embarrassing dinner with Oliver and Mirabel.

"Have three glasses and a bottle brought up to the box, there's a good fellow," said Philippe. "Better make it four glasses, in case my uncle joins us there."

With a small, rueful glance in my direction, Otto moved swiftly off on his errand. Philippe gave me his arm, and we set off, up a tall flight of stairs that led to the second tier.

"Miss Thursday, have you dropped this by any chance?"

I looked around with a start at the sound of Count Robert's unmistakable voice. He was near the foot of the stairs below us, but he was not looking at me; instead, his eyes were lowered to a scrap of paper that he held between his white-gloved fingers. My heart tripped a double beat. Breathless with sudden alarm, I fumbled in the palm of my own glove, where I had thrust Otto's cryptic note. It had gone.

"I—I think it may be mine," I faltered, and I walked

swiftly down the stairs toward the Count, leaving Philippe standing.

"It is a note," said the Count in a cold voice, "but, since it is not addressed to anyone, I thought I may have been mistaken. It *appeared* to fall from your hand."

"It—it is mine, sir," I whispered faintly, wishing that the stairs would straighten out and bear me down into the underworld.

" '*Du bist wie eine Blume,*' " he read aloud. "Now, are we to understand, miss, that among your many accomplishments is also numbered a competence with the German language?"

"I—I do not speak a word of German, sir," I breathed.

"Perhaps you would care for a translation?" His voice was loud, grating. Several people, passing us on the stairs, turned to stare in surprise.

I nodded miserably, eyes fixed on the hem of my crinoline.

"For your enlightenment, miss," said the Count, "it is a quotation from one or another of the modern German poets, whose name at present evades me. It means"—he gave a cough—"it says: 'You are like a flower.' "

Placing the scrap of paper in my hand, he turned and was gone down the staircase without another word.

The road westward from Tours closely follows the north bank of the wide and sluggish Loire, past vineyards and orchards, sleepy villages, water mills, sprawling farmsteads, and—seemingly everywhere—the fairy-tale castles that give the district its romantically otherworld flavor. I traveled the road, three days after the gala performance, in a spacious carriage, with my two cavaliers. They were taking me to my new home: to the Château Brassy.

I was by then completely recovered from my accident and had buried my fears even more deeply. Nightmares and specters had no more power to frighten me, in my new circumstances, than scarecrows in cornfields or hollowed-out pumpkin heads on All-Hallows' Eve. Nor had the incident of the note given me any lasting cause for concern; Count

Robert might very well think that I was having a secret flirtation with Otto von Stock, but, since such was not the case, my conscience was easy. I had not responded to the flattering note, nor shown either approval or disapproval to its author, but treated Otto exactly as I treated Philippe —as if I were his indulgent younger sister. Privately, I doted on him: on the way his china-blue eyes melted at the sight of me; because of his tallness and straightness; for the way he walked and smiled and talked. Otto was the object of my first love, in all its purity—and all its fickleness. On that day of our journey to the château, I found him rather irritating, because he was wearing a ridiculous hat with a shaving brush attached to the hatband. He was also laughing too loudly.

That morning I had said goodbye to Oliver and the others. Mirabel, Joëlle, and the rest of the ladies had accompanied me, during the previous two days, on a protracted shopping expedition among the smart *magasins* of Tours—the results of which were piled in new luggage at the rear of the carriage. Mirabel had kissed me and cried a little, in the big-hearted way she had, when I saw them into the train which was to take them to Paris.

Last of all, I had said goodbye to Oliver at his carriage door; striving to hide the tears, laughing too much; pretending to drop my muff so that he should not see me dab my eyes while he was stooping to pick it up . . .

"Amboise!" Philippe broke in on my reverie, pointing. "Do you see the château on the heights?"

Rounding a clump of poplars, we came in sight of the town, with the craggy shape of a fortress hugging the crest of a rocky spur above the river. From the highest tower, a banner stirred lazily in the afternoon breeze.

"The Emperor is still in residence," said Philippe. "Though he much prefers his château at Meudon, near Paris. I should imagine he sleeps uneasily at Amboise. Too many ghosts of France's past—ancient ghosts for whom he and his upstart family are merely intruders."

I tried to assemble the look on Oliver's face when he had kissed my cheek. Had he smiled? . . .

Philippe said, "Amboise has been a royal residence for

centuries. What times it has known! What splendor of balls, tournaments, masquerades. It attracted all the great names of Europe. Leonardo da Vinci spent his last days in the château and is buried there; Mary Queen of Scots was a young bride there: it is said that her royal bridegroom led her from the dinner table to watch a party of conspirators being hanged from the upper balconies. Ah, yes—a great weight of history lies upon Amboise. I should not think that our Napoleon feels much at home there."

We crossed the river and clattered through the cobbled streets of the old town, past the frowning gateways and beneath the very walls of the château, through an ancient archway overtopped by a clock tower. Thursday proved to be market day in Amboise town, and our progress was constantly delayed by farm carts and hand-barrows piled high with produce, thronging crowds about the stalls, barefoot children everywhere. At one check—where two carts had come to an impasse, face to face, and neither of the drivers would budge, but contented themselves by mouthing loud and good-natured abuse at each other—Otto stepped down from the carriage and returned a couple of minutes later with a posy of sweet-smelling freesias, which he presented to me with a courtly bow. My heart melted, and I almost forgave him for his ridiculous hat.

In the end we won clear of the marketplace and the town, and were jouncing down another country road overhung with new blossom. I sniffed at the delicate-scented freesias and told myself that everything passes, and that I should see Oliver again very soon. Meanwhile, I was admired by my two cavaliers, and was more than half in love with one of them. My whole world was opening out before me, and soon I would see my new home.

It lay at the end of a winding drive that started between tall gatehouses, beyond a screen of whispering cypresses. The first intimation was a glint of sunlight on water; next, a pair of pointed turrets, blue-gray and elegant against the sky; followed by the reflection of the low-cast sun in a score of winking windowpanes. A last turn in the drive, and the tall bulk of the great château came into view: three stories of warm golden stone and high-pitched slate roof, crested with finely wrought pinnacles and twisty chimneys. I have this to say about the Château Brassy—it was my first impression and it has remained with me forever after: that despite its size, its splendor, its declaration about the might and arrogance of its owners, there is a curious atmosphere of *friendliness* about the place. It invites to be looked at, to be admired, to be lived in.

We drew up to a wide bridge that spanned the water, and a pair of large hounds—replicas of the one that the Count had brought when he called to see me at the hotel —came bounding from the great double doors of the château and across the bridge to greet us. They cantered alongside the carriage, baying delightedly as Philippe called to them.

There were people filing out of the château: they hastily formed themselves into two lines by the doors. As Otto handed me down, they greeted us, the men bowing from the waist, the women curtsying low. I realized that these must be the servants.

At a slight signal from Philippe, one of the men stepped forward, and, touching his brow, he bowed to me again. Then, speaking in painful and obviously carefully coached accents, he addressed me in slow and hesitant English:

"Welcome—home—Mees Thursday."

Somewhere out in the night, beyond the moat and among the trees, an owl was calling. Another answered him from the coach house, whose walls showed in the moonlight beyond the sweep of lawn. I went to the window in my peignoir and looked out.

Below, a wide patch of light faded from the surface of the water, as if someone had extinguished the candles in one of the lower chambers: perhaps in the great tapestried hall where I had dined with my two cavaliers. Count Robert had not been present. They told me he was not due back for a week—and I was deeply relieved at the postponement of our next meeting.

"Home . . ."

I touched the solid walls by the window—they were two feet thick and of solid stone—to assure myself that I was in reality and not imagination. Home in the Château Brassy. Little Tessa Thursday from the parish workhouse in far-off Penruth.

I touched the pendant: the silent testimony of my birth, whose secret was very faint and far-off and receding farther every day. I told myself that none of this mattered; I was tomorrow's child, and the past held nothing for me.

It was then I saw—or seemed to see—a dark figure standing in the fringe of trees beyond the moat. I felt a strange chill envelop me, and hesitated to strain my eyes into the gloom lest I saw more than was good for me. Even as I hesitated, the figure seemed to take the shape of a female dressed entirely in funereal black, the head masked and shawled.

But when I made the deliberate attempt to look more closely, the apparition was gone.

PART TWO

The Echo of a Melody

1

"Compliments of Monsieur le Comte, mam'selle, and would you please attend him in the music room at your convenience?"

"Thank you, Henri," I replied. And the butler of Château Brassy—he who had greeted me so effusively on my first arrival—bowed and silently departed.

I knew that Count Robert was in the music room: all morning the music of his flute had been coming from the open windows above the moat, in the tower opposite my sitting room window. I could still hear it: the unearthly strains of Glück's *Orfeo ed Euridice* on the clear spring-time air, a sound that always had the power to make my skin prickle with gooseflesh and the small hairs stir at the nape of my neck. It was curious that I was able to disassociate the music—which I loved—from the player, with whom I always felt ill at ease. Of course, I was deeply indebted to the Count for his patronage; but my feelings of gratitude were always in conflict with another emotion. I did not actually *dislike* Count Robert; but, since he never treated me with anything but frigid politeness at the best, I found it curiously difficult to regard him as a real, living and breathing human being.

I glanced at my reflection in the mirror, patting my hair in place and straightening my lace collar. I told myself that I had much changed: the raw girl who had half fallen in love with the handsome Prussian boy had also half fallen out of love with him; and had done exactly the same with Philippe de Brassy. And both young men were now the best and dearest friends of my life: my true cavaliers and loving brothers. What's more, the same fickle passion had also led me to fall in and out of love with Gaston Pepin, the under-gardener—a smiling Breton, whose looks reminded me of the Cornish farmers' lads who used to call after us when we were being carted over the moor to Mr. Martel's chainworks. There had even been the time —the shame of it made me shudder!—when I had actually thought myself to be in love with the Count. This had coincided with a bad attack of the grippe, which had scourged the district in the winter of '65, when I had lain for days and nights in delirium and the doctor from Amboise had feared for my life. During that time, Count Robert's mournful countenance had seemed to haunt those moments of clarity which appeared like small sunbursts in the gloom of insensibility. I had come to connect him with light and life: that craggy face, those brooding dark eyes, were always there to greet my emergence from the delirium. So, in a curious way, I grew to love the sight of him. Of course, it was the grippe. The unhealthy passion died with my return to health!

Yes, I had much changed. One thing had remained: the girlish tendency to fall in and out of love had never obscured my ambition to be an actress, nor clouded for an instant my deep attachment to Oliver, even though I seldom saw him; even though he came to see me only about once a year at the château; never responded to my hints, both verbal and written, that I might visit him in Paris. And how I longed to go to Paris!—particularly in that year of 1867, because a Great Exhibition was to be held throughout the summer in the capital, at which all the world and his wife and children were going to be present. But not, it seemed, Tessa Thursday.

During my years in the Loire, I had never been farther than Tours—where I went thrice a week for lessons from a dramatic coach, a former member of the Comédie Française—and a fortnightly shopping visit to Orléans with Mme. Arlette, the château housekeeper. It was during these excursions, and from the pages of *Le Figaro*, that I kept abreast of the great events of the world far beyond the dreamy banks of the Loire. And stirring things had happened while I had watched four times four seasons pass in the shadow of the château walls. In far-off America, the terrible Civil War had dragged to an end after unbelievable suffering; Abraham Lincoln had fallen to the assassin's bullet; slavery had been abolished. On the continent of Europe, the enigmatic figure of Bismarck had become a force to be reckoned with; under his leadership, Prussia had snatched the little state of Schleswig-Holstein. Everyone seemed to fear Bismarck—everyone, that is, save Napoleon III, who met the Prussian Chancellor at Biarritz and charmed him out of his mind, as the saying goes.

I had a colored engraving, bought from a print shop in Orléans, that showed the Emperor standing in his study at the Tuileries palace in Paris; one hand resting on a table, the other lightly clenching the tasseled baton of a Marshal of France; the eyes looking out at the viewer with the curious, gray-blue, regarding glance that I remembered from Tours. Not a particularly dashing figure—short and running to stoutness in his uniform of blue, crimson, and gold—but undeniably a figure of destiny. The self-made Emperor. I kept that portrait in my sitting room, for I had become a tremendous devotee of Napoleon III, with one thing only clouding my admiration at that time. It concerned the Archduke Maximilian, that other distinguished figure whom I had seen on the night of the gala performance in Tours, who, with Napoleon's encouragement, had accepted the invitation to become Emperor of Mexico. At first, things had gone brilliantly for the tall blond Austrian with the ravishingly beautiful wife: he had shown himself to be an enlightened and liberal monarch, and the French troops supporting his regime had swept his enemies, the Mexican revolutionaries, almost over the border into the United States. This latter move was Maximilian's downfall: with the Civil War over, the U.S. was able to turn its attention to Mexico and demand the withdrawal of the French from the American continent. Only the previous July, the Empress Carlota had come to France to beg Napoleon III not to abandon his *protégé*, her husband. She even pleaded with the Pope. In vain. That beautiful creature who had been so kind as to smile at me that night at the opera house had been driven insane by despair. And we in France were still ignorant of the fate of her husband at the hands of the revolutionaries. This, then, was the only cloud on my hero worship of Napoleon III; in all else he could do no wrong. Had he not made France the most brilliant, the most exciting, the most prosperous country in Europe, and Paris, rebuilt by his architect, Baron Haussmann, the City of Light, the very Rome and Athens of the modern world? And was not this year of 1867 to be crowned by his supreme achievement: the Great Exhibition? Oh, if only I could go to Paris!

With a sigh, I gathered up my skirts (thanks to the influence of Mr. Worth, the crinoline had all but disappeared, giving way to the much more convenient demi-crinoline, still worn over small hoops, but more easily manageable when getting in and out of carriages and suchlike), and, leaving my sitting room, took the vaulted staircase that descended into the great hall of the château; every panel in the vaulting containing a medallion portrait, either of De Brassys long gone, or of kings, queens, and royal dukes who had resided within the walls.

Mme. Arlette was waiting for me in the hall. The housekeeper gave me a small curtsy as always, for I ate at table with the family and had always been treated as a relation—albeit a poor relation—of the Count.

"Will mam'selle wish to see the menus for the week?" she asked. During the last year or so, I had slipped into the role of chateleine of the château, a role that I did not find unpleasing.

I glanced at the neatly penned menus: not so briefly as to seem careless, nor in so protracted a manner as to suggest that I doubted Mme. Arlette's abilities.

"That seems excellent, Madame Arlette," I told her, as always.

"Thank you, mam'selle. Will mam'selle be dining alone or with the Count?"

"I have no idea of the Count's plans for this evening, but I will inform you after I've seen him, Madame Arlette."

"Thank you, mam'selle." The woman curtsied and withdrew.

Halfway across the hall, with its great painted ceiling depicting King Francis I at the boar hunt, I saw Gaston Pepin, the under-gardener, standing outside one of the long, open windows. The handsome Breton was bare-headed, holding his cap in one hand and a potted plant in the other.

"Good day, Gaston," I smiled at him.

"Good day, mam'selle," he replied. "Would mam'selle be pleased to accept this azalea? It is the first of the year, mam'selle."

I took the plant, savoring the delicacy of its scent. "Thank you, Gaston," I said. "It shall go on the windowsill of my sitting room."

He blushed with pleasure, bowed, and set off back to the formal garden beyond the bridge.

I laid the plant on a side table, near the music room door, met my reflection in the mirror above, squared my shoulders, and assumed the calm and withdrawn expression that I always employed against Count Robert's overbearing arrogance.

"Don't forget," I murmured aloud, but not too loud, "that you're as good as he, and don't let yourself be browbeaten." I told myself the same thing every time I was summoned by the master of the Château Brassy. Sometimes the injunction worked better than at others.

I tapped upon the door.

"Enter!"

I entered. The greenish glare of sunlight on still water filled the music room, coming as it did through the wide windows that spanned half of the circular tower chamber. The Count was seated by one of the open windows, throwing morsels of biscuit out to a trio of swans that swooped and circled in the sun-dappled water below. He was in shirt-sleeves, with his cravat hanging loose in two ends. His silver flute lay on a chair nearby, together with a pile of music. Roland, his favorite hound, was asleep under the chair.

"Good day, Miss Thursday."

"Good day, Count." All the time I had been at the château, we had never greeted each other any less formally.

"Pray be seated."

"Thank you." I took my place in a straight-backed chair facing him, folded my hands on my lap, and waited.

There was a newspaper lying beside him on the window seat. He tapped it.

"I see from the reviews that Craven has scored another sensation at the opening of his new season." The brooding eyes fixed me for an instant, seemed to find nothing of interest about my person, and returned to the printed page. "The critic Guyon (a fellow after my own heart) writes: 'Oliver Craven and his ensemble, playing currently at their own Théâtre des Comédiens, will certainly outshine the vulgar extravagances promised in the forthcoming International Exhibition. Long after the exhibition site in the Champ-de-Mars has been returned to its habitual pristine state—when the English have removed their Bible Society kiosk and their model farm, the Americans their rocking chair, the Turks their mosque, the Japanese their house of bamboo, the Chinamen their pagoda of porcelain and their two bazaars; when Prussia has taken home Herr Krupp's fifty-ton cannon and the mammoth equestrian statue of Frederick the Great—in short, when all these promised delights have departed from us and the fanfaronade is silent, we shall remember in tranquillity—those of us who have been fortunate enough to visit the Théâtre des Comédiens—only the pure, artistic brilliance of Mr. Craven's incomparable concert of mime.' Now, what do you think of that, Miss Thursday?"

I replied tartly, "I think Monsieur Guyon is very flattering about Oliver, but unnecessarily rude about the International Exhibition."

"But then," replied the Count, "as we all know, Guyon is a Royalist, like myself."

I knew he was looking at me, and I stared hard at my hands, willing them to lie there on my lap without showing the slightest inclination to tremble.

I took a deep breath and said, "The Emperor has commanded the Exhibition in order to promote peace and understanding between the nations of the world. I think—I think it's a very wonderful idea."

"Ah, there speaks the little *Bonapartiste!*" His voice was hard-edged, mocking. "Yes, I know that you are well-informed, Miss Thursday, and that you have a keen and inquiring intelligence. However, there are empty patches in your knowledge. You need to be informed of the reasons why our esteemed Emperor has really ordered this absurd charade—no, do not interrupt me, miss! It is for political reasons. Not to promote peace and understanding between nations, but to charm the Parisians and to fool the world that France is the supreme power on the Continent. He knows that Bismarck aims to unite all Germany under the Prussian crown, and that he has no hope of preventing it. So our Napoleon hopes to create an illusion of greatness. In place of diplomacy we are to have Strauss waltzes. Incompetent rule will be concealed under a wealth of empty pageantry. For a brief spell, the toiling masses will cease to mutter about a new revolution, while gazing spellbound at the Americans' rocking chair and Herr Krupp's black cannon. Am I boring you, Miss Thursday?"

I met his eye; remembered to keep my shoulders squared, my expression calm and withdrawn.

"Do you require me for anything else, Count Robert?" I asked quietly.

The brooding eyes were hooded by his heavy brows, so I had no way of telling if I had offended him. Presently he rose, brushing back from his brow a stray lock of his thick gray hair. "No, that will be all, thank you, Miss Thursday. Wait, though—there is one thing more. You are still pursuing your dramatic studies, so I understand?"

"Yes, Count."

"With Monsieur Martin, late of the Comédie Française, at Tours?"

"Three mornings a week."

"And how are you progressing, pray?"

"I have studied the works of the French seventeenth-century dramatists, as well as their English counterparts . . ."

"Ah, Molière and Corneille!" he cried. "And Racine. You have added the leading role of Racine's *Phèdre* to your repertoire, I do not doubt?"

I thought I detected a distinct note of mockery in his voice. Now, M. Martin had coached me very carefully in the role of Phèdre, a mature and tragic part, and scarcely less demanding than Shakespeare's Cleopatra. I prided myself—and M. Martin had kindly intimated as much—that I gave a good delivery of Phèdre. But if Count Robert de Brassy thought I was going to do so there and then, at his command, he was greatly mistaken.

So I simply replied, "Yes!" And raised my chin defiantly.

He nodded and turned away, picked up some fragments of biscuit from a plate on a side table, and tossed them out the window to the waiting swans on the moat.

"Be so kind as to inform Madame Arlette that I shall be dining this evening, Miss Thursday," he said.

I managed to reach my room and put on a bonnet, take up an umbrella and my reticule; I even left the great door of the château and was halfway across the moat bridge— and Moko, the most foolish and affectionate of the hounds, had uncoiled himself from the steps and was padding amiably after me—before the tears came.

That overbearing man—why did he have the power to upset me so?

It was always the same: whenever he summoned me it was either to goad me about my admiration of Napoleon III and the Second Empire, or to ask a lot of unnecessary questions about the progress of my acting studies. Today was typical. He must have known, mustn't he, that I would give anything to go to Paris for the Exhibition? And he, who had only to lift his finger to make it possible, had done nothing but pour scorn upon the wonderful events which were to take place in the capital that summer.

And he had already asked me twice since New Year if I had added the role of Phèdre to my repertoire!

"Moko," I informed the good-natured hound, angrily brushing a treacherous tear from my cheek, "I find your master extremely annoying. He brings out the worst in me!"

Moko responded with his cheerful, baying bark; and the sound carried to the formal garden, where Gaston Pepin and the head-gardener were trimming the maze of low box hedges that enclosed primly patterned beds of spring flowers; the two men straightened up and touched their caps to me.

The formal garden—called Mary Queen of Scots' Garden, after the tragic queen who was reputed to have spent a summer at the château—was not to my taste; I preferred the orderly wilderness of the great park, with its dark copses and mysterious hedgerows, dramatic fountains, and unexpected statues lurking in secret arbors. However bad my mood—and it was bad enough on that occasion—a quiet stroll in the deserted park was usually sufficient to soothe me. I was somewhat cheered by the prospect.

"Come, Moko!" I cried.

The Château Brassy stands on an islet in a lagoon formed by one of the lesser tributaries of the Loire, making a kind of moat. Three sides of its warm stone walls rise straight from the still waters, which are the haunt of wildfowl, swans, and all manner of fresh-water fish; as well as bulrushes and water lilies in rich abundance. Begun in the fifteenth century as the fortified castle of an early, warlike De Brassy, it was considerably rebuilt during the more gracious age of the Renaissance, and turned from a place of war into a comfortable home: its battlements surmounted by a high and elegant roof, its stern towers set with pointed pinnacles like witches' hats. The iron hand of history lies heavily upon the château, but, as I have said, it bears its weighty burden with smiling ease.

Moko and I skirted the lagoon and set off, across the trim grass of the park, to my favorite arbor: a bowery retreat hidden from sight of the château by a tall hedge of rustling yew. Behind the yew hedge was a stone bench facing a fountain bowl, in which a marble cherub wrestled eternally with a marble swan, from whose open beak gushed a stream of glistening water. The hound knew the way, since he had accompanied me there more than once; he went on ahead and was gulping noisily from the fountain bowl when I reached there.

It was a clear March day, not unlike the day, four years before, when I had driven to Brassy for the first time with my two cavaliers; but a bank of clouds to the east promised rain. I settled myself in the shelter of the hedge, on the bench, and took out the two letters that had arrived for me a week previously, both in the same envelope, and the envelope posted from Oxford, England.

Here was something which, I knew, would drive away my blues. I settled down to read them for the tenth time . . .

> Balliol College,
> Oxford
> Sunday, 24th February, 1867

Ma Chère Tessa,

Less than three weeks till the end of Hilary Term, and we shall be at Brassy by the 13th, gales in the Channel permitting.

I read in today's *Times* that the bad weather persists in Paris and that the Champ-de-Mars is still a sea of mud, with no hope on earth of the poor Emperor's Great Exhibition opening on April 1st as planned (April Fool's Day—a fitting choice, Uncle Robert would think!). Such may be the *Times*'s opinion, but it is not mine. Do you know, I have become infected by your own enthusiasm for His Imperial Majesty, and I really do believe that the old adventurer is going to succeed in the face of the weather, the Doubting Thomases, *The Times*, Uncle Robert, and all, and astonish us all on April 1st!

You will naturally want to visit the Exhibition, and I fear you will get neither encouragement nor support from Uncle Robert. However, Otto and I have put our heads together and have decided to make a combined assault upon his prejudices. I can offer no promises, my dear, but we will *try* to persuade him that long dead De Brassys will not rise from their tombs and call down the wrath of Heaven if the three of us are seen to attend "that upstart Bonaparte's folly."

On Saturday, Otto and I went to London, where we saw Henry Irving in *Hunted Down* at the St. James's Theatre. You would have enjoyed . . .

I turned to Otto's letter, which, with its spiky Germanic script and formal mode of expression, was in marked contrast to Philippe's gay, dashed-off lines. I turned to what was for me the most interesting part:

. . . I trust, dear Tessa, that I shall have the honor to be your co-escort to the Exhibition. It will provide a fitting termination to a most happy chapter of my life. As you are aware, I shall not be returning to Oxford after the vacation, but will be proceeding to Potsdam, to enter the Imperial Military Academy. Let us hope that, together, we may prevail upon M. le Comte to permit the happy excursion . . .

I was heartily echoing Otto's sentiments when a sudden onset of wind brought a splattering of rain. Moko raised his head and looked at me questioningly as I got up and unfurled my umbrella.

"We must hurry back, or we'll get a soaking, Moko," I told him. Slipping the letters back in my reticule, I set off to walk quickly to the château, with the big hound bounding on in front, nose sniffing the ground.

The rain swept down, bending the tops of the cypresses and speckling the surface of the moat with a million droplets. I bowed my head before it and hurried my pace.

I was happier now. A dip into my two cavaliers' letters had been reassuring. There was a faint possibility that I should get to Paris after all. And, in addition to all the other delights awaiting me there, what a blessing it would be to be free, for a while, from having to sit and have meals alone with Count Robert!

We dressed formally for dinner at Brassy, no matter what the occasion. I have sat at table with thirty guests and with only the two of us—Count Robert and myself. The ritual was always the same: never fewer than twelve menservants waited on us, and all of them dressed in knee breeches and powdered wigs of the eighteenth century. For two diners or for thirty, there were never less than six courses, with at least four choices for each course, from *Hors d'oeuvre* to *Dessert*. The wastage of food in the castle must have been appalling, and in an area where, as I knew from the Tours newspapers, farm laborers worked all hours for a few francs and there was real starvation in the poor quarters of Orléans. I sometimes wondered what the paupers of Penruth Workhouse would have thought, to be served with a typical dinner menu from any evening of any week at Château Brassy.

I changed into a gown of oyster satin, with no other decoration save my Maria Theresa pendant and a single white carnation in my hair. Dinner was announced three times at five minute intervals before seven o'clock, when the butler sounded the final gong stroke exactly on the hour, and I was careful always to be waiting at the top of the staircase, to start descending as the last reverberations died away in the remote stone fastnesses of the great building.

That particular evening, as ever, Count Robert was waiting at the open doors of the drawing room, where he had no doubt taken his customary glass of Scotch whisky before dinner—a habit widely popularized by our own Queen Victoria. As ever, he was in evening dress of tailcoat. He nodded stiffly to me as I made a curtsy, and motioned for me to precede him into the great hall, where the long table was laid with a dazzling array of napery and silver plate, and the servitors stood in two ranks at each end of the table, behind the two high-backed chairs—all of twenty paces' distance from each other—where we were to sit.

I took my usual place at the far end, the Count waiting till I had done so before he himself sat down. The butler snapped his fingers to his underlings. And so began a typical dinnertime at Brassy.

Soft-footed, the under-butler took his place at my side and bowed deeply. "For hors d'oeuvre," he murmured, "will mam'selle prefer turtle soup, caviar, plovers' eggs, or capon?"

I toyed with some caviar, for which I had acquired a mild liking, and sipped at half a glass of light wine. This would see me through the second and the third courses, both of which I intended to miss, then to re-enter the contest with the roast meat course in something like an hour-and-a-half's time. A little cold roast beef and a salad, followed by a piece of fresh fruit, would then suffice me. The only problem was to make it spin out the time. Count Robert—while taking only moderate portions—invariably ate his way through the entire menu, with a different wine for each course and champagne between courses. I never ceased to marvel how he managed to retain his lithe and upright figure.

Half an hour passed with not a word spoken, save for the respectful murmur of the servants. I had known the Count to address a remark to me while we were dining alone—but not often.

At the beginning of the third course (choice of pheasant, mullet with shrimps, duckling, pike), Count Robert signaled to the footman who stood by the doors, and the latter opened them to admit a tall figure in a coat of hunting green and long boots with jangling spurs. This was Colombe, the Count's huntsman and head groom, who was responsible for the well-being of the thirty or so horses and ponies that were kept in the vast stable block beyond the moat.

"Good evening, Colombe," said the Count, pouring a bumper glass of red wine and handing it to the other, who took it and bowed.

"Good evening, Count," The huntsman bowed to me. "Mam'selle."

"At what hour are the hounds meeting tomorrow, Colombe?"

"At ten o'clock, Count."

"Who shall you be riding?"

"With your permission, Count, I think Belisarius."

"Ah, Belisarius. Not Caspar?"

"Caspar cast a shoe while being exercised this morning, Count," replied the other gravely, "and returned lame."

"The groom in question has been dealt with?"

"I horsewhipped him with my own hands, Count. And he has been sent back to laboring duties on the estate."

"Excellent. Never dismiss a man for one mistake, Colombe. One mistake should not bring hardship—perhaps starvation —to a whole family."

"I will bear that in mind always, Count."

I fell to marveling at this strange and complex man, this master of Brassy, lord of life and death over a vast domain and several hundred servants and farm workers. In my four years at the château, I had never once heard him raise his voice in anger to an underling, nor address any one of them with other than icy civility. And whatever my own feelings toward the man who also ordered my life to a very large degree, one thing was certain: his people worshiped him only just short of idolatry—an attitude which I found strange, for I considered the Count to be the complete feudal tyrant.

The interview continued. The huntsman remained standing, and the Count asked questions about the horses between mouthfuls of pheasant. I had witnessed the scene many times. Count Robert took a curiously obsessive interest in every detail of Colombe's duties—which was all the more odd because he himself never set foot within the stable block.

I had heard the reason for it from Philippe soon after my arrival at Brassy. On his return from the Crimea, lamed by a musket ball, the Count had ordered his favorite hunter to be saddled, and had ridden him twice round the entire estate—alone. Whatever had happened during that time, this man whose whole life had formerly been devoted to the fanatical pursuit of fox and stag dismounted from his steed and never again set foot in a stirrup. The horses remained and were scrupulously cared for, with no regard for expense; but the Count never went near them again.

I had been told—something else.

Covertly eyeing the master of Brassy over the top of a silver epergne in the form of the Birth of Venus, after Botticelli, I thought back to a somewhat bald and sketchy account that Philippe had given me—all the facts he had—four years before; to which I had added my own embellishments, as my imagination took me.

Count Robert, it seems, had been engaged to be married to a local lady, the daughter of another Loire aristocrat. This was before the Crimean War, when he would have been in his late twenties and the hardest-riding sportsman in the province. The lady, it seems, had similar interests—which gave me the opportunity to let my imagination run riot with a vision of some breathtakingly beautiful nymph of the chase, a Diana on a milk-white palfrey, a huntress chaste and lovely. But with a heart of stone, for when Count Robert returned from the war a cripple—and having satisfied himself, by trial, that he would never be able to match his former skill in the saddle—he announced to his fiancée that he would be willing to release her from the engagement, and she accepted her release. Then went off and married another.

It was only in contemplation of this story that I was able to stimulate any sympathy for this man who, though my benefactor, and for whose hospitality I was properly grateful, I disliked and feared more than any man I had ever met in my life. Having drummed up a modicum of sympathy, I was able to tell myself that his Diana's betrayal had burnt like a hot iron into his mind and his heart, cauterizing him against any gentle feelings for his fellows, and particularly, perhaps, for young female persons like myself. Only being crossed in love, surely, could account for his total lack of human warmth.

I wondered what had happened to the lady in question, and if she had ever regretted her decision. Not, I thought, if she had seen anything of her former fiancé in recent years!

Toward the end of dessert, the Count dismissed his huntsman. It was then that he addressed his first remark to me in—my eye stole to the great clock surmounting the minstrel gallery at the end of the hall, with its burden of half-life-size nymphs and satyrs—three hours.

"Miss Thursday, we will retire to the drawing room for coffee."

"Yes, Count," I responded, as ever.

After-dinner coffee had become something of a ritual. The Count had decided that—having tried them all, one after another—not one of the château staff was capable of brewing a drinkable cup, which, in his case, was required to be black, strong, and scalding hot. More from curiosity than anything else, and certainly with no hope of success with him, I had one night repaired to the small butlers' pantry adjoining the drawing room, which was used for the convenient preparation of light collations and hot drinks at any hour, and there, under the anxious eye of the butler and two frightened footmen, I had prepared a pot of coffee, using the simple method learned from Mrs. Isabella Beeton's excellent *Book of Household Management*, of which poor Miss Cribbenshaw had had a copy back in Penruth. The Count had tasted my coffee, had drunk it all down, and had made no comment, adverse or otherwise. From then on, by mutual consent between myself and the butler, I made the after-dinner coffee.

Half-past ten was sounding as I pronounced the brew to be ready, and followed the footman who carried the tray into the drawing room, where the Count was seated in an armchair before the vast open fireplace, with the hound Roland curled at his feet.

The footman poured two cups of coffee, placed one on the occasional table beside my chair, and the other at the Count's elbow. As usual, I held my breath in anticipation.

He took a tentative sip. And another. Then he disposed of the whole cup in a mouthful, set it down, and, taking a large silk handkerchief from his breast pocket, dabbed his lips.

The huge log on the fire crackled and spat a small shower of embers onto the tiles close by the Count's feet. Roland looked up, ears pricked. Some time went by in silence. I finished my own coffee, and when I had done so, I stood up.

"Well, I will say good night, Count," I murmured.

He replied without looking round, continuing to stare into the fire, his right hand resting lightly upon Roland's head.

"Regarding Paris," he said. "I have written to my steward there. You have only to indicate to me on which day you would prefer to go—think it over, there is no hurry—and you will be met at the railway station."

I stared at him. "To—*Paris*?"

He turned his head to regard me, with some surprise. "That is your wish, is it not, Miss Thursday?" he said quietly. "To visit Paris and see the Exhibition? That was the impression I received during our conversation this afternoon."

"Yes, Count. But I never thought . . ."

"You could very well remain there for the entire summer," he said. "My nephew will be returning to Oxford for the Trinity Term toward the end of April, and I understand that Herr von Stock is to commence his military training in Potsdam about the same time; but you will have the company of Oliver Craven and the members of his ensemble, so you will not be without escorts."

I took a very deep breath. There was a tightness in my throat that told me my emotions were in peril of spilling over in tears of joy and gratitude.

"Count, I—I don't know how to thank you . . ." I began.

"Please, Miss Thursday—" he lifted one lean hand in a gesture of dismissal—"do not be demonstrative, I beg you. I cannot abide excess of feelings."

Paris! *La Ville Lumière!* City of Light!

I was there within days of the Count's declaration, for I could not bear to wait a moment longer than necessary. With all my quite considerable wardrobe packed in three large trunks, I was driven from Brassy to the station, with Mme. Arlette and others of the staff waving me out of sight, but not a sign of the Count. From Orléans, I went by train and, in the rosy glow of a perfect sunset, arrived in Paris, where I was met at Montparnasse station by an army of liveried footmen and a shortish young man with an extremely gushing manner, who removed his hat, bowed very low, and informed me that he had a message from M. Craven.

I opened the envelope, which was addressed to me in Oliver's flamboyant handwriting.

My dear Tessa,
You have come at last! I knew, when the time was ripe, your footsteps would be directed to Paris. My only regret is that I am not here to greet you, but the curtain rises at seven.

Tonight, you will be weary after your journey. Sleep well, my dear, and I will call upon you tomorrow at the Hôtel de Brassy.

Always,
O.—

I glanced up from the page, to see that the man was watching me with close and serious interest. Immediately on catching my eye, however, he assumed again the ingratiating smile with which he had greeted me.

"Are you Count Robert's steward?" I asked him.

"I am Flambard, the assistant steward, mam'selle," he replied. "And I prevailed upon my superior, Monsieur Fournier, to permit me the honor of escorting you from the station to the Hôtel de Brassy. I am, you see, a Parisian, mam'selle, whereas Monsieur Fournier is from Normandy." He made a deprecating gesture. "Not to be introduced to Paris by one of her children would be like being shown round Paradise by the devil—if you will pardon the comparison, mam'selle."

I laughed. For all his gush, Flambard was quite an engaging sort of man, with sleekly handsome looks and an air of assurance that belied his lack of inches. He was dressed neatly in dark, clerkish attire. His shoes were polished to a high gloss, likewise his fingernails, and his hair appeared to know the touch of the curling iron.

"I am in your hands," I told him.

"The carriages are this way, mam'selle," he said, bowing and gesturing with his hat for me to precede him.

There were two carriages waiting in the forecourt of the station, and the footmen were piling my trunks into the second of them. Flambard handed me into the first, which was an open landau, with the De Brassy coat of arms emblazoned upon the door. Two coachmen rode on the box, with two footmen standing at the rear, all in cockaded tall hats, gold-laced tailcoats, knee breeches. I felt like royalty. Our own Queen Victoria's visit to *La Ville Lumière* some twelve years previously could scarcely have been conducted in more sumptuous style.

We rolled out of the station yard and joined the moving throng of traffic in a broad, tree-lined street beyond. In the sunset gloaming, the street lights were strung out like two lines of fireflies for as far as I could see, with countless carriage lamps bobbing between them.

"Paris, mam'selle, has much changed in the last fifteen years," said Flambard. "Since His Imperial Majesty entrusted Baron Haussmann with the task of rebuilding the city. There are many who consider that the changes are not above criticism—" he paused, and I was aware that he was searching my face for some reaction to his words "—but I do not expect that mam'selle, being an English lady, will have any strong views about that, one way or another."

"Quite so," I replied noncommittally.

"We proceed along Monsieur le Baron's new thorough-fare, the rue de Rennes," said my guide. "Thence along his boulevard St.-Germain to the Concorde bridge. We are passing through what is known as the Latin Quarter, abode of artists, writers, intellectuals of all sorts. Over to our right, mam'selle, is the Luxembourg palace and gardens. Do you see, mam'selle—between the trees? Do you see the roofs of the palace? It was there, in the Luxembourg, that many of the great figures of the Revolution spent their last days before being brought to trial and the guillotine. The mighty Danton and his circle languished there, also Marshal de Mouchy. And the Count de Brassy, my master's ancestor —now, what do you think of that, mam'selle? Is it to be wondered at that Count Robert and his family are all Royalists to the core?"

Again, I was uncomfortably aware that those searching eyes were upon me, weighing up my reaction to what he had just said. I merely nodded.

My guide resumed his monologue. "Also on our right is the church of St.-Sulpice, with the two towers like inkwells, do you see, mam'selle. There was a very devout priest who stole pieces of silver—spoons, forks, and such —at weddings and banquets, in order to have the metal made into a massive silver statue of Our Lady, which he put up in St.-Sulpice. How is that for devotion, eh, mam'selle? You do not see the likes of that sort of devotion often. Haha!"

The coachman flourished his whip, and the horses—beautifully paired grays—increased their pace as we swept out into a wide boulevard that opened up before us. I saw the bright lights of cafés, with people seated at outside tables under colored awnings; tall-hatted men, women's bright skirts and gleaming napery; light dancing from glassware; bay trees in tubs, their leaves startlingly green in the gaslights.

"Where is this?" I asked Flambard.

He said, "The boulevard St.-Germain, and there is the church of St.-Germaine-des-Prés. This place is full of history, mam'selle. It was at the Abbey of St.-Germain-des-Prés and at the Carmelite convent nearby that the gutters ran with the blood of the poor imprisoned nobles who were slaughtered by the revolutionary mob. Terrible, is it not, mam'selle? Not a droll story, like the one about the priest who stole silverware to make into a statue of Our Lady. Such terrible days they were. Can you wonder that Count Robert is a Royalist?"

This time there was no mistaking the insinuation. He was staring quite hard at me, seated, as he was, beside me in the open landau, inviting my comment. Still I said nothing, but merely inclined my head as if in bland agreement. Why, I asked myself, was this man trying to pump me about the Count's political views? And so clumsily. Did he think me stupid?

My guide must have tired of his attempts to draw me out, because we went for some distance in silence, while the last glow of sunset died in velvet blueness. With the night came a slight wind, and a reminder that it was still only March. I drew my shawl more closely about my shoulders and blessed my good tweed traveling dress and jacket. At last came the glint of lights reflected from water, and the entrance to a wide bridge swept into view ahead, marked by two shimmering rows of lamps.

"The River Seine!" cried my companion. "If you look to your right, mam'selle, you will presently see Notre Dame riding like a great ship in the center of the river. Immediately in front, across the bridge, is Europe's finest square, the place de la Concorde. Do you see the great obelisk rising in the center? That was a gift from the ruler of Egypt to the people of Paris and it was carved over three thousand years ago to the glory of a god-king."

"It's all so beautiful—beautiful!" The words burst unbidden from my lips as we came into the great square, joining the throng of glittering carriages and high-stepping horses that circled that vast place of light and color, where flags and bunting streamed from every lamp post and column. Flambard called to the coachman to slow down, as from our left cantered a jingling double line of mounted soldiers, helmets and breastplates agleam, horsehair plumes streaming in the night wind. They passed right in front of us, under the obelisk and beyond, down a wide and tree-lined avenue, at the bottom of which blazed the distant lights of a great building.

"That is the royal palace of the Tuileries," cried Flambard. "Tonight the Emperor is holding a reception in the Pavillon de l'Horloge as a curtain-raiser to the Exhibition. As the day of the opening draws nearer, such events will occur nightly, and the crowned heads of Europe will be seen there. I tell you, mam'selle, our Paris will be at the very center of the world in this year of 'sixty-seven! And now—behold!" He pointed right round in the opposite direction, and I gasped to see a broad sweep of street lights ascending into the far distance, to a dramatic hillcrest, where the dark bulk of a great archway stood on high in a pool of brightness, with the last, lurid strip of the dying day behind it.

"The Champs-Élysées and the Arc de Triomphe!" I cried.

"The heart and artery of Paris," said Flambard. "The Arc de Triomphe, you know: the first Napoleon ordered it to be raised to his own glory, but never lived to see it complete as it is today; though—and here is an odd thing, mam'selle —they built one there in full size, of wood and painted paper, for him to ride under. Now, what do you think of that?"

"What a man he must have been!" I exclaimed. "To have left his mark like this!"

"Ah, mam'selle, I daresay you are right," commented my guide. "But there are some who would not agree with you. My master, Count Robert, to name but one. He has no time for the Bonapartes."

I turned on him angrily. "The Count's opinions and his politics are no concern of mine, Flambard!" I snapped. "Nor are they any business of yours!"

I saw the man's eyes widen with alarm in the lamplight.

He snatched off his hat and bowed his head in contrition. "I am sorry to have spoken out of turn, mam'selle," he said. "And I beg you to overlook my unfortunate lapse."

In the face of such abject repentance, I could do no other than agree to his request; but I determined to watch my step with the assistant steward in future. He seemed to me to be altogether too smooth, too sly, too insinuating. Not another word passed between us till the carriage slowed to a halt near a pair of high stone gateposts in an elegant street just beyond the place de la Concorde. While we were still moving, the two footmen jumped down from behind and had lowered the steps and opened the door by the time we were through the gates and the wheels had come to their last turn in a cobbled courtyard, by the lamplit splendor of a great mansion.

"This, mam'selle," said Flambard solemnly, "is the Hôtel de Brassy."

The private town mansion of the De Brassys would not have done amiss as a royal palace; with a massive center block and projecting wings each side, high-pitched roofs, a baffling array of windows, and enough chimneys for a fair-sized village. Lying in the heart of that vast and breathtaking city, it had the power to overawe me in a way that the château never had in all the time I had known it. And the hôtel did *not* give off an atmosphere of friendliness.

"May I say what an honor it has been to escort mam'selle," murmured Flambard smoothly as he handed me down from the carriage. His face was rapt with good humor; you would never have thought that a cross word had been spoken.

"Thank you, Flambard," I said coolly. "The journey was most delightful, and instructive."

"Mam'selle is too kind." For a moment, I thought he was going to shower kisses on my hand, but fortunately he released it. "If my humble efforts have found favor with mam'selle, may I point out that mam'selle has only to speak for me and I can accompany her on any future excursions in the city."

"I will remember that, Flambard," I replied. And privately resolved to do no such thing. Mine of information though he might be, there was something about the assistant steward of the Hôtel de Brassy that made me feel unaccountably uneasy.

On the threshold of the mansion, Flambard presented his superior, the steward M. Fournier, a white-bearded man of advanced years who seemed to defer to his junior. I then received a curtsy from a fresh-faced, sturdy lass in a high lace coif, who had been appointed as my lady's maid for the duration of my stay. I may say that I had steadfastly refused the services of a lady's maid during my years at the château, thinking myself better equipped—by virtue of having been brought up in a parish workhouse —than most ladies who live in châteaux! However, it struck me that the time had come to resign myself to the fate of being a lady. So I greeted the girl, who introduced herself as Hortense, and said that I hoped she would be happy in my service.

"Hortense will escort you to your suite, mam'selle," said Fournier.

This she did, with six footmen following after us, carrying my luggage. We ascended a great curved stair to a wide gallery on the next floor that was lined with portraits in heavy gilt frames. The faces in the pictures, particularly those of the menfolk, had the dark, craggy good looks of the De Brassys. And the De Brassys' indefinable air of being a vastly improved version of the common run of human beings. Some of them wore white court wigs of the previous century: I wondered how many of these had perished on the guillotine.

"This is your suite, mam'selle." Hortense opened double doors and stood aside.

Now, my bedroom and sitting room at the château, though splendid beyond belief to a person who has shared a poky cell with three others, were only of medium size and somewhat on the dark side, being entirely paneled with age-blackened oak, and with heavy seventeenth-century furniture of the same hue. The total effect was somber—but friendly.

My suite at the hôtel was staggering in its proportions and sumptuous in decoration. A crystal chandelier hung from the center of the sitting room ceiling, the like of which I could only compare with those in the opera house at Tours. The walls were paneled, but painted in pale shades of pink and gilded at the moldings. The furniture, also, was more gilt than woodwork, and upholstered in striped silks and satins. The clock that stood above the elaborately carved fireplace was set into a gilded chariot drawn by a pair of gilt butterflies and driven by a laughing faun. When I looked down at my feet, they were all but lost in the rich pile of an Eastern carpet.

"The bedroom is through here, mam'selle," murmured my maid.

The bedroom was in warm gold: paneling, ceiling, upholstery, and hangings all in tones that varied from buttercup yellow to deep saffron. The hangings of the tiny, delightful four-poster bed were of the true golden color. All the pictures in the room echoed the same warm tints, being scenes of sunlight, with naked pagan figures. The sitting room may have struck me as too grand by half; but it was a bedroom from out of a dream. And, looking at the enticing four-poster, I remembered that I had been traveling most of the day.

"Will mam'selle wish to give her orders for dinner?" This was from a soft-footed butler who had followed the footmen with the luggage, which Hortense was already beginning to unpack.

That four-poster was beckoning me, and I never have much of an appetite when the sun has gone down—which was why the interminable dinners at the château had always been such a trial to me. I was only too glad of the opportunity to ask for a light collation of sliced cold beef, with a salad and a pot of coffee, to be served in my sitting room. In fact, when it arrived, I myself carried the tray into my bedroom, and sat there by the window, watching the night sky over Paris.

It was very quiet in the rue du Faubourg St.-Honoré, with hardly the sound of a carriage wheel to disturb the night. Indeed, at the rear of the mansion, where my suite was situated, there was scarcely even that. My bedroom windows looked down into a town garden so cunningly devised and laid out that it could have been the great park at Brassy, were it not for the high stone wall that could be discerned, here and there, among the clumps of handsome trees and bushes. In the center of the garden, immediately in front of my windows, was a mate to the selfsame marble cherub wrestling with the swan that occupied my favorite arbor at Brassy. As I sipped the dregs of my coffee, looking at the pure water that streamed from the fountain, my mind was carried back to the château, and I imagined Count Robert in his formal evening dress, seated alone at one end of the long table in the great hall. And I felt sorry for him. Poor man.

Through the open doors of the sitting room, the discreet chimes of the gilt butterfly clock gave the hour of ten. Time for bed. One last look out into the garden and at the loom of light above the high enclosing walls that told of the presence of Europe's most exciting city. Good night cherub. Good night swan.

Something, surely, was moving in the shadows!

Over by the clump of laurel bushes, near the foot of the pair of towering cypresses, close by the wall!

I stared into the confusing darkness, whose shifting pattern of moonlight and shadow was capable of producing all sorts of phantoms for the tired eyes of someone who had risen early and had been traveling all day. Had I been mistaken? Yes. Nothing moved there, save the light upper branches of the laurels.

Or, perhaps, that was a cat—a black cat—that moved out there?

It was no cat!

I saw her as clearly as I had seen her—was it all that time ago, four years before?—on the deck of the Channel packet *Princess Royal* . . .

Tall—though not so tall as she had appeared the first time. Dressed in a black shroud from head to foot, with face hidden by her draperies. She moved into a sliver of moonlight and stood very still by one of the sentinel cypresses. Watching.

Watching. And looking up at my lighted window!

Anger conquered my terror: anger at the grotesque intrusion upon my privacy. Who was this creature? I demanded of myself. What right had she to frighten me across the years? Reaching up, I fumbled at the catch of the window, but it was stiff with lack of use, and I found it difficult to shift. In giving it my whole attention, I finally got the wretched thing to open, flung the window wide, and leaned out into the moonlit night.

The dark watcher had gone. And though I stayed there for nearly an hour, straining my eyes at the shadows, she never showed herself again. Finally I shut the window, drew the shutters, and went to bed, leaving the gas lamp burning throughout the night.

I was out early, before breakfast, searching the walled garden in the brisk air. There was certainly no way that a woman in skirts could have scaled the wall, which was not only lofty but also capped with revolving spikes against intruders. However, I was able to establish that almost anyone could enter the grounds of the Hôtel de Brassy merely by walking quietly through the gates and being careful not to attract the attention of the concierge who lived at the gate house, an old soldier who wore a kepi and other oddments of uniform and a row of clanking medals, and whose rheumy eyes would certainly miss more than they saw after dark.

In the courtyard, also, I made the brief acquaintance of a shy poodle dog whose name—so I learned from the concierge—was Sasha.

Oliver arrived immediately I had finished breakfast in my sitting room. He entered as all good actors should: with the air of having waited all his life for the pleasure of my company, with a bunch of red roses, and a brilliant opening line:

"Tessa! No—don't move, my dear! Stay just as you are— like a Greek goddess; like one of the caryatids from the temple of Erechtheum in Athens!"

"Oliver, you are a terrible flatterer!" I told him, taking

his hands and offering my cheek for his kiss. "And your roses are beautiful. Thank you, my dear. And how glad I am to see you."

He sat down and I offered him coffee. I was conscious of his eyes upon me as I poured it.

"Your hand is trembling, Tessa," he said quietly. "And you said you were glad to see me with a very particular vehemence. Is something the matter?"

"I—I think something's the matter," I admitted. And I told him everything—about the Woman in Black. And when I had finished, he put down his empty cup and saucer and looked at me quizzically, head on one side.

"Surely it's all your imagination, Tessa," he said. "Last night, after all, you had just finished a long and tiring journey. You were excited. Perhaps overwrought."

"But, Oliver, I saw her once before! Perhaps twice! On the Channel packet. And again that first night at Brassy. Admittedly, I have always thought I imagined it the second time. But the way it happened last night—the way she stood in the shadows, looking up at my window, was exactly the way it was at Brassy!" I heard my voice taking on an edge of hysteria.

"And that's all you are worried about, Tessa?" he asked me calmly.

"No, there's—something else."

"Please tell me."

I recounted my journey from the station with the assistant steward, Flambard, and was in a way relieved to see that he accepted this with more interest.

"It was as if, you say, he was trying to get you to comment on the Count's politics?"

"Yes. At least three times."

"Or perhaps—your own politics, Tessa?"

I thought for a moment. "That might have been so. It didn't occur to me at the time." I felt a chill of fear. "Oliver, why would he want to know about me?"

"He could be a police spy," said Oliver.

"A *spy*?"

"My dear, you must realize that the Emperor came to

power by a *coup* that was not entirely without bloodshed. He has many enemies amongst his own subjects." Oliver fixed me with an even glance. "The De Brassys, particularly Count Robert, are strongly anti-Bonaparte. It has to be admitted that the authorities employ people to watch the comings and goings of such people as the De Brassys—and their friends and acquaintances. This fellow Flambard may very well be one of these. But you have nothing to fear, my dear."

"I should think not!" I cried. "Why, I don't even *have* any politics."

"Of course, of course," he said soothingly. "You have nothing to fear, and neither has my patron the Count. He is a Royalist by reason of his birth and background; but (albeit with some small show of reluctance) he is as loyal a supporter of the present ruler of France as any man."

"If that fellow—that Flambard—is a spy, he should be dismissed!" I cried.

Oliver shrugged his shoulders in a very French sort of way. "Why so?" he demanded. "It cannot be proved. In any event, he is doing no great harm, and he is possibly a very good assistant steward. And now, my dear Tessa, if you would care to put on your bonnet, I will take you and show you Paris—particularly my theater."

That day began a whirl of days which, because I have never kept a diary, remains part of a dazzling kaleidoscope of impressions that I am only able to recall in part, and some parts clearer and more detailed than others—as is often the case in our lives.

Oliver had a most sporty-looking carriage of his own waiting in the courtyard of the hôtel: what he called a "light park phaeton," English-made and imported by himself, and drawn by as restless a pair of high-stepping hacks as ever I set eyes on. I marveled at the way he handled the tiny two-seater in all the bustle of midday Paris, winning for himself many a Gallic curse in the process of cutting his more manageable vehicle in and out among the slower-moving omnibuses, heavy carriages, drays, even farm carts piled high with hay. And all the time he drove with a cigar clenched between his very white teeth, a devil-may-care grin on his face, his tall hat tipped jauntily over one eyebrow.

His theater was in the rue de l'Echiquier, off one of Baron Haussmann's tree-lined, teeming Grands Boulevards. Called the Théâtre des Comédiens, it was a tiny, intimate place of red plush and gilded cherubim, popping gas lamps and the smell of garlic, tobacco, and patchouli. Count Robert, so Oliver informed me, had taken a twenty-year lease upon the place, which, though far from the smart quarters of the city, was the regular haunt of not only the most discerning of theatergoers but also of the "set" surrounding the Imperial court, and even of the Emperor himself.

At the theater, I had a most happy reunion with Mirabel and the company, whom I had not seen since the memorable night of the gala performance in Tours, four years previously—for though, as I have said, Oliver had regularly visited me during the intervening years, it had never been possible for more than one of the principals at a time to absent themselves from the performances. Mirabel had not altered one bit, neither had Jöelle the *soubrette*; and so happy and successful was the company that there had been only a couple of changes. In the corner of Mirabel's dressing room I saw the dresser called "Old Gigot," whom I had first seen on the far-off Christmas Eve in Penruth. She was crouched over a piece of sewing and never looked up.

That night, after the performance, Oliver took me to dinner at a smart restaurant called Véfour's, in the Palais-Royal. There he told me that sometime during the next few weeks and certainly before the summer was over, he intended to set me up there, alone, on the stage of the Théâtre des Comédiens and submit me to the final test of proving that I had fulfilled the promise of my early youth and indeed become the material from which great actresses are made. I was overjoyed at the prospect, and quite confident that my delivery of Phèdre would clinch the matter.

With that to look forward to and to work for, and the excitement of my two cavaliers' arrival from England in a few days' time, not to mention the forthcoming Exhibition, it is not to be wondered at that, in all that whirl of days, I was able to put my fears out of my mind.

Philippe and Otto were due to leave Oxford on the 11th and to arrive in Paris, weather permitting, on the evening of the following day. The 11th was a Monday, and it rained cats and dogs from morning till night, further putting in hazard the completion of the Great Exhibition site, which had been blighted by a bad winter of prolonged sleet and snow, so that the site—an open space of parkland called the Champ-de-Mars, which lay between the river and the military academy—was still a sea of mud, with less than three weeks before the official opening. Toward nightfall, however, the rain slackened and then stopped. I was toying with the notion of ordering a carriage to take me to the Théâtre des Comédiens to see the performance (which would have made it my third time of doing so since I had arrived in Paris), when Sasha the poodle came coyly up to me with his lead in his mouth and laid it in my lap. We had become great friends, he having overcome his shyness, and we had started a habit of taking evening walks together in the faubourg and the adjacent streets and alleyways leading to the tree-lined park of the Champs-Élysées.

Sasha reinforced his request with a bark.

"If it rains again—and it might—we shall get soaked," I warned him.

He let it be known that this was of no consequence.

"Very well," I told him, resigned.

Presently, we set off, I in a long rainproof coverall, sensible bonnet, and clutching a large umbrella; Sasha trotting ahead at the full extent of his lead. The concierge saluted us stiffly as we passed.

The lamps were lit along the faubourg, and the upper windows of the great mansions all ablaze behind their secret, enclosing walls. The rain had worked wonders, leaving the cobblestones glistening and scrubbed-looking, and the air tasted like champagne. There were very few people about. A solitary cab rattled its way out of sight. We passed the window of a smart milliner's, and a pretty young *vendeuse* smiled at me as she hung a "closed" sign on the inside of the glass door. The day was running out. Paris was settling herself down for night.

We reached the park and I let Sasha off his lead for a romp. He led me to all his favorite spots, which included a fountain whose basin was low enough for him to drink from. From there, through the trees, I could see the lights of the place de la Concorde and the carriages that forever circled it; the pointing finger of the great obelisk.

"Time to go home, Sasha," I called. "Sasha, where are you?"

He had bounded off. I could see his light-colored form darting in and out of a line of trees some distance off. I resigned myself to follow after him. We were not far from home and the rain continued to hold off. But the grass was still very wet, so I kept to the path.

It was then I heard the footsteps of someone else walking along a path some distance away. Woman's footsteps, light and slow.

Instinctively, I quickened my pace. Sasha was now leading me through the park in the direction of the Arc de Triomphe, and about three lines of trees separated me from the busy avenue, where I could see the passing carriage lamps and hear the clip-clop of the horses.

And then I lost sight of the dog.

Still with not the slightest feeling of alarm, I paused to peer around for him. And heard the footsteps again. This time they came quickly, as if the woman was almost running. And almost immediately, they slowed down to a walk and then stopped completely.

The message of the footfalls was quite clear. Realizing it, I felt my skin prickle with sudden fear . . .

The unseen woman was following me!

By this time, I was in the deep shadow of the trees. Somehow the bustle of the avenue seemed to have retreated far away. I was alone, as it were, in a wood, with no one at hand to help me, no one to hear if I called out for help. No one but—*her*!

It was then that I took to my heels and ran, gathering up my skirts, and uncaring when my bonnet came detached and flew off, nor stopping to pick it up. My hair, too, freed from its covering, began to fall down. My eyes fixed on the lighter shade of the path ahead, I simply kept going. Nothing else mattered but to put as much distance as possible between myself and my pursuer.

I do not know how it became borne in on me that I had chosen the wrong path: one which, instead of leading straight out into one road or another, merely turned in on itself and pursued a meandering course round and round the park. I only remember becoming suddenly aware that the sound of the traffic had become fainter and died away; the trees bigger, more leafy; the darkness more intense.

I stopped. Leaned against the trunk of a tree, my heart thudding, my hand gripping the umbrella defensively, my eyes straining at the darkness all round, my ears alerted to the slightest sound.

Calming myself as best I was able, I told myself that my pursuer must still be behind me, back the way I had come. It followed, then, that my safest way lay immediately in front—no matter where it led. And, after all, the park was severely bounded by busy thoroughfares on three sides at least, and by habitations on the fourth. If I went straight ahead, I would both put more distance between me and my pursuer—and win out of the park, sooner or later. Immediately in front of me, across a stretch of grass, lay a clump of bushes that might well mark the edge of a road and the limit of the park. I set off across the wet grass—and ran full tilt into a dark figure that closed upon me from my left!

I screamed and hit out with the shaft of the umbrella, but it met with only empty air. It was too dark to see my assailant, but a hand was gripping my arm as if to hold me steady to receive a blow. I had the impression of another hand and arm raised as if to strike. Then blind panic lent me the strength to break free. I felt the sleeve of my waterproof coverall rip and sunder. There came a cry of frustrated fury. Something hit my skirts—it might have been a stone. The cry was repeated; but I was already struggling through wet bushes that soaked my skirts, lashed my face, and teased out my streaming hair. I broke through and looked about me. The hard pavement was beneath my feet. Not twenty yards away, a painted gas lamp announced the presence of a café-restaurant. I stumbled toward it, burst open the door, and met a row of shocked faces.

"Mam'selle, what has happened to you? Have you been attacked?" A waiter in a long apron put down a loaded tray of dirty dishes and came up to me, taking my arm and guiding me to a seat, his honest face a picture of concern. Looking up, I saw my own reflection in an engraved mirror: hatless, wild-eyed, and tousled, I looked indeed like the victim of some savage assault.

They brought me a cognac and fussed round me, asking my name and the whereabouts of my home. Hearing the Hôtel de Brassy, the proprietor sent a lad there straightaway to summon someone to fetch me in a carriage. When I told them about Sasha, a couple more went out, as they said, to "whistle him up." They returned almost immediately with the poodle, who, when he saw me, showered my face and hands with affection.

"Mam'selle, you've got holes all over your coat," said someone.

"Such a strange smell," was another comment. "Sharp to the nose, like something burning."

I glanced down at my torn coverall, to see that its skirt was speckled with dark-edged holes of varying sizes; and as I touched the fabric, pieces of it dropped away as if charred by flame. And there was a strange, acrid smell.

"What can it be?" demanded someone.

The waiter pulled at his lower lip. "Smells to me like some sort of chemical . . ." He glanced across the room. "The Professor will know. Professor, can you spare a moment, please?"

An old gentleman with a white beard and pince-nez was supping at a nearby table, and had been too engrossed in his book, propped against a salt cellar before him, to notice the small disturbance surrounding me. He came across, peered down at my skirts, delicately probed at one of the holes with a fingertip, sniffed the fingertip, and gave a mild exclamation.

"What is it then, Professor?" they demanded.

"It is oil of vitriol," he replied. The rheumy old eyes met mine in concern and puzzlement. "My dear young lady, what have you been doing, to get yourself splashed with vitriol? Why, the stuff is terribly corrosive. If you had got it on your hands—your face . . ."

It must have been then that I started to scream.

2

I was waiting in the wings of the stage when Oliver and Mirabel took their bow, hand in hand, at the interval curtain. They were both surprised and shocked to see me in the state I was in; and I must have presented an alarming sight, with my hair still hanging down and my eyes frightened. The ruined coverall lay bundled up on the floor of the brougham which was waiting for me outside. Immediately on its arrival at the café-restaurant, I had told the coachman to drive me straight to see Oliver. Sasha was outside, too, in the fellow's care.

"Tessa lovey, what ails you?" cried Mirabel, enveloping me in her scented warmth. "Bless me, you look as if you've seen a ghost, don't she, Oliver?"

"It's nothing," I said. "Only I must speak to Oliver—alone." I saw a shadow of disappointment cross her face; but I had no intention of burdening any one else with the strange horror that seemed to be closing in on me, gradually, insidiously, from all sides.

"We've got twenty minutes," said Oliver, taking my hand. "Come along to my dressing room." I smiled wanly to Mirabel. She patted my shoulder and turned away.

Oliver's dressing room was small, cluttered, and cosy. He offered me a button-back armchair, but I preferred to go through the ordeal standing up. He offered me a glass of wine, which I declined.

"All right," he said encouragingly. "Out with it."

I told him . . .

He stared at me as if I had been a stranger; as if he were seeing me for the first time.

"So I came straight here," I added. "And I've told no one else."

"I think you're wise," he said. Then he was at my side,

arm about my shoulder and comforting me. "There must be some mistake. Vitriol, you say? Oh, no, my dear, it isn't so. I ask you—who would want to harm a sweet, innocent creature such as you? Why, you don't have an enemy in the world. Outside of a small town in far-off Cornwall and a lonely château down on the Loire, no one even *knows* you!"

"The old gentleman—the one they called the Professor—was quite certain it was vitriol," I said, and I clenched my hands in an effort to keep the hysteria out of my voice. "And the person who attacked me—the strange woman—tried to throw it in my face, but my umbrella must have got in the way. I—I can remember something—it must have been the bottle—hitting my skirt."

"No, Tessa—*no!*"

"I tell you it happened that way!" My voice was no longer my own. I felt my self-control slipping away from me. "Don't you see—someone was trying to . . ."

He smacked me sharply across the cheek. The shock of it brought me up short, drowning my cry in a sudden intake of breath. I exhaled slowly—and felt myself taking control again of my mind, of my actions.

"I'm sorry about that, Tessa," he said quietly.

"Oh, Oliver—Oliver!" I clung to him then. And the tears came, washing away the doubts and the fears; signaling my mind's willingness to accept the judgment of that strong and capable man who was more to me, surely, than any real father could have been.

"There, there," he murmured, stroking my hair.

"I—I could have been mistaken," I whispered. "In my nervousness I could simply have bumped into someone in the dark. Someone who could have been even more frightened than I was. And the stuff on my skirt . . ."

"Your Professor," he said. "You know, Tessa, there's scarcely a café in Paris that doesn't have, among its regular clientele, some old character everyone calls '*Monsieur le Professeur*,' who's as often as not nothing more than an old bookworm—an eccentric recluse with his head stuffed with fancies, who couldn't distinguish vitriol from a bar of soap. I promise you."

"Yes, yes, you're right, Oliver!" I cried. I so wanted to believe; not to believe meant accepting thoughts and fancies that could drive me mad. One doubt remained: "Oliver, what about the holes—the burn holes—in the skirt of my coverall?"

He thought for a moment. "The last time you wore it," he said firmly, "you stood too close to a hot stove—as it might have been in a railway station waiting room, or such—and scorched the fabric. Next time you wore it, the thing went in holes. That's a perfectly reasonable explanation that fits the case. There may be a hundred others. And, Tessa—" he took my face, tenderly, between his hands, and those wonderful deep-blue eyes looked down into mine— "any one of those hundred explanations would be better than the one you brought to me."

"Yes, Oliver," I told him, determined to be convinced.

The call-boy tapped on the door to inform him that the curtain went up in five minutes. He escorted me to the stage door, where the one-horse brougham waited, with the coachman holding the open door with one hand and Sasha with the other.

Oliver kissed me good night. I was driven back, through the Grands Boulevards, all lit up and teeming with strollers. Later, in a quiet street leading through to the faubourg, I took the bundle from beneath the seat—my ruined coverall—and dropped it out the window. I wanted no memories of that ghastly encounter in the Champs-Élysées. Bury the memory and smooth over its grave with comforting explanations.

It was Flambard who greeted my arrival back at the Hôtel de Brassy: all smiles and flourishes as ever.

"A surprise for mam'selle!" he cried. "While mam'selle has been out, the two gentlemen have arrived from England!"

Phillippe and Otto? "But they're not due in Paris till tomorrow evening!" I cried.

"Notwithstanding, they are here, mam'selle," he replied. "And they have gone out. For a foot-race!"

I stared hard at the man. The thought crossed my mind that he must have been at the bottle.

"A *foot-race*, did you say?" I demanded.

"Yes, mam'selle," replied Flambard. "The gentlemen left a quarter of an hour ago. The winner, as I understand it, is he who is first in a race from here to the Arc de Triomphe and back." He glanced at his watch. "And, judging from the speed of their departure, mam'selle, I would say that Monsieur Philippe and Herr von Stock—one or the other, or both—will be back with us at any moment."

I caught sight of myself in one of the gilded mirrors in the hall. Heavens! What a mess I looked. It was one thing to rush pell-mell and lay my terrors on Oliver's broad shoulders and a fig for my appearance; quite another to face my two devoted cavaliers with hair all awry, a smut on my nose and eyes red with weeping.

I darted up the great sweep of staircase with Sasha bounding at my heels. Hortense was already waiting for me in the dressing room. She swiftly put up my hair into a chignon. A dusting of rice powder, a mere *soupçon* of rouge on my cheeks, a clean lace blouse—and I was ready.

The boys were coming in from the courtyard as I walked down the staircase, looking as calm and collected as I was able, for all that my heart was pounding with excitement to see them again.

"Tessa! How splendid you look!"

"Tessa, you are divine!"

They took my hands, showered kisses upon my cheeks; gave me their arms and escorted me into the drawing room, where they called for champagne. Both, I noticed, were in shirtsleeves and soft-soled yachting shoes—the attire, I supposed, in which gentlemen of Oxford University go for casual foot-races. I had not seen them since Christmas, and they both seemed to have become disconcertingly manly and mature. Philippe, I noted, was sporting the beginnings of a moustache.

"But you're back a day early," I said.

They exchanged glances.

"You tell her, Otto," said Philippe.

"Tomorrow evening, Tessa," smiled my Prussian cavalier, "you are going to the theater. No, not to see Oliver at the Comédiens, but to the premiere at the Variétés."

I gasped for joy. "Offenbach's new comic opera with Hortense Schneider!" I cried.

"The Grand Duchess of Gerolstein," confirmed Otto. "You are pleased, Tessa?"

Pleased? All Paris was talking about Offenbach's new opera. Tickets for the premiere were being offered in the newspapers at absurd prices—and were being eagerly snapped up. All the orchestras in Paris played Offenbach's gay and lilting tunes from morning till night: you could hear them drifting through the trees in the Bois de Boulogne and coming from the cafés of the Grands Boulevards: airs from *Orpheus in Hades* and *La Belle Hélène*, the frenzied cancan from *La Vie Parisienne* that set one's feet a-dancing. Was I pleased to be going to the premiere? I gazed at them with my eyes misting for pure pleasure.

"The commencement is at seven-thirty, and we shall take a little light supper after the performance," said Otto. "I shall be ready to escort you at seven, Tessa."

There was a moment's silence, and Philippe looked into his empty champagne glass.

"You mean—you'll both be ready for me at seven?" I prompted.

Otto shook his head, "No, Tessa," he said quietly. "Only I shall have the honor to escort you tomorrow evening."

Another silence. I happened to glance down at Philippe's white shoes, slightly dusted from their swift passage to and from the Arc de Triomphe. And in a flash of inspiration, I knew the reason for a foot-race that evening, and who had been the winner.

In spite of Oliver's reassurances, I took care to shutter and bolt my bedroom windows that night. Nor did I dare to look into the garden. As for walking Sasha after dusk, that, I decided, must cease. One must assume an innocent explanation for all the strange and disturbing occurrences —but one must also take sensible precautions.

Oliver and Mirabel came for luncheon next day, and a right jolly meal it was: the like of which the Hôtel de Brassy could scarcely have witnessed since the powdered and pampered ladies and gallants sat at the long table in the huge dining room, under the painted ceiling, in the twilight of careless elegance before the Great Revolution changed Europe forever.

Oliver was in a high good mood, and he chaffed us that, though the Emperor and Empress might be present at Offenbach's premiere that evening, he would wager that His Imperial Majesty's attendances at *The Grand Duchess of Gerolstein* would never match the total of his visits to the Théâtre des Comédiens—thirty-three to date. Mirabel tried to persuade him to cancel the evening's performance at the Comédiens so that the two of them could accompany us—Monsieur Offenbach having apparently sent free tickets for the stars of Paris's most esteemed mime company—but Oliver would not hear of it. One less audience at the Comédiens, he said with almost feminine logic, was one audience the more for old Offenbach at the Variétés.

I had a ball gown that had been made for me by one of the best dressmakers in Orléans. It was of lilac Lyons silk, covered with puffs of tulle of the same shade, in which were sewn sprays of artificial lilies of the valley. I began my toilette at five with a perfumed bath, and Hortense took over an hour—and three separate attempts—to dress my hair, which she did in a high chignon, with falling curls at the nape of the neck and a band of matching lilac silk set with lilies of the valley. Dressed, I regarded myself in the pier glass. And in my pride and delight I saw myself as the future star of the Paris theater. Phèdre personified. But if only my nose were not quite so perky!

Otto was waiting for me in the hall, fidgeting with the button of his white gloves and sneaking glances at himself in the mirror. He sprang forward to greet me and, when I offered my hand, implanted a formal kiss—upon his own thumb.

"You look truly ravishing, Tessa," he breathed. Then, adding in his own language, *"Du bist wie eine Blume."*

I smiled at the recollection of those words: the first compliment he had offered me, though by no means the only. Our carriage was waiting. He handed me in. The footmen closed the door, folded up the steps, and took their places behind. We set off through lamplit Paris toward the Grands Boulevards. My escort was silent and seemed preoccupied: staring thoughtfully at the passing scene. I had the opportunity to study his face.

In the four years I had known them, Otto had changed less than had his friend. Philippe's dark, Latin good looks had increased in ruggedness till one could clearly see the resemblance to his uncle, so that they could have been brothers; Otto still looked absurdly young, and, for all his sturdy tallness, possessed an almost feminine grace. His pink cheeks were innocent of the lightest stubble, the sky-blue eyes still wide and innocent.

"Do you remember that ridiculous hat with the shaving brush?" I asked him.

"When I knew how much you despised it, after Philippe had confided to me, I gave that hat to my scout—the fellow who looks after my rooms—at Balliol," he replied, and continued ruefully, "I was very proud of that hat."

"I'm sorry, Otto," I said lightly.

He did not answer for quite a while, indeed we were nearly at our destination before he reached out and laid his hand on mine; and I could see then that my light banter about the hat had not dispelled his pensive mood. The sky-blue eyes were clouded with seriousness.

"Don't be sorry, Tessa," he said.

"Not about the hat?" I replied, making a last, desperate attempt to keep things light. "But if I had known what that hat meant to you . . ."

"Not about anything!" he cried. "You must have no sorrow, no regrets, for anything that has ever passed between us—or for anything that may ever pass between us in the future, Tessa."

Happily, I was not called upon to reply. At that moment we drew up with a flourish outside the brightly lit awning of the Variétés, where the flower of Parisian society of the Second Empire was thronging to be entertained.

After the performance, we went for supper to Bignon's restaurant in the Boulevard des Italiens close by the theater.

We were in high good humor; the note of seriousness which had been struck in the carriage on the way to the theater had been overlaid by the dazzling genius of Offenbach. How we had laughed that evening! How Parisian society and her Emperor had laughed!

Truth to tell, M. Offenbach's elaborate joke had been directed toward Otto's own people: the plot of *The Grand Duchess of Gerolstein* concerned the pleasure-loving Grand Duchess of a comical small German state and how her army was led to war by a fire-eating buffoon named Baron Puck. In the then-current situation of European politics, it was obvious to all that Offenbach's mocking finger was pointed at Prussia, and that Baron Puck was a caricature of Bismarck. Several times during the performance, when the laughter was loudest, I had found myself glancing anxiously at my companion—only to see, to my relief, that he was laughing as loudly as any. Freed of that anxiety, I had been able to relax and lose myself in the sheer delight of the performance, in the color, the music, the entrancing tunes and lyrics; in the incomparable Hortense Schneider, who played the title role.

Supper-time, then, found us at a table in Bignon's, still tapping our feet and humming the catchy airs of the opera; recalling the jokes, the many delights, the impudence of M. Offenbach's plot. As to the latter, Otto frankly stated that he was aware of a certain absurdity about Bismarck and his grandiose schemes for Prussia—and that he thought Offenbach's piece would go a long way toward the encouragement of sanity and good humor in European politics. Laughter, said Otto, with a clear-eyed wisdom, was a great force for peace and understanding among nations: people who laugh at the same things do not easily find cause to fight each other.

It was almost immediately after delivering himself of this remark that he fell silent. We both fell silent. We had run out of things to say. We had certainly said all there was to be said about *The Grand Duchess of Gerolstein.*

I addressed myself to the food, which was excellent, meanwhile searching my mind for something to set us chatting again. With a small feeling of near-panic, I thought I detected a look of melancholy descending upon my companion's features. I remembered his closing remarks in the carriage on the way to the theater . . .

"This is a marvelous restaurant," I cried. "Do you know, Otto, I first learned about Bignon's years ago, when I read *Le Figaro* in Cornwall. But I never guessed I should ever eat here."

Otto said, "It has a certain style. I will tell you an amusing story about Bignon's, Tessa. Some years ago, a rich Russian aristocrat named Count Teufelskine breakfasted here. When presented with the bill, the Count was surprised to see that he had been charged an absurd amount for the two peaches which he had eaten: something ridiculous, something like twenty francs. He said to the waiter, 'I suppose that peaches must be very scarce in Paris?'—to which the waiter replied, 'No, sir. But Teufelskines are.' "

I laughed politely. "That's very funny," I said.

"Not so very funny," he replied. "Tessa, I must tell you something . . ."

"Otto . . ." I felt the panic rising within me.

"No, please, Tessa, hear me out," he said earnestly. "First, I will tell you about myself and my background and prospects. You have known me for four years. Some—most— you have heard before; but if you will graciously be patient, I should be obliged . . ."

I fixed my eyes, avoiding his, on the wall opposite, where hung a fine print of Napoleon III seated on his throne and receiving a gift of what looked like an elaborate pudding basin from a kneeling Oriental gentleman in a curious wide-brimmed hat with a pointed crown. The Empress was looking on, and uniformed gentlemen of the court stood around.

"I come from Friedland in East Prussia," said Otto, "where my family have held estates for five hundred years and more. My mother, as you know, is half English, and it was at her wish that I have been liberally educated abroad, in France and England, before entering the army. Service in the Prussian army, you see, Tessa, is in the family tradition. The Von Stocks are Junkers of the ancient

149

mold: soldiers first and second, landowners and farmers third . . ."

His voice washed over me. So long as he continued to speak in such a general fashion, all would be well. I had heard most of his story before, for had we not been devoted friends and confidants over the years? There was more to come, much more. I was safe till he had finished. Perhaps by then I would have thought of something to say, to change the subject. Meanwhile it seemed important not to look directly at him, but to appear attentive and interested all the same. I concentrated my gaze on the picture. An engraved line underneath it seemed to read: *"Reception of the Siamese Ambassadors at Fontainebleau . . ."*

Otto was saying, "My formal education being finished, it is now time for me to commence my military career, a career upon which depends my whole future. I would not have you mistakenly think, my dear Tessa, that I shall ever succeed to great wealth, broad lands, fine castles. The Von Stocks, as Prussian Junkers go, are really quite poor. And I am a younger son. No, my only hope lies in rapid advancement in my chosen profession . . ."

There was also a date after the title of the print, but it was too far away for me to read. A waiter came up to remove our plates, and Otto was interrupted in his monologue by the necessity for ordering the next course. I gazed about me desperately for a subject of such interest as to stop the present course of his remarks, which seemed to me to be heading toward an inevitable conclusion. I searched the faces of our fellow diners, hoping to find a well-known countenance: some famous poet, painter, or politician, perhaps; but, though there were plenty of such folk in Paris, not one was present at Bignon's that night to provide a conversational diversion. And the picture of the Siamese Ambassador seemed hardly strong enough to do the trick.

The waiter departed. "As I was saying . . ." said Otto. Then he paused. I looked at him, to see that his gaze had slid past me and was fixed upon something—someone—over my shoulder.

"Is something the matter?" I asked him.

"How very strange," he murmured.

"What—what was strange?" I demanded. And I felt a prickle of a familiar dread.

"Why, there was a woman looking in at us, through the window there—" he indicated a window immediately behind me, beyond which, when I turned to look, I could see nothing but darkness—"but when she caught my eye, she withdrew in a hurry. One does not expect to be stared at by all and sundry while eating—not at a place like Bignon's. Waiter, come here!"

"Monsieur?" The waiter bowed, eager to serve the customer's slightest whim.

"There was a woman out there staring in at us."

The man's smile wavered, but returned. "With respect, I think monsieur may possibly be mistaken. The windows on this side look out to a private courtyard of the establishment, which is why the windows are uncurtained at this side. No one would be out there at this hour, monsieur. However, I will go and inquire." He left.

I clutched my hands tightly together, on my lap, below the level of the tabletop.

"Otto," I murmured. "Can you describe her—the woman you saw?"

He nodded. "Yes, Tessa. She was—she appeared to be dressed all in black," he said—as I had known he would!

"You saw her face—can you describe it?" Saying this, I drove my fingernails hard against my palms.

"No," he said. "She was heavily veiled, with some kind of black shawl drawn over her head, hiding her eyes and most of her face in deep shadow. My dear, what is the matter?" He rose to his feet in concern and came round to me, laid a hand on my shoulder. "What is it, Tessa?"

It was then that I told him. About the visitations of the Woman in Black, about my childhood, everything including the episode in the darkness of the Champs-Élysées. For full measure, I even told him about my half-thaler, a thing I had never confided to anyone save Oliver. And I showed it to him.

"I think that woman is menacing me," I said at the end. And I shuddered.

"But why, Tessa—why?"

"I don't know, Otto. I only know that yesterday I had half-persuaded myself that it was all my imagination, helped along by chance, circumstance, coincidence, call it what you like. But now, after what you saw, I'm right back with my terrors. Please take me home, Otto."

"Of course."

He called for his bill. The waiter brought it, and scarcely attempted to conceal his scorn of anyone who would think that Bignon's, of all places, would permit outsiders to enter their sacred precincts and stare in at the diners. He had found no one in the courtyard, he said.

I parted company with Otto at the foot of the staircase at the Hôtel de Brassy, and I held on to his hand a few moments longer than necessary.

"Thank you for a lovely evening," I told him.

"I am sorry it was so rudely interrupted, Tessa," he said. "We must try again—another occasion."

I nodded. But both of us knew that not even loving friendship would stretch to a repetition of his carefully planned theater and supper for two; and I think that he guessed, even then, that the bizarre interruption of the woman behind the window had really made no difference to the outcome of his plan.

When I left him, he was walking slowly in the direction of the drawing room; where I made a shrewd guess that Philippe might be waiting up for him, to hear whether or not his friend had capped his victory in the foot-race by winning the hand of Tessa Thursday.

I slept badly that night.

It was impossible to be fearful for any length of time, or unhappy, in that Paris of the spring of 1867. There was a breathless air of newness, like watching the opening of a sumptuous flower; it was like being present at the beginning of a new age—an age of which Paris seemed destined to be the brightest and most famous jewel.

I succumbed to the enchantment; put aside my fears, my doubts.

152

To the amazement of half Paris—and all of the rest of Europe—the Great Exhibition was ready on time for the opening. I went with Otto and Philippe, in a carriage that followed a turbulent stream to the great oval-shaped glass palace in the Champ-de-Mars, where the Emperor declared the great spectacle to be open to all. I was quite close to His Imperial Majesty and thought he looked much older and not of a very good complexion. The Empress, though, seemed very sprightly.

After the opening ceremony we moved slowly through the crowded pavilion of glass, which contained exhibits from the leading civilized countries of the world in a bewildering hotchpotch: there was marble statuary side by side with industrial machinery, railway locomotives vying for attention with fine paintings. Naturally, I was most interested to see the exhibits from my own country, and was disappointed to find that they mostly consisted of dull-looking machinery and even duller furniture. The United States of America (only just recovering from the wounds of that bitter Civil War) had sent a field ambulance. The item which by far outstripped all others for the attention of the crowds was the immense black cannon from Krupp of Essen: this Prussian monster, we were informed, fired a shell that itself weighed as much as two small cannon of the present day, and it won a special prize. I glanced at Otto and saw him looking up at the black monster with a certain wistful pride. For my part, it called to mind Count Robert's cutting comments on the Exhibition, when he had mentioned the Prussian cannon; and the memory filled me with a strange nostalgia for the château and my lonely walks in the comforting solitude of the parkland. I was glad to turn my back on Herr Krupp's grim masterpiece.

Outside the great pavilion, my spirits revived, for here was the real delight of the 1867 Exhibition. The whole of the Champ-de-Mars had been transformed into an enchanted park, with woodlands and waterfalls, exotic aquaria teeming with tropical fish, and buildings representative of all the countries on earth, where persons in their national costumes dispensed food and drink of their regions, sang and danced to their native music. There, for the first time in my life, I saw people whom I had only known about in pictures and through the written word: tall Russians in huge fur caps; pigtailed Chinese with their incredibly tiny womenfolk; flashy-eyed Mexicans strutting like cockerels in many-colored blankets; pale Swedes who seldom smiled.

And there was M. Nadar and his aerial balloons. Nadar, a famous exponent of the art of photography, was also a fearless balloonist. For the occasion of the Exhibition, he had had constructed two stupendous gasbags attached to flimsy-looking baskets, in which he took visitors for aerial excursions over the Champ-de-Mars and the Seine. Holding me firmly by the hands, Otto and Philippe propelled me toward the two vast, swaying globes that dominated one corner of the park. There we saw M. Nadar, who contrived to look extremely spick and debonair in a very tall hat, formal coat, and waxed "imperials" while sitting in his uncomfortable-looking basket. It became immediately apparent that Philippe and Otto had ambitions to ascend in one of M. Nadar's aerial carriages, either the *Géant* or the *Céleste*—and that they expected me to accompany them!

"But, Tessa, it will be the experience of a lifetime!"

"You will see Paris as few have ever seen it. As only the birds have looked down upon it."

"If God had wished me to fly, He would have provided me with wings," I pronounced. "But He didn't. What's more, He didn't even give me a good head for climbing a ladder, or for looking down from a high window. I think that if I went up in a balloon my heart would stop beating through sheer terror!"

They had no answer for that, and were far too considerate to try to dissuade me. Instead, they swallowed their own disappointment (which, when brought face to face with the ordeal, might not have been all that considerable) and contented themselves with watching the ascent of the *Géant*, with M. Nadar and others.

As we stared up at the great sphere swaying upward through the clear air of that spring afternoon, I was aware that Philippe was still by my side, but that Otto had moved some distance away and was out of earshot. It signified nothing to me at that moment.

Philippe took me entirely by surprise, though I had been guarding myself against the moment ever since the night of my outing with Otto—indeed, since the occasion of the foot-race. But, as I have said, I was completely taken unawares by his Gallic directness, his headlong dash into the fray, in such contrast to Otto, who had planned his campaign with typical Teutonic foresight and thoroughness.

I was still craning my neck to look up at the *Géant*, which had been caught by a gust of wind and was being carried high above the arcaded roof of the great pavilion, when I felt Philippe's hand on my arm; heard him murmur the suddenly surprising words close to my ear.

"Tessa, I don't suppose you would care to marry me, would you?"

So startled that I dropped my reticule, a bamboo fan that I had been given in the Chinese temple, and a woodentop dolly from Egypt, I could only stare at him and make movements with my mouth.

"Philippe—I . . ." was all I could get out.

"I thought not," he said ruefully. And his rugged face crinkled delightfully in a friendly grin. "I told Otto we were both wasting our time. That's the pity of appointing a girl as an honorary boy and turning her into a comrade. One can never get things on a different basis ever again."

Everyone was too busy watching the *Géant* and M. Nadar to be scandalized when I flung my arms about his neck and kissed him—everyone, that is, but Otto. Lest he should think that I had yielded to Philippe's offer, I kissed him also.

It was an afternoon that I shall remember with constant delight for so long as I live. And when we arrived home, there was a brief note from Oliver:

My dear Tessa,

Events have presented me with the opportunity to offer you the entire stage and an empty theater on Thursday evening next. This is the night of another of old Offenbach's gala performances for visiting royalty—an

event with which I have decided not to compete, so the
Comédiens is at your disposal.

Shall we say seven-thirty, with supper afterward, to
celebrate your triumph?

Always,

O.—

Between Tuesday and Thursday, I lived Phèdre and I
lived Cleopatra. Dawn light found me stalking my apartment in my peignoir, declaiming to the long mirrors and
dying in strange ecstasies upon my bed, upon the floor,
and more comfortably and convincingly upon a *chaise-
longue*. At one point I decided to starve myself, taking only
tea with lemon and dry biscuits with a small piece of fruit
for my single meal of the day, in order to achieve—or so I
hoped—a pale and "interesting" appearance, but only suc-
ceeding in making myself hungry, while retaining the
resolutely healthy appearance that had survived even my
early upbringing at the workhouse.

Not for me the frail heroines so beloved of the modern
drama; I should play the parts of those two tragic queens
with strength and force, as I had been tutored by M. Martin,
late of the Comédie Française. From morn till night, I
existed within the two roles which were to demonstrate to
Oliver Craven that he had not been mistaken in me all
those years ago. By Thursday evening I had arrived at the
feeling of serene confidence which comes with a knowledge
of one's true worth. I knew that, if I lived to be a hundred,
I should never play the roles of Phèdre and Cleopatra
better than I was going to play them that evening, in the
empty Théâtre des Comédiens.

I had ordered a carriage at seven. Flambard officiated
at my departure, his usual deferential self. Since that first
day, he had given me no further cause for complaint; but
I did not trust the man. He bowed deeply to me as my
carriage swept out into the faubourg and headed toward
the Grands Boulevards.

By the time I reached the theater, all my brave confidence
had vanished in the air. Oliver was waiting for me in the
foyer, looking tremendously distinguished in his evening

tailcoat, with the red rosette of a Commander of the Legion of Honor in his buttonhole, and an eyeglass, which he had recently begun to affect, hanging on a black moiré ribbon across his startlingly white shirtfront.

He kissed my cheek. "My dear Tessa. Ravishing as ever. Come, my dear, the theater is yours, and your most devoted admirer waits to be enchanted."

My nervousness melted in the warmth of his admiration. "Oliver, what should I ever do—what should I ever have been—without you?" I asked him.

A slight gesture of his expressive hands implied, with the economy of a great actor's art, that what he had done was only what I deserved. We entered the empty theater and he led me up to the stage.

I had always thought of the Comédiens as an intimate place; where someone sitting in the farthest seat of the single balcony, which stretched, horseshoe-shaped, round the entire auditorium, was near enough to see every fleeting expression on an actor's face. From the footlights, with my heart pounding and my palms moistly clutching a handkerchief, it looked to have the size and intimacy of Paddington Station. And Oliver was one small white spot in the middle of a sea of empty plush seats, one face among the shadows.

I took a deep breath. This was my moment. For this, I had fought for and won myself an education. In the pursuit of this ambition, I had applied myself with diligence and humility to studying some of the greatest roles ever written. This moment was the end of a long road that stretched all the way back to Penruth under the snow of a long-gone Christmas Eve . . .

"I should like to commence by playing the closing scene from Shakespeare's *Antony and Cleopatra*, where the tragic queen, her world crumbling about her, resolves to die."

I inclined my head in a slight bow to my audience. A moment's pause—and I began.

Give me my robe, put on my crown;
I have
Immortal longings . . .

There was never a moment of doubt from the first. Gone, my nervousness: I used it to give an edge of tremor to my voice, till the reality of the deathless words took charge of my emotions and I became, indeed, Egypt's queen among the ruin of her world. When Cleopatra died, it was upon the bare boards of the stage; but I seemed to feel the searing sun of the Nile upon my uncovered arms and shoulders as I closed my eyes and whispered the last words.

Oliver's handclap sounded startlingly loud in the empty theater, filling the place with brittle sound, and echoing and re-echoing along the barren aisles and among the chandeliers in the arched ceiling; then to fall silent. In that time of triumph, I remained in a deep curtsy of acknowledgement close by the footlights, calming my breath for the next effort.

I stood up. Softly, but deliciously conscious that I was able to pitch my voice to the very rear of the balcony, I said, "Thank you. And now, with your permission, I should like to play some short scenes from Jean Racine's *Phèdre*, that classic statement of the tragic gulf between passion and purity, where Phèdre, falsely thinking her husband dead, declares her secret love for her stepson, and brings calumny and death upon them both . . ."

If I had lost myself in the role of Cleopatra, I truly became myself in Phèdre. Tears—real tears—flowed unchecked down my cheeks as I felt myself being drawn into the tragic maw of my own hopeless passion. The walls of the theater receded, and it was I who stood under the great blue vault of the Hellenic sky, with the roar of the wine-dark sea counterpointing my anguish.

Le jour n'est pas plus pur que le fond de mon coeur.

It was on the high note of my passionate declaration that I left my audience. There was no need for the curtain to descend; my stillness, as I stood, head bowed, marked the end as finally as any artifice of the theater.

Oliver gave me a standing ovation, rising and coming forward down the center aisle, clapping as he came. He reached up from the orchestra and took my hands, pressing them to his lips.

"My dear girl," he said. "My own little girl. What can I say, what can I do, to express my feelings at this moment?"

We had supper *à deux* in a private room at Véfour's, and Oliver had chosen the menu in advance, in deference to my own taste for simple food. He pledged me in champagne, complimenting me upon my choice of program, on the daring simplicity of my plain black gown and unbound hair; asked what I had thought of the acoustics of the theater, which were believed to be the finest of any in Paris; he waxed eloquent upon great performances of *Phèdre* that he had been privileged to witness in the past, particularly that of the great Mlle. Rachel, who, while suffering from the consumption that was to kill her at the age of thirty-six, had seemed to communicate to the audience something of her struggles against the disease that was eating her alive, so that she had hardly stepped upon the stage before her inner fire had melted all ice with its intensity. And when he had finished telling me of the great Rachel, he poured himself another glass of champagne.

It was then I realized that something was missing: something needed to be said. And it very pointedly had *not* been said.

"In the *Cleopatra*," I murmured, "did you find that the omission of the lines belonging to the handmaids Iras and Charmian left gaps in the piece? Would it have been better to have spoken them myself?"

"Quite unnecessary," he replied firmly. "You gave the correct pauses. To anyone familiar with the text, it was a perfectly acceptable method. To have changed character would have been highly distracting, even risible."

Silence.

Presently I said, "Perhaps it would have been more effective if I had chosen two parts of more contrast. Say, if I had done *Phèdre* and then, perhaps, something from the English Restoration comedies: perhaps from Vanbrugh or Congreve?"

He shrugged. "The choice was immaterial, my dear. You amply demonstrated the range of your abilities. There is a certain comedy, even, in the character of Phèdre. The savage irony is there, you see. For all who know where to look."

I exhaled a shuddering breath.

"Oliver," I said. "Was I all that terrible? Was I so much of a disappointment to you that you can't even bring yourself to speak of it?"

An instant denial would have snatched me from my despair. No such denial was forthcoming, to save me. Instead, he silently rose and paced over to the window, where he looked out across the lamplit courtyard below. The light played upon the flecked grayness of his temples, but told me nothing of his expression.

Presently he said, "As to your delivery, no one could possibly have found any cause for criticism. Phèdre, if she had lived and spoken Racine's words, would have lived and spoken them much as you did. Likewise with the role of Shakespeare's Cleopatra—the reality was there. You have a truly regal presence, Tessa. Do you know that? You are, by nature, a creature set above others."

Silence. I heard a carriage rattle past down a cobbled street. Oliver commenced to tap lightly on the windowpane with a fingertip. Still he did not turn to face me.

"But," I prompted him. "But there is something else. Some way in which I fell short?"

"Reality," he said. "And the copying of nature. These things have nothing to do with—the Drama."

The Drama. He spoke the words with a passionate reverence, as I had many times heard him speak them in the past. A sacred invocation.

"So—I have failed?" It was scarcely a question; more a statement.

It was then he turned to me, and there was compassion in those deep blue eyes. But behind the compassion I saw a hard conviction. And I knew there was no hope for me.

"Some years ago, Tessa, I discerned in you the beginnings of a strange power. I had hopes—almost a certainty—that, given the right conditions, that power would develop."

"But—now you know that it has not."

"You have grown to great beauty," he said. "As I knew you would. You have presence—enough to put most so-called 'leading actresses' to shame. But this magical quality, Tessa—this indefinable thing that transcends reality, the artistry that lies at the heart of all great drama —has never developed in you. It has passed you by, Tessa."

"Oh, Oliver . . ." Despite my own bitter disappointment, I felt anguish for the disappointment he must have felt at that moment.

"Do not be mistaken, Tessa. I am judging you by the very highest standards. My dear, you could probably become a professional actress of sorts tomorrow, and I should be happy to give you every help and encouragement in my power. You could go on to enjoy, perhaps, a quite successful career. Given the right sort of roles, a considerable fame and fortune could be yours. You might well become a popular idol of—say—the theater of light domestic comedy, farce, or even melodrama of the more ephemeral kind. Expensive and exotic dishes would be named after you. How do you fancy 'Sole à la Tessa Thursday'? Rich and titled gentlemen would vie for your company, for your hand . . ."

"Oliver, please . . ."

"All these things are yours for the asking, Tessa. And perhaps they would suffice to satisfy you. Popular idolatry is not a contemptible goal. But you would have to content yourself with just that.

"The highest reaches of your art will forever be just beyond your grasp, Tessa. No Phèdre for you, no Cleopatra —not as Shakespeare and Racine intended them. I am truly sorry, my dear."

I cried upon his shoulder, as I had done before. And he dabbed away my tears with his own silk handkerchief.

"I don't want to be a popular idol," I told him. "I wanted to be a great artiste, nothing else."

"Nothing else will do?"

I shook my head.

"Then what shall you do with the rest of your life, Tessa?"

I shrugged my shoulders. What indeed?

"Supposing . . ."

"Yes?"

"Supposing you married me, Tessa."

I sat in the walled garden in the springtime warmth of Paris, with the fine spray from the swan-and-cherub fountain wetting the tiles close by the hem of my skirt. Sasha the poodle had fallen asleep by my side; every so often, a fitful droplet would land upon his tightly curled coat, causing him to stir in his sleep and give a small moan. It was quiet and peaceful in the garden. I had taken to spending much of my time there during the afternoons, when Oliver was giving a performance.

Oliver . . .

For the hundredth time, I tugged at the silver chain, bringing the pendant from its new, secret place within my bodice. There was now a ring threaded upon the chain, side by side with my half-thaler. Oliver had given it to me on the day after he had asked me to be his wife. A single diamond ringed with five rubies. My engagement ring to be.

I had not refused him, nor had I accepted, but had asked for time to consider, to accustom myself to the revolution that had taken place in my heart and in my mind. Oliver —typically—had agreed without demur, in perfect understanding. And meanwhile there was to be this "arrangement" between us. The ring was the symbol of the "arrangement": not to be worn till I had accepted his offer, and to be returned if I decided to the contrary. Oliver had strenuously resisted the latter idea, but I had insisted.

The diamond winked in the sunlight, turning on the end of the chain. Would it be yes, my answer? I thought so. There seemed no good reason why I should refuse to be Oliver's wife. He was the figure that had loomed largest in my life: my inspiration, part father, part guide, the one to whom I owed everything.

There was another consideration: having failed him by falling short of his high hopes for me, could I now refuse to devote the rest of my life to his happiness?

He loved me. I supposed that I had always been aware

of his feelings, particularly as I had grown to womanhood. On the night of our supper, after the disastrous episode of my trial at the theater, he had expressed his feelings in words. And—typically, as a great artiste of the stage—he had chosen words that transcended time and place, speaking out to eternity about the feelings between man and woman:

> *How do I love thee? Let me count the ways.*
> *I love thee to the depth and breadth and height*
> *My soul can reach . . .*

The sonnet by Elizabeth Barrett Browning—itself a gentle allusion to my own doubts, for the poetess had written them during the time of her own hesitation about marrying Robert Browning—touched at my heart, delivered as it was by his deep and expressive voice. Not for the first time did it occur to me what the larger world of the theater had missed when the great Oliver Craven had decided to devote himself to the art of silent mime. My heart was touched—and I all but accepted him there and then.

Only one doubt held me back. One question I put to myself, for which I could provide no answer: did I love Oliver as I believed he loved me?

Deep affection—yes; love of the kind that I might have felt for the father I would never know—all that. A delight in his presence that outmatched any other, even the delight I knew in the company of my two cavaliers.

But love—of the sort that Elizabeth Barrett Browning had expressed in her sonnet? I hardly knew. And, in my doubts, I asked him for time. And he had given it.

A voice from the terrace of the mansion dispelled my reverie.

"Tessa, we are ready to go!"

"Time for farewells, Tessa."

Philippe and Otto came down the steps toward me, both dressed for traveling. Sasha sat up and wagged his tail at them. I held out my hands and they clasped mine in theirs. I felt my eyes prickle with tears, and it seemed that the sun went behind a cloud. Their Easter vacation over, it was time for them to go: Philippe back to Oxford, Otto to Potsdam.

"It has been a wonderful time, Tessa."

"How we shall look back on it in the years to come."

"You will both write to me often?" I asked them.

"Every week," said Philippe.

Otto was not such a good correspondent. He smiled wryly, "As often as possible," he said.

Not a word of the foot-race and the attempts to win my hand that had followed. By mutual, unspoken consent, we had buried the memory in the comforting warmth of our friendship. I looked at them both. Should I tell them about Oliver and me? I decided against it—for the time being.

"Goodbye, Tessa," said Philippe, and he kissed me on both cheeks, formally. "I shall see you at the end of June, finished with Oxford forever. Then I shall have to think of something to do to pass my time. I must say doing nothing will be very agreeable."

"Idle fellow," said his friend. "Goodbye, Tessa." He kissed me. "I hope we meet again soon."

"But of course we shall meet again soon," I cried, suddenly alarmed. "Prussia isn't the end of the world. You will come back again during your furloughs from the army, of course."

"I shall try, Tessa."

One last handclasp between the three of us. They walked briskly back to the terrace. Halfway there, Otto seemed to remember something. He turned and came back to me. His face was serious, the blue eyes clouded.

"Tessa . . ."

"Yes?"

"Tessa," he said. "I truly don't know when we shall meet again, but I hope it will be soon. In any event, I should like you please to remember something I once said to you. About sorrow and regrets."

"Yes," I said, remembering. "That time in the carriage, on the way to the theater."

"I asked that there would be no sorrow or regrets for

164

anything that happens between you and me. Not now, nor in the future. Can I hope that it will be so?"

"Of course, Otto," I cried. "How could it be otherwise between us?"

"Thank you, Tessa." He bowed, quite formally. And then he was gone. I watched his tall figure disappear into the house. A few minutes later came the sound of the carriage leaving the courtyard in the front of the mansion —telling me that my cavaliers had started on the first part of their separate journeys. And I had a sudden premonition that if the three of us ever met again it would never be quite the same.

Springtime drifted almost unnoticed into high summer, and still I had not made up my mind. Oliver, whom I saw every day, made no attempt to hasten me, but was always my perfect escort and companion. With him as with no one else, I was able to forget the sense of loss that had come upon me after my failure at the theater. It is not easy to be deprived of a burning ambition, and I had nothing to take its place. There were times—when I was alone and particularly at night when I was sleepless—when I found myself crying for no particular reason that I could name. But these bouts of melancholy came more infrequently as the weeks passed. By the month of June they had all but disappeared—thanks to Oliver's attentions. And thanks to Paris.

Paris in the summer of 1867 was a never-ending festival. The very air was alive with rejoicing, with music everywhere. To progress through the narrow streets and the broad, tree-shaded boulevards was to pass from one pool of shimmering sound to the next: from some café orchestra playing a waltz of Herr Strauss, to a military band parading, to a march from *The Grand Duchess of Gerolstein*, and back to waltztime again. Every day there were parades and processions. A procession for the arrival of the Prince of Wales, for the Sultan of Turkey, the Pasha of Egypt. Processions for the crowned heads of Europe: Their Majesties of Sweden, Denmark, and Greece, Spain and

Belgium. Even the brother of the Emperor of Japan. And in June came the Czar and Czarina of Russia; also the King of Prussia and his Chancellor, the great Bismarck. All to see the wonders of Paris and her Great Exhibition.

Every night there were balls in one or other of the palaces and embassies of the city, and one morning Oliver called at the Hôtel de Brassy to greet me with the news that he had received an Imperial command to attend a great ball to be held in the Tuileries palace in honor of the Czar and the King of Prussia. He and the company from the Comédiens were to perform a selection of their mimes as part of the entertainment. It was the crowning distinction of his career, and I could see that he was proud and delighted. But what was more, I was also to attend the ball. There was no doubt about it: Oliver showed me the engraved invitation that had come from the office of His Imperial Majesty's Grand Chamberlain, the Duke de Bassano. And there—unbelievably—was my name written plainly for all to see.

The afternoon of the ball was memorable for a splendid military review held at the Longchamps racecourse in the Bois de Boulogne. I went with Oliver, Mirabel, and Jöelle, in one of the De Brassy landaus. In brilliant sunshine, we were thrilled by a spectacle of French military might and pageantry unequaled since the days of the first Napoleon. Thirty thousand soldiers paraded before us to the roar of cannon from the fortress up on Mount Valérien. Soldiers on foot and mounted; dazzling in blue and crimson, sunlight glancing from their arms and armor, banners streaming. I saw the Imperial party, which was dominated by the huge figure of Count von Bismarck in his white uniform and a great helmet with a spread eagle on its crest. I wondered if he was impressed by the spectacle.

The climax of the review came with a massed charge of cavalry: ten thousand of them; a sea of bright plumes, pennoned lances, and tossing manes. They swept at the full gallop, straight for the Imperial stand, and drew up as one man and one mount—within a few yards of the royal guests, saluting with their glittering blades. The roar of pride and admiration from the watching crowds of Parisians must have delighted the Emperor, for it was no secret—the very waiters in the boulevard cafés and the street sweepers confided as much—that the year of the Great Exhibition and everything connected with it was Napoleon III's demonstration, to his own subjects and to Europe at large, that France was as great as she had been in the glorious days of his uncle.

There was a shocking anticlimax to the afternoon's spectacle. We saw nothing of it, for our landau was inextricably caught up in the returning stream of traffic and pedestrians—all Paris, hot, happy, and surfeited with military glory—that stretched from the Bois and into the shimmering heat-haze of the city; but the rumor came back to us, passed from mouth to mouth in horror and disbelief. The Czar had been assassinated, was the cry. Some fanatic had fired upon the carriage containing the Russian and French emperors, and Napoleon III's guest had bled to death in the arms of his distraught brother-monarch. It would mean war, of course. The moujiks would never forgive France for this. The past hatreds of the Crimean War, carefully buried for the occasion, would rage across Europe all over again. Thank heaven, cried someone, that we have just seen with our own eyes that our army is unbeatable!

The truth came out later that afternoon. It was much less serious than the rumor, but still disturbing. A young Polish patriot, burning with hatred about the Russian occupation of his country, had sprung out from the crowd and had discharged a pistol at the Czar. Fortunately he had missed his target, but had lightly wounded a horse, whose blood had splattered the Czar's white gloves. So much for rumor. What did not emerge as common knowledge till sometime later was that the Czar, furious at the attempt on his life, blamed his host for failure to take proper precautions against such an outrage, and threatened to return home immediately. There had even been talk of canceling the gala ball that night.

If that had happened, the rest of my life might have

turned out quite differently. So does the working of blind Fate enmesh us all together: rulers, assassins, and ordinary folk alike.

Oliver called for me at ten-thirty. He was in court dress of black tailcoat, black knee breeches and stockings, with the medal of his Legion of Honor pinned to his breast. I never saw him look so fine, though he had carried himself with no less assurance that night in far-off Penruth when, with threadbare cuffs and cracked boots, he had brought the first touch of magic into my life.

As always, he greeted me with a well-turned compliment and kissed my cheek. I was grateful for the compliment, conscious as I was of wearing the lilac silk ball gown—my only one—in which I had gone to the Offenbach premiere with Otto. It would have been a simple matter to have gone to any couturier in Paris, even to Worth's, and to have had a gown made for the occasion. The bill would simply have been sent to the steward at the Hôtel de Brassy and paid by him without question. This was the way it had always been. The De Brassys never touched money—that was for underlings to handle. But ever since my failure at the theater I had not been able to bring myself to incur the debt of a single franc.

Heartened, then, by my escort's praises, I took my place with him in the carriage that bore us through the brightly lit streets to the splendor of the royal palace of the Tuileries, which lay beyond the wide sweep of the place de la Concorde.

The Tuileries garden was an enchanted dream of fairy-land, with garlands of white lights strung like pearls along the lines of trees, and colored globes illuminating the fountains that threw their great jets into the night air. From every window of the palace, ablaze and open to the warm night air, came the sound of a Viennese waltz and the laughter and murmur of the brilliant company. Another orchestra was tuning up outside, beneath a canopy of electric lights.

"Dancing will begin at eleven, with the appearance of the Imperial party," said Oliver. "Herr Strauss will conduct the orchestra, and it will go on till three o'clock in the morning, with an interval for a buffet supper at about one. It's then that we shall give our performance. Ah, here are Mirabel and the others. Good evening, my dears."

"Hello, Tessa lovely. My, you look a fair treat." Mirabel enveloped me to her bosom, all cachou and patchouli as ever. She held me at arms' length and winked. "And how do you think *I* look, duckie? I can tell you that this here thing I'm wearing cost me twelve hundred francs, strike me dead if I tell you a lie. How do you like it, eh?"

"Mirabel, you look breathtaking," I told her in perfect truth. She was in a yellow crepe extravaganza, embroidered with stars of silver and gold, and hung about with garlands of poppies and ears of corn. The flame coloring of her hair had received some recent assistance from chemistry and was plaited into most elaborate garlands of flounces and ringlets at the nape. A topknot of poppies completed the effect. Anyone else in the world but Mirabel would have looked overdressed. With her height and figure and her splendid carriage, she carried it off like some pagan queen of antiquity.

There was a roll of kettledrums, a shrill clamor of trumpets, and a group of figures emerged onto the balcony of the palace and began to descend the staircase into the garden.

"The Imperial party," murmured Oliver in my ear. "I wonder if the Czar has recovered from his alarming experience. He doesn't look very amiable. Do you see Bismarck bringing up the rear? Splendid-looking fellow isn't he? Like some latter-day Agamemnon, in all that military finery. They say he was mightily amused by *The Grand Duchess of Gerolstein*; recognized himself in Baron Puck and laughed louder than any."

The great Strauss bowed to the Imperial party, raised his baton, and the orchestra struck up a lilting waltz. Napoleon III was first on the floor, dancing with—as I recall—the Queen of Belgium.

"Would Miss Thursday grant me the inestimable honor of the first waltz?" asked Oliver, bowing.

"Miss Thursday would be delighted," I responded,

gathering up the train of my gown in one smooth move-ment—as I had been taught by the dancing master from Tours who had used to call twice weekly, Tuesdays and Saturdays, at the château.

The Imperial party were all dancing. Dukes, marquises, and counts followed after. By the time we swept to join the circling throng, the floor was well crowded.

"Oliver, what is this tune?" I asked my partner.

"It's Strauss's latest," he told me. "It is called 'The Blue Danube.' "

I danced with no one else but Oliver that night. When one o'clock approached, he caught the eye of Mirabel and the others and drew them aside to the edge of the dance floor. A bewigged flunky stood ready to escort them to rooms in the palace that had been set aside for them to change into their costumes, which had been delivered to the palace earlier that day.

"What's Tessa going to do while we're away?" demanded Mirabel. "She can't be left alone in this rout. Not with all these foreigners about. A poor girl wouldn't be safe in such company."

I smiled. Her years in France had done nothing to dispel Mirabel's insular convictions that all the real wickedness on earth began one step beyond the white cliffs of Dover and that, of all nations on earth, the French were the most deeply addicted to sundry unspecified evils.

"I shall be perfectly all right, I promise you, Mirabel," I told her. "While you are all changing, I shall find a nice footman who will bring me a little light collation from the buffet, and then I shall watch your performance."

"The edge of the dance floor will be crowded," said Oliver. "Without a male escort, you'd scarcely get anywhere near the front. Your best plan will be to go into the palace and watch from the balcony, or from one of the windows up there."

"I may indeed do just that," I told him. "But please don't fuss over me. Concentrate on your performance. I know you're going to be wonderful—remembered long after these people have forgotten Herr Strauss and his waltzes."

He leaned forward to kiss my cheek. Close to my ear, he quietly said, "You are all beauty and all sweetness. When shall I have your answer, my Tessa?"

"Soon, perhaps," I told him. "Yes, I think soon."

"I dearly hope so," he replied.

A last squeeze of my hand, and he joined the others. Mirabel threw a wink at me, and they followed their guide into the palace. I buttonholed a passing footman and made my wants known. The fellow was extremely helpful, providing me with a chair and side table under a lamplit lilac tree, and returning from the buffet in no time with a tray bearing a mouth-watering selection of comestibles, including a broiled lobster, various cold meats, a chocolate confection elaborately sculptured with cream and garnished with glazed fruits, a lemon ice, and a large bottle of champagne. And he stood by my chair and served me throughout my repast.

One o'clock drew near. I had sipped half a glass of champagne and nibbled at a lobster. People were beginning to drift back to the dance floor, where Oliver and the company were to perform. I saw that the Imperial party were seating themselves at a good vantage point and that the rest were massing themselves behind. Remembering Oliver's advice, I asked my faithful servitor if he would show me to one of the windows overlooking the dance floor.

"If mam'selle will please follow me," he replied.

We entered the palace by way of the staircase up to the balcony, and through tall glass doors that led into a vast room hung with blazing chandeliers under an elaborately painted and sculptured ceiling, with marbled walls that bore portraits of the great personages of France's past.

"This way, mam'selle," said my guide. "I know the very place where mam'selle can watch in comfort and not be disturbed."

He led me out a double door and into a hallway of white marble, with floors of black-and-white checkered tiles. A sweep of stairway rose two floors above us. He preceded me up the broad stairs. There were few guests about, and all were coming down, not up.

On the first landing, the footman bowed me into a smallish room decorated in blue brocade, with pretty gilt furniture, from which he selected a comfortable-looking button-back armchair, setting it by the open window. Looking down, I saw that we were immediately above the dance floor, with a perfect view of the royal party. I saw the Emperor leaning to murmur in the ear of the King of Prussia, on his right, and the Empress Eugénie fussing with her glittering tiara. The murmur of many voices rose like the buzz of grasshoppers in a maytime cornfield.

"Is there anything further that mam'selle requires?" my footman asked me.

I thanked him and said no. He bowed and left me, leaving the door ajar.

A hush fell upon the audience.

I settled back to enjoy the performance.

It was, as always, an enchantment. Oliver was superb, Mirabel also. They opened with a classical piece that Count Robert had devised from the Greek legends, a minor theatrical masterpiece that had been warmly applauded by the critics and become the talk of Paris. This was followed by a mime based on an old French country tale, where the entire company appeared as carousing villagers and Oliver played the local idiot, a piece of hilarious buffoonery that amply demonstrated the tremendous range of his artistry. Next he announced that he would perform a solitary mime on the tragic end of King Arthur, but asked for the indulgence of his distinguished audience while he changed his costume.

At the company's departure from the dance floor, the orchestra struck up a lively gallop. I relaxed in my chair and waited with the rest for the reappearance of Oliver. I had not seen the King Arthur mime before, for he had himself devised it specially for the occasion.

Some little time passed. The music closed in on me, shutting out all other sounds. I felt my eyelids grow heavy, perhaps from the effect of the unaccustomed champagne. I even slipped into the beginnings of sleep, but roused myself almost on the instant. It was quite dark in the room, which was lit only by a single candelabrum, and the brightness down below dazzled my eyes, increasing their heaviness.

I think I may have been on the verge of sleep for the second time, when some sixth sense told me that I was no longer alone in the room.

Fear struck me at once: I knew that I was menaced—as a small animal knows menace; as a rabbit senses the close presence of a stoat and knows its end has come. I felt every part of the surface of my skin turn to gooseflesh, and the beat of my heart quicken. My mouth went dry. My throat contracted. My breath was suspended.

Frozen with panic, I waited. If I had dared to turn my head, I doubt if, during those first few moments, my mind would have found the means to direct my movement.

Only my eyes seemed able to move. From the corner of my straining eyes, I saw the first intimation of the peril in which I stood.

The hem of a woman's skirt slid silently into the scope of my vision—and it was sable black!

A scream rose to my lips, and with it came the will to move. I leapt to my feet, turning to regard the intruder, in the same instant that a hand took hold of my hair, roughly gripping the thick knot of my chignon and brutally twisting my head away. At the same time, a strong arm was wrapped about my waist and I was bundled toward the window. My scream rang loudly in my ears, but no more loudly than the sound of the orchestra below.

My hands were gripping the sill of the open window and I was fighting for my life, with no means to wrest the savage grip from my hair and from my waist. I was being borne forward, slowly, inexorably, toward the void. Below me, I could see the tiled dance floor and the strings of dazzling lights. Through misting eyes, I saw the black and white of the menfolk's clothing, the kaleidoscope of color and jewelry of the women. And the music of the gallop rose to a crescendo of trumpet and timpanum.

I was losing the struggle. Gradually my grip on the windowsill was weakening; slowly my elbows were being forced to bend. Already my head, driven forward by the relentless hand gripping my hair, was half out the window.

173

My secret enemy had all but destroyed me. Within instants I would meet my end before the horrified eyes, and at the very feet, of the people below.

Screaming anew, I let go of the windowsill and reached backward with my hands, clawing with my fingernails for where I judged my would-be killer's face to be. I felt them rake against flesh, and the grip on my hair instantly slackened.

Able, now, to turn, I did so—

And looked, eye to eye, into the distorted face of Mirabel Ducane!

"You shan't have him—I'll see you dead first, you . . ." she mouthed some obscenity. "I should have guessed what you were at from the first, but it ain't too late to settle for you!" There was no madness in her eyes, only hatred and violence of the most barbarous sort. I knew instinctively that any attempt to plead with her would be entirely useless.

Baring her teeth, she tightened the grip on my hair, bending me back, till my head came in contact with the side of the window frame. Her other hand had freed my waist and had taken hold of one of my wrists. Helpless once more, I could do nothing but fruitlessly scrabble for a fresh hold upon the window frame.

The music shut out everything but the hate-filled scream close to my ear.

"Curse you for trying to steal him who was Minnie Duggan's! Fly to your grave . . ."

A clash of cymbals—and a deathly silence.

And in that silence, the terrible voice that rang over all, filling the empty void with its awful valediction:

"AND MAY YOU ROT IN HELL!"

I heard shouts from below. A woman screamed. Instants later came the sound of running footsteps on the marble steps leading up from the staircase vault. The murderous grip slackened and fell away from my hair, from my waist. Reeling back against the wall, I saw her wild-eyed glance toward the partly open door. She gave a small moan of despair, as a trapped animal will give before its capture and killing. One last look at me—it was almost a plea for help—and she turned and ran out of the room, the skirts of her black peignoir flowing behind her like the wings of the Angel of Death.

Her last cry came back to me in a rapid diminution of sound that was abruptly cut off in silence. Horrified shouts followed; more running footsteps. Someone called for the women to be kept away at all costs.

I crept out onto the landing and looked down over the stairwell; to the small knot of menfolk standing or kneeling by the sprawled figure in the middle of the checkered marble floor far below me. Mercifully, the folds of the black peignoir hid Mirabel Ducane's face from my sight.

3

The Grand Chamberlain was beside himself with fury at the impropriety of it all. The Grand Chamberlain was M. le Duc de Bassano, a fine-looking aristocrat with a hawk's nose and locks of black hair slicked forward on either side of a nobly shaped dome of baldness. He wore a resplendent court uniform of scarlet and gold, and addressed his furious remarks to Oliver, who was doing his best to comfort me.

"Nothing of all this must be breathed outside these walls—nothing! Not even His Imperial Majesty must know the truth of what happened. That wretched creature—they saw her, you know. They saw her deliberately fling herself head first over the banister. Happily, the gentlemen concerned may be relied on to be discreet . . ."

"Monsieur, will you please leave us?" cried Oliver. "Can you not see that this lady is completely distraught?"

The hawk's nose went up, affronted. "You will hear more of this affair, monsieur," said the Duke. "Conduct of this sort is not permitted to take place within the Imperial Presence, not without the gravest consequences."

"Will you be so kind, monsieur, as to leave us?" rasped Oliver.

When the door closed behind the affronted courtier, Oliver knelt beside my chair and prized my hands away from my cheeks, against which they were pressed.

"Tessa . . ." he began.

"She tried to kill me," I breathed. "Because of you."

He nodded. "Believe me, Tessa, I had no idea. I never guessed she would do such a thing. Oh, I knew Mirabel had a wild and violent temper: you yourself saw something of it the very first time you met her. But—this. To try and kill you because of some insane jealousy about me. Why, I can scarcely credit it."

Many things were falling into place within my mind, though there were still a host of shadowy mysteries beyond my reach.

"It must have been Mirabel," I said, "who tried to throw vitriol in my face, that night in the Champs-Élysées."

Oliver smote his brow with the palm of his hand. "Of course!" he cried. "That was the night she was late for the rise of the curtain. Why, they even had her understudy, Jöelle, half into her costume when she turned up. Naturally, it never occurred to me, then or afterward, that . . ."

"The Woman in Black," I said slowly. "All this time, she has been the Woman in Black who's been haunting my life." I shuddered and buried my face in my hands.

I heard Oliver cross the chamber, which was a small drawing room on the ground floor of the palace, at the back. It was quiet there, but not so remote that we could not hear the far-off sound of music. Clearly, whatever explanation had been offered to the distinguished audience for the curtailment of the theatrical performance had not had the effect of silencing the gaiety. He came back a few moments later and, laying a hand on my shoulder, he placed a glass in my hand.

"Drink this cognac," he said.

"Mirabel—she's . . . dead?" I asked him.

He nodded. "It was instantaneous."

I laid aside the glass of spirits, untasted. "Oliver," I said, "you must answer me. I have to know this. Was Mirabel Ducane, has she been, was she ever, your—mistress?"

He spread his hands. "My dear, how can you ever think . . ."

"Tell me the truth, Oliver!" I cried. "Don't act for me. I think I shall go out of my mind if you treat me to—*a performance!*"

A pause. "No, she was not," he said simply.

"Yet she was willing to disfigure me—in the end to kill me—for your sake, to prevent me from becoming your wife. I should need a lot of convincing, Oliver, that there was nothing, that there never has been anything, between you."

"The lightest of flirtations," he cried. "No more than is usual among members of a theatrical company. An affectionate kiss in times of happiness, when things have gone well on stage. A few words of endearment. Why, I've extended as much to Jöelle and the other ladies."

"And to Jeanette!" I cried.

"Jeanette!" He recoiled as if I had struck him, as if I had hurled the glass, contents and all, into his face. And I knew that my accusation had hit home.

"Why did you say that—why did you bring Jeanette's name into this?" he demanded. There was anger in those deep blue eyes. And something else—was it fear, I wondered?

"You promised marriage to Jeanette," I said. "Tell me, Oliver—to how many women have you promised marriage, apart from poor Jeanette and myself?"

" 'Poor Jeanette,' " he echoed. Throwing back his head, he uttered a mirthless, bitter laugh that grated on my tautly stretched nerves. "Merciful heaven, if you knew but half of the truth about 'poor Jeanette.' "

"Tell me," I said.

Suddenly his look was sober. He gazed down at me with something approaching compassion. He pointed to the glass on the small table at my elbow. "Drink up," he said. "You are going to need all the aid to courage that you can muster, my dear, before I have done with telling you all about Jeanette Dupuis."

I ignored the advice and continued to gaze at him steadfastly, hands folded on my lap. Waiting.

His eyes faltered, broke away from my glance. He started to pace up and down the room, speaking swiftly, gesticulating from time to time, to emphasize a point, or to fill the gap while he sought for an apposite word or phrase. I listened to him in silence and growing dismay.

"I have already told you something of her," he began. "Of her tremendous artistry during her early years on the stage. By the time she joined my company—and you must understand that she was some few years older than I—Jeanette was already past her best. The fame for which she had always yearned had passed her by. She had ruined her artistry, and was well on the way to ruining her looks and her figure, with overindulgence. Drink was her failing—that and high living. Rich men were her particular indulgence —when she could get her hands on them, which, for the leading actress in a third-rate traveling mime company, was not often.

"It was in the summer of 'forty-six, and we were playing at a third-rate theater in Deptford, near London, that Jeanette came to me in my dressing room—I shall never forget it, it was raining outside and the water was dripping through the ceiling—and confided in me that she was going to have a child. She was quite brazen about it, almost uncaring. I asked her who was the father, but she would tell me nothing. There was no question of marriage, she said; the man had abandoned her. I was her friend, her employer—it was up to me to provide for her, to help and comfort her in her time of trouble. There was, indeed, nothing else I could do. I had some little money put aside for new costumes and scenery: I gave her this to attend a good doctor. The child was born shortly before Christmas of that year. I called to see Jeanette and her infant a week or so after. She was staying in a lodging house in South London, where the birth had taken place.

"This part of my story is very distressing, Tessa. But it has to be told, in order that you understand about the nature of Jeanette.

"She had a suite of three rooms in the lodging house. I entered unannounced, for I had a key. There was no sign of Jeanette in the living room. Only an empty bottle of brandy. I called to her, but received no reply. I next went into the bedroom, her bedroom. No sign of her. The door into the room in which the baby slept was open. I went toward it. And—you have to believe this, Tessa, though everything in one's nature revolts against the acceptance of such a thing—I found Jeanette, this new mother of a new living creature, stooping over her child's cot.

"There was a pillow in her hand, Tessa. And even as I cried out in horror, she lowered it upon the face of the . . ."

It was then I pleaded with Oliver to stop, hands over my ears, trying to shut out the words.

Next day it rained before dawn. Afterward the garden smelled newly washed in the morning air. It was nearly midday, and I sat with a copy of *Le Figaro* on my lap, scarcely read, though I had gleaned that, following upon the outrage of the assassination attempt, the Czar was leaving for home that very day, and that the Prussian entourage were expected to follow suit within the week. The bright promise of the Great Exhibition seemed to be fading, and the music of the waltz taking on a hollow note. There was no mention, as far as I could see, of Mirabel's death.

Oliver arrived at midday, as he had promised. He kissed my cheek, as he always did.

"You are feeling better?" he asked me solicitously. "The doctor gave you a sleeping draft?"

I nodded. "Much better, thank you, Oliver. I'm sorry for the way I behaved last night." Poor Oliver. Burdened with a hysterical woman whom he had had to take home in a hired cab. But he had managed to quieten me before we had reached the Hôtel de Brassy.

"And you still insist that you must hear the rest?" he asked.

"Everything," I said. "Don't try to spare me anything, Oliver. I beg you. You prevented my—mother—from smothering me to death in my cot. What then?"

"Tessa, my dear," he said. "I would give anything to have hidden it from you forever."

"It has never been hidden from me, Oliver," I told him. "It seems that even a small baby has the capacity to remember such things. All my childhood, I was haunted by a nightmare of someone trying to smother me."

There was a silence between us, and we heard carriage wheels passing along the cobbles of the faubourg.

Presently, he said, "I persuaded Jeanette that I could find a good place for the child. I was anxious, you see, that she would never again have the opportunity to do it harm; though, I promise you, her remorse was pitiful to look upon.

"The company was on its way to the West Country, for a series of engagements in Exeter, Truro, Bodmin, and Penruth. Jeanette, still resting after her confinement, was not due to rejoin us till after the tour. I myself traveled down by railway and, the child with me, I spent my last shillings on a second-class ticket, so that the babe would be in a roofed carriage and not have to endure the February air."

"And you left me on the doorstep of Penruth Workhouse," I said.

He spread his hands. "What else, Tessa?" he said simply. "I had to get you away from Jeanette, and I had no money to provide for you. It was the parish—or nothing."

"But you came back to see me," I said. And, remembering it, I smiled at him.

"That was not the first time, when we gave the Christmas Eve performance," he said. "I came back to Penruth within the year and called upon the workhouse master, posing as someone inquiring about a lost child, one who had been stolen. He showed me the little ones under his care. There was only one infant—he called her by the name Tessa Thursday—who was of the age to be the one I left on the doorstep the previous February, and indeed he told me that you had arrived at that time and by that means, Tessa."

"And you came there yet again," I said. "You never really abandoned me at all, Oliver."

"I came to look for you," he said. "To find you. But, Tessa, it was *you* who found *me*."

I remembered how I had peered at him round the side of the dressmaker's dummy, while he had been engaged in an intimate conversation with—her . . .

"Why did you promise to marry Jeanette?" I asked him. "She was older than you. You didn't love her. Why, it was quite obvious even to me that you didn't even like her and that her attentions were distasteful to you."

He said, "We had a pretense between us, Jeanette and I. One day, we pretended, when our fortunes were made and we were famous, she and I would be wed. The pretense was of Jeanette's creation. I paid lip service to that pretense in order to keep her from going insane."

"Insane?"

He looked down at his hands. His voice came quietly. "She was not all evil, Tessa. You must believe that. Remorse for what she had attempted to do to you was what finally broke her. By the time you saw her in Penruth—" he met my gaze and I saw, with a pang of compassion, that his eyes were brimming with tears—"well, my dear, you remember how she was in Penruth."

I reached out and took his hands in mine. "You never deserted me, Oliver. I was nothing to you, but you have watched over me all my life. As soon as you were able, you brought me from that place, gave me the opportunity to do great things. Oh, my dear, what a disappointment I turned out to be."

He shook his head. "How can you say that, Tessa, when my only desire is to have you at my side for always? Oh, you have not been able to fulfill that half-impossible goal that, for my sins, I implanted in your mind. What a tragedy! So I have also not become the King of Tartary, nor the driver of an express train, nor any of the things I wanted to be as a boy." He gazed at me with that quizzical way he had, and his broad, good-humored smile warmed my heart as it always had the power to do.

And when that had been said, I remembered that I had to hurt him; as I had resolved to do during the long night before, when even the physician's sleeping draft had done nothing to quieten my racing mind. I took out my pendant: half-thaler, engagement ring, and all, chinking gently together on the end of their chain. And I unslipped the ring, and held it out to him.

"I'm sorry, dear Oliver," I whispered. "Please take back your ring."

"It's because of her—because of what happened last night," he said.

"That brought me to the decision," I admitted. "But, you mustn't think that I blame you in any way for what happened. I had a moment of doubt; but I accept without any reservation that there was nothing between you and Mirabel; that the jealous infatuation was all on her part. But—oh, how can I put it?" I fumbled for my handkerchief as I felt my voice breaking.

"Her death has defiled everything," he said slowly. "You believe—and you are right, Tessa—that we could not begin our lives together under the shadow of that tragedy. Isn't that what you want to say?"

I nodded. As always, Oliver had looked into my heart and mind and searched out the truth.

"I'm sorry," I whispered.

"Perhaps—one day, when the memory has faded, we can try again?" he asked.

"Perhaps. I hope so, Oliver." And I kissed his cheek.

Ruefully, he tossed the ring in his hand and put it into his waistcoat pocket. I was in the act of slipping the pendant into my corsage when I remembered something else I should have asked him.

"The half-thaler," I said. "Surely, now, you're able to tell me something about it, Oliver."

"Oh, no," he said. "My surprise and interest, when you first showed it to me, were perfectly genuine, Tessa. I had never seen it before."

"Then. . . ?"

"Why, it's clear, isn't it, that Jeanette must have slipped it round her baby's neck without saying anything to me, when I set off with the child to the West Country. It was—her secret token of contrition and remorse."

That—and the secret of my father's identity, now forever hidden.

It was three more days (and the Prussian entourage, including Bismarck, had left France on the heels of the Russians) before the newspapers printed brief reports of Mirabel's death. The leading actress of Oliver Craven's ensemble, they said (formerly, the entire Paris press had referred to her as a "star"—which, taken with everything else, pointed to a determined attempt to play down the affair), had fallen to her death while appearing at a private performance. Nothing else, but merely to add that, following this tragic accident, Mlle. Ducane's roles would be taken over by her understudy, Mlle. Jöelle Romy.

I seldom went out, and saw only Oliver, who called on me most mornings and occasionally took me to supper in one or other of the more secluded restaurants on the Left Bank. My life drifted into a limbo, where, deprived of ambition, I passed each day in imitation of the one that had gone before; so that even the slightest digression from a set routine which I had imposed on myself—as, for instance, when I decided to go out and buy a new hat but got no farther than the door of the *modiste* before I turned and ran back to the carriage—left me feeling unaccountably uneasy.

Paris herself seemed to mirror my mood. True, the heady delights of the Exhibition summer continued without check, even after the hurried departure of the Czar. By mid-June it was estimated that nearly ten million people had visited the Champ-de-Mars, and the authorities prophesied that the figure would reach fifteen million before the site was to be torn down at the end of October and all the cardboard palaces and pleasure domes thrown to a bonfire. The theaters flourished: Offenbach's triumph even eclipsed Oliver's, and both were playing to packed houses for eight performances a week, with tickets changing hands for many times their face value. Balls and masked routs took place every night at the Tuileries; and when the sun went down, the sky was alight over the place de la Concorde—I could see it from my bedroom window—where the palace gardens and the great square were ablaze with colored lights, resounding with jubilant cannon-fire, and bursts of rocketry as the initials of the Emperor and Empress were displayed in giant letters of firework in the sky.

All this revelry continued; but, as the summer wore on, it seemed to take on a meaninglessness, as when an aging roué puts on paint and powder and faces the world and his creditors with a brave smile. In my own lowered and depressed state, I sensed this atmosphere very acutely, and my impression was reinforced by disturbing reports I read in the newspapers (mostly, it has to be said, by political opponents of the Third Empire, with whom I had no truck) of the scandal of France pouring out so much money and labor in the vain hope of achieving prosperity at home and gaining friends abroad. "Has not what Bismarck and the rest of the foreigners have seen," thundered one firebrand, "only served to make them jealous of France's glories and more aware of her weaknesses?" I was not entirely displeased when this gentleman was arrested and fined.

So, in my uneasy limbo, I existed through the months, buoyed up only by Oliver's company and by the prospect of seeing Philippe again: he had written to say that he would be visiting friends in Scotland for the salmon fishing after he "came down" from Oxford, so he would not be in Paris before the end of the summer. Otto had written to me once: a brief and stilted little note that betrayed his inability to express himself in the written word. I replied to him immediately, but received no answer.

The high promise of my Paris summer seemed to be crumbling all round me. And then I received Count Robert's letter.

> Le Château Brassy
> Loire
> Monday, 24th June, 1867

My dear Miss Thursday,

Craven has written and privately apprised me of the true facts concerning the tragic occurrence at the Tuileries, to which, as I understand, you were a witness. It is a mystery why that young person should have seen fit to take her own life at the very height of her successful career, but there is no accounting for the vagaries of the human mind. So be it. May her soul rest in peace.

Craven is much concerned about your present state of health, and has suggested to me that it might be a good thing for you to return to the peace and quiet of Brassy for a while. I, of course, have not the slightest objection. But the decision rests entirely with you. Paris or Brassy—the choice is yours.

All is well here. When I gave Mme. Arlette instructions to have your rooms aired in anticipation of your possible return, the good woman asked me to convey her best wishes and hopes for your health.

I remain, Miss Thursday,

Yours sincerely,
De Brassy

It rained on the day I left Paris. Oliver drove me to the Montparnasse railway station in his English phaeton, which swiftly outstripped the two sedate carriages bringing after us my luggage from the Hôtel de Brassy. The train for Orléans was late starting, and we spent the time in the station buffet, drinking coffee and saying the same things over and over, as people will in such circumstances.

"Oliver, I do so hope that I'm doing the right thing, to return to Brassy."

"The countryside will do you good," he replied. "You haven't been happy these last few weeks. And you've been pale and tired-looking."

"That's not what I mean. You know what I mean."

"You mean that, not having become a great actress overnight, you feel that you have somehow taken De Brassy hospitality under false pretenses?"

"Oliver, you always look into my secret mind. Do you know, I had half resolved to return to Cornwall?"

"But now—as you see from the Count's letter (and, by the way, I told him nothing of Mirabel's attacking you, better that we all forget it)—nothing has changed as far as you are concerned. His patronage toward you is part of his patronage toward me. He would be gravely offended if you rejected it. Indeed, as I have told you, for you to do so would seriously affect my own position with him. And, Tessa, for all my present success, I continue to need the patronage and continued support of the De Brassy name and fortune."

"I understand, Oliver," I told him.

A locomotive, all gleaming brasswork and gushing clouds of steam, moved sedately into the station and came to rest with a gentle clink against the end of a line of carriages. A voice shouted, "Orléans train."

"Time to go, Tessa."

Later, through the carriage window, our hands touched.

"You will come and see me often, Oliver?"

"As soon as the summer season is over, and at least every three months after that. And, my dear . . ."

"Yes?"

"If you need me. If you should ever change your mind about that certain matter . . . send for me, or come to me. Do you promise?"

"I promise."

A whistle blew. One last kiss and clasp of hands. As I was taken away, a cloud of steam half enveloped him, making him insubstantial, like a ghost, waving to me out of a half-forgotten dream.

Out of Paris, through rain mists and the grayness of the long stone walls that backed onto the railway; out into the flat countryside with lines of tall poplars stretching far across the ripe cornfields. The train picked up speed, and I leaned back against my seat and closed my eyes; then the rhythm of the wheels took on the sound of a childish jingle, repeated over and over, and curiously comforting:

Home, home,
Going home.
Home, home,
Going home . . .

Mme. Arlette herself had come in the carriage to greet me at Orléans and escort me back to the château. She curtsied and said I looked very fine, but rather pale and peaky. The Count had not been at all well, she said: his leg had been troubling him; not that he ever complained, oh, no, not he. But it was plain for all to see, and a sure sign when he sat up in the music room till all hours, and one could hear his flute coming through the night. Nothing had changed at the château, she informed me. There had been no guests while I had been away, and the Count dined alone every night. Formally, as he had always done? But naturally. With never less than six courses. And what did I think of Paris? And the Emperor? The Count never had a good word to say for the Emperor, of course; but she—Mme.

Arlette—thought him a fine, jolly-looking fellow. And was it true that one could dine for eighty centimes at the Exhibition, and that there was not a room to be had in all Paris?

I listened to the good houskeeper's chatter, occasionally interjecting a comment or a brief question; but all my mind was directed ahead of me, down the dusty road that followed the broad and meandering Loire. Olivet was past and Cléry-St.-André; ancient Beaugency, Ménars, and stately Blois.

My heart leapt to see the tall gate houses at the end of the drive. As we clattered through, the gatekeeper and his wife and six children stood in line and waved to me. Welcome home, mam'selle, welcome home.

Home . . .

A tightening of the throat when I saw the tall turrets and twisty chimneys rising above the trees and caught the wink of sunlight on still water; smelled the smoke of a wood fire in the copse, the scent of jasmine and honeysuckle overhanging the old stone wall leading to the bridge over the moat. The people of the château and the estate were waiting to greet me. Henri the butler bowed and signaled forward the under-gardener, and Gaston the Breton came and presented me with a bouquet of rare flowers and herbs from the garden of Mary Queen of Scots. Welcome home, mam'selle. I was home, indeed.

"Monsieur le Comte," said Henri, "is in the drawing room and would mam'selle please attend him at her convenience?"

"I will go right away," I said.

He was sitting in his usual chair by the empty fireplace, with Roland crouched at his feet, when I entered. The old hound half-raised himself and wagged his tail to see me, uttering a small whine of pleasure.

"Good evening to you, Miss Thursday. You will pardon me if I do not rise. This confounded leg . . ." he gestured impatiently toward his right limb, which was resting on a footstool before him. The brooding, dark eyes flickered over me briefly, then turned to the hound. "Roland has not been well," he said. "I am afraid the old devil has nearly seen the end of his span. Have you dined, Miss Thursday?"

"No, Count," I told him. "But I'm not very hungry. With your permission, I'll take a light supper in my room before retiring early."

He nodded brusquely; shifted uncomfortably in the chair, as if in pain.

"Is there anything I can do for you, Count?" I asked him, tentatively, for he was not one for being fussed over. "Or shall I send for Henri?"

"Henri? No, confound it, I don't need cosseting," he growled. "But there is one thing I fancy, Miss Thursday, if it would not greatly inconvenience you after your long journey."

"Of course not, Count," I replied, puzzled. "What is it?"

The brooding eyes flickered toward me as he replied, "I tell you, I have a fancy for a decent cup of coffee. Do you think you could do the honors, please?"

"Of course," I cried.

It was soon done, and all the quicker for not having an anxious butler and two frightened footmen at my elbow in the narrow pantry. Presently I re-entered the drawing room with a steaming silver pot and a Sèvres cup and saucer of the kind he favored for his coffee. He watched closely as I poured out the strong, dark brew, then took the cup from me and sipped deeply.

Then he said, "Well, Miss Thursday, you have seen Paris, and you have seen something of the works of your hero the Emperor. The Exhibition, so I am told, is very fine. Four months from now, it will be gone and forgotten. Would that France's problems could vanish with that monumental folly, but such things only happen in the minds of ambitious emperors. Speaking of emperors, did you hear about Maximilian of Mexico? Another of your hero's grandiose schemes disappeared—literally—in a puff of gunsmoke. News has just arrived from Mexico that that poor puppet-emperor, abandoned by his master and left to the mercy of his enemies, has been shot by a firing squad of Mexican nationalists. How swiftly the glory of the world passes away.

"No one ever makes coffee as you do, Miss Thursday. No one."

The burring cry of a nightjar came to me out of the darkness of the copse beyond the moat; something stirred in the water beneath my window, a small creature swimming toward the bank, trailing a herringbone pattern on the still surface. The scent of honeysuckle was so strong as almost to make the senses reel.

I looked out without fear: nothing to harm me there. The night before, from my window at the Hôtel de Brassy, I had half-imagined that I had seen *her* again, dark-veiled under the cypresses; but I had been mistaken. There are no ghosts—this much I knew and believed. The fears and the dangers that had pursued me were all laid to rest.

My fingers touched the pendant at my breast, reminding me of the solitary question mark remaining against the account of my life. I spoke the question into the night, and the voice of the nightjar came back like an echo. Then, as I stood there, I heard the far-off, unearthly music of a flute, drifting over the dark landscape of woodland and water and ancient stone. And I knew that I was not the only one who remained sleepless in the summer night.

PART THREE

Through Discord to Harmony

1

"I am convinced," said Philippe, "that there will be a war. It's in the air, Tessa. No avoiding it."

He threw a ball—poor Moko's well-chewed tennis ball—from a lying position, and the good-natured hound bounded away after it, past the fountain and away out of sight beyond the yew hedge. He leaned back again, head pillowed in his hands, shirt-sleeved in the afternoon heat, his blue tunic draped over the back of the stone bench upon which I sat toying with my embroidery.

"It would be a terrible thing if France went to war with Prussia," I said. "The very thought of it—why, Philippe, you might come face-to-face, in battle, with Otto!"

He laughed. "That is somewhat over-dramatic, my dear," he said. "The chance of such a thing happening is very slight. To tell the truth, it's our opinion that, when the challenge is thrown down, Bismarck won't fight. And more's the pity. By heaven, Tessa—if you only knew what a splendid shape our army is in, compared with any other in Europe. Such weapons! The equipment! And the most professional fighting force this continent has seen since Waterloo."

The amiable and indolent young graduate from Oxford had found his niche in life. On his return to France, Philippe had decided to follow his friend's example. Three years at the military academy at St. Cyr, and he was now a lieutenant in the Lyons Dragoons. His moustache was bigger, his voice louder—but he was still at heart the same headstrong Philippe who had casually proposed to me in the Champ-de-Mars three long years previously, and had taken my refusal with such cheerful good grace.

"I'm sure you're splendid," I told him. "And you all look

very dashing and beautiful in your shiny brass helmets and horsehair plumes. But, my dear, I much prefer you as toy soldiers, parading on your mettlesome steeds to a rousing military band. I like you that way, and I like to think that Otto is similarly occupying himself."

Otto, that poor correspondent, was now reduced to sending a short note of greeting at Christmas. When last I had heard from him, he was attached to the 3rd Uhlan Lancer Regiment at Brandenburg and had been promoted to *Oberleutnant*, he said, which sounded very grand. I found it difficult to imagine gentle Otto, with his pink-and-white milkmaid's complexion, indulging in any sort of activity of the warlike kind. And there was Philippe, sprawled at my feet in the grass—another soldier; and actually talking of going to fight the Prussians. And relishing the prospect.

I was marveling at the strange ways of menfolk when Philippe abruptly changed the subject. "We have a guest to dinner tonight," he said. "To be precise, we have two guests."

"Really?" I replied. The event was unusual enough to excite my curiosity. "Who are they, Philippe?"

"Two ladies," he said. "A mother and daughter. The mama is the dowager Duchesse de Falconet, an impoverished old trout with the table manners of a tinker-woman and the most malicious tongue in the Loire valley. The daughter is—ah, but you must hazard a guess at who *she* is, Tessa."

I spread my hands. "But how could I possibly guess, Philippe? I know hardly anyone around here apart from the village people, the *curé*, the mayor, and Monsieur de Bailley from Tours, who comes to play chess with the Count on alternate Thursdays excepting when they fall on Holy Days. How could I possibly . . ."

"Aha!" Philippe was adopting a conspiratorial expression: one eyebrow raised, and peering at me through a loop made by his forefinger and thumb, as if it were an eyeglass. His voice was archly insinuating. "Now, if I were to give you the clue that the daughter is not entirely unknown to my Uncle Robert; that his glance has, in the fairly distant past, lighted upon the said lady with something more than—how shall I put it with delicacy?—a passing interest. In short, that she was once the repository of his passions, if I may be permitted the extravagance of phrase."

"Philippe!" I stared at him. "You don't mean . . ."

"Uncle Robert's former fiancée," he confirmed. "The beautiful Madame de Rollande. At least, they say she is still beautiful, though ten years or so of married life may have caused some small depredations to the paintwork."

"But, the lady's husband," I said, "Monsieur de Rollande —isn't he coming also?"

"I've no doubt he would if he could," replied Philippe, straight-faced, "for in my recollection the said gentleman was ever the trencherman, with an appetite that even his mother-in-law could scarcely emulate. However Monsieur de Rollande is unavoidably detained this evening, as he has been these past two years—in the cemetery of Azay-le-Rideau."

"You mean, she's a widow?"

Philippe inclined his head. "That is so, my dear. And I believe this will be the first meeting between Uncle Robert and his old love since she was bereaved. A decent interval having passed, one now presumes that she is looking for another husband."

"But—she threw the Count aside when he came back wounded from the Crimea!" I cried. And, to my surprise, I felt quite indignant.

"That was about thirteen years ago," replied Philippe with a shrug. "Madame's paintwork now being a little chipped, she is not, perhaps, quite so pernickety. Oh, she will have certain standards, still. The second incumbent, like the first, will have to be of noble family, rich, possessing considerable estates. But she will, perhaps, overlook a small detail like a crippled leg."

"Well, I think it's—it's monstrous!" I cried. "After ruining his life all those years ago, to come here—"

I broke off, as I saw that Philippe was staring at me with genuine surprise. "Well, I never knew that Uncle Robert had such a staunch champion in you, Tessa," he said.

Confused, I said, "It's none of my business, but I think he would be a fool to be taken in a second time by such a person. Come now, Philippe, don't you agree?"

"Indeed I do, Tessa," he replied. "And I'll tell you what, my dear—we must bend every effort, you and I, to prevent it from happening. Beginning tonight, at dinner."

There was a mischievous look in those dark eyes, and I had an inkling that the evening's dinner would not be the usual, uneventful Brassy occasion.

Madeleine de Rollande was still beautiful. Thirteen years earlier, when she had cast aside the Count, she must have been radiant. In—as I judged—her late thirties, her face and figure had the perfection of a specimen rose at the very peak of its maturity, before the first touch of decay withers the edge of a petal and darkens the flawless coloration.

She was tall, taller than I by half a head. Her hair was dark chestnut and richly glossy. Green eyes looked down in haughty disregard from each side of a Grecian nose. Her mouth was well-shaped, but the upper lip perhaps a trifle short. It was a mouth which, I decided uncharitably, had done more than its fair share of sneering in its time.

Like me, she was wearing a formal dinner gown with a bustle (the crinoline having finally gone out of fashion in the previous season), which was heavily adorned with lace flounces, large pink bows, and artificial flowers over deep blue velvet. The corsage was *décolleté* just short of scandal. She looked like a queen and made me feel like a waif from the country in my powder-blue and gray gown that had been made by a dressmaker in Tours.

"And this," said Count Robert, "is Miss Tessa Thursday. Miss Thursday, I have the honor to present you to Madame la Duchesse de Falconet and Madame de Rollande."

"How do you do?" I dropped the older woman a curtsy, to be on the safe side. She was a grotesque caricature of her daughter, with a raddled face and gray hair streaked with henna. She smelled of mothballs and was hung all over with brooches, pendants, beads, and other knickknacks.

The rheumy eyes that swam over me were green like her daughter's.

"Do you hunt, child?" she demanded.

"No, madame," I replied.

"How extraordinary!" She dismissed me from her mind, and never addressed another word to me all the evening.

"Madeleine, you have met my nephew Philippe," said the Count.

"Indeed, yes," was Madeleine de Rollande's reply. "I knew him as a boy." Those green eyes took in Philippe's tall leanness appraisingly. He looked fine in his frogged blue tunic and crimson pantaloons—and his fineness was not lost on her, it seemed.

The final gong stroke sounded for dinner punctually on the hour, and we filed into the great hall: the Count leading with the Duchesse on his arm, followed by Philippe escorting Mme. de Rollande, with me all alone bringing up the rear. There being an odd number of us, the placings were awkward: Count Robert sat at one end of the table, with Philippe at the other. The Count had the older woman on his right, and Philippe had the daughter on his right. I was on Philippe's left, next to the Duchesse and opposite Madeleine de Rollande.

The meal began smoothly, with the small army of servitors attending to our needs. Mindful of Philippe's scurrilous description of the Duchesse, I was amused to note that the old lady managed to sample three out of the four varieties of hors d'oeuvre that were offered, and still be the first to finish with an empty plate. Madeleine de Rollande kept up an animated conversation with Philippe on the subject of horses and fox hunting—a conversation from which she pointedly excluded me, even though Philippe made several attempts to bring me into the discussion. Nevertheless, I was aware of her eyes upon me from time to time; I would look up from my plate and meet her searching, critical gaze.

The Count made some attempt at conversation with the old lady, but he made little headway, for she was entirely taken up with eating. By the middle of the second course, he relapsed into a gloomy silence and seemed to become preoccupied with his private thoughts.

"When do you intend to return to England, Miss Thursday?"

The unexpectedness of Madeleine de Rollande's question took me unawares. I glanced sidelong at the Count, but he was having his glass replenished by the wine steward and appeared not to have overheard. No help from that quarter.

"I—I don't have any plans at the moment," I said, in a very small voice.

"Indeed?" was her comment, and the green eyes widened. "How very agreeable for you."

"I expect Tessa will stay at Brassy forever," said Philippe cheerfully. "She's practically one of the family now."

"Indeed?" The green eyes seemed to make a reappraisal of my person, as if to make sure that their owner had not missed something the first time. "Is she so?"

At the end of the third course, in which the Duchesse excelled herself by solemnly devouring the larger part of a whole cold salmon that lay on a serving dish before her, and then proceeded to nod off to sleep in her chair, Philippe glanced pointedly at the brooch I was wearing on my corsage.

"Upon my word, Tessa," he said. "That's a very fine jewel you have there. Have you had it long?"

It was on the tip of my tongue to tell him that he knew very well how long I had had the brooch, and all about it; but has face was blandly innocent, and it occurred to me that he might genuinely have forgotten.

"I had it when I was twenty-one," I said.

"Did you now?" said Philippe. "What a very attractive stone, don't you think so, Madame de Rollande?"

"Charming," she responded flatly.

The Duchesse began to snore quietly. The Count was drinking wine. He seemed to be taking rather a lot that evening.

"Jade, is it not?" asked Philippe. "Chinese work, I shouldn't wonder. You say it was a present? From an admirer, I have no doubt."

I said, "Count Robert gave it to me." And I saw a blaze of what could only have been anger start for one brief moment in those green eyes opposite me.

"Of course, of course," said Philippe smoothly. "Stupid of me to forget."

With quite unnecessary harshness, the Count called to the butler to clear for the next course. The Duchesse gave a loud snore and woke herself up, looking about her in some puzzlement.

The awkward moment was past. But Madeleine de Rollande said hardly anything for the rest of that meal, and I was uncomfortably aware that her whole attention was privately on me: that she was watching me every time my gaze was averted from her, and that she was weighing me up. It was quite ridiculous that the incident of the jade brooch should have caused her so much concern; and it was also mischievous of Philippe to have engineered it— as I suspected he had done. The brooch itself signified nothing either to me or—I guessed—to the Count. He had presented it to me on the 25th February two years before (I could only suppose that Oliver had told him the date upon which he had delivered me at the workhouse door, which I called my "birthday" for want of anything better); and he had done it with the total lack of emotion that typified everything that had ever passed between us. I, for my part, had thanked him warmly, but, mindful of his detestation of anything that smacked of emotion, not too warmly. I wore the brooch only very occasionally: to be honest, I was not very fond of jade.

I found the opportunity for a few words in Philippe's ear as we left the great hall after the meal.

"What do you mean by setting that woman against me, you mischief-maker?"

"Quite spoiled her dinner, didn't it?" he replied cheerfully. "And serves her right!"

The events of that unforgettable summer remain imprinted in my mind with startling clarity. As a devoted newspaper reader, I was aware of the steps by which the tragedy of 1870 occurred. On the face of it, the trouble began in

Spain, where a revolutionary government had deposed its ruler and offered the throne to a Prussian prince. France would have none of this, and Napoleon III appealed to his brother monarch of Prussia to force the prince to withdraw his acceptance—which King Wilhelm was obliging enough to do. Not content with this, the Emperor demanded a promise that Prussia would never consider the idea again. Wilhelm thought this to be a humiliating demand, and said as much. It only needed Bismarck to stir the brew by publishing an over-colored account of the affair, and all hope of a peaceful settlement was gone.

The English newspapers were vehemently anti-French. One of them said, "If France goes to war against Prussia, it will be the most unjust and unreasonable war that was ever started to gratify the ambition of one man. Napoleon III is forcing war upon Prussia to save himself and his dynasty. And his foolish and misguided people are in the wildest fever to attack across the Rhine."

I was able to vouch for the French people. On July 14th came news that the government had ordered general mobilization of the French army and navy. Over half the male staff of the château and estate were affected. I watched them march away, waving and laughing and calling to us that they would be in Berlin by August. Gaston Pepin was among those to go, and I confess I shed a tear for the smiling Breton. All that day and the day following, the bells of the Loire churches rang out their peals of joy. One would have thought that there was a great national carnival afoot, instead of war about to be started.

We had no news of Philippe. He had returned to his regiment shortly after the night of the dinner party, and the last letter I had from him came from Metz. It was to be supposed that the Lyons Dragoons were up near the Rhine frontier, waiting for the fateful declaration of war.

Prussia also was mobilizing. So were Bavaria, Württemberg, and Baden, who had pledged themselves to fight alongside their fellow Germans. I thought of another soldier—Otto von Stock—who must also be watching the frontier. And the thought brought a chill to my heart.

On Tuesday, 19th July, the bells rang out again. France had declared war. For the second time in little more than half a century, an Emperor Napoleon set out to stride across Europe.

After Philippe's departure, a strange restlessness had come over me, and I spent more and more time on my own, avoiding Mme. Arlette, who had always accompanied me on my shopping expeditions to Tours and Orléans. Increasingly, I found myself unable to face Count Robert's company, and took to sending him a message by footman, begging leave to be excused from dinner, and having a light meal served in my own quarters. By the outbreak of war, I had ceased to send the messages and was having my meals alone as a regular routine.

Madeleine de Rollande came often to the château. No doubt for reasons of propriety, she was invariably chaperoned by the Duchesse. I avoided meeting her whenever possible. Whenever we came face to face, on a staircase or in the gardens, those searching, hostile green eyes swept me from head to foot and then looked away. We exchanged nothing but the most frigid of greetings.

Having shut myself off from the life of the château, I found the outlet for my need of companionship by writing long letters to Oliver in Paris. Ever since the year of the Great Exhibition, he had fulfilled his promise of visiting me at Brassy every three months. Three years had changed him not at all: he was still the same brilliantly good-humored and impressive figure as the Oliver who had come into my life ten years previously. He always had the power to lighten my spirits with his wit, his gentle attentiveness. Nor did he ever bring a note of discord into our relationship by referring to the "understanding" we had briefly had during my time in Paris. It was as if it had never happened.

In my letters, I told him all about the Count, about Mme. de Rollande and her mother, about Philippe's mischievous behavior at the dinner party. Oliver was most amused; wrote back his view that "the fair Madeleine" would almost certainly ensnare the Count, and that I had better resign myself to being pleasant with her. Though I was sure that his warning was only given lightly, I nevertheless believed that there was a kernel of earnestness within it. The prospect of the Count marrying Madeleine de Rollande was something that I had never seriously considered in relation to myself and my own future. For all of seven years, I had lived on the grace and favor of the master of Brassy. He was my patron, as he was Oliver's patron; except that I had not repaid that patronage by fulfilling the promise of becoming a great actress. There had never been the slightest suggestion that the patronage would be cut off; but if Madeleine became chatelaine of Brassy, the story might be very different. I was a woman, considerably younger than she, and—without being conceited in the least, I could acknowledge it—not unattractive to look at. If I was any judge of my own sex, Madeleine was not the sort who would take kindly to a younger woman about the place. I had only to recall the look in her eye when she heard of the quite valuable twenty-first birthday present that Count Robert had given me.

As to being pleasant to her, nothing would have suited me better, if I had thought it would be of the slightest use. But I knew that it was not in my nature to try to keep a roof over my head by fawning upon someone who detested me. I was left, then, with only one option: if the Count married her, I should have to leave Brassy and make my living elsewhere. The prospect was not all that daunting. Had Oliver not said that I was capable of making for myself a career as a popular actress? Not an artiste of the highest order, but a leading lady in, say, the sort of light comedies favored by Parisian theatergoers. I had excellent French, and the slightest trace of English accent that was considered so *chic* in the smartest circles. The more I thought about the prospect, the more I liked the sound of it, the necessity for earning my own living and becoming independent quite overturning my earlier scruples about aiming at anything lower than the very highest and purest. Let there be "Sole à la Tessa Thursday"!

I arrived at my decision about a week after war was

declared. If and when the Count and Madeleine announced their intention to wed, I should immediately write to Oliver and ask him to use his influence to get me a place in one of the Paris theater companies.

Scarcely twenty-four hours after that, my whole world was blown apart . . .

It was an afternoon of high blue sky and languid warmth, with the sound of honeybees carrying on the heavy air, and pigeons calling to each other in the depths of the copse. Hatless, my hair unbound, I wended my way to my favorite spot, the arbor behind the sheltering yew. Moko went with me, bounding on ahead with his accustomed eagerness.

I had not settled down for more than five minutes, nor read more than a page of my book, before Moko raised his head sharply, ears pricked, a bass growl coming from the depths of his chest. I heard voices. Someone was coming. And from a direction which would take them past the far side of the yew hedge. With my newfound reluctance to mingle with people, I had the hope that they would come and go without being aware of my presence. Laying a reassuring hand on Moko's head, I persuaded him to be silent and still.

The voices came nearer. Women's voices. With a slight pang of dismay, I recognized them as belonging to Madeleine and her mother, the Duchesse. The very first words shocked me to numbness.

"Men, my dear *maman*, are all the same. And if Robert should insist on keeping his common English creature, I should be the last to deny him his wishes."

"I think you would be mistaken, my dear," came the reply. "For my part, I would not permit my husband to keep a mistress under my own roof. I recall that your father . . ."

I suffered the awful awareness that this conversation— this appalling conversation—was unbelievably concerning *me!*

"Nonsense, *maman!*" was Madeleine's retort. "No arrangement would be more convenient for all concerned.

I would wish, naturally, that he had chosen someone with a modicum of breeding. The English, generally, are incredibly *bourgeois*, but that creature, to me, seems positively from the very gutter. However, as I have said, there is no accounting for men in their choice of mistresses . . ."

The voices were now very close: almost at the other side of the hedge. Startlingly, it came to me that, instead of going past, they were coming round it—*to meet me face to face!*

I sprang to my feet, my book slipping from my lap. Instinctively, as if for protection, I laid my hand on the hound's shaggy neck. I knew my face would be pale and shocked, my eyes staring. I scarcely cared.

The Duchesse said, "Well, my dear, I am sure you are very well able to dispose of the creature should the need arise."

"Have no fear of that, *maman*," came the reply. "If their behavior—either of them—exceeds the bounds of propriety, I should have no scruples about crushing that . . ."

At that moment, Madeleine de Rollande came round the side of the yew hedge and met my gaze. For one brief instant, those green eyes flickered with shock. Then they were hard and steady as ever. The haughty head went up. A sneer curled on those flawed, shapely lips. And, without any further hesitation or embarrassment, she finished her remark—throwing it straight into my face.

". . . that English guttersnipe!"

I think I was never nearer to striking a fellow human in my life; but somehow I restrained myself. Left with only whatever shreds of dignity I could draw about myself, like some tattered shawl, to hide the nakedness of my humiliation, I availed myself of that, turning on my heel and striding off back to the château, calling to Moko to follow me. Remembering to keep my head up and my shoulders squared; thankful, above all, that they were unable to see the tears of shame that poured unchecked.

Blessedly, no one was about when I entered the hallway, and I met none of the servants on the staircase. And when the door of my bedroom was closed behind me, I threw

myself face-downward on the counterpane and gave way to
the bitter hurt.

"Why you must go in such a hurry, that's what I can't
understand, mam'selle. Why, what the Count will say when
he returns, I can't imagine. Surely it could have waited
till tomorrow, mam'selle."

I was on my way to Orléans, to the railway station.
Blois was behind, Ménars, and Beaugency. In the carriage
were Mme. Arlette and me. And a few clothes that I had
bundled into a wicker hamper—all that I should be taking
away from Brassy.

As chance had it, the Count was making one of his
infrequent journeys to one of his estates beyond Tours that
day, so I had not been able to go to him and tell the bald
reason for my hurried departure. Unable to say the words,
I had written them and left the letter on his desk in the
library. I shall never know if the courage to speak the
words to his face would ever have been granted me.

26th July, 1870

Dear Count,

I am sorry to have to tell you that it is necessary for me
to leave Brassy immediately, at once. Today. For reasons which would be hurtful and embarrassing, I beg
to be excused from explaining the need for this sudden
departure. Be assured that the need is very real.

I thank you from the bottom of my heart for all your
kindness and generosity in taking me in and treating
me for so many years as a favored member of your
family. My gratitude is total—and unqualified.

With my best wishes for your future health and
happiness,
I remain,

Yours very sincerely,
Tessa Thursday

Of course, I had no money: there had never been any
need for me to handle any; anything I had ever wanted

since my arrival in France had simply appeared before me. The necessity of reaching Paris—and Oliver—meant that I had to beg a small loan from Mme. Arlette, with the promise that I would return it at the first opportunity. This had meant her discovering that I was going away to Paris in a hurry, with very little luggage, and with no plans for returning. Small wonder that the good woman was puzzled. Small wonder that she "pumped" me all the way to Orléans, where she had insisted on accompanying me.

Orléans station was a scene of such chaos that we thought, at first, some terrible disaster had befallen it—such as a railway crash, or perhaps a fire. Milling crowds of excited men, most of them in military uniform, or part-uniform, filled the streets and entrances to the building. On closer acquaintance, we discovered that their excitement was largely caused by drunkenness. Our progress into the station yard was through this disorderly mob, who shouted ribald and suggestive comments to us two women in the carriage. Only the efforts of the coachman and footmen enabled us to enter the station building with my luggage, and look for seats in the first-class waiting room, which was already filled to suffocation with passengers, both military and civilian.

There was an officer—a red-headed man with an eyeglass and a fierce "imperial"—who gave up his seat to me with a swaggering salute that nearly overturned him, so unsteady was he on his feet.

"Thank you, monsieur," I said, seating myself.

"At what hour is the train to Paris, monsieur?" demanded the redoubtable Mme. Arlette, with a doubtful glance at the officer's swaying stance and tipsy smile. "And what is all the fuss about?"

"The train," said the officer, "was due to depart on the hour but has not yet been seen. And the fuss, madame, concerns the national mobilization, of which you must have heard."

"The mobilization?" cried Mme. Arlette. "But that was done nearly two weeks ago, monsieur. Our men left Brassy nearly two weeks ago—yes, I remember well that it was on Bastille Day and a Thursday."

The officer tapped the side of his nose and endeavored to look wise. "Matters military, madame," he said. "Matters military, and not carried out without some small difficulty. For instance, the excellent body of men at present awaiting the arrival of the Paris train (my own men, madame, and as fine a corps as ever wore the uniform of glory!) have, in fact, come from Paris. And now they are returning. We are Parisians, you see, madame. And our depot for mobilization was Orléans."

"Then why, monsieur, are you returning to Paris?" cried Mme. Arlette.

"In order to take an onward train to Metz and the frontier, madame," said the officer, with the air of a man disclosing an eternal truth. "And from there, we shall march to Berlin. Oh, yes, I assure you. We shall be in Berlin by the end of August." He hiccuped, saluted us both, and walked unsteadily to the door.

The train came into the station an hour later and departed just as it was getting dusk. I waved through the window at Mme. Arlette and the three liveried Brassy coachmen, and felt the tears start, for I should never see any of them again.

The journey to Paris—which should have taken an hour and a half, no more—lasted throughout the whole hideous night. There were long delays outside every town and hamlet on the way, and we frequently saw great trainloads of troops going past in the opposite direction, all of them waving and shouting to their fellow warriors on our own train. Most of them seemed the worse for drink. I recalled that *Le Figaro* had opened a subscription to present every soldier in the French army with a glass of cognac and a cigar. It seemed that the fund must have been heavily oversubscribed.

My own first-class railway carriage was crowded with civilians, mostly prosperous-looking townspeople. A stout lady in bombazine pressed me close to the corner, and slept with her head lolling on my shoulder. In this manner, I spent the long and wakeful night, too uncomfortable, almost, to be able to bother my mind with all my troubles. The thin summer's dawn found us waiting in the Paris suburbs for over an hour. More troop trains passed. More waving and shouting. There was a train with a long string of wagons bearing gleaming brass cannon. They looked very small, more like toys: I thought of Herr Krupp's big black gun and had a pang of unease. We rolled slowly into Montparnasse station at seven o'clock, and I hired a fiacre to take me to Oliver's apartment in the rue du Temple.

At that early hour, the streets were crowded with military traffic: marching men, heavily laden with great packs and jangling equipment; helmeted cavalry in long cloaks; strings of cannon rattling past on iron tires, drawn by jaded-looking horses. My driver was obliged to make many detours to avoid the crush; and I had the opportunity to see that there were army tents erected up the whole length of the Champs-Élysées, with more cannon parked in lines right up the gray bulk of the Arc de Triomphe on its dramatic hillcrest.

Oliver's apartment building was in the first block down the rue du Temple and only a stone's throw from the Hôtel de Ville, the town hall of Paris. I paid the driver, who deposited my baggage at the concierge's lodge. The latter knew me by sight and told me that M. Craven was up and had already been out to fetch his newspaper.

I tapped on Oliver's door on the third floor. He opened it, and took in my appearance with hardly any surprise— only compassionate concern.

"My dear," he murmured. "I knew you would come one day. But, oh, how tired and worn out you must be."

I slept the clock round in Oliver's spare room, and the woman who cleaned for him brought me a cup of coffee in the evening when she heard me stirring. M. Craven was still at the theater, she told me, but he would be honored if I would take a cab and meet him at ten o'clock, for supper at Véfour's restaurant after the performance.

I bathed and dressed myself in the only formal gown I had brought with me: the selfsame blue and gray that I had worn at the dinner party at which I first met Madeleine de Rollande. More than a day had passed since I had left Brassy. The Count had read my letter, had slept on it, and had by now put Tessa Thursday and all her works right out of his aristocratic mind. The unspeakable Madeleine would have been told, by her intended, of my departure, and would have put her own, no doubt perverted, construction upon my reason for doing so. A fig for her! But I thought of how the late afternoon sun cast long shadows across the moat of the château, and how it brought the scent of the honeysuckle through the open windows of my sitting room—and my throat tightened.

No repining. No backward glances. The future lay ahead, and my decision had been made. It had been a great time for decisions, those last few days. Beginning with the first resolve, which had been to quit Brassy as soon as the Count and that woman announced their engagement. Next, the flight from Brassy to Paris. And then the final decision . . .

I looked down at the third finger of my left hand, at the ring with the single diamond surrounded by five rubies —my engagement ring, no longer to be worn on the end of the chain with my half-thaler, but openly for all to see that I was Oliver Craven's intended.

He had pressed the decision upon me that morning, and I had not found any good reason to refuse him a second time. Overjoyed to see him again, weary and a little frightened after my journey, I had not had the slightest will to say no. And as I stood there in the evening's gloaming, my mind and body rested, there was no vestige of regret. I had done the right thing. Oliver and I were intended for each other: it had surely been written in our stars from the very first. I sighed with a new contentment and crossed to the window, to close the shutters against the gathering night. The spare room was at the rear of the building, with a view of a small paved area set with plane trees. There were starlings in the plane trees, singing an evening chorus. Coming from somewhere out across the darkening rooftops, I heard the unaccustomed sound of a bugle sketching out an elaborate call.

And, glancing down into the area below, I saw—*her*. The Woman in Black!

There was no mistaking her. Dressed in the sable shroud that hid face and features; but with the head raised so that I knew the hidden eyes were upon my lighted window.

The light! I reached out and snuffed the single candle flame with my finger and thumb. From that moment, I could see without being seen. I peered down again, trembling for fear of what might meet my gaze.

The figure was still there, in the dark shadow of the planes. The birds had fallen silent, or had quit the branches with the coming of the intruder.

An eternity of stillness, while I stood with my heart pounding; then—slowly, so slowly that it could have been the working of a mechanical doll—the figure raised one hand and pointed straight up at me. I knew that I was seen, that the darkness was no concealment from the gaze of the Dead.

I closed my eyes when I screamed. When I opened them again, the apparition had vanished.

Oliver was waiting for me in the porch of the restaurant. He rushed forward and handed me down from the fiacre, fussing with my cape, all concern.

"Are you sure you are rested, Tessa?" he asked me. "I told Madame Lebrun that you were not to be woken on any account, but that she was to listen for you. My dear, you're still very pale. Didn't you sleep well, even after the fatigue of that terrible journey?"

A head waiter escorted us to a quiet table in an alcove that was partly curtained against the gaze of the other diners, most of whom—the menfolk—were in uniform. I waited till we were alone; then, steeling myself, and controlling my voice as well as I was able, to mask the tremor in it, I said, "Oliver, I can't go back to that apartment again tonight."

"But, my dear, it's all arranged," he told me. "I have already moved out, to stay with one of the fellows in the company till the wedding. Madame Lebrun has agreed to move in and look after you. She will have the spare room and you can have . . . Tessa, my dearest, what *is* the matter?"

"Oliver, I've seen—*her!*"

"Seen whom, my dear?"

"Mirabel!"

"Mirabel?" The deep blue eyes widened with shock. A moment later, he smiled at me with all the kindness and understanding in the world; it was no wonder that Oliver Craven had impressed himself upon my heart all those years. My resolution—to keep calm and matter-of-fact—crumbled before his strength. All I wanted to do then was to lay my head, and all my fears, upon his capable shoulder. I felt my lower lip trembling.

"It's true, Oliver. I saw her with my own eyes." And I told him of the apparition. It made no difference. He merely became more gentle, more understanding.

"My dear, you've had what was likely the most upsetting day and night of your life," he said. "Excess fatigue, followed by a deep sleep, from which you had scarcely woken—" he spread his hands expressively—"the mind, one's own eyes, play strange tricks upon us at such times."

"I saw her, Oliver," I persisted. "I saw Mirabel, just as I saw her before. Just as she was—that last night, in the black peignoir with the hood. Looking up at my window."

He shook his head. "Overwrought imagination, my dearest. Your tired eyes were playing tricks on you," he said gently.

"It was her ghost!"

"There are no ghosts, Tessa. Only in our minds. There are times—and you have passed through such a time—when we create ghosts in our minds. But everything passes. Your ghost no longer exists."

"Oliver," I pleaded. "I can't go back to that apartment."

"Nor shall you, my dear," he assured me. "I will get you a suite in a private hotel this very night, and have your belongings brought over from the rue du Temple. You see? I am quite convinced of the sincerity of your belief; it's merely that I put a different—a more logical—interpretation upon the disturbing experience you have been through. There! I do believe I saw the beginnings of a smile."

I said, "You are good for me, Oliver."

"You never spoke a truer word," he assured me cheerfully. "And now, my dear, let us address ourselves to this magnificent bill of fare. Are you hungry? But you must, of course, be starving after all this time . . ."

I was not really hungry, but I had a few mouthfuls to please him. And I said little, but watched him covertly: this man whom I had pledged myself to marry. He went out of his way to amuse and distract me, and succeeded as only a supreme artiste could. His range of conversation spanned the latest theatrical gossip, news of the war, imitations of various absurd public figures and their pronouncements, more gossip of the theater: old Offenbach, he told me, was finished; his *Princess of Trebizond*, produced in the previous year, had been a failure.

His distracting monologue was rudely interrupted by a disturbance from the main part of the dining room, where, amidst a clash of falling cutlery and broken glass, an officer of the Zouaves leapt up upon his table—encouraged by the cheers of his companions—and gave out with a full-throated rendition of the "Marseillaise":

Allons! enfants de la patrie,
Le jour de gloire est arrivé!

The old revolutionary anthem had been banned since the days of the Republic, but I had heard it again and again during the long night journey from Orléans, from the mouths of the troops. Presently, the entire restaurant, waiters and all, were joining in the chorus. Oliver took my hand and assisted me to my feet, to be upstanding with the rest. Neither of us was familiar with all the words, but we made shift with the parts we knew and shouted *"marchons, marchons!"* with the best of them.

"To Berlin!" cried the Zouave, raising his glass on high.

"To Berlin!" we echoed.

More cheering.

"They will do it, you know, Tessa," said Oliver, when the din had subsided. "The French will walk through the German states. Bismarck's career is ended. He was a fool to have goaded Napoleon into going to war; what with France's tremendous superiority of numbers, not to mention the professionalism of the French army and their marvelous weapons. Why, do you know they have a secret weapon called a *mitrailleuse,* based on the American Gatling gun, that can mow down lines of advancing men like standing corn? By heaven, I am really sorry for those Prussian fellows!"

I did not reply. On the one hand, I had a vision of Otto's dead face lying in a cornfield; on the other, I seemed to see again that drunken officer at the Orléans station and all the chaos and confusion that still seemed to grip the French army so long after the beginning of mobilization. But I did not mention any of that to Oliver—for what does a woman know of how a war is properly conducted?

Our wedding was arranged for Saturday, September 3rd, to take place at the Hôtel de Ville; a civil ceremony, at which the mayor of the district would officiate. Neither of us wanted a lot of fuss, but Oliver was very insistent that I should wear white—a desire with which I was very happy to comply. And so, again at Oliver's insistence, it was to Mr. Worth's famous establishment at No. 7, rue de la Paix, that I took myself, where the master himself designed a typically elaborate creation of pure white Lyons silk, embellished with a mile of white Alençon lace and artificial white gardenias from Angoulême. My veil was supported by a high comb, after the manner of the Spanish mantilla. White gardenias and lilies of the valley were to make up my bouquet. The gown was completed and standing on a dressmaker's dummy in Mr. Worth's salon a fortnight before my wedding day, and every morning I went past the window of No. 7, rue de la Paix, and peered in, to feast my eyes upon its splendor.

The war, which had been in progress for five weeks, had begun brilliantly for the French by the capture of the German town of Saarbrücken. The news had been received in Paris with tremendous rejoicing. Oliver himself brought me the tidings at my hotel in the rue des Archives, and insisted that I put on my gayest hat and accompany him on a tour of the streets in his phaeton. By the time we had progressed to the end of the block, we were caught up in an immovable mass of tumultuous humanity, all waving the national flag and calling the name of the Emperor, who had personally led the French forces to victory, and that of his son, the fourteen-year-old Prince Imperial, who had been present at the battle and who, so the story went, had picked up a Prussian bullet that had fallen close by him. Like a wind that fans a brush fire came further news that the Prussian Crown Prince had been captured in the battle. The crowd's spirit soared to fresh heights of patriotic fervor. Someone recognized Capoul, the celebrated tenor, and the soprano Marie Sass, both of the Opera, in an omnibus. The pair were made to stand on top of the vehicle and lead the masses in a rendition of the "Marseillaise." I have to admit that it was an experience which brought a lump to my throat.

After the success of Saarbrücken came news of reverses for the French. At first no one thought of these as anything but the normal setbacks of war. A day later would come news of another victory, and then the flags flew from every window, and people—complete strangers—kissed each other in the streets. But all too often, as the month of August progressed, these spurious victories became known to be ghastly defeats. At Weissenburg, Wörth, and at Gravelotte —names that were on everyone's lips—the French, though inflicting terrible losses upon their opponents, were forced to fall back.

It was during these dark days that my thoughts flew to Philippe and to Otto. Had they both managed, so far, to survive the carnage? And had they, as I fervently hoped, never had the mischance to meet each other in battle?

As the last days of August brought further bad news

from the front, insurrections broke out in Paris. Led by extreme Republicans, they were aimed at the manner in which the government was waging the war. In a working class quarter of the capital, a fire station was attacked and several of the firemen killed. That night Oliver closed the Théâtre des Comédiens, and for three days after.

I think, of all the people in Paris, Oliver must surely have been the most serenely convinced that all would come well, and that Napoleon III would, as he put it, "bring something out of the bag at the eleventh hour." The Emperor was a Bonaparte, he reminded me constantly: of the same stamp as his illustrious uncle, who had led France to victory against all Europe. Even when foreigners began to pack up and leave the capital, Oliver never faltered in his conviction. Come our wedding day, he promised me, the tide would have turned and the French would be over the Rhine and driving deep into Germany. Trust the Emperor!

I trusted. And hoped. And wished for the safety of "my two cavaliers," wherever they might be. Meanwhile, our wedding day was nearly upon us, and there was my beautiful bridal gown just in sight when I stood on tiptoe outside Mr. Worth's plate-glass window.

With only a week to go to our wedding, a strange silence fell upon the military situation. We were told that the French Marshal MacMahon was executing certain strategical movements with his troops, with a view to striking a fatal blow against the Prussians. Oliver was wild with enthusiasm and took me out to supper for a celebration. The restaurant was almost empty: no sign of a foreign visitor, for they had all fled from Paris; and scarcely a uniform to be seen, for every soldier was up at the front.

Almost alone, while bored waiters looked on, we drank a champagne toast to Marshal MacMahon, who, said Oliver, was going to bring France a glorious victory on the occasion of our wedding. I had never seen him more animated, more radiant with the strange power of attraction that I had noticed in him from the first. It was almost as if he had taken France's fortunes on his own shoulders; as if it were he, and not the Emperor and Marshal MacMahon, who would be leading the troops into battle; and as if he, by a sheer effort of indomitable will, were going to bring victory.

Two days before the wedding, it appeared that Oliver's faith had been justified. Flags were flying at the news of an astounding success near Sedan, where the two armies were locked in a mortal combat. People took to the streets and rejoiced at a rumor that the King of Prussia had gone mad. By the evening of that day, both items of news were contradicted. The battle was still in the balance, together with the King's mind.

Mr. Worth's principal *vendeuse* herself delivered my wedding gown on the eve of the great day, in a smart gray box cart, attended by two flunkies in tailcoats and cockaded hats. She had been crying. When I questioned her, she burst into tears and told me that her brother had been wounded near Metz and had now been lost in the confusion of the fighting. The poor creature pictured him dying, unattended, in some ditch, with the battle raging all about him; alone, frightened. He was only eighteen, she sobbed. I offered her what comfort I could and saw her on her way.

After that, my beautiful white wedding gown seemed strangely tawdry and out of place, on its dressmaker's dummy.

Saturday the 3rd of September dawned with gray skies that promised rain. I rose early and looked down into the street, where the morning traffic was beginning to circulate, and a few people were about.

I rang the bell for the floor maid and ordered coffee and *croissants*, together with a newspaper. The breakfast was long in coming—which was unusual for the hotel, an extremely well-run establishment. And the maid was sullen and truculent.

"You forgot the newspaper," I prompted her.

"There aren't any newspapers this morning," was her reply, and she slammed the door on the way out. I had noticed an increasing dislike of foreigners on the part of Parisians during the previous few weeks, and a definite hostility toward those who were moving out with their baggage. The girl's attitude had the power to cast a cloud of depression over my mood. It did not go till I had bathed and was contemplating the putting on of my wedding gown. It was then ten-thirty. The ceremony was timed for midday.

All had been carefully arranged by Oliver ("organized down to the last gaiter-button, like the French army," had been his proud boast). The two ladies from the company— Jöelle Romy and an English *soubrette* named Felicity Mortimer—who were to be my bridesmaids, were supposed to arrive at the hotel at ten-thirty, to help me dress. The carriage was due at the hotel entrance at ten minutes to twelve. Oliver had timed the drive on three occasions and had established that, in average Saturday midday traffic, I should arrive at the Hôtel de Ville with my bridesmaids with a minute or two to spare.

At twenty to eleven—no bridesmaids. At eleven o'clock, there being no answer when I rang the bell to get assistance from the floor maid, I made the best shift I could of getting into the elaborate gown by my own efforts, telling myself all the time that I had nothing to worry about, and that Jöelle and Felicity would be along in plenty of time to help with the finishing touches, as for instance my hair and my veil.

At a quarter past eleven, I had more or less arranged the gown to my satisfaction; but the bridesmaids still had not arrived. Nor had my wedding bouquet of fresh white gardenias and lilies of the valley, which Oliver had ordered the florists to deliver to the hotel at least an hour before my departure. It was then that I noticed the first signs of panic in myself: a wildness about the eyes and a dampness of the palms.

"You've nothing to worry about," I told my reflection in the pier glass. "Jöelle and Felicity must have overslept. Why, even if they don't arrive at all, you can perfectly well get to the Hôtel de Ville by yourself."

I went to the window, in time to hear a clock chime the half hour. The traffic in the street below had scarcely increased since early morning, which was curious. By that time on a Saturday the road should have been packed with vehicles of all kinds, and the sidewalks thronged. All Paris took to the streets and boulevards on Saturday mornings, particularly when the weather was fine. And the dawn's dismal promise had given way to bright sunlight and high blue skies. Where, then, were the strollers, the shoppers, the men-about-town with their eyeglasses, the *midinettes* forever running on some errand? And where were all the smart people taking the air in their liveried carriages? It struck me as most odd—and strangely disturbing.

At twenty minutes to twelve, I knew as if it had already come to pass that the carriage would not be calling to collect me. Having decided that, I felt calmer. Had I not triumphed over every other shortcoming that morning? Then I would continue to do so.

One last look in the pier glass. A pause to tuck a scented lace handkerchief into my sleeve. A dab of powder on my nose. A stray curl patted into place. And Miss Tessa Thursday quit the room, to keep her appointment with Destiny.

I met no one on the stairs on the way down to the hallway. Nor was there anyone behind the ornate reception counter, which was usually presided over by a stout gentleman of tremendous efficiency and helpfulness. No sign, either, of the dazzlingly buttoned doorkeeper, who was so adept at producing a cab for hire from out of the most unpromising tangles of passing traffic. Only two elderly gentlemen who were sitting in armchairs at the far end of the hallway, deep in earnest conversation; they looked round in some surprise to see the woman in bridal finery trying to slip inconspicuously out of the plate-glass doors of the hotel and into the sunlit street.

I saw a fiacre almost immediately: going in the right direction, and empty of passengers. I hailed the driver and asked him to take me to the Hôtel de Ville, settling my train on the seat as best as I was able, so as not to crush it.

He turned his head at the sound of my voice. "Are you a foreigner, eh?" he demanded sulkily.

I said, "Yes."

He grunted something beneath his breath and whipped up the horse with quite unnecessary brutality. Another Parisian who had been bitten by the anti-foreigner bug. I had hoped to ask him if he had heard any news from the front, but the sullen hunch of his shoulders clearly precluded any more communication between us. We progressed in silence.

Oliver had timed my journey well. It wanted five minutes to the hour, by the clock over the center of the massive Hôtel de Ville, when my surly driver deposited me at one of the main doors, took his fare and a handsome tip without so much as a thank you, and drove off. I gathered up my train, drew a deep breath, and went inside to look for Oliver and our wedding party.

Up a flight of steps and into a vast hall of echoing marble: marble columns reaching ceiling-high; a sweep of veined marble staircases going to left and right. As I stood, irresolute, asking myself why Oliver—or at least one of the men of the company acting as usher—was not standing there to greet me, a small man in a dark coat and very tall hat came swiftly down the stairs. He had a briefcase under his arm. When he saw me, he gave a start of surprise and raised his hat in passing.

"Could you tell me, please," I asked, "where I am to go for my marriage ceremony?"

"Marriage ceremony?" he echoed. "Well, now, the mayor's office is on the second floor, you know. That is where the ceremonies usually take place. But, under the circumstances —well, I really would not like to say, mam'selle. Pardon me. Good day." He raised his hat again and was gone before I could call after him.

My gown made a rich froufrou as I progressed up the stairs to the second floor. There, I saw a harassed-looking young man slip out of a door and cross the corridor; but he had shut the door of another room behind him before I could call out.

At the end of that corridor were large double doors, open. I walked through and into a large chamber hung with tapestries and glistening chandeliers. At an ornate table in the center of the room, a white-bearded gentleman in pince-nez was writing rapidly on a large sheet of paper. Though he must have noticed me at the edge of his vision, he did not look up as I approached, nor did he till I had finished putting my question to him.

"My name is Thursday," I said. "Miss Tessa Thursday. And I am to marry Mr. Oliver Craven here at midday. Could you please direct me to the mayor's office, monsieur?"

"This is the mayor's office, mam'selle." His short-sighted eyes took in my appearance, and seemed to soften with compassion. "But I am afraid that he is at an important meeting."

"But—my wedding?" I cried.

"Mam'selle, you have my entire sympathy," he said, "but do you really expect, in the present grave situation, that the city officers are able to concern themselves with—begging your pardon, mam'selle—such matters as *weddings?*"

"But—what has happened?" I cried.

"Mam'selle, you do not know—you have not heard the news?"

"I—I've scarcely spoken to a soul all the morning."

There came a dry cough from somewhere behind me, as when a man clears his throat in preparation for speaking. Next, the scrape of a chair leg on parquet, as when someone rises from a seat. I turned to see who it was. And I felt the blood fly from my cheeks.

"France is finished, Miss Thursday. The cardboard emperor has made his last throw and failed. Late last night came news that our troops were surrounded at Sedan, and it is believed that they have capitulated. The war is over and lost, Miss Thursday. The Prussians will be in Paris within the week."

"You!" I cried. "I—I don't understand."

Count Robert de Brassy's lips sketched the hint of an unaccustomed smile. He took off his hat, revealing the thick gray hair streaked with white.

"You will pardon my presumption, Miss Thursday," he said, "but I had come as an uninvited guest to your nuptials. It appears, however, that you are not only lacking a mayor to officiate, but also a groom!"

2

It was past two o'clock in the afternoon when, after a long
and fruitless wait at the Hôtel de Ville, I allowed the Count
to persuade me to accompany him to Oliver's apartment.
There we found the concierge drunk and almost incapable
of coherence. The woman was half-laughing, half-crying,
and calling down curses upon the Emperor, the government
and the army. "We have been betrayed!" was her only reply
to our repeated inquiries about Oliver, at the door of whose
apartment we received no response to all our knocking.

Crowds were filling the streets as we made our way to the
Théâtre des Comédiens, and long lines of people were
collecting at all the newspaper kiosks. The Count ordered
the carriage to stop and sent his coachman to purchase a
copy of Le Figaro. The man returned later and grimly held
up the headlines for us both to see.

ARMY CAPITULATES AT SEDAN
EMPEROR A PRISONER OF BISMARCK

We drove in silence for the rest of the way to the rue de
l'Echiquier, with the Grands Boulevards growing ever more
crowded by the minute; the people walking aimlessly, blank-
faced, like those who have suffered some indescribable loss
which they have not yet learned to accept.

The theater doors were open and unattended, the booking
office empty. The memory of my failure as an artiste—that
hideous occasion of my self-deception upon that small stage
—came back to me as I followed the Count's tall, limping
figure down the narrow aisle and backstage to the dressing
rooms. Oliver's was deserted, like the rest. In his dressing
room, the costumes still hung upon their racks, and his
greasepaints were neatly lined up before the mirror, his

many wigs perched upon their blocks; but the other quarters showed signs of hasty departure: drawers open and empty, discarded rubbish lying about, the stale smell of abandonment.

"The company must have fled Paris *en masse* late last night, when the first news of the Sedan disaster filtered through," mused the Count. "By now, if the Prussians have not advanced so far as to cut off the railway line to the Channel ports, they will be well on their way to England. And good luck to them. But what, Miss Thursday, of Oliver Craven? What happened to your bridegroom-elect? He has not been here to collect his belongings preparative to flight. And he did not present himself at your hotel to inform you that it was highly probable that, with Paris facing imminent occupation by enemy troops, you would not find an official who would be disposed to stop what he was doing and bind you both in wedlock. Oh, dear me, Miss Thursday. Now you are crying. Do you have a handkerchief?"

I had nothing left in me with which to protest when the Count took me back with him to the Hôtel de Brassy, but just slumped in the silk cushions of the carriage and closed my eyes against the sight of the crowds, the broad and spacious boulevards under the deceptive blueness of the summer sky. I had been deserted in a doomed city. Alone— save for the chill comfort of the Count's presence. And how, I wondered, had he come to hear of my projected marriage? Presumably Oliver had written to his patron about it.

Oliver . . .

Where was he? And why had he so heartlessly, so callously, abandoned me on our wedding morning? Had he fled in panic with the rest of the company? Hardly—Oliver was not the running-away sort. Besides, he had left all his things behind at the theater.

Then—where? Why?

We clattered through the place de la Madeleine, where the sound of many voices raised in anger made me open my eyes. Crowds were massed before the steps leading up to the porticoed front of the Madeleine church, where a party of men and women bearing scarlet banners were haranguing their listeners. I heard shouts of "Down with the Empire!" and "Long Live Trochu!" General Trochu had recently been appointed Governor of Paris. Reputedly hated by the Empress and mistrusted by the Emperor, he was a popular favorite in the city.

"Matters are moving faster than I had thought!" The Count was staring intently at the scene before us, and his words were spoken more to himself than to me. "The mobs will take to the streets tonight. Within a week, we shall have another Republic. Well, it will bring peace, if nothing else."

We came at last to the Hôtel de Brassy, and who should be there to greet us and hand me down but the unctuous Flambard, perhaps now not quite so unctuous. In the years between, he had built on his air of assurance. Old Fournier had died, and he was now chief steward of the mansion.

"Such a very great pleasure to see mam'selle again!" he cried.

I had removed my veil, and the Count had draped his light overcoat over my shoulders. If Flambard realized that under it I was wearing a formal bridal gown, he showed no sign, but merely bowed, revealing a thinning patch on his sleek, curled dome.

"We should like some refreshment," said the Count. "Nothing too elaborate. Miss Thursday has—unavoidably missed luncheon. See to it, please, Flambard."

"At once, Count." The steward bowed again and soundlessly slipped out of the drawing room.

I sat down wearily, the folds of the Count's gray coat spreading about me. The garment had the masculine smell of well-oiled leather and cologne water.

The Count gave the small cough that always indicated his embarrassment in my presence, coupled, in this case, with his total inability to cope with my troubles. So he avoided them by discussing something else.

"Well, then," he said. "We have the exit of Napoleon the Third, for it is certain that his abdication will be demanded. I have spoken against him many times, but have never thought him to be an evil man at heart. Napoleon the well-meaning—'*le bien-intentionné*'—is possibly how he will be regarded by history. A pity that his good intentions should have had to bring ruin upon France."

I responded to his lead in the conversation, glad to speak —and to think—of anything other than Oliver. "I can't understand how it could have happened," I said. "Everyone was so sure that France would defeat Prussia within weeks. The English newspapers thought so. And I remember Philippe saying what a splendid condition the French army was in. And Oliver was so certain . . ."

I checked myself. Looked down at my hands. The Count gave his awkward cough.

"As to the army," he said, "I am now not qualified to speak. The disaster—and it was always with us—was the French people's conviction, fostered by the man himself, that they had in him another Napoleon Bonaparte (for whose memory, though myself a Royalist, I may say I have an enormous respect and admiration). But this was not so. In everything about him—in his deportment, his coloration— he is not a Bonaparte but a Beauharnais. For, you will remember, Miss Thursday, that his mother was sister to Josephine Beauharnais, wife of the first Napoleon. France's tragedy, Miss Thursday, is that people thought they were being led by the nephew of the great Napoleon—*while all the time they were cheering for the nephew of Napoleon's silly, erring wife!*

"Ah, here comes refreshment."

He had been speaking swiftly and without pause, as a man will do when he is filling in awkward gaps of silence. The return of Flambard with a string of lackeys, bearing silver dishes and wine coolers, provided him with an *entr'acte*, a brief interval in his self-imposed task of keeping the ball of the conversation high in the air. He directed the servitors to place the dishes here and there; he fussed over the coolness of the champagne; he feigned anger and demanded the replacement of a glass that, he claimed, showed a thumbprint when held against the light; directed the steward to close the shutters so that the dying rays of the afternoon sun should not shine directly in my eyes. He looked about him almost despairingly when the double doors shut behind Flambard and his men. I took pity on him.

"And how," I asked brightly, "is Madame de Rollande?"

There was a clatter when his elbow caught the handle of his stick, which was resting against the arm of his chair. This nearly caused the overturn of his occasional table and the spilling of his wine and food; but he deftly saved it, and with a muffled curse.

Presently, he said, "Hem! Madame de Rollande has departed for Martinique, where her late husband had extensive plantations and other properties which have now fallen to her care."

Mindful of the insult I had received at Madeleine de Rollande's hands, an imp of malice made me probe him further. "You must miss her company very much, Count," I said. "And be eagerly looking forward to her return."

I regretted the remark as soon as I had made it; but instead of showing anger at my over-familiarity, as I might have expected, he fixed me with a look of such simplicity and earnestness, such grave dignity, that I could have bitten off my tongue.

"Madame de Rollande will not be returning," he said. "Not, as I understand it, in the foreseeable future."

"Oh," I said, surprised. And, again, "Oh."

"And, in the unlikely event of that lady's return to France, and to the Loire, I greatly doubt if I—if either of us—will see our way clear to renewing the acquaintanceship."

Now it was I who was caught out. A champagne glass in one hand, the end of a piece of toast with caviar in the other. My occasional table was so far distant—a whole arm's length—and what should I do now, now that my hands were trembling so that he must surely see? Carefully— slowly—I put down the glass first, spilling a sizable puddle at its base. I resolved the problem of the caviar by putting it into my mouth—a solution that also absolved me from the necessity of making any comment upon his declaration.

He noticed my sudden discomfiture, but could scarcely have guessed at the reason for it. "Miss Thursday," he said, "you must be totally distraught after what has happened.

Would it—how shall I put it? Would it help, to talk about the situation?"

"I—I don't really know," was my foolish reply. Was I distraught? I supposed that I was. But, if this was so, why was it that I suddenly wanted to laugh and cry together? . . .

"I cannot account for Craven's behavior," he said "To have left you standing in that manner, without a word, a note." He shook his head. "I must say that such conduct does not square with my own experience, over the years, of Oliver Craven. There must be a rational explanation. Perhaps he had an accident in the street. Of course, I have had word sent to the police, so far with no result. I hope no ill has come to him."

"Oh, that would be terrible," I said. And I thought of Oliver lying injured, not having jilted me at all.

"We must hope for the best," he said.

"Yes, we must," I murmured. I met his glance and looked away. To hide a new onslaught of confusion, I reached out to take up my champagne glass again—but abandoned the project when I found that my hand was still trembling.

Fortunately the Count did not notice this. He rose to his feet, and, leaning heavily on his stick, he limped slowly over to a window; looked out into the garden. I wondered at his tallness, and felt a strange tenderness to see the way he was obliged to lean heavily against the window recess, shoulders bowed. It occurred to me that he too had had a demanding day.

"Obviously, Miss Thursday, you must remain in Paris," he mused, "until this wretched business is cleared up, one way or another: till you discover if Craven has played the blackguard, or if there is some reasonable explanation for his conduct."

"Yes," I said.

"I should deem it an honor, Miss Thursday, if you would see fit to accept the hospitality of the Hôtel de Brassy. At least till your affairs are in order, one way or another."

"Oh, but I couldn't . . ." I began.

He turned to face me, one hand raised in a mild gesture of remonstrance. "Please, I beg you, Miss Thursday. Let us

227

be frank with each other. The matter of the letter that you left for me . . ."

"Yes?" I murmured, fearful of what was to follow.

"You spoke, in the letter, of hurt and embarrassment. I may say that I am aware of the source, the cause, of that hurt and embarrassment. I am aware of the nature of the calumny—the foul slander—that was uttered. Indeed, that same calumny was repeated in my presence. Do I make myself clear, Miss Thursday?"

I nodded. "Y-Yes."

"Following upon which repetition, I not only denied the slander in the most forceful terms, but also severed my connection with the slanderer. Do I continue to make myself clear, Miss Thursday?"

"Yes," I whispered.

"The calumny having been nailed, Miss Thursday, there is no longer any impediment to your honoring me by accepting De Brassy hospitality. And, to put it in the light of brutal truth, what alternative have you? Craven, so I take it, has been supporting you, in anticipation of your marriage to him." He hunched his shoulders in that typical, expressive way the French have. "But what now?"

I took a deep breath and said, "I accept your generous offer, Count. And I hope that the day will come when I shall be able to repay you for all you have done for me."

He smiled, and that craggy face was heart-warmingly transformed by unaccustomed lines of pleasure and humor. "That will not be necessary, Miss Thursday," he replied. Then, more briskly: "I must return to Brassy almost immediately. The first thing tomorrow morning at the latest. My position in the local provincial government puts severe responsibilities upon me—and the more so after this day's dreadful news. You will be better off here: Paris will be safer than the countryside. Not that there will be any—unpleasantness; but it is likely that at least some of France will be occupied for some time by the victorious Prussians. Happily, they are, in my experience, a chivalrous people. Their army very correct . . ."

I watched him, wonderingly: scarcely listening to his words, though noticing every nuance of inflection and tone;

the way, when speaking English (as he invariably did to me when we were alone), the perfection of his accent was only marred by a slight difficulty with the "th" sound and the "st" sound, so that his brow would furrow ever so slightly with the effort of pronunciation.

I watched him throughout dinner that night. Saying hardly anything myself. Full of my wild, new, wonderful thoughts.

I was there at the window of the upstairs hallway, and keeping well out of sight, when he left early the following morning; saw him limp to the waiting carriage, nod a brief farewell to Flambard, and settle himself in the seat with a newspaper. I watched till the carriage turned out of the gate, till the crown of his tall hat bobbed away out of sight along the enclosing wall.

And then I cried tears of misery mixed with joy.

It had come to me swiftly, like a thunderbolt out of a cloudless sky, when he told me that he was finished with Madeleine de Rollande. How had he put it?—"I doubt if either of us will see our way clear to renewing the acquaintanceship."

In that instant I had known such a surge of joy and relief that it had been as if my whole life had opened up like a flower. In that same instant, the true reason for my hurried departure from Brassy had been revealed to me. Not only outraged hurt and sullied pride had driven me out; I had left because I had to put some distance between myself and Robert de Brassy, who could even contemplate marriage to a creature who could think—and speak—such things about him and me.

For I loved him. I supposed that I had loved him—all unknowingly—for a very long time. Perhaps from the time, years before, when he had helped to nurse me through the grippe. The "unhealthy passion" had not been unhealthy after all; nor had it died with the end of my illness, but had quietly grown in my heart, awaiting the call to blossom forth in splendor.

So I wept for the revelation. And for gratitude: because he had defended my honor—and his own—against Madeleine de Rollande's slanderous accusation. And he had cast her off—not that I even dared to presume any advantage in this, as far as I was concerned.

I knew—and accepted—that my love was hopeless. The gulf of birth, of breeding, of upbringing, that lay between us precluded all hope that he would ever regard me as anything more than a recipient of his patronage.

And I wept for that, also. And because I was in Paris and he in Brassy.

That day, September 4th, it was given out in the streets that the Emperor had been deposed and that a Government of National Defense had been formed in Paris, with General Trochu as President. The Second Empire was dead; the Third Republic born. Robert de Brassy had been right about that, but wrong about his second prediction. There was to be no question of making peace with the Prussians; the new government declared it would continue the war to the bitter end.

Scarcely a week later, rumor had it that Prussian lancers had been seen scouting the approaches to the capital.

There had been no news of Oliver. I had expected none. My guess was that, for some reason that I would possibly never discover, he had had an eleventh-hour change of heart about marrying me, and had decamped to London with the rest of the company, leaving his belongings behind. No other explanation offered itself.

One afternoon, I was attempting to write a prim letter to Robert de Brassy, informing him of this, when Flambard burst into the drawing room.

"Monsieur Philippe is here, mam'selle! And in such a state!"

I raced after him to the front doorway, to see a travel-stained berlin drawn up at the foot of the steps. It was driven by a soldier in a forage cap. Riding escort were two dragoons, from whose plumed brass helmets and green facings, I knew to be men of Philippe's regiment. Another dragoon—an officer with a bandaged head—alighted from the carriage and looked about him dazedly.

"If this is indeed the Hôtel de Brassy," he said, "for pity's sake, will some of your men help us to get the Captain out

of here?" He then reeled back against the coachwork and
would have fallen had not Flambard caught him.

"Quickly!" I cried. And footmen came running down
the steps. I looked into the berlin and recoiled with horror
at what I saw. There was much blood, and the remains of
a rough meal of bread and cheese. Flies crawled everywhere: they crawled upon the white face of Philippe, as he
lay slumped across one of the seats. His hand was pressed
to his chest, and it was clutching a bloodstained rag.

"We ran into an Uhlan patrol outside Reims while
covering the retreat," muttered the officer with the wounded
head. "Captain de Brassy took a lance thrust. We—we
have been God knows how many days on the road. Can the
men and horses be fed and watered, please?"

The footmen tenderly lifted Philippe from the berlin and
carried him up the steps. The two troopers had dismounted
and were leading their horses across the yard: the clatter
of their great military boots sounded unreal upon the
cobblestones.

"Take Monsieur Philippe to my bedroom!" I told them.

They laid him on the golden counterpane of my little
four-poster, and the silk was instantly dabbled with his
bright blood. I tried gently to prize away Philippe's hand
from his chest; but with no success.

"He's dying, mam'selle," said one of the older footmen.
"I've seen many go like that in the Crimea."

"Fetch a doctor!" I cried.

"No doctor to be had, mam'selle," said Flambard, who
had just entered. "I have just had this from the Lieutenant.
Our fellows have been teeming into the city since last
night. The last of the rear guard, you see, mam'selle. The
surgeons are working the clock round, and not a place to
lay a litter in any of the hospitals. That is why they brought
him here, you see, mam'selle."

"Brought him here to die," said the lugubrious footman.
"And he'll not be long."

"Shut up!" I snapped at him. "I'll show you that he
hasn't been brought here in vain. Fetch clean water. Laundered sheets, to tear up into bandages. And all of you
save Hortense get out of here and go about your business."

I turned to my lady's maid, who stood at the open door, staring, wide-eyed, at the still figure on the bed. "Unless you're upset at the sight of suffering, Hortense."

She shook her head. "My father is our village dentist back in Normandy, mam'selle," she said. "It was always my job to hold them down."

So I was going to show them that Philippe's comrades had not brought their captain home in vain. Brave words! They almost died in my heart when Hortense's strong fingers overcame the death grip of the unconscious man and took away his hand. I scissored through the stained tunic and shirt, baring the wound. The lance point had taken Philippe in the left side of his chest, above the heart, scoring across flesh and ribs, and entering near the breastbone. Air bubbled in the bright blood that oozed from the wound. The lung had been pierced.

"Oh, mam'selle, what do we do?" wailed Hortense.

"We'll do everything we can," I told her. "And keep doing it, till he's better. Give me a big piece of clean sheet, Hortense. Make it up into a wad."

With no knowledge, but only an instinct to stop up the wound and prevent further loss of blood, I proceeded to apply a firm pad across the riven flesh. This I then fastened in place with a cross bandage right round Philippe's chest. I could never have lifted him without Hortense's help. That done, we stripped him, washed him, and laid him within the sheets. His brow was hot and damp with sweat.

"Go and attend to the Lieutenant, Hortense," I instructed her. "I'll watch over Monsieur Philippe till I grow sleepy, then I'll send for you to relieve me. Get what sleep you can meanwhile."

"Yes, mam'selle." She departed, not forgetting to curtsy at the door.

I sat with Philippe till nearly dawn of the following day, with a single candle showing me the still, pale face. He made not a sound all that time, but the wounded chest continued to rise and fall—however slightly. Toward dawn I felt my eyelids begin to grow heavy, and, fearful that I might doze off and not be ready to render him any help if, for instance, the bleeding began again, I pulled the bell

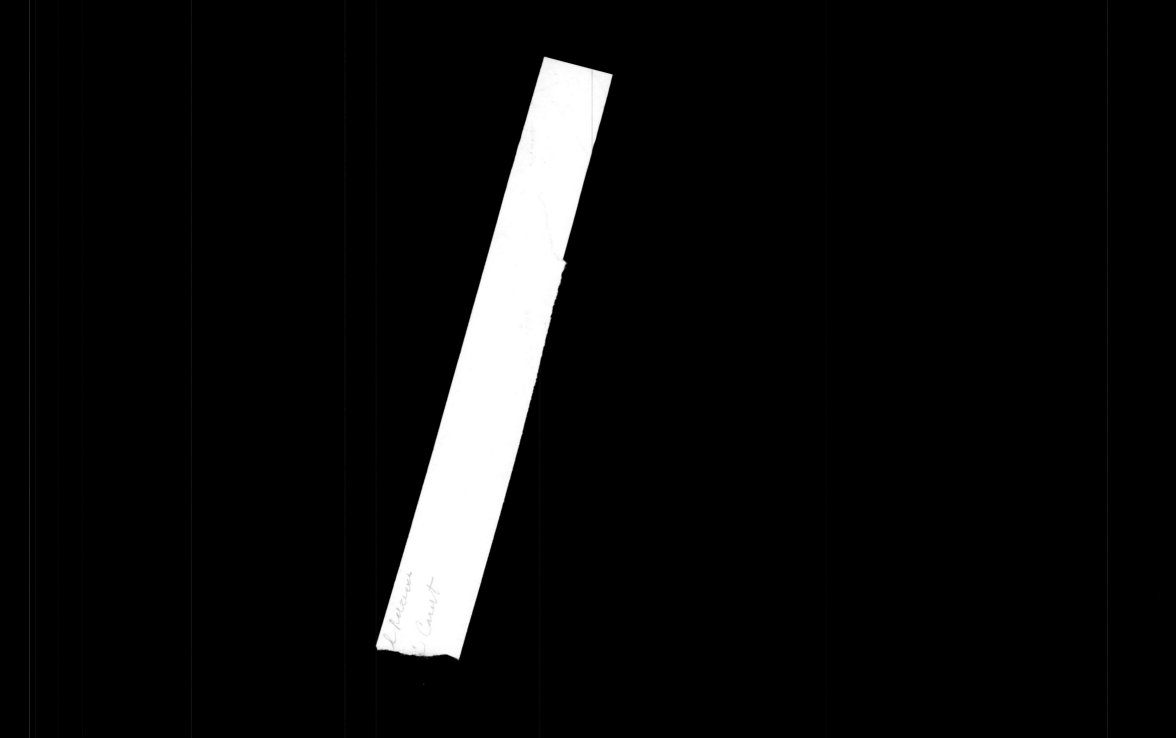

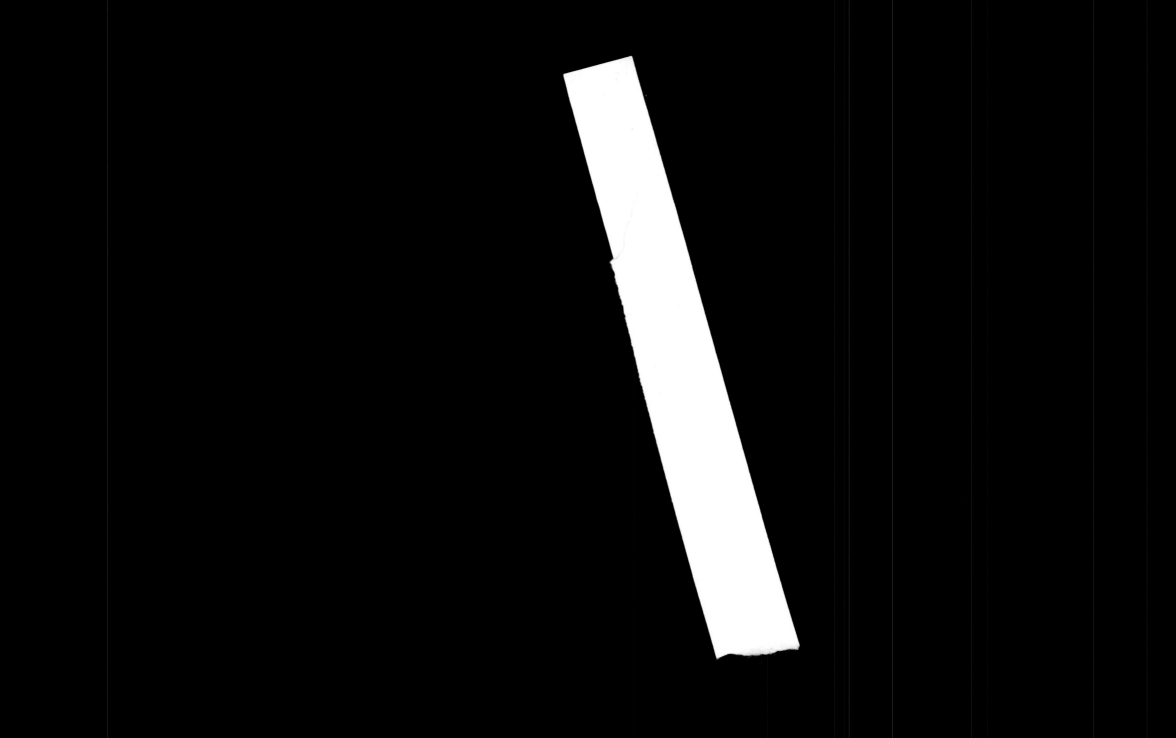

cord for a maid and asked her to summon Hortense. My staunch lady's maid had been sleeping on a mattress in the corridor outside and was with me in moments. I left her in charge, with a lingering backward glance at the face of the stricken man, and an injunction for her to summon me from the next-door room if there was any change.

Dawn broke as I lay myself down on the sofa in my sitting room. A distant sound came to me, and as it drew nearer, it resolved itself as the clash of horses' hooves and the rattle of cannon wheels on the cobblestones of the faubourg outside.

Paris was preparing to fight. I shuddered and closed my eyes.

Philippe did not die. Within twenty-four hours he was grinning weakly up at me from his pillow and sipping a few mouthfuls of broth. Talking was painful to him—but what need of words? I pressed his hand and was heartened to receive an answering squeeze.

The Lieutenant—who quickly recovered from loss of blood following a nasty, but superficial, scalp wound—was more communicative. His name was Faucher, and he hailed from Languedoc. A farmer's son who had risen from the ranks, he was brutally outspoken about the war which Napoleon III—sometime my hero—had inflicted upon his soldiers.

"It was a shambles, mam'selle. A shambles from first to last. Take the mobilization: generals walking around in tears because they could not find their divisions; not a single corps ready to take the field after fourteen days. I saw it with my own eyes: men half in uniform and half in civilian clothes, marching to the front without a loaf of bread between them, nor the transport to carry any such supplies. Oh, yes, we saw plenty of the shambles, moving about in the cavalry screen. Things that are hidden from the fellow trudging along on foot, whose horizons are bounded by the next field.

"We fought them well, mam'selle, those Prussians. Don't let them tell you that the French ran. We gave better than we took at Gravelotte—but still we had to retreat. They outnumbered us by three to one at Gravelotte, they suffered heavier losses—but still we had to retreat!

"Philippe de Brassy was promoted in the field, to captain, after Gravelotte. He was in the forefront of every charge.

"What went wrong, you ask me? I will tell you, mam'selle. Our generals. Oh, they did fine work in the past. Against barefoot Algerians, and Mexican peasants armed with farm tools. They wear medals for their fine work in the Crimea— but the Crimea ended fourteen years ago. I shouldn't wonder if the Emperor wasn't a better general than any of them. He was with the army. I saw him. My God, how ill he looked. They say he suffers from the stone. How can a leader apply himself to war when he's suffering the torments of the damned, I ask you, mam'selle?"

I poured him a glass of wine.

"Rest," I told him.

That day, I went out into the streets for the first time since Philippe's return. My carriage was several times held up by marching mobs, bearing red flags and calling for all patriots to prepare themselves for the coming struggle by joining the National Guard. This citizen army—which was to play such a tragic role in the grim months that lay ahead—was made up of volunteer battalions from different parts of the capital. Those from the "smarter" areas, who had the means, provided themselves with colorful uniforms of their own choosing; while those drawn from the poor districts, such as Belleville, made shift with what they were given—which was seldom more than a cap, an ammunition belt, and a gun. The pay was thirty sous a day—not a lot, but a great inducement to the very poor. So it was that the Guard quickly became the refuge of the most wretched— and most dissatisfied—elements of the great city.

I watched them march past, in all their motley rig, all out of step and many of them clearly the worse for the cheap wine which their thirty sous had provided—and I feared for the future of Paris. Rumor had it that the main mass of the Prussian army was not far away, and coming on fast. The roads to the south—to the Loire—were still open, and I yearned to leave the city before it was too late;

before I was shut in with the rest. But I knew that I could never leave Philippe, and he could not be moved in his present state.

That evening, after many fruitless attempts, I managed to compose a letter to the man I loved.

> Hôtel de Brassy,
> Paris
> September 14th, 1870

Dear Count,

I must first tell you the news, both tragic and hopeful, that your nephew Philippe has been gravely wounded, but appears to be on the mend. He is safely in this house and under my care. An hour ago, I managed to secure the services of a doctor, who examined the patient and was able to confirm that the worst of the danger is past. With good nursing, he told me, Philippe should make a complete recovery.

Regarding my own affairs, I have made extensive inquiries, but can find no one who can give me any information about Oliver Craven's whereabouts. It seems clear to me that I may have heard the last of him, and a chapter of my life has now ended.

Every day comes fresh news that the Prussians are closing in on Paris. It may be that this letter will not reach you before we are surrounded. But if it does, I would wish you to know that I shall remain forever grateful for all your many kindnesses. And be assured that Philippe's safe recovery will be my first consideration.

Until we meet again, Count,
I remain,

> Yours very sincerely,
> Tessa Thursday

That letter was dispatched the following morning. Two days later the Prussian army reached the outskirts of Paris in the east and began a giant encircling movement to surround the city and shut it off from all outside help. Before that came to pass, the defenders showed their spirited defiance by counterattacking. In doing so, they unwittingly provided Tessa Thursday, failed actress, with a new vocation. A fresh reason for living.

Shortly after dawn on Monday the 19th, I was awakened by the distant thunder of cannon fire to the south. Hortense, who was watching over Philippe in the bedroom, rushed into my sitting room, where I had just risen from the sofa.

"Heaven help us, mam'selle!" she cried. "The Prussians are here!"

We opened the shutters and looked out, over the treetops of the Champs-Élysées, to where the dawn sky was illuminated with the sparkling red flashes of guns. The sound was like that of a continuous roll of thunder.

"That can't be far away," I said.

"Perhaps they've already broken through the fortifications," said Hortense. "Oh, mam'selle, what are we going to do? What's to become of us?"

"We must wait and see," I told her, with more calmness than I felt. "And whatever happens, no harm will come to us, never fear."

The gunfire continued, with some pauses, well into midmorning. By nine o'clock, rumor was spreading through the streets like brush fire. Our old concierge at the gate house had only to stand at the corner of the faubourg to pick up the latest information as it was passed, by word of mouth, the length and breadth of the city.

The fighting was at Châtillon, we were told. I remembered Châtillon as being on a high point just south of the capital. On a summer's day four years before (it seemed so long ago), Oliver had driven me in his phaeton to the heights of Châtillon, to show me the breathtaking view it commanded of the towers and domes of the distant city, etched clearly in the still air. It appeared that a certain dashing General Ducrot had decided to deny those heights to the Prussians, and was leading an attack upon the enemy. The attack, said rumor, was going well. Victory was well in sight, for were not those splendid fellows the Zouaves spearheading the assault? The Zouaves, red-pantalooned elite of the French army, inspired everyone with confidence. If they were acting as General Ducrot's good right hand, no Prussian would set foot on Châtillon heights.

At midmorning, the gunfire slackened—and the voice of rumor fell strangely silent. At that time I had a visitor: the doctor whom I had previously managed to secure for a brief examination of my patient. His name was Dr. Dupont, and he had formerly had a smart practice in the faubourg but was now attached to the army. He arrived in a military carriage. He looked pale, tired, and distraught, accepted a glass of cognac, and drank it down in one gulp.

"Doctor, what has happened?" I asked him fearfully.

"The attack has been a disaster," he said. "Our fellows are falling back through Montparnasse. Casualties have been very severe. Mam'selle, I call upon your assistance."

I stared at him in astonishment. "I would do anything to help," I told him. "Anything. But of what possible use could I be?"

He gestured about him: to the spacious drawing room, and the vast hallway and chambers beyond. "In the hospitals of the city there is still scarcely room to move for the wounded of Sedan," he said. "This new disaster will break what is left of our fast collapsing medical organization. We must have more helpers, more equipment, more space!"

"Bring some of the wounded here!" He had scarcely finished before the words were out of my mouth. I added, "I know that, if he were here, Count de Brassy would agree to it without hesitation."

A tired smile of relief creased his pale face. "I can get you some helpers," he said. "Volunteer women, a handful of nuns. But you will have to find others for yourself. And we have no sheets or blankets."

"I'll find more helpers," I told him. "And there is enough bed linen here to supply a small army."

"No bandages."

"We'll tear up sheets for bandages." I was possessed with a wild surge of enthusiasm, the like of which I had never before experienced.

"I cannot guarantee that you will have the services of a doctor for days on end," he said. "You will be left to your

237

own devices, with perhaps the assistance of a half-trained medical orderly, if I can spare one."

"We will do the best we can with what we have," I told him.

He took both my hands in his, and there were tears in his eyes when he thanked me.

The wounded started to arrive at the Hôtel de Brassy by the middle of the afternoon. They came in farm carts, in market barrows, in crested carriages; on foot, carried upon the backs of their comrades. Some were already dead when they arrived. More than anything, I was shocked by the youthfulness of most of them. The Zouave regiment, of whom so much had been expected, was composed almost entirely of young recruits. They had received their baptism of fire on the heights of Châtillon, when the Prussian shells fell among them. There were tales of panic and cowardice. Wounded men of other units told bitterly of how the young Zouaves had broken and fled, and how others had followed at the sight of the famous red pantaloons in full flight. Some spoke of betrayal. They were betrayed by their officers, they said. By General Ducrot. By the government—who really had no heart for carrying on the war, and wanted to save their own skins by delivering Paris into the hands of Bismarck, even at the cost of Frenchmen's lives. As I passed among the wounded, who lay in long lines upon the priceless carpets of the mansion, whose blood stained the silk and brocades of the sofas and easy chairs, I learned much about the canker that was savagely gnawing at the heart of defeated France.

With the wounded came our new helpers: a dozen countrywomen from outlying villages abandoned to the enemy, who had volunteered for nursing duties as much for the pay—which was thirty sous a day, like that of the National Guard—as for patriotic motives; also four young novice nuns, who were not of a nursing order, and who looked as if they might faint away with sheer terror if a man so much as glanced at them. Sixteen potential nurses —eighteen, counting Hortense and myself. I next took stock of the staff of the mansion. Most of the menservants were by that time in the army or National Guard. Of those remaining, six were capable of fetching and carrying the patients; the others—the old and infirm—I put to work in the kitchens. And there were six maidservants, all of whom volunteered to nurse.

Twenty-four nurses and six male orderlies. And a kitchen staff, to prepare food round-the-clock for our "guests." There would be no formal meals at the Hôtel de Brassy, not for a long time to come. When that terrible day drew to its close, no less than two hundred and three soldiers who had set out to fight at dawn lay wounded—and in some cases, dying—in the spacious rooms and long corridors of the great house.

That night, Lieutenant Faucher came to say goodbye to me. He had made a good recovery from his head wound and was off to report for duty at the Paris Army Command. He called me a saint, which made me smile, and said that he would come to visit Philippe as often as he was able. I never saw him again. I heard afterward that he had been killed the very first time he went on duty at the fortifications.

After Faucher had gone I took a candle and made the rounds of the makeshift hospital. Only a small minority of the wounded having had any attention—and that of the most rudimentary nature—before arrival, my nursing staff and I had had to tend to them all, the more gravely injured first. By eleven o'clock that night every man had a fresh dressing on his wound and, if he was capable of getting it down, a bowl of nourishing soup inside him. I had sent three-quarters of the staff to bed. The remainder were watching over the long lines of figures lying in the dimness, in a silence that was broken only by the occasional moan of pain and the thin babble of delirium.

In the passage outside the dining room I came upon one of the young novices, whose name was Sister Assunta. The girl was crying. She pointed to a figure at her feet. The soldier's face was covered by his blanket, and she told me, brokenly, that he had just passed away. I comforted her as best as I could; but, remembering how this nervous, sheltered child had worked unflinchingly through the long day, I marveled that her fortitude had carried her thus far.

At the end of my rounds I went to see Philippe. He lay in my four-poster, and a trick of the shifting candlelight made him appear much older, much more like—Robert. I had only to reach out my hand, and it was as if I was smoothing Robert's brow, settling his pillow more comfortably, tucking his arms under the edge of the blanket. And when I stooped to kiss the sleeping forehead, in my make-believe I was also saying good night to that proud, stern master of far-off Brassy, who owned all my heart.

My "hospital" at the Hôtel de Brassy would have ended in a shambles but for the kindness of Mr. Elihu Washburne. Mr. Washburne came to my aid the following day—which was also the day upon which the two arms of the Prussian advance joined hands near Versailles and completed the encirclement of Paris. He was the American Minister, who had courageously elected to remain in the capital when so many members of the foreign diplomatic corps had fled— a tall, fine-looking gentleman with piercing eyes and a mane of hair worn long at the neck. I took to him immediately.

Mr. Washburne, it seemed, knew and liked Count Robert (which naturally commended him to me), and, having heard that the Hôtel de Brassy had opened its doors to wounded soldiers, had come to see if there was any way he could help. My response was to show him round my "hospital" so that he could see for himself where our many shortcomings lay. The Minister said nothing during that grim tour of the mansion, but listened intently as I explained the simple system of accommodation that I had devised: the most severely wounded on the ground floor; the less badly hurt on the upper floors; and a room set aside for "walking cases," which had a door opening out to the garden so that the men could take exercise in the fresh air.

At the end of it, it was obvious that Mr. Washburne was deeply affected by what he had seen. Clearly, what I needed, he told me, was equipment and expert medical aid. He promised to do all he could to provide both of these. We had tea together in my sitting room, and he spoke sadly of happier days he had known in the "City of Light," in the gay and carefree times of Napoleon III's brittle, fatally fragile Third Empire. He had frequently been the guest of the Imperial family at both the Tuileries and the palace of Compiègne, and he treasured valuable pieces of Sèvres china with which he had been presented by his hosts as souvenirs of his visits. And now the disaster of war had swept away all the gaiety, silenced the laughter and the music. And worse was to come, he prophesied: the present government walked upon a knife edge, with the Prussians staring it in the face and Red revolution breathing on its neck. Meanwhile, the people of Paris were gripped by the wildest fancies. This week, he told me, it was spy fever. Would I credit it?—the Anglo-American school which one of his boys attended had been ransacked by National Guards, for no other reason than that someone had reported seeing a pigeon flying out of its garden and heading toward the Prussian lines. Mr. Washburne shook his fine head in despair.

The American Minister's despair, however, did not act as a brake upon his energies. That very day a vanload of medical supplies—of bandages, drugs, instruments—arrived on our doorstep. With it came a tall and gangling young man in a rusty brown frock coat and an over-large hat. In a lazy transatlantic drawl, the newcomer amiably introduced himself to me as Dr. Elmer G. Brewster, of Buffalo—"at your service, ma'am." We had got ourselves a doctor!

Blessedly, Dr. Brewster was able to confirm that Philippe was on the mend. Laconically, he did not put it down to my treatment, but to the patient's strong constitution. The healing process, he said, must have started days before Philippe had been brought to the Hôtel de Brassy—otherwise he would have been dead by then.

Our American doctor speedily brought some order to the chaos caused by our ignorance. He made a reappraisal of the patients' conditions. Those who were in need of surgical treatment he sent to one or another of the city's hospitals—and disarmed all objections by offering to take twice the number of lightly injured patients in exchange. In this way we swiftly increased the population of the Hôtel de Brassy, but with patients who made less demands upon the slender nursing capabilities of the staff. And, naturally, our lightly injured patients were soon able to leave us and return to their soldierly duties. By mid-October we had only twenty remaining, and most of those were walking cases. And it was at this time, to my great joy, that Philippe was able to take his first few, hesitant steps across the bedroom, unaided—an event that inspired me to write again to Count Robert.

Naturally, with the city entirely surrounded, we were quite shut off from news of the outside world, or all but: there were occasional brave or foolhardy souls who came into the city by creeping through the Prussian lines (in later months, when the food shortage became acute, there were even those who, for the wage of a franc a day, were willing to sneak out under cover of darkness and grub up vegetables that lay in the untended fields and gardens between the lines). If incoming news was scarce, however, a constant stream of communication soon began to flow *out* of Paris, and it came about in this manner: someone remembered that there were several aerial balloons in the city. These were taken out, repaired and refurbished, and put to use. I myself saw the first balloon rise above the besieged city—it was during the last week of September— and rise above the Arc de Triomphe on its way south, over the Prussian lines and into the unoccupied provinces. Within days, a postal service by balloon had been set up. To save weight, one had to write the letter on a special form of flimsy paper. On such a form, I briefly informed Count Robert of his nephew's return to health, and con- trived, without actually saying anything of the kind, to convey a fraction of the yearning that I felt for the recipient. That night, I sat up at my window, with its view over the treetops of the Champs-Élysées, and waited for a sight of the balloon that carried my poor, inadequate love letter southward to the Loire. I waited in vain. That night the wind blew from the east, and the balloon—no more than a piece of chaff flying before the fickle wind—left the beleag- uered city in a different direction. And my heart went with it.

242

At the end of October came news that the city of Metz, which had held out against the Prussians for two months, had surrendered, and with it the last of the armies of the Third Empire. Coupled with this tragedy, there was a disastrous attack by the Paris garrison upon the village of Le Bourget, which changed hands, but was recaptured by the Prussians at heavy cost in French lives. As if to add fuel to the flames of discontent in the city, word got round that the government was considering peace terms with the enemy. It was on the morning of Hallowe'en that we were awakened by the sound of military bands and marching men. Led by would-be revolutionaries, certain of the National Guard stormed into the Hôtel de Ville, where General Trochu was holding a Cabinet meeting, leapt upon the conference table, and demanded the election of a new government more to their taste. In the anxious hours that followed, I recalled Mr. Elihu Washburne's dismal prophecy of revolution. On this occasion, General Trochu and his ministers kept their heads, the "Reds" were outmaneuvered, and their ringleaders arrested. But, as events were to prove, the fire of revolution had only been damped down, to burst forth later with renewed fury.

November brought snow, rain, and biting cold. The sort of weather, you would think, when no sane man would willingly perform an unnecessary task out of doors. Yet on a cold, raw day, when the snow on the ground turned to an evil slush that was already freezing in the biting wind, the sort of day when a sensible person would wish to stay by his fireside instead of marching out in the cold to get himself killed, the Paris garrison made its most determined attempt to break out and join with another French army that was believed to be marching up from the south. The venture went by the name of the "Great Sortie," and we were told that it would free France from the invader and wipe out the shame of Sedan.

All one night the cannons roared, and there could not have been a soul who slept in Paris throughout the long dark hours. The early news of the sortie was displayed outside the Hôtel de Ville. It told that General Ducrot's force had crossed the River Marne at Champigny and Bry, which are some six miles east of the city ramparts. What it did not impart, this cruelly optimistic piece of semi-fiction, was that when Ducrot's men came up against the Prussian outposts beyond, they were mown down like ripe corn. Nothing of this reached our ears in the city—for a time. And—just like the Parisians—the early news was treated as a prelude to certain victory. As on so many previous occasions, complete strangers kissed each other in the streets, the "Marseillaise" was sung in cafés and wherever a few were gathered together. And the sound of the guns continued to rumble, day and night, from the east.

On the third night of the Great Sortie an ominous silence fell upon the city. No sound of guns, and a heavy fall of snow cast its blanket of quietness so that it masked even the rumble of carriage wheels along the faubourg. I never heard the coming of my midnight visitor till the strident clang of the doorbell echoed through the mansion. I took a candle and went down the great staircase, a shawl wrapped around my shoulders over my peignoir.

Flambard was there before me. The steward was still fully dressed, save for his neckscarf. His smooth face still bore the day's growth of stubble, and the appraising manner in which his eyes swept over me made me hug the shawl more tightly across my bosom.

"It is Dr. Dupont, mam'selle," he said.

The doctor entered, stamping the snow from his boots and brushing it from the shoulders of his military cape.

"Doctor, what is it?" I asked him.

"Disaster, mam'selle!" he cried. "The sortie has failed and failed tragically. Our fellows lie out there in their thousands, beyond the Marne, the dead with the dying. Mercifully, the Prussians have granted us a twenty-four-hour truce to remove the wounded. You have room here, for some of those stricken souls?"

I gestured about me. "As you see, Doctor, the place is now nearly empty. We have discharged all save a handful."

"Then I beg you to join my convoy of vehicles, which will be setting off from the place de la Concorde within the hour, mam'selle. Bring every carriage you can lay hands on, together with helpers, blankets, bandages, food, and water. There is not a moment to be lost, for we must be over the Marne at the first light of dawn."

"We will be there!" I cried.

I gave my orders to Flambard. At that time there remained four vehicles in the stables of the Hôtel de Brassy: a victoria, two landaus, and a dog-cart—though there were only five horses to serve all four. I decided to take the two landaus for the wounded, with the one-horse dog-cart to carry the supplies and helpers. For helpers, I chose Hortense, one of the strongest and youngest of the footmen, and myself. Word was sent to Dr. Brewster's lodgings for him to hold himself in readiness for our return with the wounded.

We set off into the night, with the snowflakes dazzling in the light of the coach lamps, coachmen hunched up on high, horses' hooves muffled in the whiteness beneath. There were few people about at that hour, though the street lamps burned, and the smart milliners along the faubourg showed new season's hats in their lighted windows.

The center of the great Place was massed with carriages and wagons of all sorts. I espied Dr. Dupont's gaunt figure at the base of the obelisk, surrounded by a group of cloaked officers, who had a large map opened out against the ancient stonework. There seemed to be some difference of opinion about which route we were to take, but it was presently resolved.

Dr. Dupont pointed. "That way! Follow me!" he cried.

Past the Hôtel de Ville, with the twin towers of Notre Dame rising beyond it, we were joined by another line of vehicles coming from the northern part of the city. At the place de la Bastille, center of the great web of streets and boulevards, they came from all directions, till we progressed five abreast. Five abreast and more, we passed through the fortifications of the city, where National Guardsmen stamped their feet against the cold, hugged their long rifles and bayonets close to their chests and blew on their hands. A few of them shouted and waved to us as we clattered through the unbolted gates and over the rough draw-bridges that had been lowered across the trenches. Then we were out into the darkness and the gathering blizzard—where the stricken thousands awaited our coming.

Fort Vincennes came out of the darkness on our right, and we could see the gunners standing up on the ramparts, by the long muzzles of their cannons. They too waved down to us, till the swirling snow squalls shut them from our sight.

Shortly before dawn on the morning of Thursday, December the first, we came in sight of the Marne at Joinville: gray, wind-driven water, swollen with the snow and rains. Two arches of the town bridge had been destroyed and were spanned with a flimsy footbridge, along which we could see lines of figures walking back in our direction, slowly moving silhouettes. A more solid-looking pontoon bridge had been constructed close by, and it was across this that the relief parties were moving. No question of its being strong enough to bear wheeled traffic; we should have to leave our carriages on the west bank and do the remainder of the journey on foot. It was about two miles to the Prussian lines, in front of which lay most of the French casualties.

There was still some sporadic gunfire to the east, but it slackened and ceased as dawn broke. In the dawn light, also, a large white flag bearing the red cross was broken out on the tower of Joinville church. The twenty-four-hour truce had begun.

I cannot attempt to recall all the details of what I saw and experienced during that long and hideous day, for my mind has done an admirable task of blotting out the most harrowing of the memories, as nature has mercifully ordained it should in such circumstances. Two things, however, stay in my mind: the pathetic youthfulness of so many of the poor, wounded creatures who lay in long lines on the riven, frozen ground; that, and the awful sight of the many dead horses that lay scattered over the entire battlefield.

We worked through the day, the three of us, giving what comfort and assistance we could. We disposed of the blankets we carried with us, wrapping them round the seemingly most needy cases and those whose outer clothing had been torn or blown off during the fighting. We gave the food and water we had to the first wretches we came upon who were capable of swallowing it. When that was done, it was simply a matter of helping in the removal of the wounded from the battle area—a task which was to go on till dawn of the following day. We should then return to Paris and the Hôtel de Brassy with—I had reckoned—as many of the lightly and medium-heavily wounded as we could load into our carriages. I had thought about thirty at a pinch. In the event, we took over fifty.

Champigny and beyond, where the worst of the previous two days' fighting had taken place, was a flat and unlovely landscape studded with ruined farm buildings, broken trees, and the tall chimney of a brickworks standing sentinel over silence and desolation. And among it all stalked the groups of helpers, stooping to pick up the wounded, to gather the dead for burial. A few farm carts had been obtained, and it was to these that Hortense, the footman, and I helped the walking wounded and somehow carried those who were beyond walking. Toward sunset it seemed that most of the stricken had been moved. By that time, all unknowingly, we had moved very close to the Prussian outposts.

My first sign of the enemy (strange, how I had come to think of them, the enemies of my adopted country, as my own enemies also) was when I looked round and saw a group of gray-clad figures watching us from the other side of a narrow canal, no more than twenty paces distant, and standing there all unconcerned, some of them smoking long pipes. I could scarcely accept that they were indeed Prussian soldiers; only when I saw that some were wearing the characteristic spiked helmets, and noticed the prevalence of blond whiskers among them, did the full realization dawn upon me. I felt my anger rise. Sickened and embittered by the suffering I had seen, I wanted to shake my fist at them and shout my hatred. But I contented myself by staring.

It was then I saw—*him*.

Unfamiliar in his long gray greatcoat. Hair close-cropped round the sides of his stiff-peaked military cap. Face leaner and paler, and more drawn, than it had been before. The eyes no longer wide and innocent, but narrowed against the chill wind. And looking directly at me.

It was undoubtedly Otto; and I think he recognized me an instant afterward, despite the fact that my head was muffled by a scarf wrapped over the top, hat and all, and knotted under my chin. I saw his eyes widen with sudden surprise; saw his mouth open as if to call out.

But I turned my back on him and walked swiftly away, to where Hortense was trying to assist a weeping boy soldier to his feet.

There was a great gulf between me and the lad I had known as Otto von Stock. And it was wider, deeper, than the dark canal that separated us on the stricken battlefield of Champigny.

Dr. Brewster had things well in hand when we arrived back at the Hôtel de Brassy next morning. He had prepared the dining room as a surgery and had already dealt with a score of cases. The mansion was packed with wounded, directed there by Dr. Dupont's staff. Our additional fifty-odd swelled the total to over three hundred.

"We sure are gonna need some more help," drawled the tall American. He reached out, and with his huge thumb he gently pulled down my lower lid and peered into my right eye. "Miss Tessa," he said, "if you don't get yourself some sleep, lady, you're gonna die right there on your feet."

"I slept a little on the way back," I lied. "Can't we unload some of the worst cases on the city hospitals, like we did last time?"

He shook his head. "Miss Tessa," he said, "they're already packed up. And this is only the beginning . . ." He nodded toward the window, the frame of which was rattling in unison with the sound of heavy gunfire that had been thundering across Paris since just after dawn. "How do you imagine things are gonna be by the end of the day, ma'am?"

I nodded numbly. All the way back to the city, we had

passed long columns of regular soldiers and National Guardsmen marching toward the sound of the guns at Champigny. The Prussians, we had been told, had launched a counterattack immediately on cessation of the truce. The haunted eyes of the men marching into battle had told, more eloquently than any words, that the heart had gone out of the Great Sortie.

"I'll change out of my wet things and help with the bandaging," I told him.

"Miss Tessa, lady, you'd do a whole lot better to get yourself a few hours' sleep," he admonished me.

Up the wide staircase, with wounded men packed tightly, elbow to elbow, at every turning. My own bedroom—vacated by Philippe, who had reported for light duties at the Paris Command and was quartered there—I now shared with Hortense and the four novices, who slept upon camp beds. There was no one in there. Thankfully, I shed my wet outer clothing, took off my boots, and chafed my numb feet into life. The window rattled to the sound of the guns. I crossed over and looked out, sitting on the deeply recessed sill and resting my head against the paneling.

Somewhere out there, beyond the treetops and the gray roofs, Otto von Stock was either still living, or he was newly dead or wounded.

My other cavalier . . .

I should have acknowledged him, if only by a look, a brief gesture of the hand.

His words came back to me, with a new and ever more poignant meaning . . .

"No sorrow, no regrets . . . for anything that may ever pass between us in the future, Tessa."

I closed my eyes, expressing a tear. When I opened them again, it was already nightfall, and I thought—with a sudden start of alarm followed by a crawling dread—that I could have been sitting there in the dark while *she* was watching me from the shadowy garden below.

A providential fog came down and masked the bitter end of the Great Sortie. The full force of the Prussian counterattack had fallen upon the hotchpotch of reserves that

General Ducrot had sent against them. The battle had swiftly become a rout. The French poured back over the Marne pontoons, with the blanketing fog mercifully hiding them from the Prussian sharpshooters. Not for another two days was the full import of the disaster broken to the people of Paris, immediately throwing the capital into the deepest despair; for not only had the Great Sortie failed, but the promised help from the south—the army which was to have joined hands with the victorious Paris force— was also defeated, near Orléans.

In bitterness and despair, Paris faced the stark winter of the new year.

We at the "hospital" of the Hôtel de Brassy were left with our hands too full and our minds too occupied to think of any future beyond the immediate working day. My most pressing worry, after we had managed to sort some order out of the chaos following our new influx of patients, was the question of food. At the opening of the siege, the meadows of the Bois de Boulogne had been stocked with large herds of sheep and cattle; enough, one would have thought, to feed the capital for years. They disappeared well before the end of the year. After November, fresh vegetables were no longer available in the shops. Horsemeat, which had been the cheap meat diet of the city's poor, became the only provender to be seen on the butchers' counters. Horsemeat stew fed our poor wounded soldiers— but only for a short time; by the new year of 1871 there was not a joint to be had in any butcher's shop, and all our carriage horses, save one, had been disposed of.

It was on an afternoon just after Christmas—and I was alone in the bedroom, seated at my dressing table with the housekeeping book before me, puzzling my brain as to how my slender store of provisions was to be stretched to feed so many mouths in the week ahead—that a tap came on the door.

"Come in," I called.

Flambard entered. Neatly dressed as ever, with the air of mingled deference and assurance that was his stock in trade. And something else—something different about him

—struck me as he closed the door behind him and took up a position a respectful three paces from my chair, and stood, head slightly on one side, waiting for my permission to speak. I could have sworn, if I had not known the man better, that Flambard had been drinking.

"What is it?" I asked him.

"It is a matter of some delicacy, mam'selle," he said, clasping his well-manicured hands together and treating me to a suave smile. "A personal matter."

I felt a sudden spasm of irritation. I had no quarrel with the man's efficient running of the household. He obeyed my every command and anticipated many of my wishes; but in all the time that the mansion had been given over to the care of the wounded, I had never once seen him so much as address a kind word to one of the stricken soldiers, smooth a man's blanket or make his pillow more comfortable, spoon a few drops of soup into a thirsty mouth.

"If it isn't too pressing," I said, gesturing toward my housekeeping book, "I would much prefer to listen to your personal matter later, when I've finished."

"Not *my* personal matter, mam'selle," he said. "It is a matter that concerns *you* personally, mam'selle."

"Me?" I stared at him, surprised.

"Just so, mam'selle."

What business, I wondered, could this man possibly have that concerned me personally?

"Then you had better tell me about it," I said. "As briefly as you can, please."

"It is not a matter, mam'selle, that can be dealt with in a few words. It is—a somewhat lengthy matter."

"Then you had better sit down," I told him, pointing to a seat.

He made a self-deprecating gesture. "Oh, no, mam'selle. I know my place, I hope. I am but a servant, and a servant does not sit down in the presence of—the mistress of the house."

I looked keenly at him. There had been the lightest suspicion of a sneer contained in his last remark. Once more it occurred to me that he had been drinking.

251

"Remain standing then," I said coldly. "But please proceed with your—lengthy matter."

Still clasping his hands, Flambard looked up at the ceiling, furrowed his brow as if in remembrance, and began, "I recall to your mind, mam'selle, the circumstances of the day, last September, when you returned to the Hôtel de Brassy with Monsieur the Count."

"The third of September, it was," I replied. "Yes, I remember it well." (And did I not!)

He clucked his tongue against his teeth. "Tch, tch! Indeed it was, mam'selle. The third of September. The black day on which came news of the disaster at Sedan. Ah yes, and you, mam'selle, arrived here with the Count. You came into the drawing room, the Count ordered refreshments. You, mam'selle, sat in the small armchair facing the window. I recall that you had over your shoulders, at the time, the Count's gray coat. Is that no so?"

I felt a slow anger begin to rise within me. That—and something else. A touch of a nameless unease?

"Flambard," I said, "what, pray, is all this leading to?"

His eyes were still directed to the ceiling. His brow still furrowed, as if with a slight puzzlement. "The Count's gray coat," he repeated. "And under it, as I recall, mam'selle, you were wearing a white gown. Is that not so, mam'selle?"

"Yes," I replied.

"A white gown. Well, now, that does not necessarily have a special significance in itself. White is favored by many ladies, for evening and ball gowns. But for a lady to wear a formal gown of white in the middle of the afternoon, one would think—one would suppose . . ."

"It was a wedding gown," I said flatly.

The eyes came down from their regard of the ceiling—by easy stages—to meet mine. And they crinkled with pure pleasure.

"I am honored," he purred, "that mam'selle has made me her confidant."

"You spoke of a personal matter concerning myself," I said coldly. "What else is there?"

"Might I be so bold, mam'selle, as to inquire the name

of the fortunate gentleman?" And, when I did not reply: "Might I hazard a guess at the gentleman's first name? Might it, perhaps, begin with—*O*? And might not the gentleman's second name begin with the letter *C*?—making the initials *O.C.* in all?"

I cried out at him, into that smirking, smooth face, "Why are you interrogating me, Flambard—why? What right have you to torment me like this?"

The mask was down, then, from that smooth face. The eyes were suddenly hard, calculating. The curved lips set in a tight line.

"You must want to know what happened to your missing bridegroom-to-be, mam'selle. Well, I can tell you. I can take you to him—discreetly. You can see him without being seen by him. Now. Tonight. What do you think of that, hein?"

Flambard did not want money; he made that quite clear. Not that I had any, as he must have known very well. His was the hand that drew any cash that was needed, for the running of the establishment, from the Count's bank in the rue Royale. All he wished, he told me, was to place himself in a position of credit in my estimation. I had no inkling of what he might have meant by that phrase, but it filled me with a certain unease.

It was after dark when we drove out of the courtyard in the dog-cart, which was drawn by the last of the horses—a skinny and run-down creature, for hay had been unobtainable since the beginning of the siege. Flambard drove, and we traveled in silence. He had given me no inkling of our destination, but it proved to be in the direction of the Left Bank. We crossed the Seine and were soon in the maze of narrow streets beyond the military academy, in the heart of Bohemian Paris, the haunt of artists, writers, and intellectuals. Coming at length to a cul-de-sac lit only by a single guttering gas lamp, Flambard drew rein and nodded in the direction of a dark archway close at hand. From its mysterious depths came the sound of many voices raised in raucous song.

"We are here, mam'selle," he informed me.

He handed me down, and I drew my shawl more tightly about my shoulders, fearful and apprehensive of the coming encounter. Was it possible, I asked myself, that the steward of the Hôtel de Brassy had indeed located my missing fiancé? And, if so, how had he managed to do this? And what was Oliver Craven, the former idol of the Parisian stage, doing with himself in such a place as we were now entering?

It was a low cabaret of the type favored by Parisian workmen, poor students, impoverished artists, and the like. In Paris's violent past—as in the present—such places were hotbeds of revolutionary activity. We descended a steep flight of steps that were lit by a tallow dip stuck into a bracket on the damp brickwook of the wall, and were met at the bottom by the smell of tobacco and crowded humanity. We were also met by a wry-necked dwarf of truly hideous appearance, who greeted Flambard and gestured toward a door at the rear of the cellar.

"This way, m'sieur," he hissed.

The cellar was packed with dark figures, all seated at rough tables, their backs toward us. Up on a small stage at the far end, a blowsy woman was leading the audience in song. Limelight picked out the stark paint that lined her eyes and lips. The song was familiar to me: I recognized it as one of the revolutionary tunes much favored by the tatterdemalion National Guard battalions of Belleville and St.-Antoine.

"After you, mam'selle," murmured Flambard in my ear. The dwarf was leading the way through the door. I followed.

A narrow, steep staircase brought us to a small room that was entirely empty of furniture. There was a candle set into a niche in the wall, and its light showed the place to have the appearance of a monk's cell. I looked about me in dismay and some apprehension.

"You have not long to wait, m'sieur," whispered the dwarf. "I will leave you." He bobbed his head, grinned wildly at us both, and sped swiftly back down the stairs.

I looked at Flambard. "What now?" I demanded.

As clearly as if it had been in the next room, we could still hear men's voices raised in song, with the woman's shrill counterpoint soaring above them.

"Watch this, mam'selle," said Flambard, smiling.

He crossed to the wall opposite, where there was a wooden shutter, like a blind window. This he partly opened, and gestured to me to look. I did so. We were indeed in the next room to the cellar, but above it and looking down from ceiling height. Directly below us, and presented to us in profile, was the singer, who had finished her piece and was taking a bow before her enthusiastic audience. They thudded beer mugs upon the rough tabletops and called for more. She responded by blowing a kiss and, flicking up the hem of her skirts to show a button-booted ankle, went off the bare stage to a roar of appreciation.

I felt my nerves grow taut, and my fingernails were driven hard against my palms.

There was silence in the cellar below. By the flickering light of candles stuck in bottletops, half a hundred faces were gazing expectantly toward the empty stage.

After a time, someone called out, "Why are we waiting, then? Bring on the clown!"

"Bring on that clown!"

He came out onto the stage, and I knew him at once, despite the clownish motley: the white face, the cherry-red nose, the diamond-painted eyes. And all that could not conceal the ruination that had taken place in Oliver Craven. All the paint in the world could not have made up for the life that had gone out of those once-brilliant eyes, nor hide the sickness in the face, with its skin tautly stretched across the too-prominent cheekbones. Numb with compassion and horror, I gazed down upon the wreckage of the man who had come into my life all those years before and changed me utterly.

Then the audience began to laugh at him, but not out of good humor: mocking, contemptuous laughter, as the former idol of the Paris stage began to dance, a graceless, shuffling dance, to the tune of a penny whistle coming from somewhere in the wings. And it was painfully obvious, from his unsteady movements, that the clown was far gone in drink.

Soon they grew tired of baiting him with their laughter. And they began to throw things. It was then I had to close the shutter and press my forehead against it, so that my companion should not see all of my hurt.

3

"How did you come to find him there—how?"

I flung the question at Flambard when we arrived back at the Hôtel de Brassy, not having spoken all the way, but having sat in a dazed silence, my very thoughts cauterized by shock.

"Mam'selle," he replied, "I have certain—connections. By one means and another, I happen to know much of what goes on in the city."

It came back to me then: how Oliver himself had once suggested that Flambard might be a police spy.

"What—what else do you know of him?" I whispered.

Flambard hunched his shoulders. "There is not much to tell, mam'selle. As you are aware, Mr. Craven disappeared with the news of the Sedan disaster. At first, they—that is, the authorities—assumed that he had fled the city with the rest of his company, for England. At the beginning of December, however, a vagrant was picked up during a routine police search following an anti-government riot in Belleville. This man—half-starved and ruined with drink—refused to give his name, but his accent betrayed him as an Englishman. Because no charge could be laid against him, he was released after a night in the cells. But the police continued to retain an interest in this Englishman."

"Are you—a member of the police, Flambard?" I asked him quietly.

The shifty eyes flared slightly at my challenge; then he gave a smooth, practiced smile. "You are probing me, mam'selle," he said, mockingly chiding. "Suffice to say that, as I told you before, I have certain—connections. For this reason, I became aware of the vagrant Englishman. I learned that he had taken up employment as a mime at a cabaret in the Bohemian district—a well-known haunt of Reds and malcontents. Some imp of curiosity prompted me to go and witness the performance of this English mime, and I did so yesterday evening. I went. I saw. I recognized. The rest you know, mam'selle."

"Is anyone else aware of who he is?" I murmured.

Flambard shook his head. "No one but you and I, mam'selle," he said. His sleek face was all guile. "And the fact that the former star of the Théâtre des Comédiens has taken to drink and fallen upon evil times is of no real interest to the police, so they will not learn it from my lips. The secret is ours, mam'selle. Yours and mine."

"Why are you doing this, Flambard?" I asked him.

"But, mam'selle, did I not tell you before?" he cried. "It is my earnest wish to put myself in credit in your estimation."

And what, I still wondered, did he mean by that?

There was nothing I could do. I racked my brains for ideas, but no sort of action made sense. I suppose I could have obtained money—Robert de Brassy's money—and sent it, anonymously of course, to Oliver. But my conscience would not bring itself to do anything of the sort, though I was sure that Robert would have approved under the circumstances. And, I reasoned, what good would it do, if Oliver spent the money on drink, the further to ruin himself?

Go and see him? Confront my former fiancé? I shrank from the prospect. One thing I knew of Oliver Craven: however low he might have fallen, the knowledge that I had seen him in his present state—had been there when that jeering crowd had pelted him with beer slops and bread crusts—would have finished him forever.

There was nothing—nothing on earth—that I could do for him. To leave him alone was the greatest kindness I could perform.

That decided, I threw myself into the work of my "hospital."

The victims of the Great Sortie who had been brought to the Hôtel de Brassy fell into three groups: those who had died of their wounds; those who had recovered and been discharged; and those who still remained. The latter group, numbering nearly a hundred, were the gravely wounded, amputees, young soldiers driven half out of their minds with the horror of their experiences. All of them sorely in need of care; and, in view of the rapidly deteriorating situation in the beleaguered city, gravely lacking that care.

Food, by January of 1871, was unobtainable in any quantity. Moreover, the prices of what still remained had risen astronomically, with butter increased from 4 francs to 35 francs a pound, eggs from 1.80 francs to 24 francs a dozen—and hardly ever to be seen, at that. There was some talk of rats being eaten, though I never saw anything of it. Cats and dogs were certainly added to the diet of the Parisians, and priced at around 6 francs a pound. I could not bring myself to touch them, or to provide them for my poor soldiers. Happily, there was no shortage of money at the Hôtel de Brassy: Flambard drew as much as we needed from the bank. Such rationing as existed was rationing by price, and I was glad that our patients benefited; but it filled me with dread to think of the poor people of the teeming slum areas of Belleville and St.-Antoine, where starvation and disease were providing such a ready breeding ground for violent revolution.

The obtaining of sufficient food, then, was my greatest problem. In this I was greatly assisted by my good friend Mr. Washburne, but for whose generosity even the bottomless De Brassy purse would not have availed us. One day the American Minister himself called to see me with an outsize basket, in which reposed a large and soggy package. It was, he explained, a supply of meat "for your poor soldiers, ma'am." By persistent questioning, I learned the truth of the matter. For some months, certain of the animals at the Paris Zoo had been put down, either because there was no food available for them, or for themselves to provide butcher's meat. That day the newspapers had been full of the dispatch, by gunfire, of the zoo's greatest pride, two elephants named Castor and Pollux. Their trunks were available to the well-to-do at the ridiculously inflated price of 40 francs a pound. And Mr. Washburne had dipped deeply into his own pocket to provide enough elephant trunk to make nourishing soup for three days' meals for my poor soldiers. Thanking him from the bottom of my heart, I quenched a feeling of queasiness—and turned the basket over to our cook.

That same week—on January 5th—the Prussian shells began to fall upon Paris, providing a hideous background to the misery of near-starvation, disease, and despair which were slowly and inexorably squeezing the life from the former City of Light.

It had begun some weeks earlier, with the bombarding of Avron, to the east of Paris. On the 5th, the enemy shells were directed into the very heart of the city, mainly on the Left Bank, in Montparnasse and around the Luxembourg Palace. The church of St.-Sulpice was hit, as was the Odéon theater and the Salpêtrière hospital. Within days there began a mass movement of people from the Left Bank: a stream of frightened refugees crossing the Seine bridges to get away from the hail of explosive death that poured down at the rate of three to four hundred times a day. We opened the doors of the Hôtel de Brassy to over fifty of these unfortunates. Yet more mouths to feed. And more frozen bodies to make warm—for the bitter winter weather, added to the desperate shortage of fuel, had laid yet another intolerable burden upon the people of the besieged city. Everywhere, one saw hordes of fuel scavengers—mostly poor folk, men, women, and little ones—hacking away at the very bark and branches of the trees; ripping up wooden fencing; making off with anything that would burn. The tall and elegant cypresses in the garden of the Hôtel de Brassy had long since been chopped down to provide warmth for its inmates.

I was brooding on all this, and considering the prospect of ordering the elegant paneling to be removed from the interior walls and used for firewood, when Philippe came to see me. One glance at his face, and I knew that something very much out of the ordinary had befallen him. And I was right.

"I have just seen Otto, Tessa!" he cried. "Less than half an hour ago. And I spoke with him!"

Philippe, newly recovered from his grave wound, had been appointed aide-de-camp to General Ducrot, commander-in-chief of the Paris garrison. In that capacity, he was close to the center of things. Still too weak to take his place in the firing line (which he would have much preferred), he accompanied his general everywhere: on tours of inspection of the fortifications; to interminable government conferences, from which, white-faced and drawn with fatigue, he would sometimes return in the early hours to the Hôtel de Brassy for a hot drink. And on that day, he had been present at a secret meeting between his chief and a delegation of Prussian officers who had come to parley.

"Otto was with them!" The excitement brought two vivid spots of redness on his cheekbones, startling against his pallor. "We recognized each other at once, of course. And here's something for you, Tessa. He saw you that day—the day you went out to collect the wounded."

"He told you that?"

"We had the opportunity for a few words together." There was a suppressed excitement in his voice. "Tessa, do you know that he made a special point of volunteering for this delegation—in order to have an opportunity to see you?"

"To see me?" I cried. "But—how could he possibly arrange that?"

"The Prussian delegation is still in Paris," said Philippe. "Under conditions of the greatest secrecy, in a house at Auteuil, where they are guarded only by trusted officers of Ducrot's staff."

"But why all the secrecy?" I asked him.

Philippe crossed to the door, opened it, and looked out. Only then did he answer me, and in low tones. "Tessa, there is a move afoot to make peace with the Prussians. If the Reds had the slightest suspicion of it, they would denounce the government for a pack of traitors and take over Paris by force. Oh, they could do it: the majority of the National Guard is seething with discontent and ripe for mutiny. Because of this, the peace negotiations are being conducted under a blanket of total secrecy. The Prussians are in civilian clothes, and they are seen by no one but picked members of the government and Ducrot's staff. And now you, Tessa, are a party to that secret."

"Why me?" I cried. "Why do you tell me all this, Philippe?"

"Because," he replied, "you are going to see Otto. At his earnest—I should say desperate—request. He has asked me to smuggle him here, tonight, from Auteuil."

"Here? To see *me*? But—why? Why should he go to all that risk—that danger?"

"He has something to tell you, Tessa," replied Philippe. "He didn't confide in me precisely what. But he said to me, Tessa, that he had to speak to you—*for he had the answer to the riddle of your half-thaler!*"

Nighttime in the great house. I was in the garden room, which was the room that had doors opening out onto the terrace, and a view of the fountain, now silent and covered with a glistening skin of ice. There was also ice on the surface of the terrace. I shivered and drew my shawl more closely about my shoulders. A small log of wood burned fitfully in the large open fireplace—my pitiful gesture of welcome for my expected visitors.

I glanced at the clock on the chimney piece; ten minutes to midnight. The poodle Sasha stirred at my feet and went back to sleep again.

Not a sound in the great house. The inmates—patients and refugees—would all be lying snug within their blankets. Thank heaven we had blankets enough for all of them. Tomorrow, I decided, I must go shopping for more meat. The sack of moldy potatoes that I had bought at Christmas from a street market at Issy—for a sum which, in happier times, would have amply paid for one of Mr. Worth's most exotic creations—were all but gone. There were no other vegetables to be had. And scarcely any meat. Even dog and cat had become priced beyond the means of ordinary folk, and were served in the gourmet restaurants and in the Jockey Club, smothered in fine sauces, to mask the taste. Yes, I would decidedly quench my revulsion and buy cat or dog—if any was available . . .

I gave a start to hear a footstep on the terrace outside. Sasha sat up and growled.

A moment later, two tall figures loomed into my view, and Philippe's face stared in at me briefly as his hand was laid upon the latch of the glass-fronted door. The opening of the door brought a rush of cold air that threatened to extinguish my candle, so I shielded the flame with my hand, which had the effect of throwing my visitors in deep shadow. When I took my hand away, the light fell directly upon Otto's face.

"Hello, Tessa," he murmured.

"Hello, Otto."

He was much changed. More so than Philippe, even allowing for the ravages of the latter's wound. Lean-faced as a hawk, and hardened by the years between. Even the eyes had changed: they stared out at me narrowly, blue as cut sapphires in the candlelight. From the corner of his right eye, a livid duelling scar scored his cheek to the angle of his jaw. He smiled—and he was Otto again.

"Du bist wie eine Blume."

"Please, Otto. No," I entreated. "You'll make me cry, and I was so determined not to cry. Oh, you look so thin. Both of you look so thin. Why do you men have to make war? Where's the sense in it?" I fumbled in my reticule for my handkerchief.

A distant rumble of gunfire rattled the window frames.

"I think we should close the shutters now," said Philippe. "It is hardly likely that we should be spied upon, but Otto would face a court-martial—and worse—if news of this venture reached the ears of his superiors."

"And what of you, my friend?" commented the other dryly. "I much doubt if your part in tonight's business would greatly advance your military career, if it came out."

"Neither of you should be here," I told them firmly. "I don't need you to tell me that you are both putting yourselves in considerable peril for my sake."

Philippe turned from closing the shutters. His face was grave in the candlelight.

"Concerning the confidential matter mentioned," he said. "You will naturally wish me to leave you alone with Otto while he speaks to you about it." And he made to leave the room.

I checked him with a gesture of my hand. "No, Philippe," I said. "We've known each other for long enough, we three. There should be no secrets between us, particularly since you're risking so much for me tonight." I turned. "Otto, I understand that you are able to throw some light on—the secret of my birth?"

He nodded gravely. "Yes, Tessa."

"Then please proceed," I asked him. "And sit down, do, both of you."

Otto took his place in an armchair before me. He was wearing a broadcloth frock coat of dark blue, and he looked—save for the brutally cropped hair and the scar on his cheek—every inch an English gentleman. His hands, lean and capable, toyed briefly with the poodle's head, and Sasha cast him an adoring, upward glance.

"It began, Tessa," he said, "in Sedan. I was with my regiment, the Third Uhlans. We spearheaded the attacks at Wörth, at Spicheren, at Gravelotte, and St.-Privat. Oh, they gave us hell, these French." He glanced at his old friend, a glance composed of bitterness mingled with grudging admiration. "At Gravelotte, they caught our cavalry in a trap. From that death-ride, my regiment emerged with only twenty lances. I was summoned to the headquarters of General von Moltke, who asked to hear my version of the action. After that, he pinned an Iron Cross to my tunic and told me he was decorating the whole of the Third Uhlans, alive and dead. He then commended me to Count Bismarck, who appointed me his aide-de-camp." He gave a short, bitter laugh. "They considered, you see, that the Third Uhlans had done enough. So I spent my time riding behind Count Bismarck's big bay mare with the two white socks. Oh, how I came to know, so well, the back of Count Bismarck's neck."

Philippe had quietly crossed to the cabinet and poured three glasses of cognac. He placed mine on a side table and it remained untouched. Otto refreshed himself with a swallow.

"So you were at Sedan?" asked Philippe. "At the capitulation."

Otto said, "It was late in the afternoon. Count Bismarck had lunched long and late, as is his habit, even in the field. I remember there was goose with olives, Reinfeld ham, and Varzin wild boar. And more captured French wine than you would believe. The entire staff rose from table with no more ability to conduct the war than a pack of children in a kindergarten. All save Count Bismarck—he was as incisive as ever. Luncheon over, he rode toward Sedan, with me following.

"As I have said, Tessa, it was late afternoon. Bismarck did not quicken his mare's pace when we saw the carriage ahead of us. It was halted in a lane. An open landau it was, with a liveried coachman, escorted by a troop of our guardsmen. And in the coach, the Emperor of the French."

"Napoleon!" cried Philippe. "You were actually present at the surrender of that fraud, that mountebank?"

"I never saw a man look so ill," said Otto. "He was in such pain, I was told that he could hardly sit a horse. Yet he had remained for two hours in the shellfire before Sedan, while his officers were being killed all round him. I know those who saw him. Bismarck, who knows the quality of men, treated him with the greatest respect and consideration."

Otto took another draft of his cognac, and Philippe refilled his glass. I, who had been listening to his account with interest and growing impatience, found myself drumming with my fingers on the edge of the table. If only, I thought, he would bring that—admittedly engrossing— account to a close, and come to the matter that concerned myself.

265

At that moment, Sasha stiffened and gave a growl. Our eyes followed the direction of his: to the window.

"Is that someone outside?" said Philippe, crossing to the window and part opening the shutters. "I don't think so. I see no one. Calm down, Sasha."

The dog sat back on his haunches and licked his lips.

"To resume," said Otto. "As a fluent French speaker, I was delegated to attend the Emperor and his staff. They were a pleasant enough lot. The generals mostly self-indulgent and thoroughly woebegone, as you might expect. Wherever we went in the presence of surrendered French soldiers, they were hissed at and booed by their own men. The Emperor particularly. He bore it with great fortitude, though I saw him weep once. You look at me with impatience, Tessa. I will be brief with the next part . . .

"It was in view of this—because of the Emperor's health, the pain he was in, and his low spirits—that Count Bismarck gave me the task of ensuring that he did not have the means wherewith to end his life. A dagger, you understand, or a vial of poison secreted about his person. It was stealthily done. At a nearby château, we obtained for him a bath. While he was taking it, I searched the Emperor's clothes and belongings. As I told you, Tessa, I will be brief. I trust that the brevity will not come too harshly, with too much of a shock.

"In the Emperor's wallet, discreetly hidden from all eyes, I found . . . *this*."

He was holding something in his hand that revolved on the end of a silver chain; winking, winking in the candlelight, till it was still. Then I saw that it was a half-thaler, and the mate to my own.

With trembling fingers, I took it from him; took the pendant from my own neck, and placed the two together.

They joined closely, smoothly. For they had once been one.

"Impossible! It's impossible!" I cried.

"Some logical explanation will present itself," said Philippe soothingly. "It cannot be the first time a coin has been cut in half to make a keepsake. They are from two different thalers."

Wordlessly, I passed both halves over to him, watched the expression of realization pass over his face when he put them together again.

"Tessa, my dear," said Otto. "I have had time to consider this. Will you listen to me? I will give you what evidence I have, and you must then make up your own mind."

"They are two halves of the same coin," murmured Philippe in an awed voice. "Even to the slight irregularities of the cut. The same!"

"Please, Otto," I cried appealingly.

Otto had a piece of paper in his hand, and I could see that it was covered in his own tight handwriting and figures. At the top of it was a date: 1847—the year in which, on a February night, Oliver Craven had laid me on the doorstep of Penruth Workhouse, on the date that passed for my "birthday."

"Twenty-five years ago," said Otto, "he was known as Louis Napoleon. A dashing man in his late thirties. A man with a star that led him on, invested him with a strange and powerful attraction. A man determined, by any means, to claim his uncle's throne and be emperor of the French. For this the French imprisoned him. In the early summer of 1846, he escaped from prison, disguised as a laborer. And—not for the first time, for of all places on earth he loved it next to France—he went to England, to London."

"No!" I cried. "No!"

The summer of 'forty-six. It all came back to me. As Oliver had told me. They were playing at a third-rate theater near London . . .

"He was not there for long," said Otto. "Little more than eighteen months later, a revolution in France set in motion a chain of events which was to carry Louis Napoleon to his destiny."

Jeanette Dupuis would not reveal the name of the father. There was no question of marriage—the man had abandoned her . . .

"You make a convincing case, Otto," said Philippe.

"Certainly the dates fit. But what else? Tessa has never confided in us about her mother. The question of whether she may have met Louis Napoleon and become his mistress must surely rest upon the character of the lady herself . . ." He glanced questioningly at me. They both looked at me.

I took a deep breath, and said, "I think—I believe—that you have found my father, Otto."

"My dear . . ." Otto leapt to his feet, crossed over to me, knelt and took my hands in his. "I wrestled with my conscience on this matter, Tessa. Undecided whether I should tell you."

"I'm glad you did, my dear," I said. "But tell me one thing else: did he—the Emperor—discover that you had taken the half-thaler? And, if so, what explanation did you give?"

"I said nothing of it," replied Otto. "Neither to the Emperor, nor to anyone else. I merely—appropriated it. The spoils of war. That same evening I saw him for the last time, and he made no mention of his loss, so I assume that he was not in the habit of regularly taking the pendant from his wallet. Next morning, he was escorted on his way to Prussia. When he discovers the loss—as indeed he must, sooner or later—he will scarcely connect it with me."

In the silence that followed, the clock on the chimney piece thinly tinkled the hour of one. Philippe stirred and rose to his feet. "Tessa, we must leave," he said. "We have a covered carriage waiting in a cul-de-sac off the faubourg. Every minute we stay here increases the chances of Otto being missed at Auteuil. If we are delayed during the return journey, it might prove fatal."

"You must hurry!" I cried. "I'm grateful to you both for what you've done tonight."

Otto took my proffered hands in his. His deep blue eyes —no longer shy as they had been in youth, but wise and watchful—looked into mine. "Are you truly glad, Tessa?" he asked.

I nodded. "I promise you," I told him.

"Good night, Tessa," said Philippe. "If these peace talks

are successful—and pray God they will be—I shall be bringing you the good news in a few days. Till then."

"Good night, Philippe." I kissed his cheek.

"Till we meet again, dear Tessa," said Otto. *"Auf Wiedersehen."*

"Till we meet again, Otto." I kissed him.

"You will remember what I once said?" he asked me.

" 'There must be no sorrow, or regrets, for anything that passes between us, now and in the future,' " I replied, repeating his words as well as I could remember them. "You must have foreseen that war would come and set us apart, the three of us."

He nodded. "What we had, we three, was too perfect: a long summer's idyll that had to end in night, or storm. Cruel Fate is jealous of perfection."

The three of us joined hands, briefly. Then they were gone. Out into the freezing night. I heard their soft footfalls fade away across the garden.

I sat and watched the sullen flames slowly devour the log in the fireplace, till, with the coming of the late winter's dawn, it was only a heap of charred embers. And in the long hours, I had decided what I must do.

Morning brought the distant rumble of guns from the south. I listened to them as I stood watching and waiting, while the sole remaining coachman of the Hôtel de Brassy harnessed our pathetic horse to the dog-cart. The man was sulky and close to disobedience, for I had told him that we were going to the Left Bank, and that if he was frightened to go, I would make the best job I could of driving the dog-cart myself.

We left shortly after nine. National Guards lolling at the end of the Concorde bridge warned us that shells had already landed, so early that morning, in the Montparnasse cemetery. Even the dead, they said, were not safe from the accursed Prussians, so what hope for the living? Death to the Prussians, they cried. Let the government give the order for the lads of the National Guard to march out, and they would end the siege. By their unkempt appearance, I recognized them as men from one of the "Red" battalions. At that early hour, they were clearly the worse for drink. I ordered my coachman to drive on, which he did with a great show of reluctance.

The streets of the Left Bank were all but deserted: only the occasional forlorn figure, wrapped in rags against the freezing cold, padded out with scraps of newspaper, dragging a piece of firewood perhaps, or hugging a bundle of something—presumably edible—that might have been the product of a night's foraging. We passed close by the Champ-de-Mars, scene of the triumph of the Great Exhibition. Could it have been only four years ago when Paris was Queen of the World? The change in her now!

Beyond the military academy, we saw and heard our first shell: a cloud of dust and smoke rising high above the rooftops to the south, followed by the rumble of the explosion. Our horse snickered with terror and reared up. My driver flashed me a wide-eyed, appealing glance when I ordered him to carry on. We were getting close to our destination.

Though the possessor of a good sense of direction, I had some difficulty in identifying the cul-de-sac to which Flambard had brought me. The surroundings looked different—and even more sordid and dilapidated—in the daylight. But, by trial and error, I led us to the dark archway with the lantern above it. And there was also a roughly printed poster stuck on the wall, describing the delights of the cabaret within: the singers, the versifiers, the jugglers, the clowns. Next to it was a glaring red poster calling for the government to be replaced by what was described as a "commune," and for the National Guard to be sent out against the enemy.

"Wait here," I told the coachman.

Daylight showed my way down the steps, and I was suddenly nauseated by the reek of stale tobacco. Inside the cellar, stools were upturned on tables; and the wry-necked dwarf was sweeping a line of sawdust across the stone floor, whistling to himself between his teeth the while. He paused when he saw me, head on one side, little eyes taking me in from bonnet to hem.

"Where is the clown?" I asked him. "The Englishman. I want to see him."

"I was not paid for last time," replied the dwarf. "The man said I would be paid, but he never gave me a sou."

I had a small amount of money in my reticule. I took out a five-franc piece and held it out to him. The dwarf approached me with disturbing alacrity, snatched the coin, tested it between his broken and discolored teeth.

"Where is he, the Englishman?" I repeated.

The dwarf jerked his head for me to follow him, setting off toward the stage; scrambling up there and leaving me to mount it as best I could. He was waiting for me in the narrow wings. There he pointed to a door close by.

"He's in there."

My guide went back the way he had come. Moments later I heard the sound of his sweeping brush on the stone floor. By then I had decided not to knock on the door, but to go straight in. I did so.

The room was lit by daylight coming in through a begrimed basement window, high up. The sole furnishing was an iron bedstead set under the window. On it, partly covered by a tumbled pile of old gray blankets, was Oliver Craven. He was lying on his back, one arm pillowed behind his head. His eyes were open—and looking straight at me.

"Well, what a surprise," came his familiar, deep, actor's voice. "If it isn't little Tessa Thursday."

From afar there came the heavy rumble of a shellburst, and a flake of grimy plaster detached itself from the ceiling and drifted to the stone floor. The man in the bed—he was fully dressed in the rough garb of a Paris workman—reached under where he was lying and took out a black bottle, removed the cork with his teeth, and blew it across the room.

"Drink?" He held out the bottle to me, and when I made no answer, he put it to his lips and tossed back his head.

Freed of the merciful mask of the clown, Oliver Craven's face was revealed to me in all its ruination, with the sum of his self-destruction written large: the sick pallor, the wasted flesh, eyes sunk deeply in darkened sockets; and of his former dark mane of hair nothing remained but a vestige of the widow's peak and a few lank gray strands lying across a wrinkled cranium. It was the head of an old, ill man.

The lackluster eyes were still watchful. He lowered the bottle and smiled.

"I see you are making a sum of my decrepitude, dear Tessa," he said with a touch of mockery. "The decline is not *quite* so dramatically sudden as you might think. For instance, I have worn a transformation—the unkind would call it a wig—ever since you have known me. And I have held at bay the ravages of my advancing years with the aid of my consummate skill at the art of make-up. All that, however, is now behind me. I no longer avail myself of the artifices of the *toilette*. Add to that, I have been ill. Very, very ill. " He took another long draft from the black bottle.

At last I found my voice.

"I have come to tell you, Oliver," I said, "that I now know the identity of my father."

The black bottle was lowered from his lips.

"Do you, by gad?" he exclaimed with genuine amazement. "Do you, now?"

"The reason I have come to see you," I went on, "is that I think you have known who he is all along. I believe, furthermore, that you have deliberately deceived me all these years. And to suit your own ends. But I can't for the life of me understand why. Why did you do it, Oliver— why?" My voice broke off in a cry. It was counterpointed by another distant shellburst.

He rose from his bed. Unsteadily. Carefully laid the bottle on the floor, and walked slowly across the narrow room. At the far end, he turned and regarded me.

And he said: "My father was a London crossing-sweeper, a worthless fellow who kept eleven children on the verge of starvation by clearing away a small area of accumulated mud and filth, hard by Charing Cross Station, so that fine ladies should not soil their hems, nor fine gentlemen their dove-gray spats, while crossing the road. Six days a week he labored, as the Bible instructs us, and on the seventh day he went fishing in the Thames. Have you ever tasted Thames chub or roach, Tessa? Not a gastronomic revelation, I assure you—being coarse, full of small bones, and tasting of the river. But Thames chub and roach provided the only decent meals I ate for the first ten years of my life. At the age of ten, I ran away from home and joined a traveling troupe of mummers."

I felt compassion for him. "Oliver . . ." I began.

He said, "By heaven, Tessa. Can you ask why I deceived you? Do you know—do you *really* know—what a prize you offered?" He threw up his arms and stalked the length of the narrow room and back again, gesticulating all the time and muttering to himself. Facing me again, he pointed straight at me.

"You are a Bonaparte!" he cried.

"Oliver! I . . ."

"The first Napoleon," he cried. "You know, do you not, what he did for his family? Made them dukes and princes! Kings, even! If the uncle would do that, why not the nephew? What would he not do for his only daughter— even if she were a natural daughter, a love child?

"And what of the husband—your husband? A dukedom for certain, perhaps the title of prince. And some tremendous state appointment, at some discreet remove from metropolitan France, of course, in view of the delicate nature of your relationship to the Emperor. Governor-general of a North African province, or of Madagascar, perhaps. Picture it, Tessa—to have been lord of all I surveyed, in a private Xanadu devised by the great Emperor Napoleon for the consort of his beloved daughter!"

I recoiled from him; from the strange and disturbing light in those sunken eyes. "You're insane!" I cried. "Insane!"

"Not insane, my dear Tessa." He smiled, with something of the old, self-mocking wryness that had always been so much a part of his stock in trade, part of his disarming

273

charm. "Rather, I am—or I was—obsessed, you could call it *possessed,* by this dream of splendor. For what you do not know about me is this, Tessa: great artiste I may have been in my time; but, above all, I was also a tremendous snob! How do you like that, eh?" And he was convulsed in a paroxysm of laughter that ended in breathless choking, so that he had to lean against the wall, racked with coughs and gasping for breath. And all the while I stared at him, slowly comprehending, but with my mind still in a turmoil.

I waited till he had composed himself, and then I said, "You would have married me for that—for a title and position?"

But he was not listening to me. His brain had taken another turn of thought. The eyes, now narrowed, peered this way and that, in a fury.

"Emperor of the French!" he grated. "By heaven, I hitched my wagon to a fine star! Twenty-four years I had that dream, and not a day passed without the glory of it filling my life. And all destroyed in a night. In a night!

"I believed in him, Tessa—in that Imperial sire of yours, even when others doubted. Even at Sedan, I believed the stories about his grand strategy. When we had the first news of the disaster—it came during the evening performance at the theater, and the house emptied immediately—I still believed that there must be some mistake, that my future father-in-law, like his mighty uncle before him, was too great a commander to be taken so easily. I pleaded with the company to stay, even while they were throwing their things into hired carriages and making for the station.

"Then there was this officer. A captain of artillery, wounded in the early days of the war. Stage-door hanger-on and a friend of one of the girls of the company. I told him everything would come right and that the Emperor would win the last battle. He laughed in my face.

"I heard the whole of it then, Tessa, from his lips: the muddle and the delay; the cowardice and incompetence of the generals; the lack of any real plan. The inevitability of defeat.

"That night, Tessa, when my twenty-four-year-old dream crumbled to dust in the smoke of Sedan, I went into a café close by the theater and drank cognac.

"I have been drinking cognac—give or take a few hours here and a few hours there, when I slip into sleep or unconsciousness—ever since!"

He finished his declaration—as if symbolically—by picking up the black bottle and draining it.

I said, "So you put me into the workhouse, knowing all the time that you meant to bring me out, to talk me into marrying you one day."

"My father," he said, "a dull fellow, the amateur fisherman, had what he called a 'keep-net,' which was a large net where he stored live fish till such a time as he needed them. I looked upon Penruth Workhouse, my dear Tessa, as the keep-net in which I stored you, my little fish, till you were ready for me."

"And all the talk about my becoming a great actress," I said, fighting against the bitter tears, "all that was just—talk?"

"As Cleopatra, you were magnificent," he said. "As Phèdre, a revelation. How could it have been otherwise? You are a Bonaparte, a descendant of one of the most astonishing families ever to stalk upon this earth. The blood of queens and empresses flows in your veins. Impersonate Cleopatra? For you, nothing easier. But an actress—never. Never, from first to last. I am sorry to have deceived you, my dear."

Behind the flippancy of his tone, I sensed, for the first time, the callousness that lay at the heart of Oliver Craven. And the most terrible suspicions began to spring to my mind, all unbidden. Before I could speak again, however, a thunderous crash shook the cellar, filling it with dust and broken plaster. I reeled back against the wall, my hands to my ears. The shellburst must have landed very close, and my thoughts flew to my coachman and the dog-cart waiting in the cul-de-sac. I wondered if man and horse had come to any harm.

Oliver Craven seemed scarcely to have noticed the turmoil of sound and fury. He sat down heavily on the bed and stared across at me with a flat, reflective gaze.

Presently, I said, "Did Jeanette Dupuis—did my mother —reveal to you the name of her lover?"

He shook his head. "No, she did not."

"Then how did you find out?"

He laughed shortly. "How do you imagine? Here is this woman, this brazen creature, asking—nay, demanding—my help and the pittance of money that I had put by. Would I not first want the name of the man, in order to make that scoundrel pay the piper? So I asked her his name. And she refused to give it."

"So?"

He grinned, and I saw that most of his teeth were missing. "So I beat the name out of her!"

"You—beat her?" I stared at him in horror. "A woman in her condition! You used violence on her?"

"That I did. And when she gave me the name of Louis Napoleon, the man whom all Europe tipped to be the next ruler of France, you may be sure that I quickly dabbed her eyes and comforted her. Oh, my dear, from then on, there was nothing too good for poor Jeanette. And, of course, there was no question of approaching Louis Napoleon. My plans concerning that gentleman were already laid—but well into the future. All that was required was that the child should be born a girl. And so it transpired."

Another shellburst shook the room. The atmosphere in there—already tainted with the unwashed odor of its inhabitant—was thick with dust, so that I was obliged to hold a handkerchief to my mouth. My time there was running out. Nauseated by the very presence of the creature before me—the person who had once been the inspiration of my life and was now revealed, out of his own mouth, as a very monster of depravity—I had only one wish, and that to put as much distance between myself and him as possible. And forever. But one thing more needed to be asked . . .

"Did my mother ever know, ever guess, of your inten-

tions?" I demanded. "Of your future intentions concerning
—me?"

"That she did," he replied. "And you may be sure that
she thought very little of the idea. I have had, in my time,
something of an unfortunate reputation with the fair sex.
In your own experience, there was the ridiculous business
with Mirabel Ducane. I see you look at me with horror
and alarm, my dear. Yes, I am afraid I lied to you over
that matter also. Mirabel was my mistress. Unfortunately,
when she found out about my plans concerning you, she
acted after the manner of the street arab she really was.

"But to return to your question: yes, Jeanette realized
what I intended to do with you, and she tried to stop me.
But I had—a certain means—to prevent her."

The door of that wretched cell was behind me. Before
I could trust myself to speak again—to blurt out my
accusation—I felt for the handle, took it between my
fingers. Only then did I hurl the accusation across the
fetid, dust-laden air:

*"You bent my mother to your will by threatening to kill
her baby! It was you, and not she, who put the pillow over
my face!"*

I saw the words strike home. His eyes widened, as if from
shock. A moment's pause—and then he threw back his head.
There followed a peal of unholy laughter, the like of which
I pray never to hear again. The creature rocked himself back
and forth on the bed, clutching his emaciated chest with
his bony arms; helpless in his demoniac mirth.

Petrified with the horror of the sound, I was some moments
in summoning the will to escape; but escape I did, wrench-
ing open the door and fleeing out of the room, and from
that building, watched by the wry-necked dwarf, who paused
in his work to see me go, up the stairs and into the wintry
sunlight and the biting air.

When I looked about me, up and down the cul-de-sac
and the street beyond, there was no sign of dog-cart, horse,
or driver. Only a pall of smoke rising from a shattered
rooftop opposite, the empty, eyeless windows marking the
explosion of the shells.

．　．

The shelling continued as I set off on foot. Once, I heard one whine overhead and speed on with a roar like a railway train passing over a bridge; it was followed by an explosion away on my right, and a rising cloud of smoke and dust. Minutes later, turning a corner, I came upon a group of men—all roughly dressed and bearing in their countenances the marks of starvation and despair—foraging in the shattered ruin of a shop window. Looters—though what they found to loot there (it was a monumental stone mason's establishment) was beyond all imagining. When they saw me, they stopped what they were doing and muttered to each other, eyeing me covertly. Conscious of their glances, I quickened my pace. And when I reached the next corner, I broke into a run, gathering my skirts about my calves and racing, pell-mell, down a long stretch of street lined with stumps of hacked-down lime trees and strewn with broken glass and the debris of fallen houses. Two hundred yards away—less—was another corner. I told myself that if I could reach that corner I might live to see the day out. Behind me, I knew, the gang of looters were in full pursuit. What they would do to me, after overhauling me and robbing me of everything I carried, I did not dare to think. And the only reason that they had not caught up with me already, surely, was because I was better-nourished and stronger than they.

A lifetime seemed to pass, and I had been running all that time, before I reached out my hand and grasped hold of the stonework of the building on the corner of the street. There I paused, sobbing for breath. Blinded by fatigue. I had come thus far and could run no farther. If the effort had not been enough, if my pursuers had not been shaken off, then I had no more effort to give.

The pounding in my ears grew less. I opened my eyes, slowly, dragging my gaze for fear that I should see them standing before me, gloating, perhaps waiting to grasp me, and I turned to look back the way I had come.

The long road was empty. But not quite empty . . .

At the far end, by the corner at which I had started my

run, stood the familiar veiled figure in her funereal black. Standing there, regarding me across the wide space between us.

Sobbing with horror, I found wings of panic to take me on. Nor did I stop or check my pace till the Concorde bridge and the wide Seine lay between me and the apparition.

The demands of my work at the "hospital" flung me immediately into a frenzy of activity that precluded any thought of what had taken place in my life since my momentous reunion with Otto. If I gave any thought to it, it was only for the few moments before sleep snatched me away, when, after long hours of work, I dragged my weary footsteps to bed. And I deliberately never took to my bed, during that period, until sheer dog-tiredness shut out all memories.

The bombardment continued, but Paris grew used to it. As my friend Mr. Washburne remarked, "The carelessness and nonchalance of the Parisians in all this business is wonderful. Ladies and gentlemen make excursions to see the shells fall." The truth was that the Prussians' frightfulness in unleashing random destruction upon the men, women, and children of the beleaguered city had had a counter effect to the one intended: instead of beating Paris into submission, the bombardment made her people all the more willing to continue the siege to the bitter end. Nor was the city's resistance lost upon the outside world. What few scraps of news entered Paris (news was still going out, by regular balloon service, but only came in by the hands of brave men who crept through the Prussian lines under cover of darkness) told how the opinion of the civilized world had swung against Prussia and toward France. No longer looked on as innocent victims who had turned the tables on bullying France, the Prussians were now regarded as arrogant victors who could not be content with conquest, but must utterly humiliate the conquered.

In all this, I thought of the secret talks that were going on in that certain house in Auteuil. I hear the murmurings about me, growing ever more loud, for another Great Sortie against the besiegers—and I feared for the hopes of peace.

It was on January 17th, a Tuesday, and I had just finished the issue of evening soup to our patients, when Philippe arrived at the Hôtel de Brassy. One look at his white, drawn face and I knew that he was the bringer of ill news. I was not mistaken.

We went together into the garden room and shut and locked the door behind us. Philippe threw off his military cloak and, slumping into an armchair, he buried his face in his hands.

"We have failed," he muttered. "The talks have come to nothing. Otto and the rest of them departed for their own lines an hour ago. The bombardment—and the war—will continue."

"Why, Philippe—why?" I cried. "Surely even the Prussians want an end to it."

"It's our people who oppose it," said Philippe bitterly. "The Reds, that is. Certain discreet representations were made to some of their leaders—to Delescluze, Blanqui, and Flourens—asking their reactions to the prospect of an armistice. Their answer: any armistice will bring civil war in Paris."

"Oh, my dear," I fell on my knees beside his chair and smoothed his brow. "After all your efforts. And you look so worn out."

"I haven't told you the worst, Tessa," he said. "The worst is almost too frightful to believe. I shouldn't tell you, but I think I shall go insane if I don't tell somebody."

"Tell, my dear," I said, continuing to stroke his brow.

"The National Guard," he said, "our ramshackle civilian army, numbers four hundred thousand. In equipment and in training it is totally inadequate to face up to a first-class military force like the Prussian army, but it is more than enough to bring about a successful revolution in Paris. As our government very well knows. So we have the situation where the Red leaders howl for a continuation of the war, and for the National Guard to be sent out on a massive sortie. And, on the other hand, we have a government terrified of revolution and of the National Guard."

"And so?" I asked, puzzled and fearful.

"And so, with cynical brutality, the government is going to send the National Guard against the Prussians," he cried. "As a distinguished member of that august body said this morning in my hearing, 'When there are a hundred thousand National Guards lying on the ground, opinion will calm down!' "

"Philippe!" I replied. "But that's monstrous. Can't something be done to stop it?"

"Who will stop it?" he demanded. "Not the government. And not the leaders of the National Guard themselves; *they* are convinced that tomorrow's attack will lead to victory. But, oh, how wrong they are, how tragically wrong!"

"Tomorrow, you say?"

"They begin the approach march tomorrow," said Philippe. "Toward Buzenval, in the direction of Versailles. And they don't have a chance. Best look to your arrangements, Tessa. You are going to be busy—hideously busy—by dawn on Thursday!"

Philippe de Brassy never spoke a truer word! All the next day the kettledrums rattled and the bugles blew, as the men of the civilian army marched through the streets of Paris to give battle to the city's besiegers: old men and boys; clerks and laborers; ragged volunteers from Belleville and high-stepping gentlemen from the rich quarters in their bespoke greatcoats and striped pantaloons; with wives and sweethearts lending a hand with packs and rifles; with gay *vivandières* strutting alongside in their high-buttoned boots and carrying their neat kegs of cognac. I wanted to cry to them to turn and go back; to tell them that they were the unwitting dupes of their government and their political leaders; that they were being kettledrummed and bugled to maiming, disfigurement, and death. But I knew no one out of all that procession would listen; so, to my shame, I kept my peace. I went back to the Hôtel de Brassy and prepared everything in readiness, as Philippe had advised me.

By the midafternoon, the sound of the Prussian guns all along the west and southwest of the city told that the sortie was being held. We stood by our posts all that night: Dr. Brewster by his operating table, and me with my staff of nurses, ready to give what aid we could when the wounded were brought in. I nerved myself, all that long night, to face the new ordeal; for in all the time the "hospital" had been running, I had never become accustomed to the sight of suffering and death.

The rattle of iron tires on the cobblestones of the faubourg heralded the arrival of the first of the field ambulances. All through that first, long day I remained strong in the face of the weeping, frightened boys whom they brought in and laid out along the elegant staircases and corridors, to await their turn with Dr. Brewster's knife. I listened, unflinchingly, to their cries of pain, to their repeated assertions that "We were betrayed!" I could have told them of their coming betrayal—but I had chosen to remain silent. All that was left was for me to help pick up the pieces.

I think it went on for five days. Somewhere along the way, day and night became fused together in a timeless road that stretched ever onward into a dark infinity. Somewhere during those days and nights, the Prussians threw back the French sortie with almost contemptuous ease—and even found time, in Louis XIV's ornate Hall of Mirrors in Versailles palace, to proclaim their king as First German Emperor. During that time, also, the people of Belleville, enraged at the futile slaughter of their National Guards, marched upon the Hôtel de Ville and brought Paris to the brink of civil war. But I remember nothing of those events. I remember nothing but the suffering, and the ineffable sense of my own failure to have prevented it.

They told me afterward that I collapsed on the morning of the fifth day. They may have been right.

I woke to the sound of a starling calling from the ragged stump of one of the cypresses outside my window. It was morning, and the new sun had an unaccustomed warmth. I was alone in the room. The five cots used by Hortense and the novices were neatly made up. I heard someone walking down the corridor outside, and a murmur of voices. From the distance came the rumble of cannon fire.

I felt guilty to be lying there, for I knew that there must still be plenty to be done. The clock told me it was half past nine. In ten minutes, I promised myself, I would rise and go about my business. Meanwhile, it was strangely pleasurable to lie there and let my mind wander, avoiding hurtful and distressing things, and embracing golden memories of the days at Brassy: sunlight on the moat, with golden carp flickering in and out of the shadowy weeds; the joyful sound of the hounds gamboling at play; the rattle of a carriage wheel on the long drive; the sound of Robert's voice . . .

Where was he at that moment? I gleaned from the fragments of news that Tours was a center of provincial resistance to the enemy, and I guessed that Robert must be playing some important role in the local government there. One thing I prayed: that his lameness had kept him from the fighting, for in the provinces, as elsewhere, ill luck had dogged French arms.

I tried to picture him at work in a quiet and elegant room, perhaps in his own library at Brassy, his white mane bowed over a pile of documents, his keen mind pondering on the problems of his unhappy country.

Did he ever think of me? . . .

My time was run out. I put aside my daydream and rose, washed and dressed myself, and went downstairs, stepping between the rows of men who lay there, regarding my passing with their numb and patient eyes—like the eyes of sheep in a slaughter pen. Hortense was kneeling by one of the men in the hallway, close by the doorway. She looked up from her task of tying a bandage and told me I looked much better for the rest, and would I please go along to the kitchen and get myself a hot drink and something to eat?

I was about to reply to her, when a movement caught my eye. Glancing sidelong, I saw a face peering in at me through the window by the door. It was the dwarf from the cabaret. He was looking straight at me, and one small hand came up and jerkily gestured a summoning motion. He wanted to speak to me.

I went out into the portico. He was standing by one of the pillars, wearing a long coat that trailed about his feet, and a hat too large for him. Despite his comically grotesque appearance, he exuded a sense of tragedy.

"What's happened?" I asked him.

The dwarf plucked at his nether lip and rolled his eyes. "I was sent to tell you to come," he said. "Will you give me the money first? He said you'd give me money. The Englishman. The clown."

"Yes, I'll give you money, but tell me what's happened!" I cried.

"The cabaret was hit last night," he said. "A shell landed by the steps and brought the roof down. I was not there. I saw the people being dug out this morning. They were all taken to the hospital, to the Saint-Michel."

"The Englishman! Is he badly hurt?"

"I don't know. He was lying in the wagon with all the rest when I saw him. He told me to come and find you. Said it was important. Said . . ." the small face twisted in a grimace as he strove for recollection . . . "said there was something else you had to know. Said you'd give me money."

"I'll give you money," I promised him. "You say he was taken to the Saint-Michel hospital?"

"They were all taken to the Saint-Michel," he replied. "Except the dead ones."

There was no question that I had to go and see Oliver immediately. He might be seriously injured. Dying. No matter what, the man who had imprinted himself so deeply upon my life demanded that much consideration. And there was something else—something else he wanted to tell me. What could that be?

I gave the dwarf ten francs and he went on his way. We had no means of transport about the place, for the coachman, horse, and dog-cart had never been seen again: it was to be presumed that he had sold the wretched horse to a butcher and disappeared with the proceeds. However, I had scarcely left the faubourg when I was overtaken by one of the few cabs that still plied for hire in the city. The driver looked dubious about going to the Left Bank. The shelling had been very heavy, he said, and it would cost me double —in advance. I paid, and we set off across the Seine, heading for the sound of the guns.

We came to the hospital, which itself had a gaping hole made by a shell in the enclosing wall. Inside, I found all the familiar atmosphere of overcrowding, of overworked and harassed helpers driven almost to breaking point. There was a nun, however, with a face as serene and calm as if she had been at prayer instead of trying to calm a screaming child. In answer to my question, she told me that the victims of the cabaret disaster were in one of the out-buildings; she then turned her attentions again to the child.

The outbuilding in question was across a yard. There was a bearded young man leaning against the open door, a mug of coffee in his hand. He was taking the fresh air, and he looked as if he had been up all night. I took him— correctly—for a doctor.

"The people who were injured in the cabaret . . ." I began.

"You are a relation?"

"I am—a friend of the Englishman. The clown," I said.

I saw the compassion flicker in his tired eyes, and I knew the answer before he framed the words.

"I much regret to tell you that the clown is dead," he said. "He died almost on arrival. Isn't that so, Sister?" The last remark was addressed to an elderly nun who had just come out the door.

"Indeed he did, Doctor," she replied.

Oliver was dead. I was numbed by the shock of the news. It seemed unbelievable. The human derelict whom I had seen a few days before—yes, he had had the marks of mortality upon him. But the man I had known for half my life—the original and unforgettable Oliver Craven—had been so vivid and vital as to seem completely indestructible.

"There's the other who was with him," said the young doctor. "The old woman. How is she, Sister?"

"Not long for this life," replied the nun.

"There was someone with him?" I asked, puzzled. "But who?"

"They say she was his assistant," said the nun. "Played a tin whistle, for him to dance to. She calls herself 'Old Gigot,' poor soul."

"Gigot?" The years sped away, and I was back in that room at the Penruth Workhouse, with the princess's fairy-tale gown on the dressmaker's dummy, and the beautiful, self-destroying woman—my mother. And the old dresser they called Gigot.

"Can I see her?" I asked.

"Of course," said the nun. "It can do no harm, my child. She has not much time left, and a kind face will ease her going. Come with me."

They had made shift with the outbuilding by setting a line of cots down both sides of a long, narrow room, and these were all occupied with patients, most of whom were heavily bandaged about the head and arms. At the far end was hung a rough curtain. The nun pulled aside one end and motioned me to precede her. There was one cot behind the curtain, and the old woman lay upon it, her face in deep shadow.

"Someone come to see you, my dear," said the nun. She nodded at me, smiled, and went away.

"Gigot," I whispered. "Gigot, do you know me? I'm Tessa Thursday. We never met since that evening in Cornwall all those years ago, but you have been with Oliver Craven's company ever since, and you must have heard about me. And perhaps seen me backstage."

For a moment I thought she was asleep; but as my eyes grew accustomed to the gloom, I could see that she was watching me.

The mouth moved, and the whisper came back: "You came. I prayed that you would come—my Tessa."

I felt my skin crawl. I took a pace near the cot and peered down into the ruined face that lay, wreathed in a haze of white hair, upon the rough pillow.

"Who—who *are* you?" I breathed.

"I am—I was—Jeanette Dupuis," said my mother.

4

She would not have me draw the curtain that cast the narrow corner in deep shadow; the vestige of her woman's vanity forbade that I should see what she had come to. She remained a shadowy shape upon the pillow, with only the large and luminous eyes that never left me, and a thin hand that lay like the skeleton of a small bird in mine, while I listened—and wondered.

"The first Gigot died in Naples," she said. "It was small-pox. I had it also and it did—this—to me . . ." Her other hand briefly sketched the outline of her face. "After that, I was finished for the stage, but Oliver let me stay with the company. I became the dresser. I became Old Gigot."

"He told me that you had died," I said.

"It was a kind of truth," she said. "Jeanette was dead. There was nothing left in her life. Not until that night in London, when I saw you and knew who you were. And then Jeanette became alive again."

"In London?" I shook my head in puzzlement.

"It was at the hotel," she explained. "That night when you cried out in terror and everyone came running to see what it was, I was there. I looked in through the door, past all the people standing there—I was last to arrive, for I had come down from an attic room, where the servants slept—and I saw you sitting up in bed, and I knew. I knew . . ."

I had a blinding flash of revelation. "You saw the half-thaler, the pendant, round my neck!" I cried.

"Oliver had tried to take it from you," she said. "It was he who stole into your room. He admitted it to me when I saw him afterward."

"But why—why did he try to take the pendant?"

"So that I should not see it and know who you were, Tessa," she replied. "But he failed in the attempt, and then he had to admit everything to me. How he had brought you from the workhouse in Cornwall. How he was going to turn you into a great actress. But I never trusted him. And then I overheard him quarreling with that girl, that Mirabel Ducane. She screamed at him that she would disfigure you for life rather than have him marry you, so I knew then that you were in danger. After that, I watched over you even more closely."

Lying on top of the blanket that covered her—spread out like a counterpane for extra warmth—was a black cloak and hood. I took the material between my fingers. It was coarse-textured, substantial; not the stuff of which apparitions are made.

"You were there, following me in the Champs-Élysées that night," I whispered. "You prevented Mirabel from throwing the vitriol in my face."

"I struck her arm down," came the reply. "And she cried out with rage. She never guessed it was me, Old Gigot. On the night of the ball at the Tuileries, I was beside myself with anguish, for there was not a chance of my gaining admittance there, to be at hand to watch over you, to protect you. And then I heard that a young woman had fallen to her death. And I thought that I had lost you again, this time forever."

The thin hand tightened in mine, and I gave a gentle, answering squeeze.

"The last thing in the world I want to do is to upset you," I whispered. "But would you like to speak about that first time—the time when Oliver took away your baby?"

"He said it was for the best," she replied brokenly. "That I was not fit to take care of my own child. That I was too far gone in drunkenness, and only half a person. I listened to him and believed him. And I let him take away my baby to another home. I never asked him where—and he never told me."

"He was evil beyond all belief," I cried. "The lies he told me about you. The things he made me believe. Why, he even said that he had to prevent you from suffocating me with a pillow."

The hand in mine began to tremble. I reached out to touch her cheek, and felt the tears that were falling there.

And she said, "He did not lie to you—not that time. May I be forgiven—for I did do that awful thing!"

The short, winter's day was dying, and the darkness closing in on the narrow space behind the curtain. I sat by my mother while her life ebbed away. She had told me more, much more. Of a love that had come like a sunburst into her life and carried her to unimaginable heights of ecstasy —only to be dashed to earth again. He—my father—had wanted to marry her; had even been prepared to throw over his high ambitions for the sake of love; but harder, more cynical counsels had swayed him. In the end, he had given way before the advice of his followers and had broken with her; returned to France to make his bid for the throne, to marry Eugénie. And his last act had been to give her the half-thaler and to keep the other half for himself—as, indeed, he had kept it close by him all the years between.

Deserted, distraught, she had easily fallen prey to the dreadful lowering of the spirits that so often afflicts women after childbirth. Alone in the lodgings where Oliver Craven had put her, with no one to talk to, with nothing but the memories of her lost love, she had crossed the narrow margin that separates the world of the sane from the nightmare hell of the unbalanced. She had, indeed, made an attempt —a fumbling, futile attempt—to destroy her screaming child, as a prelude to taking her own life. Oliver Craven had arrived in time to witness it; had used the situation in order to get the child away from her forever; to put it in his "keep-net," to await the time when he could carry out his plan. Sixteen years later, chance had showed to her that the girl named Tessa Thursday was her lost child. By that time, weighed down with guilt and shame, and hide-ously disfigured by disease, she could not possibly have summoned up the courage to declare herself to me. Knowing this, Oliver Craven had even used the threat of betrayal to prevent her from warning me about his intentions, and she had been forced to look on, a helpless witness to her child's seduction at the hands of a ruthless adventurer.

She was sleeping now, her hand still in mine, her thin breast rising and falling with her faint breathing. At peace. She had begged my forgiveness, and I had freely given it; for had she not repaid one moment's madness with years of devotion? Ever since I came back into her life, she had watched over me. On the packet crossing over to France, and on innumerable other occasions. Of course, I did not tell her that, far from bringing me comfort, her attentions had been a living nightmare; that the hand that she had held out in blessing had been mistaken for a gesture of menace; that I had latterly come to identify the Woman in Black as the phantom of Mirabel Ducane come to haunt me. I told my mother none of those things.

Oliver Craven was no more, and even the bitter memory of his evil had been softened by his last act. From the message he had sent with the dwarf it was clear that the "something else I had to know" was the truth about my mother's identity.

All things pass, even anger and bitterness. Oliver Craven had paid in hard coin for his schemes, and I could not bring myself any longer to think ill of him. Instead, I preferred to remember him as he had been on that far-off and enchanted Christmas Eve: the shepherd who loved the princess.

And she—the princess—while I held her hand, slipped peacefully out of life with the last of the winter's day.

It was on the day of my mother's passing that, their hands strengthened by the disaster of Buzenval, the government began open peace talks with the enemy, and four days later a bewildered Paris was informed that an armistice had been agreed. The French were permitted the "honor" of firing the last shot, and the guns fell silent upon the disastrous Franco-Prussian War.

The Hôtel de Brassy was still filled with badly wounded soldiers and was likely to be so for many weeks—perhaps months—till the hospital accommodation in the city returned to something like normal. Nevertheless, despite my many responsibilities, I was seized with an urgent desire to leave Paris at the earliest opportunity, to travel to the Loire, and to see Robert again. Some movement in and out of the city was already taking place under the terms of the armistice, and I was certain that my friend Mr. Washburne would be able to secure a passport for me. But before I was able to do anything about this, from out of the blue came a letter from the man I loved.

                                            4, rue Condé,
                                            Bordeaux
                                            January 30, 1871

My dear Miss Thursday,

The welcome news of the armistice leads me to hope that this communication will suffer no great delay in reaching you.

I have to thank you for yours of September 14th and October 28th last, giving news of my nephew's wound and of his return to health. In the intervening months, thoughts of your plight in Paris have seldom been far from my mind. I beg you to write to me, at your earliest convenience, dear Miss Thursday, and apprise me of the present circumstances at the Hôtel de Brassy.

As for myself: as you will be aware, next week will see France electing a new government, which will assume the solemn task of negotiating peace terms with the German Empire. I have the honor to have been chosen as a candidate for election. If successful, I shall take a seat in the Assembly, which, for the time being, will be held here in Bordeaux. It is to my lodgings, here, that you should address your communication—which I look forward to receiving.

I remain, Miss Thursday,

                                    Yours very sincerely,
                                    Robert de Brassy

Those stilted phrases—so typical of the man who often averred that he "could not abide excess of feelings"—dashed my plan to go to Brassy, but brought me the joy of knowing that he had safely come through the war in the provinces. From an atlas in the library I discovered that Bordeaux was impossibly remote, far beyond Tours, on the Atlantic coast. What excuse could I possibly make up, to go to him there? And he spoke of lodgings: I could not expect him to accommodate me in his lodgings.

When next I saw Philippe (who by then had been transferred to an appointment as liaison officer with the Paris civil authorities at the Hôtel de Ville), I showed him the letter. In Philippe's estimation, his uncle would certainly gain a seat in the Assembly. And as soon as a peace treaty was signed, he said, and the Prussians had departed to their homeland, the Assembly would return to its rightful seat of government—in Paris.

And so, with that wonderful prospect before me, I quietly and contentedly threw myself back into the work of the "hospital." This was a burden blessedly lightened, about a week after the declaration of the armistice, by the arrival of food supplies from the outside world. The first consignment, from Britain, provided me with the opportunity to give my poor soldiers the first decent meal—of beef stew, with freshly baked bread—they had had for many long months. Yet even the arrival of the relief food caused trouble: the poorest could not afford to buy it; there were riots and acts of pillage. The long siege had left mortal scars upon the hearts and minds of many Parisians. And the real trouble had scarcely begun.

The elections and the peace treaty that followed brought storms of protest in the city, where it was felt that the opinions of a few men in faraway Bordeaux had no writ in Paris. "Paris is France" became the cry. On the day before the signing of the treaty, the Red battalions of the National Guard marched in their thousands, to be harangued by their leaders, who called upon them to overthrow the government and set up the Commune in Paris. The new word "Commune" was to be heard everywhere—

in the food queues; in the shabby, rubble-strewn streets of the Left Bank—and was whispered with fear in the "smarter" districts, such as the Faubourg St.-Honoré.

The flames of revolt mounted. The new Assembly, seemingly unaware of the powder keg that was Paris, ordered that all debts and rents were to be paid within forty-eight hours. These had been held in abeyance throughout the war and siege; many were the poor Parisian housewives who had only scraped by and seen their children fed because the landlord had not been able to demand his rent. To make matters worse, the pay of the National Guard, which, though only a miserable pittance, had enabled the poorest to keep body and soul together, was immediately stopped.

But worse, far worse, was the shameful humiliation of Paris herself. The former City of Light, who had borne herself not unworthily throughout the long and bitter siege, was, by a stroke of a pen, condemned to defilement. As part of the peace treaty, the Prussians were permitted a triumphal entry and a nominal two-day occupation of the city.

On that first day—March 1st, 1871—I and most of the remainder of Paris stayed inside, behind shuttered windows. They tell me that shortly after dawn on that first day, thirty thousand of the German Emperor's soldiers marched up the Champs-Élysées, with drums beating, with bugles playing and banners flying. I have heard—and it is scarcely believable that so callous and unfeeling an act could have been carried out—that they marched in procession through the Arc de Triomphe, that part-mystical, half-sacred symbol of France's past glory. I can only say that I am glad not to have witnessed it. Two days after, with admirable "correctness," the Prussians left the city and took up positions on the outer perimeter, to the east, in accordance with the terms of the peace treaty.

It was then that the Parisians reacted as only Parisians could.

Out into the streets they poured: to the Champs-Élysées, to the great Place in which the Arc de Triomphe stands;

bearing buckets, brooms, washcloths; men and women, little children even. And there, from morning till night, they scrubbed the defiled paving stones with elbow grease and Condy's fluid. And when they had done that, they made great bonfires, to burn away the taint of alien footsteps. I saw the flames from my window.

"Tessa, you must get out of Paris! Now—at once! Immediately!"

Philippe had put on some weight, thanks to good food, and seemed totally to have recovered from his wound—though I noticed that the March weather, the freezing rain, had given him a bad cough, which troubled him greatly.

"Not while I still have fifty badly wounded and ill men in the house," I told him firmly. "Not till they have either recovered, or the competent hospital authorities have taken them off my hands. And, besides . . ."

I checked myself. I could have added that I had no intention of leaving Paris and going off to Brassy, or to anywhere else, while I imminently expected the arrival of Robert. For it had been announced that the Bordeaux Assembly had adjourned itself and was to reconvene in Versailles on the 20th. And the 20th was the following day!

Philippe's reply was checked by a fit of coughing. When he had recovered himself, he dabbed his lips with a handkerchief and said, "Tessa, you must listen to me. At the Hôtel de Ville I am in a position to see what is hidden from most people in the city—which is that the control of Paris is slipping out of the hands of the government, of law and order, and into the hands of the mob. Why, you know what happened yesterday . . ."

"I am a busy woman," I reminded him. "I have no time for politics and I am sick of war and suffering."

"My dear, you will hear me out," he persisted. "At dawn yesterday, such regular troops as we could muster were sent up to Montmartre to bring back two hundred cannon that the National Guard took away—as they said, to keep them out of the hands of the Prussians. At first all went well. It seemed that the guns were back in government hands without the spilling of a drop of blood. Then—disaster. I don't know how it was done. Don't ask me. Somehow the mob were amongst our fellows, pleading with them, bending them to their will. The regulars—mostly young and untried —were completely won over. Soon they too were shouting Red slogans, and calling for the downfall of their own officers. There were two generals up there in Montmartre, Lecomte and Thomas. Old men, both. They were taken into a garden, put against a wall, and shot like dogs."

"Philippe, how awful!" I cried, appalled. "I had no idea—"

"The writing is on the wall," he said. "The government is losing control of Paris. We reckon that there is no more than a fraction of the National Guard who can be counted on in any new emergency."

"Are you going to flee from Paris, Philippe?" I asked him.

He squared his shoulders. He was the old Philippe again: the young dragoon of the golden days before the war, full of idealism and honor. "I shall stay at my post," he said simply, "till I am given orders to leave."

I gestured about me, at the walls of the mansion that enclosed fifty men in need of my care. "And I shall stay at my post, also, Philippe," I told him.

Realizing that I was not to be moved by any further argument, he left to return to the Hôtel de Ville. Flambard saw him out and opened the door of his cab. When the steward turned away, there was a strange expression upon his face—like that of a cat contemplating the fate of a mouse within its grasp—which caused me a sudden pang of alarm. But when he looked in my direction again, his smooth countenance was as bland and servile as ever.

Alas for my hopes of seeing the man I loved on the morrow, or soon after. Next day the members of the government left the city to join the Bordeaux Assembly, who were gathering in Versailles. Swift to move, one of the Red leaders rounded up a force of National Guards, marched upon the Hôtel de Ville, and took control of the building.

That night the red flag flew from the Hôtel de Ville; and,

for the first time since the Great Revolution, the Paris mob were rulers of the capital.

And all roads out were guarded by revolutionary bayonets.

A week later, all Paris rejoiced. There had been nothing like it since the heady days of the Third Empire, with banners, with parades, with salutes of guns. The new Municipal Council had declared itself the "Commune of Paris," and people danced in the streets, complete strangers embraced and told each other that a new order had descended upon earth and that freedom was reborn.

Philippe still remained at his post in the Hôtel de Ville, where he was known and respected as a good soldier who did not dabble in politics—or so he told me. But one morning, as I was taking a hasty breakfast in the garden room at the Hôtel de Brassy, I came to learn of the peril in which he stood—in which we both stood.

A slight movement at the edge of my vision made me look up with a start from the newspaper that I had been reading.

"Flambard!" I exclaimed. "You gave me such a shock. How long have you been standing there?"

The steward stood, as ever, at the respectful three paces; but something was quite different: had he not entered the room, soft-footed, without knocking, and closed the door behind him? And the smile that greeted my question— surely that was over-familiar; mocking, even.

"I have been here a little while, mam'selle," he replied. "And have had the inestimable pleasure of watching mam'selle deep in concentration upon her reading. Mam'selle moistens her lips from time to time while concentrating —and so prettily."

"How dare you?" I half rose, confused, and angry at his sudden and distasteful familiarity. But his next words, and the manner in which he delivered them, shocked me to silence.

He looked about him, around the garden room, and said, "This is a very fine room, don't you think, mam'selle? The privacy from the rest of the mansion. The shuttered windows. The door conveniently opening onto the garden. So suitable for—let us say—*secret meetings with old friends!*"

A finger of dread coursed its way down my spine.

"What—what do you mean?" I demanded of him, in a voice that sounded like someone else's.

He faced me again, smiling. "Oh, come, mam'selle," he said, gently chiding. "You surely remember the occasion. During the time of the Prussian bombardment, was it not? Just after midnight. Two callers. Both of them gentlemen familiar to this establishment, though one of them had not been a guest here for some time. Might one hazard a guess as to the name of the latter gentleman? Might it not start with the letter *O*? And might not the second name start with the letter *S*? And might there not be a *von* joining the two?"

"What are you after?" I cried. "What is all this leading to?"

He raised a well-manicured hand deprecatingly. "Mam'-selle is over-hasty," he said smoothly. "As to what I'm after —well, that can wait awhile. As to what it might lead to— well, it might lead to very great trouble for those concerned. Though perhaps not to the latter gentleman of whom I spoke, who is possibly far away in his own country by now."

"You are a spy!" I accused him. "And you've always been a spy—ever since I first set eyes on you!"

My accusation drew a flicker of anger in the sly eyes, but it was quickly quenched. He continued to smile. "A man without a fortune, without family and friends, must find his own way in the world," he said. "I have always made myself—accommodating, I think that is the word—to those who hold the purse strings, to those in power."

"You were a police spy before the war," I cried "And now . . ."

"Yes, mam'selle?" His smile broadened. "What am I now, pray?"

"You are a spy for the Commune!"

He turned his back on me. From the movements of his shoulders, it almost seemed as if he was overcome with a paroxysm of helpless laughter. He crossed over to the window, looked out. When he turned, his face was bland, expressionless.

"Consider your position," he said, "and that of Captain de Brassy. You received here an enemy officer during a time of siege and bombardment—a meeting which will damn you both as enemies of the People. I do not know how my friend, the new Prefect of Police, would view *your* position, but I have no doubts about the gallant captain's fate . . ." So saying, he pointed his forefinger at me as if it were a gun, and brought down his thumb like a hammer. I shuddered.

"You have already reported us to the Commune?" I asked him.

"Not yet."

I took a deep breath; let it out with a shudder.

"What do you want?" I demanded.

He smiled that sleek, catlike smile.

"Can you not guess, mam'selle? On one other occasion, I performed a slight personal service in order to place myself in your credit. If I—withhold—this information from my friend the new Prefect of Police, thereby sparing the life of Captain de Brassy and possibly your own—well, I ask you, mam'selle, could you refuse me anything? Anything at all!"

The sly eyes swam down my body. I drew my shawl more tightly about my shoulders and bosom, feeling defiled.

"You are—unspeakable!" I hissed at him.

He gave a short laugh and crossed over to the door; paused there for a moment, one hand raised, finger pointing at me.

"You give yourself the airs of an aristocrat," he said. "But my inquiries have revealed to me that you are nothing of the kind. We are living in changed times here in Paris. You could do worse for yourself than to have me as your protector. Think it over. I give you—twenty-four hours."

He left me.

• •

My first thought was to get help. And from whom but Philippe? I toyed with the notion of seeking him out in the Hôtel de Ville, but was daunted by the thought of braving the cordon of National Guards who lolled in their scores in the open space before the building, by the barricades which had recently been erected there, among the cannon that dominated all approaches. In the event, it was Philippe who came to me. He arrived just as we were about to serve soup to the patients. One look at his face was enough to warn me that something was terribly wrong.

"Follow me to the garden room," he murmured close to my ear. "I must speak with you alone."

I glanced nervously about me. There was no sign of Flambard. Motioning to Hortense and the others to commence the serving, I went after Philippe. He closed the door behind me, crossed to the commode, and poured two glasses of wine, one of which he laid on the table at my elbow. And with it, he placed something else: a small pistol.

"But—what's that for?" I cried.

"For you," he said. "Though I pray you will have no cause to use it, Tessa. You are going to leave the city tomorrow night. It is all arranged. The very worst has happened. The government at Versailles is determined to topple the Commune by force: on the face of it they can do no other. This morning we had news at the Hôtel de Ville that two squadrons of Versaillais cavalry made an attack upon the Communard outpost at Neuilly, sent a handful of National Guards packing, and frightened a dog or two. It was all that was needed—the spark that lights the fuse. Now the Commune is going to march on Versailles in force. It means civil war. And a second siege of Paris, which will be even more bitter and bloody than the last. And that isn't all. I saw a confidential memorandum today. The Commune is bringing back the old Revolutionary Tribunal, with dictatorial powers of arrest, trial, and execution. It will be the Terror of 1793 all over again; with secret informers, guilt by association, no opportunity of defense, and death within twenty-four hours. I insist you

300

leave the city, Tessa, and I have made arrangements for you to do so tomorrow night."

It was then I told him of my interview with Flambard, omitting only the humiliating demand that the steward had made upon me, but intimating that we were safe only till the following morning.

"Tomorrow night will be too late," I told him. "For both of us. He says he will denounce us as enemies of the People."

Philippe smote the tabletop in fury, upsetting my glass. The wine streaked across the polished surface in long fingers of redness. I shuddered at the sight.

"Everything must be brought forward by twenty-four hours!" he cried. "I will make the new arrangements immediately. Listen, Tessa—here is what you must do tonight . . ."

Midnight approaching. Shielding the candle with my hand, I stole into the box room on the top floor of the mansion, under the eaves. It was packed with chests of drawers, boxes, trunks, and portmanteaux. Here, so Philippe had told me, I would find a tin trunk containing some of his civilian clothes. Laying the candle down, I looked about me and soon found the trunk with his initials on the lid.

Inside were suits of clothes, pressed and smelling of dried lavender and potpourri. There, also, were crisply laundered linen shirts, cravats, socks, and handkerchiefs; several pairs of boots on boot trees; a hatbox containing a tall hat.

I slipped off my peignoir. I was naked underneath. Picking up the first shirt to come to hand, I pulled it over my head. It was hopelessly too big, but I turned back the sleeves to fit. The pantaloons presented no problem: well braced-up under the armpits and the bottoms tucked into the tops of my own button-boots (no question of my being able to avail myself of Philippe's footwear, which was much too big). A frock coat fitted me like a shroud, but there was an opera cloak that covered a multitude of sins. Regarding my reflection in a pier glass that stood in a corner, I perceived a slightly built young man in someone else's clothes. The tall hat, with my hair piled up underneath it, sat neatly upon my ears. Blowing out the candle, I left the room and set off down the stairs, feeling my way inch by inch, my hand on the banister.

Moonlight lit my way, coming as it did through the large windows at the top of the first flight of stairs that led down into the hall. Below me lay the doors to the courtyard—and freedom.

But between me and freedom—standing at the bottom of the stairs and looking up at me—was the shortish but undeniably powerful-looking figure of the steward of the Hôtel de Brassy.

"Well, now," came the mocking voice. "And where is this fine young gentleman going, one asks? And at this hour!"

Steeling my nerve, I continued my descent. Ten more steps separated me from Flambard, who had taken up a stand by the bottom stair.

"Get out of my way!" I said.

"I think not," he replied smoothly.

I stopped. The palm of my right hand, the hand that held the pistol beneath the concealing folds of the cloak, was slippery with my sweat.

"Will you stand aside and let me pass?" I breathed.

For answer, he slowly began to ascend the stairs toward me. His smile was mocking, assured, the eyes looking up at me tantalizingly, as one teases a wayward child.

"I think the time has come," he said, "when I must teach mam'selle a lesson. I think that I must demand a small advance upon the credit which I have placed to my account."

Throwing aside the fold of the cloak, I pointed the pistol full at him. His eyes widened with shock.

"Get away from me or I shall fire!" I cried.

For an instant I really thought he would obey my order. But then the hateful smile returned. He held out his hand toward me.

"Give that to me," he said gently.

"I shall count to three, and then . . ."

He shook his head. "Oh, no mam'selle. You will not fire."

"One . . ."

He began to walk up the stairs toward me, his palm still held out.

"The pistol, mam'selle. Into my hand, please."

"Two . . ."

He came on. His face still mocking, seemingly unafraid. My hand wavered. I felt my whole body begin to tremble. With a mounting sense of horror, I knew that I had only instants in which to make my decision: to kill—or to submit. He was only two steps below me, and his hand was already reaching out to close about my wrist. My finger tightened on the trigger.

Suddenly, a skittering sound across the polished floor of the hallway below. Flambard half turned. We both saw the white shape of Sasha bounding up the steps. His urgent, angry bark echoed loudly in the stairwell.

It was over too quickly, almost, for my mind to encompass.

With a curse, Flambard turned his foot and aimed an awkward kick at the dog. Sasha yelped with pain as the boot connected. The man directed another wild swing, lost his footing. Fell.

His staring eyes, wide-open mouth, receded swiftly from me. His scream, briefly shattering the silence of the sleeping mansion, was cut off on the instant of impact with the carved finial of the bottom banister. He sprawled there, silent.

The eyes still stared sightlessly at me as I crept past and ran across the hall. Sasha paused for a moment and sniffed at the dead head, then came after me. Out into the night.

A fiacre was waiting on the corner, by the junction with the rue Royale, just as Philippe had told me. I saw the glow of the driver's pipe in the darkness. When he sighted me, he reached and opened the door.

"Hurry, ma'am," he said. "The patrols are out tonight. Don't want to end up in the Roquette jail on a charge of spying for the Versaillais. There's a crazy spy-fever around this city." He spoke English with a transatlantic burr.

I got into the cab, pulling Sasha after me.

"Have you seen Captain de Brassy?" I questioned him anxiously.

"Ain't heard tell of no Cap'n de Brassy, ma'am," replied the driver. "Mr. Washburne gave me my orders: 'Sam,' he tells me, 'you pick up this lady at the junction of Royale and Saint-Honoré right after midnight. She'll be in men's clothes. Take her to the Gare du Nord.' No talk of no cap'n."

"But he'll be here," I cried. "He told me he would be here. We must wait."

The face above me was a dark shape under the brim of a tall hat. I had no way of knowing his expression.

"We'll give it five minutes," he said. "And, while we're waiting, your name from here on is Abel James Barker, a clerk of the United States Embassy. We don't have no ladies on the payroll, which is why you had to be in men's clothes. Got the name right?"

"Abel James Barker," I repeated.

The horse snickered and changed its stance. The clash of its iron shoes on the cobbles sounded shockingly loud in the dark and empty street. Somewhere far off, I thought I heard a gunshot, and then a burst of tipsy laughter. Silence fell again. I strained my eyes for movement. Prayed for the sight of Philippe's tall figure striding out of the gloom toward us. Time went by.

"That's it ma'am," said the driver. "Five minutes and no more. Maybe your cap'n will be waiting for you at the Gare du Nord." He shook the reins and we set off.

There was little traffic about, and we moved at a smart trot. Near the junction of the Grands Boulevards my heart quickened its beat at the sight of a barricade: a line of National Guards lolling in flickering torchlight that pinpointed the tips of their bayonets. My driver slowed his horse's pace, and one of the men came forward to meet us.

"What's your business, citizen?"

"Business of the United States Embassy," was the reply.

"Indeed, citizen? Where are your papers?"

They were handed down. The guardsman wore sergeant's chevrons and a red sash. I shrank back into the shadows and took a firm grip on Sasha's collar as the sergeant scanned the papers that had been given to him.

"Samuel Wayne Steadman, coachman, American citizen?"

"That's me."

"Abel James Barker, clerk, American citizen?" The sergeant peered forward toward me.

"Yes," I faltered.

"Proceed, citizens. Long live the Commune!"

The driver whipped up his horse. We went through the barricade, and I saw the gleaming barrel of a brass cannon trained the way we had come. The barricade had been built of paving stones, and our progress was over rutted, uneven earth for some distance. My heart scarcely returned to its normal rate until the dark bulk of the Gare du Nord came up on our right. The great building was in darkness. My driver directed his course round the back of it, down an alleyway that opened out into a yard. At a far corner of this yard, a tall figure stood in the light of a lantern.

Was it Philippe?

"This is as far as I go, ma'am," said the driver. "Good luck to you now."

I thanked him. Without more ado, he turned his horse and was gone, clattering down the alleyway into silence.

I turned, as the figure with the lantern came toward me.

"Hello, mam'selle. It has been a long time." A familiar voice, but not Philippe's.

"Who is it?" I cried. "It surely can't be . . ."

He lifted the lantern and showed himself. A smiling, ruddy-complexioned face. Older now, but scarcely changed. And wearing a sailor's cap with the red pompon.

"Gaston! Gaston Pepin! But what are *you* doing here?"

The under-gardener of the Château Brassy bobbed me a bow, then remembered his current status and changed it to a salute.

"Monsieur Philippe gave me my orders, mam'selle," he said. "All is in readiness, mam'selle. Please to come this way." And he motioned toward the great fretted bulk of the station building, open at one end, with the spider's web of dark rails emerging from it and trailing off into the gloom.

"But surely, Gaston," I said, "there are no trains running out of Paris yet. And the city's in a state of siege again."

"Trains, mam'selle?" He sounded surprised. "No one knows that better than I, mam'selle. I tell you, mam'selle, we've been doing a very different kind of business at the Gare du Nord—and at the Gare d'Orléans—since last October. This way, mam'selle."

He stood aside for me to precede him through a door. I stepped into a vast enclosed space. There was a sound, as if of metal striking metal: it echoed hollowly in the high vaulted roof of steel and glass. There were pinpoints of light here and there: more lanterns. As my eyes grew more accustomed to the semi-darkness, I picked out the arched end of the station, with the lighter-colored patch of night sky. And something else: a large spherical shape hung there, suspended between the top of the arch and the ground.

"It's—a balloon!" I exclaimed.

"That it is, mam'selle," said Gaston. "Would you credit it? Here's me, a Breton. One of the seafaring race. My father a sailor and his father before him. And now me—*pfui*! Drafted to the balloon service in Paris." He raised his voice in a shout. "Are you there, André? Is that you, Jean-Louis?"

"All's well, Gaston!" Two figures came toward us, both carrying lanterns. They were revealed as two more sailors in pompommed caps, blue collars and pea jackets. Both of them heavily whiskered.

"Better be off smartly, Gaston," said the other. "The wind is veering and you won't want to be carried northward. Not to the coast."

A terrible suspicion was beginning to form in my mind.

"Ready to get aboard, mam'selle?" asked Gaston. The balloon now loomed above us, swaying gently in the draft through the great vault. Gaston had his hands on the edge of a large wickerwork basket. "We can take the dog also, mam'selle. He's not much of a weight."

"You're taking me—in *that*?" I breathed.

"That's right, mam'selle," came the answer. "The last of the Paris balloons. This will be the sixty-seventh—and a bit small and patched-up, I'm afraid. Also quite unofficial. It was all Monsieur Philippe's notion. Can I help you up into the basket, mam'selle?"

Another thought broke through my sudden alarm. "But, where *is* he?" I cried. "Isn't he coming too?"

"Monsieur Philippe couldn't be here to see you off, mam'selle," said Gaston, "but he particularly told me to say he wished you a safe journey, and that he would be thinking of you. It wouldn't have been possible for him to have come, for, you see, this patched old balloon will only carry one passenger and me—the trained balloonist. Are you all right, mam'selle? Hang on tightly to these ropes, do you see?"

So that was it: in Philippe's instructions, he had been vague about the exact means of our leaving the city; and, come to think of it, he had only implied that the two of us would be leaving.

Unresisting, numb with my personal fear about the ordeal ahead of me, stricken silent at the thought of Philippe left behind, I clung to the ropes that connected the frail basket to the great globe above, closed my eyes, and waited.

There was a bump as Gaston landed in the basket beside me. He called down to his two companions. The basket gave another lurch. Sasha whined and crouched more closely against my leg. I heard one of the men shout out as if in farewell—but nothing happened. No sense of movement. Perhaps there was a hitch: some fault in the balloon's mechanism. Suddenly the thought of staying behind in Paris, to share Philippe's perils, seemed a blessed release. The nobler course.

I opened my eyes.

The spider's web of railway lines was opening out below me, and the roof of the great station stood like the ribs of an upturned boat, with moonlight winking from its million panes of glass. It was soon gone.

Next came rooftops with chimney pots, all moving very

quickly past. Afterward, more slowly, the pattern of streets and wide boulevards: dotted lights exploding into the shape of the whole, lit-up city.

And, lastly, the river—a band of beaten silver. Wisps of cloud. An awesome silence.

5

I threw the last of a crust of bread to the swans beneath my window: they gobbled up the pieces and swept away, wings arched and preening, about some other business.

The last of the mayflies, hovering too close to the still surface of the moat, was taken in the maw of a giant carp: a slight rippling of the glassy water, one swallow, and it was gone. The ripples died away.

I leaned back against my window seat and closed my eyes, luxuriating in the languorous stillness, the warmth. They had told me at Brassy that the winter had been so hard—the moat frozen to a thickness greater than ever in living memory, the grass blackened, young trees uprooted in the icy blizzards—that one would have thought the normal succession of seasons to have been forever suspended. But here was a June of such burgeoning richness that the branches sagged under the weight of blossom, and wild flowers sprouted from every crack in the ancient stonework of the bridge.

Two weeks had passed since the last of the killings in Paris. And there was no news of Philippe.

A bare forty-eight hours after my flight from the capital (and after landing safely in a meadow near Chartres, some forty miles away), the civil war between the government forces in Versailles and the Paris Commune had blazed into terrifying life. Early defeats had soon driven the Communard leaders to desperate measures: there had followed, in the city, a regime of terror, of total dictatorship. This had been brought to an end in one week of fighting that had raged from one end of Paris to the other; with the Versaillais relentlessly driving forward, and the men and women of the Commune disputing every barricade, every street corner, every window—and winning a kind of flawed splendor for themselves. The Commune perished in flames: the flames of the Hôtel de Ville, of the former royal palace of the Tuileries, of wide acres of the city. Notre Dame itself had narrowly escaped the torch. And, after the fighting—the expiation. The reprisals. It was not forgotten that the more fanatical of the Communard leaders had ordered the execution of innocent hostages, including the Archbishop of Paris. For that, and for all the destruction, those who had manned the barricades paid dearly. In the dark days after the surrender, it was death to be found with hands that were blackened with gunpowder. The killing went on till someone cried out, "Let us kill no more!"

News of this had reached peaceful Brassy. But no news of Philippe. It seemed certain that he had been arrested along with scores of others, officers of the old regime, aristocrats, churchmen. And had met the fate of so many of them, during the death throes of the short-lived Commune.

The tears welled under my closed eyelids, and I let them fall unchecked. Then the warmth must have lulled me to sleep for a while, because the shadow of the cypresses beyond the moat had reached my window and the tears had dried upon my cheeks when I opened my eyes again.

Something had woken me. And not the slight chill caused by the shadow of the trees cutting off the late afternoon sunlight. I had heard something. I could almost place it: the sound of carriage wheels on the gravel driveway leading to the great doors of the château. It occurred to me that it might be the postman from Tours with a package of letters. Perhaps with a letter from Paris.

The idea inspired me to rise and go out of the room, to go down and see for myself. Down the corridor and toward the staircase, my ears pricked for the telltale sound of the bell that hung by the great porch. The postman from Tours had a certain way of ringing the bell that was peculiar to him alone: a double-double ring. I heard no bell: only footsteps ascending the staircase.

"Is that you, Madame Arlette?" I called out. "Did I hear the postman's van arrive?"

No answer. The footsteps ceased. With a slight prickling of unease, I also stopped, ten paces from the staircase arch. "Who's there?" I called.

No answer. It was out of the question that one of the servants should be playing the fool with me in that way; but I knew for sure that there was no one else in the place but the servants and myself. And the postman from Tours would scarcely have the temerity to enter the portals of Château Brassy without so much as a by your leave. It followed, then, that whoever it was on the staircase must be someone who had just arrived—someone who had a perfect right to enter the château.

Someone . . .

Then I was running. And the footsteps ascending the stairs joined with the sound of mine. We met at the top of the staircase, and I threw myself into his waiting arms, enveloping him in mine.

"Philippe! Oh, Philippe!"

"Tessa, my dear."

"You're alive—alive!" His uniform tunic was ragged at the collar, and loops of gold braid hung in tatters across his chest. He smelled strongly of carbolic soap and was close-shaved and well-brushed. Hatless, his hair appeared to have suffered from the shears of a somewhat ruthless barber. But he looked well; better than when I had last seen him in Paris.

"Philippe, what happened to you? We've been out of our minds with worry for you."

"It's a long story," he said. He slipped one arm round my waist and guided me back down the stairs, back the way he had come. "But tell me about yourself, Tessa. How was the balloon flight?"

"Terrifying and wonderful," I said. "The experience of a lifetime. Never mind about me, what happened to you. Were you arrested?"

"Not quite," he replied. "I was eventually denounced to the Revolutionary Tribunal of the Commune as a Royalist, a spy, and an enemy of the People, but I had more friends than I guessed: one of my colleagues at the Hôtel de Ville—though himself a dedicated Communard—warned me in time. I managed to leave the city under cover of darkness and make toward the east. And now I am home, my dear Tessa."

We reached the bottom of the stairs, in the great hall. The late afternoon sun from the deeply recessed windows cast long shadows across the elaborate patterning of black and white tiles of the floor. A shadow shifted. There was someone standing in one of the window recesses, someone who turned and looked toward us.

"*Du bist wie eine Blume.*"

"Otto!" I cried.

We embraced, the three of us: I and my two cavaliers, reunited—while I laughed and cried by turns.

"How did you manage to find each other?" I asked them.

"I blundered straight out of Paris and into the Prussian occupation lines to the east of the city," explained Philippe. "There I was greeted with the deepest suspicion and a distinct atmosphere of the firing squad—till I revealed myself as a member of the former secret peace commission at Auteuil, and invoked the name of the Herr Rittmeister Otto von Stock, Third Uhlans. It worked like a charm. Unfortunately, Otto was on furlough in Berlin and had to be sent for, to establish my *bona fides.*"

"I was given leave to wear civilian clothing and escort Philippe to Brassy," added Otto. "And here you see us!"

"Monsieur Philippe! Monsieur Otto!" Half-laughing, half-crying, Mme. Arlette rushed into the hall. "Oh, to see you both safe and well, messieurs . . ."

They embraced the good housekeeper, for she had always adored them both and spoiled them shamelessly from boyhood. She then dabbed her eyes on the corner of her apron and went to bear the good news to the kitchen quarters. And she paused at the door, addressing me.

"So it will be four to dinner tonight," she said. "Oh, what a blessing that we chanced to include some of their favorite dishes. Oh, I am so happy, Madame la Comtesse."

"We are all very happy, dear Madame Arlette," I assured her.

"Yes, Madame la Comtesse." She dropped a curtsy and rushed out.

By degrees, I brought myself to meet their expressions. Surprise mingled—rather unflatteringly, I thought—with incredulity. Manlike, neither of them had spared a glance for my wedding finger. I smiled at them both—and was overjoyed to see the shock give way to delight.

"Tessa!" cried Philippe. "When did it happen—when?"

When did it happen? For me, it had happened on that unforgettable afternoon in Paris, when I had realized that I had loved Robert almost from the first. As for Robert—I had had it from his own lips that he had loved me for as long . . .

"We were married a few weeks ago," I said. "It was a civil wedding, but, happily, you have arrived in time for the ceremony at Tours cathedral next Saturday. It will be a very grand affair. You will both receive an invitation in due course. Is no one going to offer congratulations?"

"Oh, Tessa! How wonderful! How wonderful for you both!"

"Tessa, it is really *wunderbar!*"

They embraced me, yet again.

"But it must have happened so suddenly," cried Philippe. "When we parted company in Paris, I had no idea—no idea at all—that you were destined to become—to become —well, I suppose you must be my aunt. And *that's* a thought!"

It had happened suddenly, as the most splendid things often will. I had steeled myself to meet Robert again: to be matter-of-fact, polite, amiable, detached, serene. I had been none of those things, but had melted at the sight of him, at the expression in his eyes at first sight of me that had told me the unbelievable, the blessed truth of his feelings . . .

"I arrived back here on a Friday afternoon, from Orléans station," I told them calmly. "And we were married the following morning at the town hall in Tours, by a special dispensation. These things can be arranged, given influence—though the Count has now resigned from the Assembly, in protest against the government's treatment of the Communard prisoners."

"Bad things were done in Paris," said Otto. "That

313

accursed war that began it all!" He eyed me watchfully as he continued, "You have heard, have you not, Tessa, that the Emperor—I should say, the ex-Emperor—has been released and has joined his wife and son in England?"

I nodded. "The Count made inquiries for me. They are living in Chislehurst, in the county of Kent. I hope they will find some happiness there, some consolation. He—the Emperor—is a very sick man. Perhaps with not much longer to live."

"You will, perhaps, not—visit him?" It was scarcely a question. More a statement.

I shook my head and touched the pendant that hung at my throat. A whole thaler now, with both pieces fastened together by a jeweler—never to be separated. My only legacy. The answer to the question that had clouded my life.

"But where is Uncle Robert?" cried Philippe. "I long to offer him my congratulations on securing for the De Brassy family our finest acquisition in eight hundred years of our turbulent history."

Was I much of an acquisition for the De Brassys? I doubted it. It was with great apprehension that I had confided the secret of my parentage to Robert—he who had always held the ex-Emperor in such scorn. But, to my joy and relief, he had applauded the news, saying that, unlike my father, I was a Bonaparte through and through, not a Beauharnais. In the Borghese palace in Rome there was a statue, so he had told me, of Pauline Bonaparte, favorite sister of the great Napoleon. And the first time he saw me, in that conservatory of the Tours hotel, I had reminded him of Pauline . . .

I jolted myself out of my reverie. "I'm sorry, Philippe. What was that you asked me?"

"Uncle Robert," he repeated. "Where is he, Tessa?"

"Why, he's gone for his afternoon ride."

"But, Tessa. Uncle Robert never rides. He hasn't been near the stables, let alone thrown his leg over a horse, since he came back from the Crimea and declared himself to be a cripple, worn out before his time."

"All that," I told him, "is now changed."

•   •

Sunset—and I waiting by the open window in the hall, the one that gave an uninterrupted view across the moat bridge, past Mary Queen of Scots' Garden with its trim privet borders, down the long, straight avenue of ancient plane trees patterned light and dark in the ebbing sunlight.

Philippe and Otto had retired to their quarters to make ready for dinner, no doubt availing themselves of the château's excellent bathing arrangements to free themselves of the military aroma of carbolic.

Sunset . . .

My heart leapt . . .

A movement, barely perceptible at first, at the far end of the long corridor of trees: a flickering of light and dark, a rising and falling, fickle and sometimes fading, then growing hard and clear. Tall rider on tall horse, coming down the long avenue toward me, in and out of the bands of light and shade.

Gathering up my skirts, I rushed out of the great hall and out of the château; across the moat bridge and past Mary Queen of Scots' Garden. Now he had seen me and was waving his hat above his head. And the hounds with him—Moko and old Roland—gave tongue in greeting, and so did Sasha, the poodle, trailing far behind them.

As I called out my wonderful news, he was already checking the headlong pace of the big black stallion Belisarius; and when I was near, he leaned down in the saddle and reached out an arm to snatch me up, lifted me and gathered me to him, setting me before him and burying his face in my hair.